"I OWE YOU MUCH, SIR HAWK," CATRIONA SAID SOFTLY.

He watched her with unwavering intent. "Remember that when you reach Blackburn Castle."

Cat was no stranger to propositions, and she had learned early how to turn men aside while flattering them in the same breath. But this man had been nothing but distant and respectful since the first moment they had met long ago. Had the Hawk changed since then? Had he become like so many others?

"You wish something of me, Sir Hawk?" she asked, her tone cautious and level.

"Aye." He nodded once. "I would ask that you not start a war until you leave our keep," he said, and turned away on the heel of his boot.

A flash of anger sparked through her. She had not asked to be harassed by his soldiers. "Only if more men are as foolhardy as these were."

A spark of humor lit his eyes. " 'Tis said, lass, that a bonny face can make a fool of any man."

LOIS GREIMAN

Highland Brides

HIGHLAND HAWK

AVON BOOKS NEW YORK

This is a work of fiction. Names, characters, places, and incidents either are the product of the author's imagination or are used fictitiously. Any resemblance to actual events, locales, organizations, or persons, living or dead, is entirely coincidental and beyond the intent of either the author or the publisher.

AVON BOOKS, INC.
1350 Avenue of the Americas
New York, New York 10019

Inside cover author photo by Barbara Ridenous
Published by arrangement with the author
Library of Congress Catalog Card Number: 99-95339
ISBN: 0-380-80367-4
www.avonromance.com

First Avon Books Printing: January 2000

Printed in the U.S.A.

WCD 10 9 8 7 6 5 4 3 2 1

To Tara, who is everything I expect
my heroines to be—and so much more.
When I dreamed of a daughter
I never imagined anyone as perfect as you.

If one must stray from the nest, better to soar with the hawk than to waggle with the goose.

RODERIC THE ROGUE

Chapter 1

In the year of our Lord 1524

The lance pointed directly at Catriona's heart.

"Put back your hood at once," the soldier ordered. He was young, red-haired, and very straight in the saddle.

Catriona eased back the dark fabric with an unsteady hand. The sunlight, falling sharply from the west, struck her eyes at a hard angle, and she could not see the soldier's immediate reaction. But she heard his intake of breath, and the lance near her chest wavered for a moment before he steadied it.

"You are . . ." he began, then paused. "Gypsy." He said the word like a denouncement, his tone as stiff as the weapon he held with such youthful zeal.

"Aye, good sir. That I am."

"Where are you bound and how many in your party?"

Catriona tightened her hands on the reins and prayed from the depths of her soul. She could ill afford to be turned back now. Lachlan's very life depended on her success.

"You shall travel to the castle of the king," Blackheart

had said. *"And there you shall do as you are bid."*

"We go to the castle for the king's celebration. And there are only the two of us you see here and one more asleep inside the cart."

"Man or woman?"

"A woman, good sir."

"Is she . . ." For a moment the soldier faltered and leaned closer, as if to determine whether his eyes betrayed him. "Is she like you?"

From the top of the willow stick cage secured to the side of the cart, two greenfinches quarreled, then fluttered to the nearby treetops.

"Like me?" Catriona knew what he saw—a dusky-skinned, cat-eyed woman who showed the traits of a thousand foreign tribes in her features.

"Is she . . ." he began, but a noise from behind warned him of someone's approach. He straightened his back stiffly and hardened a determined scowl. "Tell her to come out where we can see her," he ordered.

Catriona mentally winced. With diplomacy and luck, she might be able to soften the soldier's mood. But Marta of the Bairds had long ago outlived her love of finesse.

"She is weary and needs her rest," Catriona said, hedging carefully.

The boy-man behind the lance scowled uncertainly, then twitched his gaze to the rear and hardened his expression once again. "You shall have her come forth immediately or suffer the consequences," he said, but just then his mount was jostled aside.

"Oh, for God's sake, put up your weapon, Galloway." The man who spoke was perhaps a dozen years older than the first and scowled at the other before dropping his gaze to hers. His brows rose as if in surprise. "I see now why the lad made himself a fool." He smiled, slowly, as if that expression alone could accomplish much. He was dark-haired, fit, and bonny, and would be the last person on earth to be surprised if such was said aloud. That much Catriona knew immediately. "So you are Gypsies," he said.

"We are Rom," Rory corrected from beside her on the narrow wagon seat. His tone was terse, and like the young man called Galloway, he too could manage disdain. It was not an emotion Catriona condoned—not when surrounded by a score of soldiers, well armed and well mounted.

"I and my cousin have been invited to entertain for the king's birthday festivities," she said, hurrying to draw attention from Rory's haughty demeanor.

"Have you indeed?" asked the dark man, and canted his head as if impressed.

"Lieutenant Brims," Galloway began. "They are Gypsies, and as such . . ." He paused, then leaned closer to his superior, dropping his voice as he did so.

But in truth, there was little need to hear his words, for it had all been said before.

The elder man straightened with a grin, not pulling his gaze from Catriona's. "I think the king's guard can manage a few Gypsies in our midst."

"Are you certain, sir?" asked another as he urged his steed closer. He too was dark, but narrow faced and narrow lipped. "It looks as if this lass might take a bit of handling."

"Are you offering your assistance, Wickfield?" Brims asked, still smiling at Catriona.

"That I am," said the other, his eyes bright in the setting sun.

"Very generous of you. But I see no reason for you

to stay," said the officer. "You may return to your post with the others."

"Sir—" Galloway argued, but Wickfield interrupted him with a companionable hand on his shoulder.

"Not to worry, lad," he said. "I am certain the good lieutenant knows what he's about."

Galloway hesitated for a moment, but finally turned to the men behind him and ordered the troop away.

Their retreating hoofbeats sounded muffled in the still evening air. Celandine tossed her flaxen mane at the midges, and from behind, Cat heard Bay flirting with the soldiers' mounts.

"So you are entertainers?" said the lieutenant, leaning on the high pommel of his saddle as he stared down at her. "What do you do?"

"We are tumblers of sorts," Catriona said. "You may remember us from some years ago."

" 'Twas surely before I came to be in the king's employ," Brims said, nudging his steed closer. "For I would not have forgotten the likes of you."

Catriona smiled. Long ago she had learned that when the advantage of both flight and fight were against her, a ready smile was her best defense. And since her cart horse was tired and her gelding not the type to outdistance Brim's mount, she made certain her smile was effective. "I am flattered indeed, kind sir," she said, glancing demurely at her hands. "But I am certain a man of your stature has more pressing things to hold his attention."

"More pressing?" he said and laughed. "That I doubt. But tell me, sweet lass, what do I call you?"

He was uncomfortably close now. Close enough for her to feel the heat from his horse against her leg.

"They call me Catriona."

"A fine, bonny name, but one I've not heard before. It makes me curious as to its origin. Mayhap we could take a stroll in yonder woods and discuss it." He leaned from his saddle to brush the back of his gloved fingers against her cheek.

She was careful not to draw away, though she could feel Rory's jealousy like a tangible force on her opposite side. "Truly I would love to," she said. "But I fear I must press on toward the castle."

"Why the rush, wee Cat?"

"The king requested that we come." It was only a partial lie. "It seems unwise to make him wait."

"Certainly true," Brims said. "But the king is young and well involved with the preparations for the festivities. I am certain he will not notice a few minutes delay. Come with me," he ordered and reached for her.

But in that instant the tiny door behind her swung open.

"And what of me?" rasped a voice as melodious as a squeaky wheel. "I have a bonny name. Would you not like to discuss *it*?"

The lieutenant jerked back involuntarily as his gaze snapped to the face framed in the narrow door. Catriona knew what he would see—eyes as black as coal set in a toothless, dried-apple face.

"Speak," commanded the old woman. "Or has my beauty bewitched you?"

The lieutenant stared for a moment, then laughed. "Indeed I am quite stunned. And what might your name be?"

"My name is Get the Devil Out of Our Way Before I Cast a—"

"Grandmother!" Cat interrupted rapidly. "This gentleman is but ensuring our safe passage to the castle. Best that you rest until we arrive there."

"Aye," said the lieutenant, but his jovial mood seemed to have darkened, and his gaze did not leave the doorway. "Shut yourself away, old one. Your granddaughter will only be gone for a short while unless—"

"She'll not be gone at all!" vowed Rory and lurched to his feet, his dirk already in his hand.

A movement flashed behind him. Something rose and fell, and suddenly Rory crumpled over the seat like a doll of rags.

From the far side of the cart the narrow-faced soldier smiled as his steed pranced in place.

"Back so soon, Wickfield?" Brims asked dryly.

"I told you she'd take a bit of handling, sir."

"And now I suppose you think to share."

The soldier shrugged, still grinning at her. "When there's a banquet . . ."

"Very well then," said Brims and reached for her.

Catriona stepped quickly sideways, but Rory's lax body impeded her retreat. "I regret my haste, gentle sirs," she said. "But truly, the king is expecting my imminent arrival. I dare not disappoint him."

"You dare not disappoint *me*," warned Brims, and reaching wide, snatched her sleeve.

The time for finesse had passed.

Catriona slapped the reins against her mare's back and yelled a command. The cob leapt forward, jerking the cart into motion.

Catriona was yanked backward, but the captain's hold broke and suddenly she was loose and flying down the road toward the castle, her heart thundering like the mare's wild hoofbeats.

Behind her, the two men bellowed and cursed. Beside

her, Rory bounced closer to the whirling wheel.

"Fly!" she yelled to the mare, and lurching sideways, grabbed hold of Rory's collar. Tugging on a bounce, she wrenched him toward her. He bumped against her legs, nearly upsetting her, but she gained her balance, grabbed the reins in both hands, and urged the steed on.

The mare was fleet and game, but fatigue and her burden were against her. Catriona saw Brims's steed inch forward, saw his hands come into view. She yelled again, but clearly the race was already lost. She frantically scrambled for a way out.

Something brushed her shoulder and she spun sideways, ready to do battle, but only a blackened, long-handled kettle met her gaze. Snatching it from her great grandmother's hands, she dropped the reins, steadied them with one foot, and prepared herself.

Another second . . . One more . . . Brims's head was almost in sight—nearly there. Cat waited another instant, and then she swung.

Hot, pumping panic welled through Catriona, but her swing rang true. The kettle banged against Brims's forehead like a thundering mace. His head snapped backward. His body followed, and he torpedoed off his steed and out of sight.

"Cat!" Grandmother shrieked.

Catriona pivoted to the right, her pot ready for the next attacker, but in that instant, she was snatched off her feet by the man called Wickfield. The pot banged against the side of the cart, numbing her fingers before it fell away.

She was yanked over the saddle, her breath was torn from her lungs by the force of their speed. The earth blurred beneath the steed's galloping hooves. With her legs dangling on the horse's near side, Catriona struggled for a hold, one hand in her captor's shirt, one in the mane.

"There's a good lass," Wickfield gritted, his arm wrapped hard about her waist. " 'Tis best you know when you've been mastered."

She couldn't reach the knife at her waist. Couldn't . . . Suddenly Catriona realized her fingers were wrapped about a rein. Instinctively, she jerked.

She had only a moment, only the briefest flash of time before the horse stumbled, but she was ready. As Wickfield grappled to right the reins, in the second when he realized they were about to fall, she wrenched her legs beneath her and launched herself from the steed's back.

She hit the ground hard and somersaulted, and when she rose to her feet, she saw that the horse had done the same, but Wickfield had not. Instead, he lay holding his right thigh and cursing, swearing revenge in staccato tones.

It was then that she heard the hoofbeats. Heart in her throat, she swung toward the noise. Horses thundered up and a dozen uniformed men were upon her in an instant. The nearest rider threw himself from his steel-gray mount.

Soldiers! And she had injured two of their own!

Catriona backed up a trembling step as the soldier approached. Limned by the sun behind him, he loomed over her like a castle wall. There was no hope against him and his men. Unless . . . Wickfield's mount still stood behind her, and seemed uninjured. If she could make it that far she might have a chance of reaching the castle and falling on James's mercy.

But she must be clever.

"Please, good sir . . ." There was no need to fake the quaver in her voice. Indeed, her knees threatened to buckle. "I meant no harm. I am but a poor innocent lass traveling—"

He reached for her, and she reacted. Not like a poor innocent lass at all, but like an acrobat trained from infancy. Her heel struck his face as she tumbled away and his head snapped to the side. She rose to her feet with a jolt, but a hand was already closing around her arm in an unbreakable grip. She was jerked toward him, face to face, inches apart. Frustration and anger boiled inside her, and then, like a cat at the end of her defenses, she spat.

The saliva hit him square on the cheek. She felt him tense, sensed his anger.

And then he nodded.

"Catriona," he said.

"Hawk?" She said his name on a breath, certain she was mistaken. "Sir Hawk?"

"Aye." Around her upper arm, his big hand relaxed, though the muscle in his jaw did not. There was, she noticed, a swelling beginning to form just in front of his left ear. "Galloway informed me that there was a Gypsy lass who might have found some trouble with Lieutenant Brims. So I came to . . ." He glanced sideways, noting the man on the ground, the riderless horses. "Rescue her." He sighed and a bit of tension left his stance. "I was not expecting you, Catriona. My mistake, I see."

"Nay, I did not plan to—"

"Sir Hawk!" Brims stumbled up, his voice breathless and raspy, his nose purple and swollen in his usually handsome face. " 'Tis not as it seems. I saw this troupe heading toward the castle. Knowing they were Gypsies, I feared they meant the king some harm. Hence, I detained them."

Sir Hawk dropped her arm and remained perfectly silent for a moment. "And your men?" he asked quietly.

"What?"

"The rest of your men—where are they, Sir Brims? Knowing you were dealing with wild Gypsies, did you not keep your men close at hand lest the lass overwhelm you?"

"I . . ." Brims paused for an instant to glance at his fallen comrade, but Wickfield merely stared, his face ashen as he gripped his injured leg. "I saw there were only the few of them, hence I thought it safe to send my men back to their posts."

Silence.

"But?" Hawk urged.

"What?"

"But what happened?"

Sir Hawk had changed little since Catriona had seen him last, nearly two years before. Square jaw. Bowed nose. Mayhap a bit more silver in his hair. A new scar nicked diagonally across his chin, but his voice was the same; low and even, as if every word was carefully measured before it was loosed. "What went amiss, Sir Brims? I would think you could have managed to escort a lass to the castle without breaking Wickfield's leg and your own nose."

"Broken!" he rasped, covering it with one hand as he grabbed his sword with the other. "Damn—"

Catriona didn't even see Sir Hawk move. It almost seemed as if the lieutenant's blue doublet became entangled in his fingers of its own accord. As if it were Brims who pressed his chest up close to Hawk's fist.

"I am too old to enjoy such wild displays of passion," Hawk said softly. "Therefore I shall warn you now. Not only do I myself owe Lady Catriona a personal debt of gratitude, but she is a friend of His Majesty, King James, and therefore a friend of Scotland herself. Do you understand me?"

"Aye. Aye, Sir Hawk."

"Good. Then let us proceed." Hawk loosened his fingers, letting the lieutenant's doublet spill out of his hand. "What happened here?"

Brims cleared his throat, chanced one glance in Catriona's direction, and spoke clearly. "I sent the others back to Blackburn as I said, but I did not want the lady to travel alone. Hence—"

"Alone?" asked Hawk, glancing at her.

"Not entirely alone," she said quickly, wishing his eyes weren't quite so piercing. "Grandmother and Rory are with me."

"What of the others?"

She refused to turn her eyes away, though it was difficult. "They had no wish to make the long journey north and joined up with kin instead."

"Young Lachlan too?"

"Aye."

"I would not have thought—"

"Sir Hawk," Brims interrupted, impatient and in obvious pain. "I fear we have lost the thrust of this conversation."

Hawk turned slowly back toward his lieutenant, his expression inscrutable. "And what is the thrust, Brims?"

"I merely offered to escort the lady to Blackburn, nothing more."

Hawk shifted his attention back to her. Their gazes met.

The memory of rattling fear swamped Catriona. But with it came the knowledge that she was the outsider here. She could ill afford to cause trouble among the ranks. Still, if she could not have justice, at least she would have truth. " 'Tis not what he offered," she said softly.

"Lying—" Brims rasped, but Hawk interrupted with a raised hand.

"You will return to Blackburn, collect any monies due, and leave posthaste." His tone was low and level.

"But—"

"And if your head has no wish to be separated from your body . . ." Hawk watched the lieutenant with silvery, deadly earnest eyes. "You will be gone before I arrive there."

For a moment Catriona thought Brims would argue, but he drew himself up and turned away.

Not a soul spoke. Somewhere off to the side a man groaned, but whether it was Wickfield or Rory returning to consciousness, Catriona could not tell.

"I owe you much, Sir Hawk," she said softly.

He watched her with unwavering intent. "Remember that," he said, "when you reach Blackburn Castle."

Cat was no stranger to propositions. She was Rom, she was young, and she possessed an allure for men that she could not explain but had long ago accepted. She had learned at a tender age how to discourage men without lessening her own prospects. How to turn them aside while flattering them in the same breath. But this man had been nothing but distant and respectful since the first moment they had met, since she had rushed to Blackburn Castle so long ago to inform him of his beloved niece's plight. Had the Hawk changed since then? Had he become like so many others?

"You wish something of me, Sir Hawk?" she asked, her tone cautious and level.

"Aye." He nodded once, slowly. "I would ask that you not start a war until you leave our little keep," he said, and turned away on the heel of his boot. No, he had not changed. His plaid flared and settled around corded thighs as he strode away—a quiet, kilted bear among yapping lap dogs.

"Sir Hawk," she said, screwing up her courage. "May I request one favor?"

He turned back, his brows pulled low over his moon-mist eyes. "Does it involve any more of my men being broken or bloodied?"

A flash of anger sparked through her. She had not asked to be propositioned or pursued. "Only if the men in question prove to be as foolhardy as the first."

Something in his eyes changed almost imperceptibly—a spark of humor, perhaps, though his lips remained immobile and stern.

" 'Tis said, lass, that a bonny face can make a fool of any man."

"Then 'tis hardly my fault, is it? For this is the face I was given." She felt indescribably weary suddenly, far older than her twenty-two years. "In truth, it has caused me far more trouble than joy."

"Indeed?" He did smile now, though the expression was wry and fleeting as he gave her a shallow bow. "Then I must do what I can to lighten the load of your beauty, Lady Cat. In what manner can I assist you?"

Chapter 2

Catriona took a step into the great hall. Her heart thrummed in her chest, and her muscles felt taut, like brass wires stretched too tightly along the neck of a gittern. But these sensations were nothing new, only sharpened with the urgency of this impromptu performance.

"I cannot do it," she had said. But Blackheart had only laughed. *"The Princess Cat unsure of herself? Surely not. Nay, you shall deliver the young king to me, and when you do . . . Well, your reunion with your wee brother shall be quite touching, I am sure."*

Off to her right, a young nobleman noticed her and turned from his conversation with a pale young woman dressed in pink. His lips parted, but his words had ceased. The drinking horn slipped from his fingers to clatter noisily to the floor. Around him, heads turned toward her. The hall fell to whispers, then to silence. 'Twas then that the music of a lute began, softly at first, then rising like a musical moon. As if from nowhere, it trilled around her.

She took another step forward, balanced on the balls of her bare feet. One step and then another. More heads turned her way. A path was cleaved in front of her. She twirled once, then again. Her skirt, crafted of fabric as light as air and as bright as holly berries, twirled with her, billowing away from the dark, cuffed garment beneath. Stretching her arms overhead, she danced for a moment, then tipped her body over, positioned on her hands for an instant before finding her feet again. Her flaring skirt made a continuous arc through the air, and when she landed—voilà—there was a goblet in her hand. A goblet filled with wine and not a droplet spilled.

She handed it off to a nearby gentleman and danced on. One stride, then two. From the corner of her eye, she saw the raised dais in the center of the gargantuan room.

The rhythm of the music sped along. Not far away there was a space between two men who sat on the table's benchlike seat. She leapt easily into that opening, her feet a light patter against the wear-smoothed wood as she spun again and again.

In an instant, she was atop the table. Platters and saltcellars and goblets and food crowded the great wooden expanse. But it was no great feat for her to avoid the clutter, to dance across the surface, to scoop up a tart, somersault from the table, and offer the dessert to the nearest bystander. No great feat to twirl and dance and mesmerize until she fell forward in a heap of gauzy fabric at the foot of the king's chair.

The music fell away. The hall was as silent as a mausoleum. She sat up slowly, lifting her arms above her head, unfolding like a flower to the sun, and with her movement came the birds, fluttering from her on delicate yellow-green wings.

She watched the king lift his freckled face to the ceiling, watched him giggle with glee, before finally turning back toward her.

"Lady Cat." His voice had deepened somewhat since her last visit there, but the smoothness of his cheeks still evidenced the features of a lad. "You have returned."

"Aye." She rose to her feet amid raucous applause, bowed low, and smiled. "Did I not say I would?"

"Aye. But it has been forever and beyond."

She laughed. "Mayhap to a lad, but surely not to a king," she said softly.

"Am I not a person first, and a king second?"

"Aye. That you are, Your Majesty," she said. "And a young man, I see. You are twice the height you were when last I saw you."

"I am nearing twelve years of age." There was excitement in his voice. "The day of my birth approaches."

"Does it?" She held her breath, awaiting his next words.

"Aye. There will be much merrymaking. You must come."

She could feel her heart knock against her ribs in thrumming relief. "But, Your Majesty, I have—"

"Nay, you must!" he said. "I insist. You will perform at the festivities."

Thank you, God. "A simple Rom lass at such a lavish festival? What will your council say?"

"They will say . . ." He scowled and cast a mischievous sidelong glance toward Lord Tremayne, his most senior and most unbending, advisor. " 'These gypsies are the very devil incarnate and must be cast from our midst.' "

"Will they?"

"Aye. And I will say . . ." He raised his chin and

flipped a casual hand. " 'Accept my friends or forfeit your heads.' "

"Can you say that?" she asked, making certain her tone bore the proper awe.

He shrugged and leaned close to whisper. "Oh, aye, I can say it, but thus far no heads have actually been forthcoming."

She laughed. " 'Tis good to see you again, Your Majesty."

"Say you will perform for my birthday."

"Or I must forfeit my head?"

Beside her, Sir Hawk strode up and bowed slightly.

"Why did you not tell me she had come?" James asked.

"Mayhap I did not know," Hawk said, but the king scoffed.

"A maggot could not enter this keep without your knowledge. Nor can I breathe without your consent."

Hawk tilted his head. The black plume in his deep green bonnet bobbed. "I am but trying to keep you safe, Your Majesty."

"Then I would suggest keeping me informed as to our guests," said a voice at Cat's elbow.

She turned. Lord Tremayne looked no different than he had at her last meeting with him. He was a man of indeterminate years with cheekbones sharp enough to draw blood. He stared at her with pale, watery eyes and pursed lips that blended into the parched color of his face.

" 'Tis a pleasure to see you again, my lord," she lied.

He raised a single brow. "Explanations, Sir Hawk," he said, without turning his attention from her.

"Catriona of the Bairds is a friend of the clan MacGowan and a friend of the throne," Hawk said, his low voice not reaching past their small ring of listeners.

"But I did not give permission for her presence here," Tremayne said. "Therefore—"

"Who is this person?" asked another gentleman, elbowing his way forward. He was a good hand shorter than Tremayne, though his increased girth made him appear considerably less. He struggled to free something from a pouch at his side. "And why is she here?" he asked, still wrestling with the recalcitrant pouch.

"My apologies, good sir," Catriona said, curtsying gently. "The fault for my rude interruption is entirely mine."

"It is . . ." began the man, but just at that moment, he managed to fish out his wire spectacles. Behind the curved glass, his eyes grew wide before he blinked like a blinded owl. "Who is she?" he asked again, but the question was asked in a breathy whisper now.

"She is Catriona of the clan Baird, Your Grace. Some call her Princess Cat. 'Tis naught but a courtesy name, for her origins are humble, unless you believe the wild tales about her antecedents." Hawk's tone was parchment dry. "And Lord Tremayne is correct, of course; she should not have been allowed to disturb this royal assemblage. Off with you now," he said, turning dramatically toward Cat.

"Surely you jest," argued a gentleman who pushed through the crush. Dressed in mustard-yellow hose and a slashed crimson doublet, he was the very picture of polite refinement. "We can hardly toss the lass out on her ear. 'Tis practically the midst of the night. She needs a place to retire." Reaching for her hand, he bowed smoothly over her knuckles, bestowing on them a lingering kiss. While the duke was squat and balding, this man was narrow and refined, with bonny features and perfect teeth. "Marquis de la Faire," he introduced himself. "But you may call me Boswell the Fair."

"I did not say we should toss her out," insisted the myopic duke. "I but meant . . ." For a moment he floundered for words and perhaps for breath itself, then, "After all, we would not want the king to be thought of as uncharitable."

"But what of his safety?" Hawk asked.

"Safety!" The stout man scoffed, turning his gaze back to Catriona with a labored sigh. "What harm could one wee lass do? And such a . . ." He paused as he examined her more closely—her face, her bodice, laced tight to keep all the necessities in place, her waist, and then down to where her hands clasped each other beneath her slashed red and black sleeves. "Such a delicate thing at that."

She had just catapulted from the table and into their midst. "Delicate" did not seem a fitting description, but Catriona was not one to argue when things were going her way.

"Aye," said Sir Hawk, his dry tone suggesting he had forgotten neither Wickfield's agonized moans nor his lieutenant's purple nose. "She is indeed a delicate lass."

"She is perfection of form," said de la Faire.

She smiled, trying to encompass the gathering of lords and ladies that crowded in for a better view.

"Had I realized the cordiality of Blackburn Castle, I would have come sooner," she said.

"You have never been to our fair keep before?" asked de la Faire.

"Long ago," she said. "And then only for a short visit."

"Then I must show you about," said the Frenchman.

"I know the castle as well as any," argued the spectacled duke. "Therefore—"

"As much as I appreciate your kind offers," Catriona interrupted. " 'Twas a long and arduous journey. Truly, I desire nothing more than a bed and—"

"I've got a bed," piped a young noble with crooked front teeth and a lopsided grin.

"And solitude," Cat finished. Ignoring the crestfallen expressions of the men around her, she turned toward the king. "Your Majesty, I thank you for your kind audience."

He rose from his chair with the energetic haste of youth. "Tell me you shall stay and perform for my birthday."

She turned her eyes toward Tremayne and his nearsighted counterpart. "I've no wish to cause rancor amongst your loyal advisors."

"Nay, nay," crooned Lord Spectacles. " 'Tis a royal request. What can we do but comply?"

Tremayne said nothing.

"Then I shall gladly agree," Cat said.

"I have been practicing my horsemanship since last we met," James said.

For a moment she wondered what he meant, but then she remembered their time together—the young king's grave efforts as he tried to achieve a few of the simpler tricks she had shown him.

"You must demonstrate when next we ride." She curtsied. "My thanks, Your Highness," she said and turned away.

"I shall see you again then surely," said the duke, tottering along after.

In all honesty, that depended on if he had his spectacles close to hand.

"Can I see you to your chambers?" asked the Frenchman as others pressed close behind him.

"Sir Hawk promised to escort me," she said, glancing toward the huge soldier.

He raised a single brow a fraction at her lie, but stepped up with a bow.

"Do not forget me, then, if you wish for a tour," said de la Faire.

"How could I?" she asked and tucked her hand beneath the Hawk's elbow. Against her fingers, muscles honed by years and battle jumped to life as he bore her through the pressing crowd.

"Mourning the sad state of your beauty again?" he asked quietly, not looking down at her as he pulled open the hall's heavy door.

She smiled, nodding once at a young gentleman who cocked a knee and bowed to her. "I but said it gave me more trouble than joy," she reminded him. "I did not say that I was too proud to use it."

"Then use it to your best advantage, lass," he said, "for the king's celebration begins in less than a fortnight. And I doubt Tremayne will tolerate your much bemoaned beauty after that."

"A fortnight!" The words caught in her chest.

"Aye." He glanced sharply down at her. "Is something amiss?"

"Nay. 'Tis just that there is much to plan if I am to entertain for such a grand assemblage. Costumes, routines . . ."

"Your performance tonight was quite impressive."

She couldn't tell if he referred to her acrobatics or her conversation afterward, but his next statement answered her unspoken question.

"The Catriona I remember was not so designing."

"I was younger then." Far younger. Indeed, she felt as old as the curving stone stairs up which they climbed. "Is there something so dreadful about wanting to perform at the king's celebration?"

"Not at all. But you might have simply asked."

"Who? You or Lord Tremayne?"

He acknowledged her point with a simple nod. " 'Tis lucky that the Duke of Ramhurst is not entirely blind, or your ploy might well have failed."

She laughed as they reached the door of the chambers she had been given to use. " 'Tis good for me to flex my manipulative muscles now and then."

"I fear I do not understand."

" 'Tis because you are not an entertainer."

"True. I am naught but a—" he began, then turned in surprise as a pair of greenfinches fluttered up the stairs toward them. They flitted to her shoulder and squabbled, but she opened the door and shooed them inside. "You were saying?"

"I was saying I am but a scared old warrior."

"False modesty, Sir Hawk?" she asked.

"Painful honesty," he countered.

"I think you underrate yourself," she said, glancing up through her lashes.

"And I think you should find younger game on which to hone your hunting skills."

She laughed aloud and pulled her fingers from his arm. Her knuckles brushed his chest, and for an instant she almost thought she heard him draw in a sharp breath. "I think you would make a fine entertainer, Sir Hawk. In truth, being able to judge your audience is an important asset. It seems you would do well in that regard, and you would look quite dashing with your fierce scowl. Perhaps a sweeping cape to add to the drama.

But . . ." She shrugged. "Mistress Hawk might take offence."

He said nothing.

She cleared her throat and eyed him askance. "Mayhap you do not know the rules of this game," she said. "I am asking, and quite subtly I might add, if you are wed."

"Marcele died some fifteen years past."

"Oh." She suddenly felt very foolish and rather callow. "My apologies."

The silence stretched uncomfortably.

" 'Twas a marriage arranged between her family and Lord Beaumont."

"A Frenchman?"

"He was my liege lord for some years."

"And you impressed him with your skill and loyalty."

He did not deny it. "I should have refused. She was . . ." he began, then paused.

"What?"

"Fragile," he said. "She died carrying my child."

"And so you have no children . . . except for the king, of course."

"You could see me beheaded with that sort of talk, lass," he warned wryly.

"I only meant that I imagine most guards don't share such a closeness as you do with young James."

"An old soldier's means of recapturing his youth, I suppose."

"How old?"

He raised his brows in mild humor. "I hope you find the room to your satisfaction, Lady Cat."

"You've no intention of answering me?"

"Quite astute for a babe just out of swaddling."

They stared at each other in silence for a moment. A

strange sort of breathless tension stole over her. She dropped her gaze.

"My thanks for rescuing me from Lord Tremayne. It seems he bears no fondness for me," she said finally.

"Rescuing?" He gave a mild expression of surprise. "I was hoping to see you cast from Blackburn before you caused more trouble. Unfortunately, the duke of Ramhurst found his spectacles too quickly."

She would be wise, she knew, to ignore the odd trickle of pleasure caused by his off-hand compliment. "Which goes to prove that everything happens as it should," she said.

"Or that there is no fool like an old fool."

"How old?" she asked again.

"The duke? Too old for you," he said.

"And you?"

"He is decidedly too old for me."

She smiled, then sobered. "My thanks again, Sir Hawk."

"My debt to you has too long been unfulfilled," he reminded her.

"Not true." She glanced toward the nearby window, remembering the first time she had met him. " 'Twas a simple enough thing to hustle to Blackburn and tell you that Rachel and her Liam had found some trouble. I owed them that much at least. Liam taught me a great deal about sleight of hand, and Rachel . . . Rachel was a saint, and a friend when a friend was needed."

"And she is my kin always," he said, still watching her. "I owe her mother, Lady Fiona."

"Truly?" she asked, intrigued. "The great hawk of the Highlands. It does not seem possible that you could owe anyone."

He canted his head. His was not a pretty face, but

solid and masculine, chiseled by years and character, with a groove on each side of his mouth like elongated dimples, and a bowed nose that suggested a colorful past. " 'Twas a time when I was even younger than you, wee Cat."

"Nay!" she said, managing to sound surprised.

"Aye. Well before the dawn of time, of course."

"Ah. So tell me, before the dawn of time, what Rachel's mother did for you."

"Naught but save my life."

The arched hallway around them was silent.

"Tell me," she said softly.

"I thought you were quite weary."

"Tell me."

He shrugged and settled a brawny shoulder against the wall. There was a casual strength to his movement, interwoven with a unique, unconscious grace. "My half-sister took me in when I was small and sickly and had none other to care for me. 'Twas *her* sister-by-law, the Lady Fiona, who nursed me into health."

She glanced at the muscle that bulged beneath the sleeves of his russet doublet, then swept her gaze up the bulk of his chest to his unreadable eyes. "You jest."

"There are those who say Lady Fiona could change a toad into a prince. Which, if you dwell on it, makes her miracle with me seem somewhat less miraculous."

"So Rachel inherited her healing touch from her mother."

"Aye."

"And she is your kinswoman."

"In actuality, she is my half-sister's husband's brother's daughter."

"Very nearly twins."

His eyes smiled "Close enough, I suspect, that they

had no wish to see me die. In truth, they insisted that I live. Regardless what my lungs thought of the matter."

'Twas difficult to think of him as a child, for he seemed to be the embodiment of looming masculinity. As she stared at him, she imagined the lad he had been—dark hair, a somber expression, a fleeting shadow of what he would become. Not unlike Lachlan—burning potential in a wee small frame. But she would not think of that just now. "Who are 'they'?" she asked.

He paused a moment, then straightened from the wall. "Is anything amiss, lass?"

"Nay." She brightened her smile. "Nothing. 'Tis just . . . difficult to imagine you as anything but a rock."

His gaze didn't waver from her face. "Rory has recovered?"

"Aye. An ache in the head, nothing worse."

"And your Lachlan. He is well and lively?"

"Oh, aye. If he were any livelier I would have to sell him to the Gypsies." She laughed.

"Young James would have been happy to see him."

" 'Twas sorry I was to leave him behind. He is as clever and troublesome as ever, but I feared Blackburn might not have enough supplies to sate his appetite. He eats as much as Bear."

"So the bear stayed behind too?"

"Aye. They are probably even now squabbling over herring pie." Her throat closed up, clogged with terror and tears. If only Bear had been with Lachlan when Blackheart's men had come upon him in the woods, her brother might still be with her now.

She forced down the fear. Now was not the time for helpless sentiment. Now was the time for action, for planning, for clear-headed thinking and bold deeds. But she was neither clear-headed nor bold. She was scared and lost and out of her depth, but she dare not show it—so she forged on, trying to turn Hawk's attention aside. "Just before I left him, he asked me a riddle," she said. "Who is gray at birth, fair at maturity, and raven-haired in her dotage?"

Hawk thought for a moment, his eyes unwavering. "Mistress Day," he reasoned quietly. "Dark in the morning. Fair at midday. And black at night."

"A warrior and a scholar," she said.

"A frail, wee child with nothing to do but plague the Rogue with riddles."

"The Rogue?"

"The Flame's husband."

"The Flame?"

"My half-sister."

"They sound quite intriguing."

"A troublesome lot, intent on plaguing the Highlands."

And he adored them. 'Twas as obvious as his quiet strength.

"The Lady Saint, Dugald the Dragon, Liam the Irishman, Roderic the Rogue, Fiona the Healer . . ." He shrugged.

"Tell me, Sir Hawk, is there anyone in your family with a normal name? An Arthur or a Malcolm perhaps?"

"My Christian name is Haydan."

She nodded. "Haydan, the Hawk of the Highlands," she mused. It seemed right somehow. But would the hawk be her doom?

Chapter 3

"We shall know immediately if you tell another living soul. We shall know," Blackheart whispered silkily. *"And then the boy will suffer in ways you can only imagine."*

How would he know? How? Who was he? She called him Blackheart but she did not know him. Did not even know if she had ever met him before her one horrid audience with him. But he was a coward. That much she knew, for he had taken an innocent boy and declared his demands without ever allowing her to see his face. He might be at Blackburn even now, watching her from inches away.

Blackburn's great hall was filled with raucous noise—the laughter of children, the music of a psaltery, and a hundred voices all speaking at once.

Catriona scanned the high-beamed room as she shepherded her grandmother through the throng toward an empty spot at a trestle table. Around them, lords and ladies and soldiers milled with servants and hounds.

Sowens made of oats and barley steamed in pots, nestled against round loaves of fine white bread, roasted venison, and a dozen tempting delicacies. Ale was served far more readily than milk. Mead and beer were plentiful.

Marta settled creakily onto a seat and scowled at a server until he offered her a wooden bowl and a nearly flat ladle. Occupied then with stirring honey into her porridge, she gummed her breakfast while Catriona filled her leather mug.

"Here then, allow me."

Catriona glanced up to see de la Faire taking the ale from her hands with a smile.

"Good morningtide," he said. "I trust you slept well in our bonny castle."

"Aye." It was an outright lie. She had barely slept at all. "Very well."

"And what of you, Grandmother?" he asked, turning his perfect smile on Marta with the confidence of the privileged who also happen to be comely.

"I am old," she muttered, glaring up at him through her darker-than-hell eyes.

"You jest." He brightened the brilliance of his smile. "You don't look to be a day over—"

"I am older than the warts on your father's arse," she said. "And I have no time for your—"

"She slept well too," Catriona interrupted quickly.

"My father's—" He stopped. "How did you know he has warts?"

"What is your name?" Marta asked, keeping her hard gaze pinned on the Frenchman.

De La Faire blinked, taken aback, but struggling to find his balance. "I am the Marquis de la Faire of Marseilles."

"If you are from Marseilles why are you here?"

He laughed, but the sound was nervous as he shifted

his gaze to Cat's. "My father wished me to ask a favor of the king."

"Then why not ask it and be gone?"

He shuffled on his slippered feet. They were pointy-toed, red on one side, white on the other. But it was the rest of his costume that was truly stunning. Sunflower-yellow hose; a red, lavishly slashed doublet; and a pearl-encrusted codpiece the size of a melon. Had Cat had any difficulty awakening, this ensemble would have done the trick.

"I came for His Majesty's birthday," said the Frenchman, then looked somewhat embarrassed. "Father thought it wise to come bearing gifts."

"Hmph," Marta grunted.

Catriona watched her breathlessly. But when the old woman looked up, her eyes were uncertain. She shrugged shallowly with a weary shake of her head.

Cat turned away, glancing across the crowded room, but there were too many unknown faces, too many uncertainties. Suddenly she could sit still no longer.

She rose restlessly to her feet.

"Princess Catriona, 'tis good to see you again," said the spectacled duke from the night before.

"Catriona." Another man entered the fray. "What an unusual name. My wife's name is Catlina. We are here with our Roberta," he said, glancing at a pale girl in pink who seemed barely bold enough to raise her gaze from the table. "She is to be engaged to Lord Drummond."

"I saw your performance last night," said another. "I must say, I've never seen the like."

" 'Twas quite magnificent."

Men crowded in on all sides.

"I saw a portrait of an Indian princess once. You bear an uncanny—"

"I cannot think for all the yammering!" Marta rasped. "Lad!" She snapped her devilish glare to the soldiers at the next table. "Tell them to be still."

Catriona felt, rather than saw, Haydan's approach. Though courtesy demanded that she focus her attention on the man who still spoke to her, she turned to watch the Hawk. For a man of such size, he moved with a hunter's easy stealth.

"It has been some time since I've been called lad," he said, his gaze on Marta's dried-apple face.

"All things are young when compared to something. The oak tree is only a babe in comparison to the sun," said Marta, glaring up at him.

His expression changed only slightly—though Catriona couldn't have said how. A crinkling at the corners of his eyes, perhaps.

"Gentlemen," he said, addressing the throng that pressed in on them, "I believe Widow Baird needs some room."

Not a soul moved.

Haydan's left brow shifted up the slightest fraction of an inch.

"Monsieur de la Faire," he said, glancing at the brightly colored lord. "Did you not promise the lady a tour this morn?"

Nay, Cat thought.

"Indeed, I did," said the Frenchman, and taking her hand, placed it firmly on the crook of his elbow. " 'Twould be my greatest pleasure."

He turned, and there was little Cat could do but turn with him. Thus, they left the mob to disperse with grumbling irritation behind them. Catriona allowed herself only one evil glance over her shoulder at Hawk, but there was little satisfaction in the glare, for he had already turned his attention back to Marta.

"So, tell me, Princess Cat, what are you princess of, besides my heart?" asked the Frenchman, leaning close.

Catriona glanced surreptitiously to her right. Two men watched her from near the hall's great double doors. She saw them lean their heads together and listened intently as they spoke. Not to what they said, but to their tone, their inflection. But there was nothing familiar there. No purred silkiness. No plural references to any one man.

"Lady?"

"Your pardon?"

"What are you the princess of . . . besides my heart?"

It didn't sound quite so romantic the second time, apparently not even to the Frenchman, for he winced slightly when he said it.

"Oh. Nothing." In the hallway outside the great chamber, a trio of men and a fashionable lady spoke together. Cat watched them until they passed.

"You're the princess of nothing?"

" 'Tis simply a title I use to draw the crowds."

He stared at her from too close. "I find that difficult to believe."

"And why is that, good sir?" The hallway opened in both directions. She memorized how the ceiling arched above them, where the next door was located.

"With your bearing and your . . . well . . ." He leaned closer still, perhaps thinking she hadn't noticed how perfectly straight his teeth were. "I thought the first sight of your face might well be the death of the poor Duke of Ramhurst."

"Are you saying I am comely?" she asked.

Throwing his head back, he laughed, then squeezed

close again. His arm crushed against her breast. "It shall take me some time to get accustomed to your candor," he said. "But, aye, I am saying you are stunning beyond description. Magical. Eyes like a sleepy wildcat. Hair like . . ." He searched for words with a flip of his pale hand. "Like starlight and moonbeams and gilded midnight all swirled into one." He touched a wayward lock of the curly, recalcitrant hair that fell past her shoulder. "Never have I seen the like. 'Tis bewitching against your velvet skin." He grinned at his own poetry. "You could be naught but royalty."

An arched, iron-bound door was planted in the stone wall on her left. "So you think my features a direct result of my royal heritage? And if I were born to a wandering bard and a basket weaver, I would be homely as a flea-bitten hound?"

He laughed. "I admit I have trouble imagining the daughter of a bard and a weaver being as entrancing as you."

"Then your imagination is a bit shortsighted, sir," she said. "For that is just what my parents were."

"You jest."

"I do not."

"Then your mother must have been a dazzling weaver, if she gave birth to a daughter as extraordinary as—"

"What is behind that door?" she asked.

He glanced up, distracted. "The Widow Charmain is staying there. Since her husband's death she is so much more . . ." He paused with a suggestive grin. "Entertaining."

"Oh. And that one?"

"Sir Guy. From where do your people originate?"

" 'Tis said my family came from a place called Khandia many years ago during a time of turmoil."

"Turmoil?"

"It seems the peasants grew weary of starving and overthrew the royal family."

"So that is why they fled?" His tone was breathy with awe.

"Aye," she said. "To save themselves from starvation."

He laughed. "Or to save themselves from the peasants."

"Mayhap every lass in Khandia looks exactly as I do."

"Then Khandia's loss is my gain," he said, and covered her hand with his.

She pulled her hand away and pointed to the molding above a particularly broad door. "What marvelous scrolling," she said. "What lies through there?"

"Come and see."

She followed him inside, then drew in her breath. "Such splendor," she said, gazing at the ceiling painted with cherubs and angels and heavy-crested steeds.

"Aye. 'Tis splendid," said the marquis. "But when you are royalty . . ." He shrugged, grinning at her. "James IV often relaxes here. But royal guests are welcome as well."

" 'Tis a soothing place," she said, moving to a window to look out. Below her, a small garden welcomed the coming of spring.

"My chambers are soothing," he murmured in her ear.

She turned abruptly and found him practically on her shoulder.

"My chambers here are not nearly so large as those in Marseilles, but they are quite lovely, nevertheless. 'Tis there that I dream of you at night."

"Monsieur," she said, endeavoring to sound scolding and flirtatious at once, when she really wanted to drag him from room to room and demand descriptions of each occupant. "We've only just met."

"Aye. But that meeting has launched a thousand dreams."

She turned away, hoping she oozed charm instead of impatience. "That door over there—"

"Come to my chambers. There is time before the hunt."

"What?"

"Come with me," he whispered, so close she wanted to shake him off, like an overly zealous hound. "We shall have a bit of time before the royal hunt."

"I fear I am still too fatigued to join a hunt of any sort."

" 'Tis perfect then. You can find repose in my chambers. I share the space with two others, but they shall surely be afield. We shall have time and to spare."

"Time for what?" she asked, looking him directly in the eye.

For a moment he seemed taken aback, then, "I think you know, Princess," he said.

"But I *certainly* would if you would tell me."

"I am not an unwealthy man. I could give you much."

"In exchange for what?"

He reached out to stroke her hair. His fingers brushed her arm before lifting a heavy coil to his lips. "Your companionship," he murmured.

"You already have my companionship, monsieur," she said and tugged at the wanton lock that curled about his fingers, but he refused to release it. "Why not give me whatever prize you deem appropriate now and we can go our separate ways?"

He stared at her in blank surprise for a moment, then laughed. "I am not accustomed to such splendid wit."

"And there lies the difference between us," said Cat. "You call it wit; I call it honesty. But I am Rom, a wanderer by nature and force. I've no time for subtlety." Not unless it would aid her cause in some way.

"Then I shall be forthright," he said, sobering dramatically. "I want you in my bed." He tugged her closer by the multihued length of her hair. "Indeed, I have wanted you since the moment I first saw you."

"Which was only a few short hours past."

"It matters not. You are in my blood."

" 'Tis lucky for you then," she said, managing to tug her hair from his grasp while only losing a few strands. "For this way a part of me will be in your bed even though the rest of me is not."

"You say you are too weary for a hunt," he said. "But I see 'tis not true. 'Tis simply a different kind of chase you lead. But I do not mind. In fact—" He reached out quickly, grabbing her arm again. "I will go to any lengths to have you."

She smiled, though the expression felt stretched as thin as her patience. "For all I care, you can go to—"

"Princess Cat." A man approached from her left.

She turned with a scowl in the tiny space afforded her between the Frenchman and the wall—rather like the proverbial rock and hard place. But it was good that she'd been interrupted, for it seemed she might have inherited her grandmother's unpredictable tongue after all.

"We have not yet met," said the man just entering. He bowed with a small man's grace. De la Faire moved away a fraction of an inch, as if to get a better view of the interloper. "I am Lord Samuel of the clan MacKinnon." His face was round, his hair bright as copper.

"I have no wish to disturb you if you are otherwise occupied."

"Nay, not at all," she said, glad for the chance to move out of the Frenchman's reach and sidle along the wall to the next window. "Monsieur de la Faire was kind enough to show me about the castle."

" 'Tis quite impressive, is it not?"

"Aye."

MacKinnon smiled shyly, his teeth flashing against his short-cropped beard. "I will not keep you," he said. "I only wished to say how I enjoyed your performance of the evening past."

"Thank you, my lord."

"You reminded me of my daughters when they were wee small things."

"I am not that small, my lord."

"Nay. Just full of life and energy."

"How are your daughters?" de la Faire asked.

"They are well. Well indeed."

"And your wife?"

A shadow crossed MacKinnon's brow. "Aisla died some months past."

"I am so sorry," said the Frenchman. "I had not heard. An illness?"

A moment of taut silence stretched between the two men.

"An accident. Her horse threw her on the way home one eve."

"Home from?" de la Faire asked. But MacKinnon had already turned toward Cat.

"Again, I beg forgiveness for my interruption, Princess."

"I am not really a princess," she told him.

"The title fits. Will you allow me to escort you back

to the hall? Or to your chambers mayhap?"

Out of the frying pan and into the fire, she thought. But the fire did not look quite as hot as the pan.

"Catriona."

She raised her gaze to the doorway, only to find Rory striding toward her.

"Grandmother needs you."

"Grandmother?" Her heart beat wildly. "Is she well?"

"You'd best come," he said, but she was already rushing toward the door, skirt hiked up in one hand.

Rory strode alongside her into the hallway, down the long corridor.

"What happened? Is she in the great hall?"

"Nay. She is in your chamber. I helped her there when I saw you were not about."

"Is it her heart? Is she breathing well?"

" 'Tis probably worry for you. Where have you been?"

"Discovering the lay of the castle."

"It did not look as if that was all you were discovering."

She gave him a sidelong glance as she trotted down the stone stairs. "I have no time for your jealousy, Rory."

"But you have time for the Frenchman, and the round-faced laird?" he asked, but she was already at her chamber's door.

It creaked open beneath her trembling fingers and she rushed across the room. Marta lay on her side, one gnarled hand cushioned beneath her frizzled hair.

"Grandmother!" Cat fell immediately to her knees. "Grandmother, what ails you?"

The dark, ancient eyes opened. "What is amiss?" she asked, moving to sit up.

"Nay. Lie back. Are you feeling better?"

"Better?" She turned a baffled scowl on her granddaughter, then at Rory, who remained tense and unapologetic in the doorway. "I am as old as dirt and I long for a peaceful nap in my own cart. Yet I feel as well as can be expected," she said. Turning her gaze back to Catriona, she softened her expression. "But what of you? Have you learned anything?"

"Nay, Grandmother," she said, refusing to acknowledge Rory's duplicity. Forever and always he had been the jealous one. When in truth, that right should have been hers. "I have learned nothing, except perhaps . . ." She smoothed Marta's white, crinkled hair away from her forehead. "Perhaps I have learned what is most dear to me in all the world."

The bead-bright eyes glittered. "There is little point to getting sentimental over a rumpled old witch like myself, child."

"I could not bear to lose you too."

Marta covered Cat's hand with her own. Her fingers felt dry and smooth against her skin. "All will be well, little dove."

Tears threatened and weakness spilled over Catriona. "Are you certain?" she asked in a whisper.

"Aye." The old woman nodded jerkily. "I feel it in my soul. And when one is as old as I, God dare not fool her. Worry not, lass. We shall have the boy back."

Chapter 4

Catriona tried to rest but daylight and terror conspired against her. And so she waited for the hunt, trying to still her thoughts, trying to control the swirling worries that threatened to drown her.

'Twas well past noon when she heard riders assemble in the courtyard. Horses nickered and iron-shod hooves rang against the cobblestones. Rising from bed, Catriona cast a glance out the window. 'Twas a goodly group of hunters. Surely the castle would be almost empty. Careful not to waken Marta, she opened the trunk that housed her garments. From it she drew and then donned a simple costume, no more elaborate than the king's servants wore. 'Twas that fact that gave her hope of anonymity.

From the courtyard, she heard raucous laughter. Tying on a grayish wig, she strode to the window. They were still there, so she paced, her bare feet silent against the worn grain of the floor, until finally she heard the riders depart.

"Your bewitching charms will not help you in this, Princess Cat. For if you tell anyone of your plight, we shall know. Indeed, it might be that it is we whom you are trusting with your secrets. Scotland's court is full of

intrigue. And we shall be watching you." Blackheart had laughed, a flowing breathy sound, but then he had dropped the object with which he had trifled all through that conversation. For a moment it had gleamed in the firelight, but she could not see what it was—not even when he bent to retrieve it.

The next day she had crept back to that spot and found, crushed into the soft ground, the imprint of a medallion. Her hands had shaken when she'd traced that image onto a ragged piece of vellum.

'Twas that medallion that she must find, for 'twas that medallion which would tell her Blackheart's true identity.

In a moment she was hurrying down the hallway, the scrap of vellum tucked into the pouch that hung beside the simple bone dirk on her girdle. A serving maid passed with a nod, carrying a bucket.

Catriona nodded back.

The castle was immense, but she had some concept of its design now, and her plans were simple; find the medallion; find Blackheart. Perhaps he wore the piece around his neck, but she couldn't afford to passively wait until she might chance to see it. She had to search for it.

It would be wise to first check the rooms of the men who were gone on the hunt, but she had no way of knowing which rooms those were. Thus, she would begin at one corner of the castle and search each room, mentally checking off each chamber until she found that for which she searched.

Another servant passed carrying a board and goblet.

Catriona bobbed her head and hurried on. Nervous and uncertain, she glanced from side to side. Then, seeing no one, she stepped up to the nearest door and knocked quietly. No one answered. One more furtive glance to her left and she was inside. It was a narrow chamber. Without benefit of a window, it was quite dark. Nevertheless, she closed the door behind her and managed to ascertain that a pallet occupied the majority of the space. Two trunks vied for room, one leather and one wooden. She searched the leather one first, since it was smaller and likely to hold the most valuable items. But it proved disappointing.

The wooden one was no better, filled with nothing more than cloth and garments. The entire search took only a few seconds. Straightening quickly, she glanced about the room. There was little enough that would help her here. But . . .

Hurrying to the bed, she snatched up a pillow and hustled back to the door. It opened noisily and closed the same. But the hallway was empty, and now she had a burden of sorts, a reason for hustling along the passageways.

Acting as if she had a lively purpose, Catriona strode along until she came to the end of the hall.

The chamber there proved to be larger than the first, boasting a tall narrow window and a fair-sized bed. Her search was quick and thorough.

The next room was locked. This was a problem she had not considered. She *must* get inside.

Then again, the medallion did not seem to be so priceless that it must be locked away. Blackheart had fiddled with it as if it were something he habitually kept with him. Of course, that might mean that he kept it tucked under his tunic. But she could hardly go about asking each guest if he possessed a medallion that bore six gemstones surrounding intricate knot work. Thus, she would keep the locked room in mind and think of a way to breach its security.

In a moment she was knocking at another door, then slipping silently inside.

The room was dark. She paused, letting her eyes adjust. It seemed as though she must be searching for a man of some wealth. Therefore, he would probably inhabit one of the larger rooms. Still, she could not afford—

A shape rose out of the shadows.

Catriona gasped and jerked back.

"Forgive me! I—"

The shadow materialized into a dark robed man who seemed to stumble toward her.

"Forgive me!" she rasped again, and pivoting away, wrenched the door open and lurched into the hall.

A matronly woman stopped dead in her tracks, her chin drawn back into the folds of her neck.

"Good Christmas, lass, what be you doing?" she asked.

"I . . ." Catriona searched blindly for an explanation. "Lord de la Faire said he was in need of a pillow."

"De la Faire!" The matron looked at her askance. "Then what you be doing in the holy man's cell?"

"Holy man?"

"Aye. Blackburn's very own saint, he is. 'Tis said he has been here as long as the castle itself. He's as deaf as a stone." She scowled again. "Are you new here?"

"Aye. Aye." Catriona was still grappling to catch her breath and her wits. "I was asked to come and help out, what with the feast and all."

"Well, need you we do," said the other. "But you mustn't be wasting your time with pillows and whatnot. Not when . . . Ahhh . . ." She nodded with a clever expression, as if she'd just realized something that most would not. "Lord de la Faire! Might that be the fellow what thinks himself such a ladies' man?"

"Aye, I think that might be him."

"Uh huh, and you a bonny lass delivering a pillow upon his request. Come along. You may call me Mildred. And what be your name?"

Catriona glanced frantically toward the door once more. "Mary," she said. 'Twas the first name that slammed into her mind. She welcomed it readily. "Mary of Kilchurn."

"Kilchurn?" asked the older woman, surprise in her tone as she herded her new ward down the hall.

It was obviously too late for Cat to change her place of origin. "Aye."

"Might you know Duana?"

"A . . . a stout maid with dark hair and a little mole just so on her cheek?" she guessed breathlessly.

"Nay, nay," said the other, waving an impatient hand as she hurried down the hall. "Duana is as slim as a reed with fine, fair hair."

"I fear I do not know her then," murmured Cat, glancing behind. "But she sounds to be a bonny maid. Whose room is that?" she asked, motioning nervously toward the door she had found locked some minutes earlier.

The matron shook her head. "I cannot keep them all straight in me mind. But I believe his name be Drummond. But this Duana, she is not bonny at all. Teeth like a braying ass, she has. 'Tis a shame, too, seeing what a prince she married. Might you know her Shay?"

"I—"

"Ooch, but you wouldn't. Not if you have not met Duana. She gives her man not a moment's peace. Just like Sophie, she is." She waved her arms expansively and shook her head.

Another hallway branched off to their left. Catriona stepped quickly into it as the other woman continued on.

"Her man has to do for her every minute or 'twill be hell to pay. In fact, 'twas not a week ago when he had a pint or two, she—"

Around the corner of the hall, Cat heard the matron's voice come to a halt. Ducking into the nearest room, Cat pressed her back to the door. Breathing hard, she prayed that her talkative friend was not the type to hunt her down.

"Mary?" The voice from the hall came nearer, footsteps meandering along. "Mary?" There was silence for a moment, then, "Now where the devil did that lass get herself off to?" A small gasp. "Supposed to bring de la Faire a pillow, indeed. 'Twas probably the twit's own ploy. Course he is not an unhandsome man." Her footsteps turned away. "Come to think on it, I wouldn't mind a bit of that myself." She chuckled. "What would Sophie say of that? Always thinking she has the only . . ."

The voice faded into oblivion.

Catriona let out a deep breath and wilted in the darkness, but just at that moment she heard someone chuckle out in the hall. Against her side she felt the door handle move, and she jumped away as if it had come alive. Dropping the pillow and grabbing her skirts, she dashed wildly across the room, leapt onto the bed, and dived to the floor on the opposite side.

The door groaned open.

"*Mon Dieu*!" a woman sighed. "So eager."

"Fayette." A man's heavy breathing rasped through the room. "I could not wait a moment longer."

"Truly?"

"Aye. There is not another like you. You are temptation itself. I can no longer resist."

Dear God, they were approaching the bed. Cat crouched lower, eager to crawl underneath. But it took no great wit to realize that the space was too small.

"You need not resist any longer."

"How I longed to have you alone. To touch you. To cherish you."

Already, Cat could hear the rustle and scrape of fabric.

"Cherish me now."

More rustling fabric, then a man's rasped breath. "You are so bonny. Too bonny to hurry through like a cheap repast. I must take my time, savor you like a succulent meal."

Nay, Cat thought fanatically.

"Succulent." Fayette rasped the word, and pulled a sharp breath between her teeth. "I have heard intriguing things about you. I wonder now—are they true?"

"You shall know me in a matter of moments, my sweet. But first I will know every inch of you. Your neck, as shapely as a swan's."

The woman's moan was accented by the unmistakable sound of nails against clothing.

"Your shoulders. Soft as a lambkin."

"Poetry *and* big stones," she moaned.

"Breasts." He whispered the word like a reverent prayer. "Like two roe deer."

"Take me, Matthew. Like a roe in the meadow."

"So sweet."

Crouched behind the bed like a whipped cur, Catriona heard his kiss, Fayette's heated groan.

"So full, like a cup of sweet wine."

"Taste my wine," she rasped.

"A sip." There was a pause, an utter lack of sound for a moment, and then a moan of hopeless pleasure. "Just a sip, sweet lass. For there is so much more. I've no wish to ruin my appetite."

"Damn your appetite!"

He chuckled. "Patience is a virtue."

"Patience be—oh!" The word was high-pitched and sharp. "Do that again."

"But there is more. Each perfect rib demands a kiss. Each . . ." He paused again as he, apparently, did as proposed. "Each tiny dip requires my attention."

"Aye."

"Your navel. Your belly."

Fayette moaned again, and just above her head, Cat felt the mattress shift as someone pressed into it.

"Your hips."

The sound of a gown slipping to the floor seemed to swallow every particle of air in the room.

"Your legs."

The mattress ropes groaned as Fayette settled onto it.

"Damn my legs," she said. "Kiss me there."

There was a moment of reverent silence, then, "Sweet mother of God!"

"Kiss me."

"Aye," he said, his voice so guttural, it was barely heard.

The bed and the woman groaned in unison. "Aye. There."

The ropes creaked again, beginning a rhythm.

"Take off your clothes. I want to feel you," she rasped.

"Shameless Jezebel."

"Aye," she agreed.

Cloth rustled. Matthew groaned.

" 'Tis nothing so wondrous as a shameless Jez—" His words stopped abruptly.

"Leona was right," she sighed. "They hardly fit in my hands. Like a bullock, you are."

"I am your beast of burden," he rasped.

"Then take me like a beast."

"Come here," he growled.

"As you wish, beastie."

Catriona scrunched backward toward the head of the bed.

"Turn around."

"I want to feel them against me."

"Hold on to the rail."

The bed creaked in earnest as she did so.

Backed against the wall, Catriona waited in horror, but the woman's eyes were closed in ecstasy. Her pale, plump breasts were bare, drooping forward as she leaned down to grab hold of the rail.

"Take me," she moaned.

"Aye," he grunted and thrust forward.

Fayette gasped. Her eyes snapped open. Her gaze struck Catriona.

She screamed, jerked away, and grappled with the bedsheets.

Cat leapt to her feet.

"What in the name of God?" Matthew rasped.

Momentarily paralyzed, Catriona stared. His hose were gone and his penis, long and narrow and pink, pointed directly at her from a mass of red hair.

Fayette shrieked again. The sound spurred Cat into motion, launching her from the floor and onto the bed. For a moment she floundered in the deep, straw tick, but she caught her balance and threw herself toward the door.

She scraped wildly at the handle. For one frantic instant it refused to open, and then, like a winged angel, it flew wide. She rushed into the hall and without thought galloped off to the right and careened wildly around the nearest corner.

A sword swept past her face. She shrieked and jolted to a halt. A voice rasped an expletive, and then hands, steady as stone, grabbed her shoulders.

"Good saints, lass, what's your—" The words stopped. Cat glanced up, still breathing hard as she stared wide-eyed into Sir Hawk's scowling face. "Catriona? What the devil are you doing? I very nearly beheaded you."

"I just . . ." She tried to calm her heart, but in her mind she imagined a naked man storming up behind her, and the only thing she'd be able to recognize was his wick. "I, um . . ."

Hawk continued to stare at her, his brows drawn low over silver blue eyes.

"Who is it?" he asked, his tone deep.

"What who?" In her scrambling mind, Fayette's husky, pleasure-soaked voice still echoed in her memory. "Who what?"

"Who is it that be giving you trouble?"

"No one." The words came out too fast and a bit high-pitched.

Hawk lowered his brows a bit more, then strode past her to glance down the corridor.

Apparently no naked man was storming down on them, sword unsheathed, so to speak, for Hawk came back looking as perplexed as before. "Come along," he said, his tone gruff as he put away his own weapon.

"I tell you, there's been no trouble that—"

He interrupted her with a wave of one square hand.

"I beg to differ, lass. I always consider wounding the king's friends a problem."

"Wounding?" she asked, baffled.

"Your temple," he said, and taking her hand in his, led her away.

"My . . ." She touched her hand to her hairline, and felt, to her utter surprise, a trickle of something warm and sticky. Bringing her fingers before her eyes, she saw that it was blood. "How—"

"I think I have never seen a woman run that fast," he said, wending his way down one corridor and the next. "And I wonder why."

There was little she could tell him. After all, there was no logical explanation for why she would be hiding in another's private chambers. " 'Tis nothing," she said, practicing a shrug. "I heard a noise and became spooked."

"Spooked?" He turned to her, his expression quizzical. "Lady Catriona, I've seen you fight men trained to war and honed for battle. Even then you were not spooked. Here." He opened a door and motioned her inside.

She glanced about as she stepped in. "What is this place?"

"The infirmary. Physic," he called, glancing about. "Physic!" But the room was empty, except for baskets and bottles that cluttered the floor and table.

"You've no need to concern yourself," Cat said, fingering the scratch that began at her hairline and skimmed backward for two fingers' width. " 'Tis naught."

"It may turn septic," Hawk argued. "Sit."

"Are you an expert then?" she asked, striving for levity—or at least normalcy.

"Of a sort." He motioned her toward a nearby wooden stool.

She took a seat and watched him as he searched for and selected a bottle. Uncorking it, he smelled the contents.

"So you've spent some time here, Sir Hawk?" she asked. It wasn't the first time she had noticed the scar beside his left eye. It was narrow, no more than a pale line that swept toward his cheekbone. It merely made him look a little more dangerous than before, but at one time he must have been in grave danger of losing his sight. "Was it your eye that brought you here?"

"Nay, it was not."

"How did you come by that scar?"

"There was a disagreement," he said simply. If he was trying to dissuade her interest he was doing a poor job of it. But if he hoped to intrigue her . . . "And what of you, lass? How did you acquire the mark on your throat?"

She touched a forefinger to the tiny blemish he'd mentioned. " 'Twas a mark from my birth, I think. I have not had so many disagreements as you."

He raised a brow as if he doubted her words, but was too polite to say so. Dumping a bit of the chosen liquid onto a scrap of cloth he'd found in a leather basket, he towered over her. "What were you running from?"

"I told you," she said, looking up at him from her defenseless position. He hovered over her, large as a destrier. "I had a fright, is all. I heard a noise and went to investigate."

"And you found . . ."

She cleared her throat and blinked. "What?"

His scowl deepened. "What did you find?"

" 'Twas nothing to concern yourself with."

"I beg to differ," he argued. Steadying her chin with one square hand as he dabbed at her wound.

His fingers felt warm and strangely protective, for if he knew the truth of her mission . . .

She winced at the thought.

"My apologies." He drew the cloth away, but his fingers remained on her jaw, cradling it as if she were a tiny lass. "I fear gentleness is not my greatest characteristic."

He was wrong, she thought with surprise. Kindness seemed as much a part of him as the deep timbre of his voice, despite his intimidating scowl and size. His stature was emphasized by his native Highland garb: a green and blue plaid, high leather boots, and a simple saffron tunic tucked into his tartan with sleeves rolled high over the dark skin of his arms. His wrists were flat and broad. Sprinkled with sable hairs, they looked taut with sinew and bone. Higher up, his arms swelled with muscle that disappeared under the pale fabric. And higher still, his shoulders looked impossibly wide beneath the simple garment. There was nothing small about this man. Everything about him seemed larger than life. The width of his sun-browned throat, the bulge of his thigh as it shifted inadvertently against hers. If Matthew was hung like a bullock, Hawk would be . . .

Catriona stopped the thought with a flare of hot discomfort. Her harrowing experience in the unknown bedchamber had been frightening and nothing else. Certainly it was not stimulating. Still, she felt strangely breathless and sensitized, as if Hawk's every movement were some kind of primitive dance. The flex of his arm, the bend of his knee, how the cords in his neck sliced into a valley when he turned just so, and how that valley pointed toward the rising slope of his chest.

He drew his hand from her jaw and she shifted her gaze quickly to it.

A scar sliced between the two knuckles closest to his thumb.

She cleared her throat. "Another reason for your knowledge of the infirmary?" she asked, doing her best to wrest her overheated mind from places hidden beneath yards of tartan wool.

There was quiet for a moment. She could feel his gaze on her face, and finally, when the silence became breathless, she lifted her eyes to look at him. Still, she could not read his thoughts. She could not even tell if he were scowling at her.

"Sir Hawk?" She said his name softly.

"What?" He seemed startled by the sound of her voice, as if his thoughts had been far away.

She was here on a mission, she reminded herself. Nothing else. And regardless of the power in his arm or the gentleness in his hand, she did not know him well. Indeed, he might be Blackheart himself. Therefore she had best keep her head now or lose it forever. "I asked about the scar on your hand."

He turned it distractedly upward to stare at it. " 'Tis naught. Lass—" He reached for her as if to draw her chin upward again, but at the last second, he drew back. "I would know what had you spooked."

A thousand possible lies skimmed through her mind. But his gaze was as steady as the falcon for which he was named. And a lie did not seem wise.

The scar beside his eye dipped. "Is someone bothering you?"

She remembered Fayette's moans, Matthew's hoarse poetry. The memories *were* liable to bother her for some time—though perhaps inappropriately. For while she should have been repulsed, her skin still felt flushed and her senses overwrought from the sound of their husky voices.

"Surely you can see, Sir Hawk," she began, trying to ignore the heavy feeling in the pit of her being, "this matter is something I've no wish to discuss."

" 'Tis my task to guard the king," he said. "And I cannot do this if I am unaware of the goings-on of the castle."

"Must you know everything that transpires at Blackburn?"

" 'Tis my preference."

"Every clandestine . . . joining?"

For a moment he seemed stunned to silence, then, "You witnessed—"

"Aye." She interrupted him before he could voice the embarrassing truth.

"Oh."

She cleared her throat and tried to think of somewhere to look, but there was nothing to see but him. "Oh, indeed."

His presence seemed to fill the entire room, and she saw that he was as uncomfortable as she. Lifting a hand, he rubbed his chest as if easing some half-forgotten wound, and when her gaze fell there, she realized that she could indeed see the end of a whitish scar that pointed directly to his heart.

"Blackburn Castle is . . ." He paused. " 'Tis a far shot from a monastery. I try to keep young James isolated from such things, but 'tis difficult."

"Are you speaking of your own behavior or others'?"

The question fell into the heat of the room like tinder on flame.

"I am the captain of the king's royal guard," he said. "My post keeps me quite busy."

"The two I saw seemed quite busy."

His eyes were deadly steady, his brows low, but his lips quirked slightly.

"Are you inquiring about my carnal experiences, lass?"

No. Maybe. Yes. Good Lord, what was wrong with her? The room seemed strangely airless, their gazes tied.

"Have a care who you hone your flirtations on, lass," he said, his voice a midnight rumble in the dim room.

"Are you so dangerous then?"

"Nay. I am so old. My heart may be unable to bear the strain."

He looked as tough as a scared oak, as intriguing as a winding trail. She almost laughed at his description of himself, but the sound would not quite leave her throat.

"Not so old, I think," she murmured.

He reached out and ever so slowly, as if he tried to stop himself, stroked the backs of his fingers against her cheek. A dozen unwanted emotions swamped her—desire and hope and host of others she could not even name. She closed her eyes to the sweet brush of his caress, but in that second a rustle of sound came from the doorway.

Hawk yanked his hand away, then pivoted jerkily toward the noise. "Physic." His tone seemed to carry an unwarranted relief. "The lass has been wounded. I leave her in your care." Without another word, he dropped the cloth on the table and strode from the room.

Chapter 5

Haydan paced the confines of his bedchamber. It was a small room, comfortable but humble. Long ago, he had been offered more elegant quarters, but he had found that he could not relax there—for the greater the distance from the king, the more his nervousness increased.

Now he resided less than fifty feet from James's bedroom door, and yet he felt as high strung as a wild barb. But why? All was well. True, the king was planning to celebrate his twelfth birthday, and true, the castle and grounds beyond were becoming mired in guests. Still, there was no reason for any great worry—for although James was the sovereign monarch of Scotland, his was a title in name only. He had no true power. The French Duke of Albany governed Scotland, and although both his interest and his involvement in Scottish politics seemed to be waning, he still held the country's reins. Therefore, 'twas *his* life that was most in danger.

It was true that there would always be those who wished the throne harm, but Hawk's men were ready for any eventuality. They were loyal, well trained, and well armed.

But that thought propelled an unwanted memory—the memory of a slim Gypsy lass fighting off the advances of a man Haydan had trusted to protect the fairer sex, not to compromise it. A man who had been Haydan's own soldier.

Damn! He paced again. Although Brims had been new to Blackburn's defenses, he had come highly recommended. Haydan had thought him above such deplorable actions. An image of Catriona wavered in his imagination. Any man might be made temporally insane by her nearness. It was not that she was beautiful; mayhap she was not even particularly bonny. She was simply . . . entrancing. And yet, what it was that made her so mesmerizing, he was unsure. Perhaps it was her eyes. Wide set and slightly slanted, they seemed to change hue with each mercurial mood. But nay, it was not simply her eyes. It was *she*. She was uncanny, unearthly. That had been evidenced that very evening in the great hall. For when she entered, all sense seemed to be driven from the mind of every man present. They were willing to make fools of themselves just to spend a moment by her side, to feel the light of her smile on their faces, to hear the sweet whisper of her voice.

And he? Haydan ground his teeth. He was just one among the crush. True, he had been able to keep himself from her, to keep his distance when others crowded close, but he could not help but be thrilled by every moment of her attention, or enraged by every inane compliment from the ever-present posturing swains.

He paced again. Why had she come here? To perform, she said. But there were things she wasn't telling him. A man didn't become the king's captain of the guard without developing some kind of sixth sense.

But why was she holding back the truth? She was not

a dishonest sort and he had never given her reason to distrust him. Indeed, since the first time he'd met her years before, they had gotten on well together. She had been a lass of only eight and ten years when she had first come to Blackburn Castle. Even then Haydan had felt an indefinable attraction to her, but years and his own aversion to taking himself too seriously had warned him that he, like every other breathing man, had merely been enamored by her unearthly sensuality. Thus, he had been careful not to act the fool. Careful to pretend that he thought of her no differently than he thought of his own high-spirited niece—rather troublesome, but a decent sort.

Still, he could remember every moment he had spent with her. He had been a fool to take her to the infirmary, for now he had even more memories—the feel of her flesh beneath his fingers, the glimmer of her eyes—so vibrant, so alive. She was not like other lasses—neither coy nor silly, but—

But what? He paced again. She was a babe, little more than half his age. Just the thought of her miniscule years made his knee creak with the years he'd put behind him. He grimaced as he walked, reveling in the pain. For with pain came reality. And the reality was, he was an old man—and the king's man, vowed to protect and serve, to put none above his sovereign lord.

And that was just what he would do. Turning toward the door, Haydan wrenched it open and stepped into the hall. In a dozen strides he had reached James's room. A sconce burned beside each of the iron-bound double doors. And beneath each light, a soldier in dark hose and blue doublet stood with his back to the wall, ready and alert.

"Galloway," Haydan said, nodding to the nearest

guard. He was a young man of humble birth, too young for such a post, some would say. But it was he who had reported Catriona's trouble with Brims, even though he had been unable to disguise his distrust of Gypsies. "All goes well here?"

"Aye!" Galloway snapped, his stance so stiff and erect it might have been hammered out on an open forge. "All is quiet, Sir Hawk!"

Haydan gave him a wry look for his overly zealous attitude, but Galloway didn't even turn his gaze sideways to note the expression.

"Nothing to report, Cockerel?" Hawk asked the other guard.

"Nay, sir," he agreed, only raising a dark brow at the other's wild enthusiasm. "You may rest assured that young Galloway here would have reported so much as a flea's entrance to the room."

Haydan stifled a grin. There was much to be said for young blood.

All was as it should be. And yet, Haydan could not quite squelch the desire to look in on the lad for himself. With a nod to the guards, he stepped silently into the room, careful to make no noise. After all, the king was nearly a man now and no longer wanted to be coddled and watched. Indeed, he sometimes chafed at the confinement that royalty brought. As captain of the guard, Haydan realized that, yet he found he longed for the days when the lad was not too large to ride on his shoulders or to fall asleep in his arms on a long day's journey.

There were those at Blackburn who would be eager to say that it was not a guard's place to become so enmeshed in the king's life.

Haydan only wished he could disagree. But as he neared the large, scarlet draped bed, he felt the familiar tug at his heart. A single candle splashed light across the room. Beneath the covers, young James slept peacefully.

Haydan watched him in silence, remembering him as a tiny lad, a chubby handsome child with a mischievous grin and hair as bright as a Highland plaid. The sound of his laughter, the look of admiration on his gamin features as Haydan taught him one thing or another—how to perform a proper riposte, notch an arrow, or hood a restive gyrfalcon.

Those days were dwindling so quickly now. Just the thought of it made him feel as old as the stone beneath his feet.

Near the door, he heard the shuffling of a guard. Turning almost guiltily from the bed, Haydan paced back through the doorway.

"Sir Hawk," said Galloway, keeping his face turned forward and only moving his eyes as Haydan stepped alongside him. "Is something amiss?"

"Nay, all is well," Hawk said, and turned away.

"Sir Hawk?"

"Aye," he said, glancing back at the lance-straight guard.

"I wished to thank you for this post."

"Already you have thanked me thrice."

The lad's stance stiffened even more, though Haydan would not have thought it possible. "I will not disappoint you, sir."

"I am sure you will not," Haydan agreed, eager to be off.

"And sir?"

"Aye."

"My apologies regarding the incident outside the gates."

"The incident?"

"With Lieutenant Brims and Wickfield. I did not know you had befriended the lass." His brow puckered. "I should have escorted her safely to Blackburn, even though she is a Gypsy."

Haydan narrowed his eyes. "You do not like Gypsies, Galloway?"

The young man swallowed hard enough to show the bob of his Adam's apple. " 'Tis difficult not to like them, now that I have seen—"

There was a whisper of amusement from the other guard.

Galloway stopped abruptly.

Haydan turned his gaze on the soldier called Cockerel by all those who knew him. Perhaps it was the wide, plumed hat he wore when off duty. Or perhaps it was simply his bearing that had initiated the name.

"Something amuses you, Cockerel?"

"Nay, Sir Hawk. Certainly not."

"Then why do you smile?"

"I was merely thinking of the Gypsy lass, sir." He paused, and the jaunty corner of his grin perked up a scant quarter of an inch. "She *is* rather . . . bonny. Is she not?"

Haydan sharpened his glare. "I had not noticed."

"Truly? Then let me inform you, sir: Lady Catriona is, without a doubt—"

"Not for the likes of you."

"What?"

"You will not touch her," Haydan said. "Do you understand me?"

Though Cockerel struggled to conceal his surprise, he was not so judicious about his grin. "I believe I do, sir," he said.

Haydan glowered for a moment. " 'Tis good." Turning abruptly away, he cursed the pain in his knee and his own grinding foolishness.

He walked for some time down the endless maze of hallways, but the castle seemed to hold no air, no freedom, no peace. He finally strode for the ramparts, hoping the wind would blow the moldering worries from his mind.

They were foolish worries. After all . . .

He stopped, aware suddenly of a small scratch of noise.

It was probably nothing more than a rat looking for a meal, but his nerves had already been on edge and now they were cranked as tight as a readied crossbow. Turning quietly down a darkened hallway, he followed his instincts, hoping he was heading in the right direction. Hoping—

There! A shadow just ahead, hovering in front of a door. Hawk paused, ready to jerk back into a hidden alcove. But already it was too late. The shadow turned toward him, the face pale in the darkness.

"Who goes there?" he asked.

There was a squeak of surprise and suddenly, like a skittish colt, the shadow turned and fled.

"Halt!" Hawk demanded. But the other was already fading into the gloom.

Haydan slammed into motion, straining to see in the darkness as he thundered along in pursuit.

Gone! He was gone! A hallway opened at each side. Hawk glanced in both directions. There!

He shot into action, leaping after his quarry like a hound, eating up the distance between them. The stairs! He saw the shadow turn, saw him lunge up the stone steps, but Haydan's stride was longer. He leapt after, swallowing several at a time. Close now. So close. He reached out, trying to snatch the intruder back to him, but his fingers just brushed his tunic. There was a squawk of dismay. His prey burst up the last stair and around a corner.

Haydan leapt after, ready to drag him to the ground. But the ramparts were empty. He flew to the parapets and glanced down. The bailey was a hundred feet below. Had the scoundrel jumped? But no, he couldn't have!

He was hiding in a crenel. He had to be!

Haydan leapt on, peering into each gap of the stone battlements. But there was nothing. No one. He had disappeared—like smoke, like magic, like a wild figment of his imagination.

The next morning, Haydan's head groaned a complaint as he sat up in bed. His knee ached as he swung his feet onto the floor. He had spent most of the night pacing. After his frustrating chase, he had returned to the king's quarters. But one quick glance had assured him all was well. He had then hurried back to the spot where he had first seen his quarry and swept the door open without knocking.

A sleepy "What the devil are you about?" was hurled at him from the bed. It was obvious there was no trouble afoot there.

After a half hour or so of fairly aimless wandering, Haydan had finally returned to his own room. But sleep was a fickle mistress, and refused to lie with him. Thus he had paced until the wee hours of the morning, until fatigue had finally pulled him under.

Belting on his plaid, he slipped the blade of his sgian dubh, his black blade, into his boot so that only the antler hilt showed. These simple rituals made him feel better, and in a matter of minutes he sat in the great hall, trying to concentrate on his breakfast and ignore the knot of men that hovered near the corner of the noisy room. He knew why they congregated there; knew that hidden behind them was the lass called Catriona. But he would not care. If he had learned anything last night, either from his time in the infirmary or his time in the chase, he had learned that he was getting old.

Good saints! He felt as if he had run a hundred miles, as if he had battled a dragon with nothing more than a prayer and the dull end of a quail bone. When in actuality, he had done nothing more than run up a few stairs. And lost his quarry.

Frustration burned through him again. Who had it been and what mischief had he planned? Haydan would have been willing to believe there was no harm meant if the lad had stopped and explained his actions, but his flight had condemned him.

Lad! The word had come to him unbidden. It *had* been a lad at the door. Haydan was sure of it suddenly, for the boy had moved with swiftness and dexterity, and although the darkness may have been distorting, the figure did not seem very large.

Haydan glanced about the hall with a new perception. Among the servants, there were many youths. Near the front door, for instance, there was a boy about the proper size, but . . . nay. He was a wee bit too small.

Kitchen Elsie's daughter appeared. She was a comely lass of about fourteen years, plump and . . . Could his quarry have been a girl?

Haydan grimaced at the thought. He was not a vain man, but he had no wish to believe he had been outdistanced by a plump girl just coming into womanhood.

Ah, there. Another lad, near the cluster of men determined to make fools of themselves. Haydan watched the boy offer wine and ale as he moved among the long tables. He was a graceful boy and quick. Dressed in tan, slightly stained hose and a too-large tunic, he went efficiently about his task. His head was covered in a gray cap that drooped down the side of his face, but Haydan was fairly certain he was Sara's boy. A good lad, if a bit high-spirited.

The boy turned slightly, granting Haydan a slanted view of his face. Ale splashed over the brim of Haydan's mug and his curse was loud enough to make his tablemates turn toward him with quizzical expressions.

Damn it all—the lad had done it again.

"I tell you," Catriona said, laughing at the latest jest. "I have no claim to a throne, here or elsewhere."

"But have you ever returned to your homeland?" asked the slight man with the crooked teeth and the unruly hair. He looked vaguely familiar, but when he had introduced himself as Arthur Douglas, Earl of Harrowhead, she did not recognize the name. He had a boyish habit of hugging his left arm against his side as if he were shy. Those around him called him Lord Hogshead, but he seemed to bear no ill will, perhaps because of the stunning amount of ale he had already consumed, or perhaps because of his own disarming and unassuming temperament.

"Nay. I have never had the opportunity to return to Khandia," she said.

"That explains it then," said another. "If they saw your face, they would surely hasten you to the throne."

"If they were still conscious after the first glimpse of her," Hogshead said, and the others around him laughed.

Nearly a dozen men surrounded her. She knew a few

names. MacKinnon with the round, bearded face. De la Faire with the perfect teeth. Lord Drummond, a dark, handsome man who sat beside the pale girl called Roberta and who seemed engrossed by her every whispered word. 'Twas he who kept his door locked, if Mildred had been correct.

Could any of them have issued that evil ultimatum?

"Widow Charmain," someone said. "You look well rested."

"I have been told that there is nowhere like Blackburn to get . . . rested."

Catriona caught her breath. There was something about the purred tone of 'rested' that tweaked her memory.

Fayette!

Cat snapped her gaze to the woman, but though the lady turned to look at Catriona there was neither recognition nor horror in her eyes, but rather the hint of an emotion Cat could not quite read.

"Lady," said a lad who appeared beside her elbow with a pitcher. "May I offer you some ale?"

"Nay, I fear I . . ." Cat began, but in that instant her gaze met the lad's mischievous green eyes. "Your M—" she began, but he lifted a finger unobtrusively to his mouth and motioned for silence.

"No ale?" he asked, his lips crinkled in an impish grin. "But 'tis an excellent brew."

"If . . . if you recommend it," she said, and sat transfixed by the sight of the crowned king of Scotland in soiled britches and a droopy bonnet.

He leaned close to pour. His cap dangled lower, threatening to be doused in her unrequested ale. "You promised me a ride," he whispered.

"Aye," she agreed simply, tearing her gaze from his face.

"Princess Cat," crooned de la Faire from near her elbow. "I missed you on the hunt yesterday."

She turned toward the speaker, wondering with stunned awe if none other had recognized the lad. "I was quite fatigued," she explained simply, and skimmed the faces that surrounded her. None was staring at the king in shocked dismay. "I fear I spent the afternoon in bed."

"An image to ponder," someone murmured.

There were chuckles.

"In the stable," James said softly. "Directly."

She nodded. He slipped away.

"Excuse me, gentlemen," she said, rising. "I must see to my grandmother."

"I hoped you might ride with me this day," someone said, but she made her excuses and hurried away.

Once outside the great hall, she turned left, trying to avoid anyone who might delay her. But just as she was about to escape, a priest in a black robe turned toward her.

"Catriona of the Bairds," he said. His hair was red, his voice soft, his hands hidden in the sleeves of his opposite arms. "I had hoped to meet you."

"Oh, Father, I . . ." She glanced down the hall she had planned to be escaping down even now. "I fear I have no time to delay. I received a message that my grandmother is feeling unwell."

He drew an expression of concern. "Mayhap I should accompany you."

"Nay!" Cat said quickly and searched frantically for an excuse. "Nay, Father," she said. "If I brought a priest into Grandmother's room she might imagine 'twas her last rites you'd come to give, and not your good wishes."

He smiled, a warm expression on his kindly face. "Very well, but please, lass, be not ashamed to come to me if you should have a need of any sort."

"My thanks," she said, and trying not to seem too impatient, hurried away.

She took a circuitous course to the stables, glancing quickly over her shoulder now and again. Her heart thundered like a running horse. It was not time! There would be no purpose in riding yet.

"You shall bring him to us. Alone and unarmed."

Not now. Not yet. That was to be her last resort, her final act if all else failed. If she could not determine Blackheart's true identity. If she could not stop him. 'Twas too early, and yet, it was not her place to refuse the king. She needed his friendship, required his trust, or all would be lost.

The stable door creaked open under her hand. From a heavily beamed box stall to her right, a groom glanced her way, then stood staring until she hurried past.

"Hello," she called softly.

No answer.

"Your Majesty," she whispered.

"Here." The voice came from up above.

She glanced up, just as James scurried down the leather-bound rungs of a slanting ladder. A smattering of straw rained down with his descent.

"We must hurry," he whispered, then glanced over his shoulder toward the stall that held the distant groom. "Most of the horsemen are breaking their fast. We've not much time."

"Time for what?" she asked, her heart still hammering in her too-tight chest.

"Our escape."

"Escape!"

"Shh. We've little enough time before someone realizes I am not in my chambers."

"You plan to ride out alone?"

"Not alone. With you."

"With me?" Her stomach cranked into a hard knot. "Truly, Your Majesty, I do not think this is a good idea. What if—"

"Shh," he warned again, and grabbing her hand, pulled her toward the nearest stall.

She stepped inside. He glanced nervously past her as he pulled the heavy door shut.

"I've already saddled Courtier. Sir Hawk taught me how to—"

" 'Twas a mistake."

James gasped and spun toward the voice. Catriona's heart twisted tight as she did the same.

"Hawk!" The name sounded like a reprimand coming from the rumpled, frowning lad.

"Aye." Hawk pushed himself from the wall where he had been resting. " 'Tis I. Were you expecting another?"

"I was expecting no one!" James snapped, his mouth puckering in concert with his brow. "How did you know?"

"I spied you in the hall and guessed your intent. When I saw that Courtier was saddled my suspicions were rewarded."

"Well, it makes no difference," James said. "I will have no guards this day."

The stable fell silent.

"So you think so little of Scotland?" Sir Hawk's voice was deep and quiet.

"This has naught to do with Scotland!"

"You *are* Scotland, lad. What befalls you befalls her."

The boy's scowl deepened, but he dropped his head

and gazed at his scruffy, oversized shoes. "I but wanted some time alone."

Hawk stepped closer. "With *one* companion," he reminded.

"Aye," James admitted reluctantly.

"I suppose it is but a coincidence that she is beautiful."

The words were no more than a murmur, but Catriona heard them.

The boy flushed, but a grin lifted one corner of his impish mouth. He turned shyly toward her, then hurried his glance away.

"I am on the threshold of manhood," he reminded Hawk quietly. "You said as much yourself."

"Aye, you are that. But I want you to step over the threshold and live in that room for a hundred score days before you do something so rash as this," Hawk murmured.

"Thirty score!"

Looping an arm over the lad's shoulder, Hawk urged him out of the stall. "How long would that be?" he asked.

"A long time!"

"How long?"

"Don't *you* know?"

"Perhaps I do not."

"Then why should I?"

"Because you are the king."

"Then I do not wish to be king."

They stood in the wide aisle of the stable, James glaring up, Hawk staring down as they locked proverbial horns.

"Then you shall not be," Hawk said with the slightest French accent. "For this day, you will be naught but

Jock, a merchant's son who is assisting me in my duties."

The boy's jaw dropped. "Jock? A merchant's son?" The boy's tone was awed.

"Aye, *Jock*," Hawk said. "Who did you think you were? The king of England? Now quit your lollygagging, lad. Fetch the lady's mount and be quick about it, or I'll give you a beating you will not soon forget."

"Aye." He bobbed an affirmation, trying to be solemn, though his grin threatened to peek through. "Aye," he said again and, spinning on his soiled shoes, thundered off down the hard-packed aisle.

Chapter 6

They rode three abreast down the beaten road. Behind them lay the gates of Blackburn. Ahead lay freedom.

James glanced up at Haydan on his mammoth gray stallion. The boy had many royal steeds, but Courtier, with his fine velvet blanket and smooth flowing stride, had been left behind with the others. Instead, the king was mounted on a spavined, flea-bitten roan with a lumpy head, a blanket made of twisted chaff, and a dried-out saddle. No trappings adorned his gear and nothing about his attire gave away his station. His homely bonnet jostled here and there, half hiding his face at any given moment, but never had a boy looked happier. "Where do we go this day . . ." He paused. "Uncle . . . Harry?"

Hawk gave him a jaundiced glance, but was willing to play along with the part he had initiated. "I must speak to the Baron of Isthill," he said. "About some spices he requires."

"Oh." The grin was turned on Catriona this time. "And you, Mistress . . ." He paused, searching for a name.

"Catherine," she supplied.

"Mistress Catherine," he said, giving her a wide smile for her quick answer. "Do you have plans of your own or do you come simply to accompany your husband?"

She opened her mouth to object, but one glance at Hawk changed her mind. For in his expression she saw his willingness to walk through hell and back to give the lad this moment of unbridled happiness.

She shifted her gaze back to the king. "I need a bolt of linen for a new gown," she said, falling easily into the part. "I had thought to mend my old woolen one, but the king is coming, you know."

"Indeed?" He grinned.

"Indeed," she said, leaning closer. "And I've no wish to offend him. He is as shallow as a poor man's grave and might well take offense at my shabby appearance."

For a moment James stared at her, then he threw back his head and laughed.

The tone of the day was set. Silly riddles, easy laughter, and foolish poems filled the morning, and if James noticed the retinue of guards that followed a quarter mile to the rear, he made no mention of it.

Sometime before noon they came to a village, where they visited the market.

Hungry and excited, James eyed a cart of fat mutton pies, but Hawk prodded him away.

"I do not ask you to dine only twice a day as many do, lad," he said, draping an arm over his shoulder. "But your old uncle can afford neither the time nor the coin for the likes of these. Here." Prodding him toward another stand, he urged the boy to choose from an array of stinky bricks of cheese.

Later, when the village was far behind them, they stopped their mounts on a lush hillock and spread their meal before them. They dined on nothing more than cheese and bread and a bottle of sweet wine, but the weather was fine and the laughter plentiful.

Half a mile's distance, a dozen guards stopped too, but not one of the trio spoke of them.

"So your father was a merchant also, Aunt?" James asked, slurping the wine straight from the bottle.

"Aye." Catriona glanced over to where her shaggy bay gelding grazed on the hillside. She had turned him loose, for he was not the sort to stray from the others. He was a powerful animal and well trained, but he was no more loyal than a hunk of brownstone. If the other steeds left, he would be gone like a loosed arrow. But the trio of horses were content to forage for now on the lush grasses.

It was a fine spring day, with a smattering of puffy clouds that threatened nothing more dire than a stirring of imagination if one should stare at them too long. Hawk had removed his gray plaid cloak, and now it lay spread upon the grass for them to dine on.

"Aye, father was a merchant of sorts," Catriona said, "but he was more."

"More?" James set aside the bottle to tear off another hunk of bread. It was dark and grainy and somewhat dry, nothing like the fine white loaves baked in Blackburn's vast stone ovens. Scowling at it for a moment, he set it aside.

"Aye," Cat said. "He was a spy."

"Nay."

"Aye. He was a spy and thwarted an evil plot against the king."

"*Our* king?" James asked, as if awed by the very thought of such royalty.

"Of course our king," she said.

"But you said the king was shallow and petty," James reminded her with a tilt of his head.

She thought for a moment, then, "I but said *shallow*, lad. I believe petty is your *own* description."

Hawk laughed. "Careful, Jock," he said, using that intriguing hint of French. "Lest you give away more than you mean to."

James granted him the hint of a wry smile, then turned it on Cat. "If you say the king is shallow, then why would your father spy for him? Surely 'twas dangerous. Why risk his life for a shallow man?"

Catriona grinned. "Let me tell you a terrible truth, nephew," she said, leaning close as if she were about to share a forbidden secret. "All men are shallow."

James drew back, looking uncertain and a bit peeved. "*All* men?"

"And what of women?" Hawk asked.

Catriona turned her gaze to his. His expression was unreadable, but there was something in his ice-blue eyes. Laughter, perhaps.

He lay on his side, propped on an elbow. One huge thigh was bent upward, knee toward the heavens, while the other lay flat on his cloak beside his sword. Lying there, he reminded her of a huge wolfhound. Powerful, yes. Protective, yes. But completely tame? Never. And even if he were, it was not *she* he was bound to protect. Nay, it was the boy that sat beside them. It was the boy for whom he would gladly die—for whom he would gladly kill if there should be a need.

She swallowed the thought and calmed her nerves. All would be well. Grandmother had promised her, and Grandmother saw things that others did not.

"Are women not shallow?" James asked, giving her a safe haven on which to anchor her wilding thoughts.

"Aye." She nodded, first at the boy and then at Hawk. "I should have said, all *people* are shallow—at some times. Even Durril, I suppose."

"Durril?" James asked.

"He was the bravest man in all the world." She said it simply, as if he should have surely known.

"Braver than me, Uncle Harry?" James turned an impudent expression on Hawk.

She glanced once more at Hawk. It was foolish of her, for there was something about him that conjured up weakness in her. Perhaps it was his attitude, watchful and confident. Or perhaps it was his mere physical prowess. Even now the thought of last night made her shiver, for she had almost been caught. She had been prepared to search yet another room when he had apprehended her. Like a great bird of prey, he had swept down the hallway. It had been all she could do to escape up the stairs and onto the ramparts. Then, when there was nowhere else to flee, she had slipped over the side and hung by her fingers until he'd passed.

It had been no mean feat. True, in the full light of day, when the stone was dry and her mind steady, it would not have been so difficult, for she had trained all her life for that sort of activity. But as it was, 'twas all she could do to hold on until he was past and she could sneak back down the stairs.

"I do not know if he was braver than your uncle," Catriona said, pulling her gaze away. "You shall have to judge for yourself."

"Tell me of him then," ordered James.

She raised a brow. "I do not know if I like your tone, young Jock. I think mayhap your uncle has spared the rod and allowed you to forget your place."

His brows lowered for a moment, but soon he spoke,

making it clear he was not willing to give up the game, even for his considerable pride. "I beg you, Mistress Catherine," he said, his tone the very definition of contrition. "Tell me of this Durril."

"Very well then," she said, and pulling her knees up under her chin, she began her story.

"Long ago and far away a child was born. His parents were young and poor, but they were not destitute for they had gifts."

"Gifts?"

"Aye." She smiled, remembering the firelight on her grandmother's face as she had relayed the tale. "Aye, they had the magic." She whispered the word with reverence and slanted her hands, palms upward, toward the heavens. "Wonder in their fingertips. Wings on their feet."

"They were entertainers," James deduced easily.

She shook her head, but did not look directly at him. "Not merely entertainers. Woodsprites. Fairies. They were as free as the wind, as wild as the falcons. Everything they did was magic. Everything they said was music. And so they traveled throughout the country, performing and training their young son in their arts.

"He was a bonny lad, was Durril. Quick as a whip, bright as a sunrise, and the joy of his parents' lives. But as the years passed, times became difficult. A plague tortured the land. Winter came on hard and cold. Yet they had little choice but to travel from village to village in an effort to earn their keep. But one day as they traveled, the wind rushed suddenly from the north. They could find no shelter. It began to snow, blowing with biting cold into their faces.

"Their cart horse floundered in the drifts and Durril's father was forced to help the beast along.

" 'Twas then that the wolves came."

She paused. It seemed that she could see the scene in her mind, as if she had lived it herself, as if she had felt the fear in her own soul.

"Since the plague, the wolves had become both bold and numerous. They surrounded the little cart, snarling and snapping, their fangs gleaming in the cold light of evening. Their attack was savage. Durril's father tried to fight them off but it was no use. There were too many. Inside the cart, his wife heard his screams. She was torn with anguish. She must stay with her son; she must save him. But she could not abandon her husband. And so, like a wildcat protecting her mate, she lunged into the fray."

All the world seemed quiet, as if a battle had been quelled and peace finally settled in.

"Did they live?" James asked, his voice hushed.

"Nay." She shook her head. "They did not. But the horse, terrified of the snarling beasts at its hocks, finally lurched free of the snow and bore young Durril away.

"Finally, after days of roaming, the boy came to a village. He was nearly frozen and he was starving, but he survived because he had—"

"The magic," James whispered.

Catriona studied the lad's rapt expression. "Aye. He had the magic, and as he grew, the magic grew with him so that his gift was even greater than his parents'. He was as quick as an adder, as strong as a steed. All the world adored him.

"Indeed, no woman could resist his charm, for he was as handsome as he was bold. And so he married—the most beautiful woman in the land. Her name was Beti. She had the voice of a wood thrush, the grace of a doe, and when she smiled, the world sang for joy.

"They lived by their wits and their skills. Free as the wild hills they were, going where they pleased when it pleased them. They were beyond happy together, and soon Beti bore a child, a daughter as comely as her mother. They named her Martuska. Durril's joy knew no bounds. Life was good. They wanted for nothing.

"But again winter came, and again Durril found himself in the cold with the wind blowing hard against him. They were alone betwixt villages and the sky was filled with swirling snow. Inside the wee cart, his wife and daughter huddled close. Fear lay on him like a blanket of ice, for he remembered the horrible death of his parents."

She paused for a moment, then began again, her voice hushed. "And then it happened. The wolves came."

She heard the king draw a sharp breath.

"But they did not come for him. Nay." She shook her head, remembering the tale. "They were following a lad.

"Durril heard the pack's evil howls even before he saw the boy. But soon a steed thundered into view. The rider was a shabby-looking lad, his eyes wide with fear, his face pale as death. Beneath him, the steed plunged and neighed in panic. A wolf leapt from the pack. Big as a bear, he was, leaping straight for the boy.

"The horse reared madly. The lad tried to hold on, tried to steer his mount toward safety, but there was no hope, and he fell. The huge wolf leapt in. Durril saw it all, and in his heart he knew a fear so great it threatened to consume him. And yet, even so, even with his family huddled in fear only inches away, he could not forsake the beggar boy.

"Grabbing his staff, he leapt from the cart and charged the leader of the wolves," Catriona said, fisting her hands as if she herself held the staff. "The battle was long and hard. Blood sprayed into the air, turning the snow as red as sunset, but there could be only one outcome."

James watched her, unblinking, unquestioning. Sir Hawk's regard was solemn.

"He abandoned his family and gave his life for a nameless beggar?" James whispered.

Catriona drew a deep breath. "He was prepared to do just that," she said. "Aye, he was willing. But as I said, he was as strong as a steed and as swift as an adder. He killed the leader of the wolves."

"With naught but his staff?"

"His staff was broken," Cat said. "He now had nothing but his bare hands. And yet he defeated the wolf. And when the other beasts saw that . . ." She shook her head and shrugged. "Perhaps they were filled with respect. Perhaps it was fear. But they turned and fled."

"Durril lived?" James asked, awe in his tone.

"Aye, he lived. And as it happened, the lad he saved was not a penniless waif at all, but Endorai, the crowned prince of Khandia. And so Durril was twice blessed—but forever after he was scarred. And it is said that to this day, every child born to his line bears the mark of the wolf upon his neck." She lifted her head and touched the base of her throat.

James's eyes followed her finger, and when she drew her hand away, his gaze shifted to the small birthmark on the left side of her neck.

He voiced no question, though his eyes asked much, until finally he could remain silent no longer.

"Then it is all true? He killed the lead wolf and sent the others running?"

Catriona shrugged. " 'Tis a good tale and oft told. Whether 'tis true or nay is not for me to decide."

James watched her in silence for a moment.

"And what of the wound on your brow, Lady Cat? How did you come by *that*?"

"Oh." Nervousness swelled inside her at the memory of husky groans and sordid poetry, of her panicked escape into Haydan's arms. "I fear that is not so magical and sadly realistic."

"Tell me," the king insisted.

"James," Hawk said, his tone deep and low. "A gentleman must always leave a lady with some secrets."

"But I fear for her safety," said James. "Mayhap she is in some danger at Blackburn."

"No danger," Cat assured him quickly. "Your palace has been like a home to me."

"Then how did you become wounded?"

" 'Tis naught to worry on," Cat assured him.

James scowled. "It seems you are guarding the wrong person, Sir Hawk."

"What?" Haydan's expression was as sharp as the bird for which he was named.

James rose to his feet just as Hawk did. The great warrior towered over him, but the lad looked up into his face and explained without pause.

"It seems to me that 'tis your duty to guard the lady."

"My king," Hawk rumbled, his brows drawn low over stormy eyes. " 'Tis you and none other who—"

"Is it not your duty to do as I wish?"

" 'Tis my duty to see that you are kept safe and—"

"Safe!" James laughed. "Look at yonder hillock."

Hawk turned away to gaze behind them. "Aye?"

"What do you see?"

"A dozen of the king's soldiers."

James grinned. "I suppose they just happen to be traveling in the same direction as we?"

Haydan's scowl deepened.

"The truth is this, Sir Hawk: If you are within fifty leagues of me I am certain to be safe. 'Tis in your blood to make sure it is so. Therefore—"

"Your Majesty . . ." Hawk growled.

"Therefore," the king continued more forcefully, "there is no reason why you cannot look after the lady." He turned.

"James," Hawk said, striding closer, but the boy was already waving an arm to the soldiers on the hill.

Immediately there was a flurry of motion, and in a minute, the little picnic area was surrounded by men on horseback.

"You have need of us, Your Majesty?" asked the senior guard.

"Aye," said James, nearly smirking. "I have need of an escort. Sir Hawk here has other duties."

"Your Majesty!" Hawk said, his tone stiff.

"Lady Cat." James bowed to her, a regal half-grown boy in shabby garment. "I leave you in the care of the Hawk, for . . ." He reached for her hand, and lifting it to his lips, brushed a gallant kiss across her knuckles. "I could not bear to see brave Durril's line end with you."

Catriona opened her mouth to object, but his guards were already surrounding him, and in a moment they were gone.

Chapter 7

Catriona tightened her grip on Bay's reins. Beside her, Hawk scowled after the departing king. It took her a moment to find her voice.

"My apologies."

No answer came.

"Sir Hawk?"

"What?" He turned abruptly, as if startled to find her there.

For a moment she was tempted to step back, for his eyes were filled with a hundred indefinable emotions, from flaring anger to a love so deep it almost hurt to look upon it.

"I said, I am sorry. I did not mean for this to happen."

"What was your intent?" His voice was little more than a rumble, his scowl deep and intimidating.

She straightened her shoulders with an effort. "I only meant to entertain him."

"With tales of how free others are? How they can go where they will whenever they please."

"I never—"

"Surely you must know how he chafes at his restrictions. The boy is fast approaching manhood and eager for free rein. Why encourage him to rebel?"

"I did no such thing," she lied.

"Didn't you? What did you think would happen? You blow in like a spring breeze, bonny as a blossom, free as a pipit."

"So 'tis my fault I am not royalty, with a royal's restrictions."

"I did not say that," he said, his tone rife with frustration.

"Then 'tis my fault that I am beautiful?" she snapped.

Hawk was silent for a moment, and then he chuckled. "Aye," he said, rubbing the old scar on his chest. "Aye, that much is your fault. Mount up, lass."

"Is that an order, Sir Hawk?"

"Aye."

"And I thought you just said I was as free as a pipit."

"Ah, well, even the pipits take orders from the Hawk."

"Do they now?" she asked, her tone carefully moderate.

"Aye," he said. "When the king orders me to guard them."

"I will not be guarded."

He shrugged. " 'Twas not my own idea."

"You are not listening." Panic was reaching for her. She could not have this hulking Highlander breathing down her neck. There were things that needed doing. Life-or-death things. "You do not understand," she said. "I cannot be restricted. I am Rom—"

"Lass!" He interrupted her with a deep tone and a deeper scowl. "I am not a young man. Indeed, I am too set in my ways to desert my post, and too decrepit to be thrilled by the prospect of guarding a young woman who makes men . . . a young lady such as yourself."

She scowled. "What does that mean? Such as myself?"

"It means that you are more trouble than the king any day of the week, lassie."

"I doubt that."

" 'Tis true," he said, tightening her mount's girth. "The boy may have men trying to kill him, abduct him, or influence him, but never yet . . ." He paused as he dropped her stirrup back into place. "Never has he had a passel of crowing swains trying to coerce him into their beds."

"Is that your worry?" she asked.

"One of them," he said, turning toward her. His chest was as broad as a Viking's shield.

"Then let me set your mind at ease, for unlike the king, I have been fighting that battle for as long as I can recall."

There was a moment of silence, then, "Successfully?"

"What?" Surprise slapped the air from her lungs. Did he care?

He stared at her for a fraction of a moment, then turned rapidly away. " 'Tis nothing," he said.

She watched him unblinking. " 'Twas indeed something. What was it you said?'

He caught his own mount's reins and refused to turn toward her. Instead, he fiddled with his girth, then stepped into the saddle.

"Might you be inquiring about my virtue?" she asked, barely able to force out the question as she mounted her gelding and hurried up beside him. "Sir Hawk—"

"I would know!" he said abruptly. "So that I am prepared."

"Prepared?"

"I do not like surprises," he said finally. "Do I protect

you from all comers, or are there some that you welcome?"

"Some? Do you ask now if I am a wanton?"

"Listen, lass," he said, his voice very deep with unexplained tension, "I did not ask for this duty, but I shall take it if 'tis thrust upon me. But 'twas you who said you cannot be restrained. I've no intention of crushing your freedom. And so, I ask."

"You need neither guard me nor worry for me. I will cause you no trouble."

He snorted, his big hands tight on the reins. "Lass," he said, his voice deep as he turned toward the castle, "you *are* trouble."

The great hall was particularly boisterous at the evening meal, but Hawk sat alone and silent, nursing a mead and his foul mood. How the hell had he gotten himself into this mess?

He should never have taken the boy riding with a Rom. They were too . . . Too what? Without straining his neck to see past the cluster of men that surrounded her again, he could remember every detail about the Gypsy lass—how her eyes seemed to change color with her mood, how her lips tilted just so when she was deep in thought, how each movement seemed like poetry set to—

He pushed away his board and knife in pounding frustration and took another deep quaff of mead. He was too damned old to be mooning.

"Sir Hawk."

Haydan glanced up, but the sight of his visitor did nothing to improve his mood. "Lord Tremayne," he said by way of greeting, and glanced back into space.

"Might I ask what you are doing?" Tremayne said.

His voice held that royaler-than-thou tone that never failed to set Haydan's teeth on edge. But now probably wasn't the time to tell him so.

"I am drinking mead," Haydan said, glancing into the depths of the horn mug as if the answers to the world's mysteries might lie there. " 'Tis not a bad brew."

"I am quite relieved to know you are content with the drink."

"My thanks," Haydan said, not acknowledging the sarcasm in the other's tone. Tremayne was bound to explain his presence soon enough. There seemed little need to rush the inevitable.

"Mayhap we should hire another to replace you as the king's captain so that you might have more time to spend with your mead."

Haydan glanced slowly up. "And mayhap I should tell James how you planned my niece's death some years past. The MacGowans were quite put out."

Against all odds, Tremayne managed to stiffen even more. "If you recall, my spies informed me that she was plotting to kill His Majesty."

It had been nearly five years since Shona MacGowan had planted a counterfeit king in the castle and taken James, incognito, under her wing. She had, in fact, saved him from the person who had *really* been plotting against the throne.

"The MacGowans are a wild lot," Tremayne added. "And your Shona was too close to His Majesty. I could not afford to take a risk on the king's life."

"I'll be certain to tell him that too," Hawk said, and moved to rise. But Tremayne's hand was already on his shoulder, urging him back down.

"It matters naught now."

Haydan raised a brow as he settled back onto the

bench. "I would say it matters to Shona's husband."

"Dugald and I have come to an understanding."

Hawk did nothing to stop his chuckle, though he was certain that if he were a diplomat of any sort, he would make an attempt. "An understanding," he said, taking another drink. "In other words he said he would hang you by your own entrails if you so much as entertained an evil thought toward Shona?"

Tremayne's sour expression said plainly enough that he had guessed correctly, but Haydan had sense enough to hide his grin behind his mug this time. It had been some years since his niece had been in such dire danger—some years since young James had enjoyed the freedom of the peasantry. Shona was now safe on the Isle of Fois with her overly protective husband and a babe of her own. And young James was safe too, though restive.

"Why are you not guarding the king?" Tremayne hissed.

Haydan stifled a sigh and glanced up toward the lean scavenger he had almost managed to forget.

"Young James needs a bit of room to grow," Haydan said. He should have said that he *was* guarding the king. That, from his position in the hall, it was simple enough to keep an eye on James and the Gypsy girl at the same time. But perhaps he was a little too old and crotchety to care that much for Tremayne's peace of mind.

" 'Tis what I worry about," Tremayne said. "That the king has a *chance* to grow. 'Tis, in fact, your entire purpose in life."

"Is it now? And always I thought our Lord God determined each man's own purpose. Or have you now taken the Almighty's role, Tremayne?"

The scrawny lord drew himself up to his considerable

height. "I heard of your outing with the king and the . . . Gypsy wench." He said the words with a peculiar pinching of the nostrils.

"Then you know the king ordered me to guard the lass instead of himself," Haydan surmised.

"The king does not make those decisions," Tremayne gritted. " 'Tis for the council to decide. And the council decided long ago—against my advice—that you should be the one to oversee his protection."

"James asked that I—"

"I do not care what he asked. He is young and impetuous and does not realize what pain Scotland would suffer if some ill befell him." Haydan wondered for a moment if the narrow lord might burst into tears. Good saints, both he and Tremayne had probably been with the king far too long. "You shall guard him and none other. And—"

"As you wish."

Tremayne's words came to a snapping halt, then, "What say you?"

"I am certain you know what is best," Haydan said, inclining his head slightly. "I will immediately resume guarding the king—from here."

"You will stay at his side so long as you have nothing better to do with your—"

"I've no wish to disturb James with this news of your plot against Shona," Haydan warned softly. "He loves her like kin, you know. And, I might add," he said, leaning slightly toward the pinch-faced Tremayne, "he feels much the same about the lass called Catriona." He glanced toward the girl. The mob around her had parted slightly, granting him a ray of her unearthly allure. "They have similarities, don't you think?"

"She is a wanton," Tremayne hissed. "Just like—"

The dinner knife fell easily into Haydan's hand. And it felt so right, like a quill might feel in the hand of a scholar. And just as easily, it tipped toward Tremayne.

"I suggest you do not continue on your present course, my lord," Haydan murmured. "For 'tis said that any man who could look on a good woman with derision is no man at all." He skimmed the area just below his dagger's point before glancing into Tremayne's pale face. "Do not tempt me too greatly to find out."

Tremayne pursed his lips into a bumpy double line. "The council will hear of this."

"I'll make certain it does," Haydan said, and with that, Tremayne turned and stalked away.

Haydan sighed, took another draught, and scanned the room. The situation had changed little. James was playing a game of ringo with Kitchen Elsie's youngest lad, and Catriona was still surrounded by idiots. But . . . Hawk counted heads. She might have lost an idiot or two. Yes, the toothy de la Faire had left. And a good thing, for he'd been becoming a bit too enthusiastic for his own good. Hawk would have considered discouraging him if he hadn't thought the others would gladly do it for him.

He must have either drunk himself into a stupor and been tromped beneath the pack, or had managed to make it out of the hall before relieving himself. Either way, judging by the amount of ale he had consumed, his bladder seemed to be the most astounding thing about him.

At least de la Faire had left, Catriona thought. His departure had given her an opportunity to study the others more carefully, to listen to the rhythm of their voices, to search for that eerie, skin-shivering plural reference to himself. But she did not hear it—not in de la Faire's clipped importance, or MacKinnon's soft brogue, or a hundred other voices that echoed around her as Lord Douglas Hogshead told a tale about a warrior, a scholar, himself, and a comely tavern wench.

She shifted her gaze away from his animated features, and a pair of steady eyes caught her.

Lord Drummond perused her with half-lidded, unflinching eyes, then lifted his goblet toward her in a sort of unspoken toast. Cat skimmed her gaze sideways but his betrothed-to-be, young Roberta, and her hovering parents were nowhere to be seen, and with their departure Drummond's charming attentiveness seemed to have slipped away. Cat's heart kicked up a wild beat in her chest as her gaze sprinted down the table. Could he be Blackheart? Could he be the one she had come to find?

"You'll not recognize us," he had said. *"And yet we might be in any crowd. And all the while 'twill be our pleasure to know that of the countless fools who drool over you, 'tis ourselves who hold your reins. 'Tis ourselves who might take you to our bed at any moment. And you would come, for you are not too good for us now, are you, Princess Cat?"*

Catriona's stomach twisted. Could he be the culprit? Could he be so cruel? She could not tell. Indeed, she could think no longer. Fatigue lay on her like a sodden blanket, muffling her thoughts, dulling her mind. Tonight she must search the castle again, but first she must sleep.

Lord Hogshead's story came to an ending. All around her, the listeners laughed and nodded.

"So you won the wench's admiration by default," someone said.

"Aye," agreed Hogshead, taking another swig of beer from his pewter mug.

"And was she worth the trouble?" another asked.

"Indeed, she was. She was the strongest woman I've ever known." A few suggestive chuckles followed his words, but he gave his listeners a self-deprecating grin. "After I passed out with the other two sods, 'twas she who carried me to my chambers and dumped my corpse onto the bed to sleep out the night."

Catriona stood up amid the laughter, moving slowly, meeting no gazes in the hopes that she would not be noticed.

They let her pass with little enough trouble. Perhaps her ubiquitous presence was causing her to lose her allure for them, she thought as she exited the great hall.

"Leaving your amorous suitors so soon?"

"Rory!" She turned with a start toward the hallway on her right. "What are you doing here?"

"Waiting for you. After all . . ." He took her elbow in one hand and escorted her toward her room. "You are my betrothed."

"You have been drinking."

He chuckled. "Aye. What with your constant occupation with Blackburn's noblemen, I have had little else to do but become friends with Blackburn's fine ale."

"And to lie about Grandmother's well-being." Frustration and fatigue burned like acid in her stomach.

Rory ground his teeth and tightened his hand on her arm. " 'Tis not right that you risk yourself, that you expose yourself to those preening fools and their filthy stories. I will find the blackguard for you," he whispered. "I will return your brother. 'Tis my place. I am your betrothed."

Catriona drew him to a halt. "I do not deny that I

need your assistance, Rory. And indeed, always and forever I will remember that 'twas you who helped me. But I am no longer your betrothed."

"Catriona," he whispered as he smoothed his fingers across her cheek. "We are one and the same, you and I. Freedom is in our blood. Who else could understand you? Those pale-faced noblemen? Nay. We are Rom. We are all that is left of the line which—"

"Is that what you truly think?" she rasped. " 'Tis not true!" Her voice shook with the force of her emotion. "Lachlan is well and fine, and he . . . he will be returned to us."

"Cat." Rory reached for her but she stumbled out of his grasp.

"He will be returned!"

"You are right," he murmured finally. "We must think of Lachlan first."

"Aye." She swallowed, but her throat was tight and her head ached. "Now I must go to Grandmother," she said and turned to leave.

"Had you stayed at the castle you would know she is not in your fine chambers. She missed her bed in the cart and said she needed air to 'feel.' She sleeps in the cart just beyond the bridge."

"Is she safe there?"

"Do you care?"

Fatigue rode her cruelly. "Please, Rory—"

"I made certain she was safe and content before I left her," he said sharply, then exhaled and took her hand between his own. "And you, Catriona? Are you safe?"

"Aye." She stared down at their joined hands. 'Twas a strange thing. At one time it had seemed so right, so natural, so inevitable. "I am safe, Rory, but I must bid you good night."

"Why?" He pressed closer, his brow furrowed. " 'Tis not right that you stay here alone. You should join Grandmother. She—"

"I cannot."

"Then let me come in. I will sleep on the floor."

"Nay." She pulled her hand from his grip.

" 'Tis because I failed you, isn't it?" He ground his teeth. "I should not have let them take him. I should have died defending him."

"If you could only remember how they looked. Remember—"

"But I cannot!" he rasped. "There was the rope about my neck, the whispered voice from behind me, demanding that you meet the bastard that night. And then all was black. But I shall make it up to you, Catriona. Let me stay with you this night."

"Nay. Please take care of Grandmother," she said, and pulling her hand from his, she turned rapidly away.

He let her go with only a little resistance and she quickly stepped inside her room. There was solace of sorts here. Private and quiet, but for a single chirp from the cage of willow sticks that stood beside the door. One small finch was perched atop the cage while the other dozed inside.

Retrieving a tallow candle from a sconce on the wall, Cat lit it from the one in the hallway before setting it back in its place.

Golden, mellow light softened the shadows.

Closing her door, Catriona leaned back against it and sighed. All seemed peaceful except for herself. But she should not feel so distraught. At least Hawk had felt no need to follow her here. Either Lord Tremayne had convinced him to leave her to her own defenses, or he had simply refused to follow the king's orders. Did he dislike her so much? she wondered, but halted those turbulent thoughts with a single reprimand.

She had no time for such foolish worries. It mattered little if the hulking Highlander cherished her or hated her. That was the least of her problems. If he learned the truth . . .

She stopped the thought abruptly, for if he learned her true reasons for coming to Blackburn the consequences would be unthinkable.

Turning rapidly toward her trunk beside the door, she pulled it open, drew out a simple, dark chemise, and tossed it over the open cover of the wooden chest. Untying her girdle, she slipped her pouch and knife from her hips and dropped them to the floor, then set her hands to her laces.

The day had been long and wearing. The night promised to be the same, but for now she would rest and let the castle settle into silence.

Her gown slid down her legs and onto the floor. Her undergarments followed. She rolled her shoulders and stepped from the rumpled linen. The night air felt soft against her skin, like a lover's caress.

But she had no lover. Even now, when her mind should be occupied with a thousand other details, she could not help but remember the intensity of Hawk's eyes when he had questioned her about that. She should have told him that she had no lovers, but pride was as fickle as the wind and could blow in any direction. He had called her troublesome, and she had no desire to confirm or deny his belief with tales of her innocence, especially when his very nearness confused and titillated her. When his voice evidenced the same raspy quality as Fayette's partner. But where Matthew had been pink and narrow, he would be dark and thick. Catriona's nipples tightened at the thought, puckering in the cool night air and plunging her back into reality.

What the devil was wrong with her? she wondered, and turned, angry and frustrated, toward the bed.

A shadow rose from the floor on the far side of the mattress. "So," said a voice. "You have finally arrived."

Chapter 8

"Lord de la Faire!" Catriona gasped.

"Aye." He leered at her, then let his gaze slip sloppily to her nipples. "I see you are ready for me, Princess."

Backing away a step, Cat snagged her dark chemise from the trunk's edge and whisked it in front of her.

"Nay." He staggered forward a step or two, but didn't manage any more. "Do not cover yourself. I have been waiting here for an eternity."

"Waiting?" she stalled and glanced quickly to the right in search of some kind of weapon. But the knife she'd taken to dinner had been dropped to the floor with her discarded gown.

"Aye. I knew you would eventually break away from the crowd. So I waited here on your bed." He waved wildly at the mattress he had just managed to skirt.

She shook her head. "I did not see you."

"Well, in truth, I may have slipped onto the floor." He grinned. " 'Tis a wild pallet you keep, Princess Cat."

"Aye." She nodded at his nonsensical words. " 'Tis indeed a wicked bed. Mayhap you'd best leave and find your own."

He chuckled. "A wild pallet for a wild wench, I am thinking. But I believe myself up to the task of taming them both."

He stepped forward. Catriona stepped back.

She had dealt with intoxicated men before, and while they were often disoriented and ungainly, they were also sadly immune to good sense.

"My lord de la Faire," she began, still holding the gown in front of her, "You should not be here."

"You are right. I should be in yonder bed. I am certain that together we can wrestle it into submission," he said, and grinned crookedly at his own brilliant wit.

"The truth is, sir, that I am a friend of the king."

Nothing but a blank expression.

"He is my guardian of sorts, and I would do nothing to cause him distress."

"Ah, well, I will not tell if you don't," he said and stumbled forward.

Catriona glanced sideways. She could edge along the wall and try to escape, of course. But there was little point of putting him between her and the door.

Thus, she had no choice. She would have to dart into the hallway and hope she had a chance to wrestle the gown over her head before anyone saw her. One more tiny step backward and she eased her fingers onto the door handle.

"But regardless if I tell James or nay, he will surely find out," she said, giving reason one last chance. "And he will be angry."

Apparently those words managed to penetrate the Frenchman's foggy brain, for he stopped for a moment, eyeing her blearily. "So you . . ." He halted briefly and grinned. "You're *laying* the lad?"

His accusation stunned her.

"Nay," she rasped, but in that instant, de la Faire leapt. His fingers snagged in her chemise, tearing it out of her hands.

Spinning around, she lunged for the door, but he grabbed her about the waist.

She grappled wildly, trying to fight her way free.

"Relax. Relax, little wildcat," de la Faire hissed. His arms wound tightly about her midriff, his hips pressed into her buttocks. "Do not fret." He swiped a kiss against her neck, but her hair was in the way. "I've no intention of ruining your place with the king. In truth, I rather like the idea of tarrying where His Majesty has been. And 'twill do you good to remember what it is like to be with a man fully grown." With those words he ground his member into her backside. She stiffened. "Feel that?" he crooned. "Big as a log, it is. I have been ordered to stay away from the stallions, lest I make them feel inferior." He laughed at his own humor. "Come now, lass," he whispered, and managed to plant a kiss on her neck this time. "Let us tame yonder wild bed."

Squeezing her eyes closed, Catriona forced her muscles to relax, and her stomach to settle. "Are you certain James will not find out? He is so young and tender."

De la Faire chuckled. "I am certain he has heard of my prowess," he said. "Surely he will understand your weakness."

"I only hope you are right," she said, and snapping her knees up, thumped her feet against the door with all her might.

De la Faire careened wildly backward, landing on his rump. She landed on his belly.

The air whooshed from his lungs in an audible rush, and she scrambled away on all fours.

But he was already after her. His fingers brushed her ankle. She squawked in bursting terror, kicked him in the jaw, and lunged forward. She couldn't reach the door and she knew it. Scrambling for her gown, she dipped her hand beneath it, found the knife, and spun toward him.

He slammed into her, pinning her back against the wall and forcing the air from her lungs with the weight of his body.

"My God, I love your fire!" he rasped. "You make me feel like a great destrier called to battle."

"De la Faire," she said. Fighting for breath, she raised her hand just slightly. It shook like a reed in the wind, but her voice was steady. "If you do not loose me, you will look more like a lopped donkey than a horse of war."

He chuckled. "I—" he began, but in that instant, he felt the prick of her blade against his groin. His eyebrows rose and his baby-soft mouth went round. "You have a knife?"

"Aye." She said the word through gritted teeth and steadied her hand. "And—"

The door burst open.

Catriona snapped her head sideways and found herself staring into Sir Hawk's icy eyes.

For a moment the entire world seemed silent, then, "Catriona," he said, nodding shallowly as he skimmed his gaze down to the knife in her hand. "I came to make certain you were well before I found my pallet." His gaze moved back up to settle on her face. The hard tension of his body lessened a small bit. "But I heard a noise and thought you might need assistance." A pause of several heartbeats, then, "I did not realize you were entertaining."

Either anger or fear made her tremble. She wasn't certain which, but the blade wobbled against de la Faire's groin. "You may find this entertaining, Sir Hawk. I do not."

"Truly?" Hawk stared at her, his expression inscrutable. "Do you mean to say that you've found some trouble after all?"

She could not even manage a nod.

"So de la Faire is here uninvited?" Hawk's voice had lowered even more.

"Aye."

"Then . . ." Hawk turned almost regretfully toward the young lord who stared wide-eyed and immobile at the king's notorious captain of the guard. "You should prepare for pain, my lord."

"This was not my idea. I thought this was my room. The wench came in and disrobed," de la Faire rambled. "I told her I had no wish to lie with her. But she grabbed a knife and insisted—"

Hawk raised hand. The motion looked peaceful, but something in his eyes was not. "I fear I must stop you before you dishonor yourself further." Grabbing the back of the Frenchman's doublet in one fist, he thumped the marquis's head against the nearest wall.

For a moment de la Faire's face expressed absolute astonishment, and then, like a soggy rag, his head dropped forward onto his chest and his legs went lax, spilling him to the floor.

Catriona stared in dumbstruck astonishment. "Is he dead?"

"Nay," Haydan replied. "Fools do not die that easy, even if they are gentry."

The room went silent. Catriona raised her gaze nervously to Haydan's. "I didn't mean to cause you trouble."

She watched the scar beside his eye twitch slightly. Watched his chest expand and his shoulders lower a mite, as if he endeavored to relax.

"One cannot bring a wildcat to his table and expect it not to bite. Are you well?"

"Aye. I am fine."

"You're trembling," he said, and taking his cloak from his shoulders, swirled it around her back. It settled in deep folds about her ankles. His fingers brushed her throat as he drew the cloak together beneath her chin. "Are you hurt?"

"Nay."

"Scared?"

"Nay, I . . ." she began, but realized suddenly that the knife wobbled in her uncertain grip. "I just . . ." She could find no words, and suddenly his hands were on hers, warm and strong against her cold figners. Urging the blade from her grip, he tossed it into her trunk. "Come," he said.

She tried to follow him, but her legs refused to cooperate. Turning back, he lifted her into his arms. Cradling her against his chest, he bore her toward the bed, then stopped only inches from her mattress and gazed down into her face. For a moment she thought he would place her on the pallet, but she trembled again, and so he turned and sat with her in his lap, his arms firmly fitted about her.

Silence filled the room. Beneath her, his thighs felt as firm and large as oaken boughs. Against her shoulder, she felt the rise and fall of his massive chest, and across her back, his arm was tight and broad. His strength surrounded her just as surely as his cloak did, holding her close, keeping her safe. And for the first time in as long as she could recall, she felt she could give up the fight, could relax and let another meet her battles.

'Twas a weakness, she knew, a weakness she should not give in to. But it felt so good, so easy to sink into his strength, his kindness, and for a moment she wished it could go on forever—that she was not who she was, that she had not come to Blackburn to ruin his life and perhaps to forfeit her own.

Catriona squeezed her eyes closed. Her throat felt tight and her chest ached with a pain that was indefinable. A tiny mewl of self-pity crept up. His arms tightened, and though the change was almost imperceptible, she recognized the movement as pity.

She cleared her throat and straightened slightly. "I am sorry."

It took a moment for him to respond. "Of all the people in this place, I think you should be the last to apologize." His soft rumble made her feel small and strangely nurtured.

She tried to fight the feelings with every weapon in her armory. "Oh?" The word that was supposed to sound flippant barely managed to be audible. "And who should be the first?"

Silence again, as deep as the night outside her window.

"Me."

His answer startled her, and she turned to stare into his eyes, but he didn't look toward her. Instead, his gaze remained fixed on the wall ahead.

"You?" she asked. From such close proximity, she could not help but notice that his eyes were clefted like a hunting falcon's, and the scar on his jaw twitched. "You were the one who saved me."

"Saved you!" The words were little more than a growl, and though she expected more, he did not continue.

"Aye," she said softly. " 'Twas you."

He jerked toward her suddenly as each sinew and muscle was pulled tight with increasing emotion. His eyes sparked silver light and one corner of his mouth twitched. "I am a guard," he said succinctly. She merely stared, waiting for him to go on. "I am a guard," he repeated, "by nature as much as by command."

She shook her head. "I do not understand your—"

"What good have I done here but make certain you did not kill him?" He glanced angrily toward the limp form on the floor. A pulse ticked in his temple, just below the dark sweep of his hair. "Truly," he rumbled, "I do not think I've done the world any great favor."

"Then the favor was for me alone," she whispered, and reaching up, she laid her fingers against his cheek. The stubble of a day's beard felt rough against her skin, and beneath that, the muscles in his cheek were taut. "Thank you," she whispered, and because the emotion was as weakening as strong wine, she leaned forward and kissed him. Not passionately, not full on the lips, but softly, gently placed at the corner of his mouth as her breast pressed intimately against the hard wall of his chest.

He felt as still and solid as Blackburn itself.

"It seems that again I owe you," she said.

Beneath her fingers, a muscle in his cheek ticked. His nostrils flared.

"Nay. You owe me naught. Now, 'tis best that I remove the rubbish before it awakes," he said and shifted his weight, jostling her slightly.

His cape, untied and unfettered, slid sideways, slipping insidiously from her shoulder.

Catriona twisted about to pull it back into place, but his hand was already there. Their fingers met with a fire-bright shock of emotion. She drew her breath in sharply as their hands trailed in tandem across her shoulder. His fingers touched the tiny dell at the base of her throat. Their gazes met and fused, and suddenly there seemed to be nothing standing guard between her body and his. She felt hot and alive and naked, nestled in the warmth of his cocoon.

"Catriona," he rasped.

"Aye?" she whispered.

"In truth," he said quietly, " 'tis I who owe you."

"Oh?" She could barely force out that single word, for the heat of his body seemed to be seeping through her thighs into her very soul.

"Aye. 'Twas my duty to protect you, and I failed."

She tried to keep breathing, to keep thinking. She was no newcomer to desire. For as long as she could recall, men had wanted her. But for the first time she felt it herself, and it surprised her that in twenty-two years, she had never truly understood their need until this very instant.

She tried to shake away the feelings, for she had no place for them, no time.

"You have hardly failed," she said, trying to sound casual. "There is little harm he can do asleep on my floor."

"Had I been alert he would never have breached your chambers." The muscle danced in his jaw again. "A wee lass like you . . ." He paused for a moment, swept his heated gaze down her body, then drew a sharp breath and continued. "You should not have been put in such a position."

She was not a small woman. Nay, she was tall and strong and, by direst necessity, independent. But in his arms she felt fragile and feminine and adored. "What position is that?" she asked softly.

"This position." His gaze swept over her. "Naked and . . ." He drew his cape more firmly about her shoulders as the seconds ticked away. "I will not be so lax next time," he said, his tone dire.

"You will not let me disrobe?" she asked.

His gaze snapped to hers. They stared at each other from inches away, neither breathing.

" 'Tis no laughing matter, lass," he said.

But the temptation to do that was very strong. For regardless of his emotionless tone and rock-steady gaze, it felt as if he cared for her. As if, after the long line of men who had pursued her, one had arrived who cared for *her* and not just the pleasure of her body. "I am well, Sir Hawk. The man was drunk and none too bright, and I have been defending myself for many years."

"Many years!" He growled the words, then narrowed his eyes and steadied his voice again "My plaid is older than you and—"

His cloak was slipping away again. He snatched at it, catching it just before it fell into infamy.

"And why the hell won't this damned thing stay up?" he snapped, grasping it roughly beneath her chin.

She couldn't help but laugh.

"Is there some jest I might be privy to?" he asked, his tone deep as the night.

"Nay."

"Then why do you laugh?"

Because honesty was as much a part of her as the air

she breathed, she said, "More than a few times men have tried to remove my clothes. Never have I known one so determined to keep them on."

"I am a guard, not a man," he said.

"I did not realize it had to be one or the other."

His scowl deepened, and though she knew he meant to intimidate her, she only felt more protected, more sheltered in the blast of his glare.

"In fact," she whispered, feeling his blood pulse hot and strong beneath her thighs. "I would have sworn you were both."

His fist still held the cloak pulled tightly at her throat, but for a moment his grip faltered, and in that moment, she acted.

Chapter 9

Catriona pressed her lips to his. Desire burned through Haydan like the flare of a torch. He tried to retreat, to push her away. His fist tightened in the cape with the intention of doing just that, but suddenly his hand was inexplicably lost beneath the garment's folds.

She was as soft and warm as an eaglet, her waist as small as the hilt of a fine sword. He pulled her closer.

The cloak slipped away. Like the walls of a fortress, it tumbled down, and suddenly her breasts were pressed warm and soft against his chest, and he trembled. The king's bodyguard trembled!

It was that shiver of weakness that strengthened him, that snapped him back to reality. He drew away, breathing hard and feeling as though his very heart were being torn from his chest.

Her eyes were the first things he noticed. They were dark pools of emotion, the pupils so wide and deep that he felt he might drown in their mystery.

"I am . . ." He tried to clear his head, to find his wits. "My apologies."

Her lips moved. He could not help but notice, for they

looked as ripe and succulent as forbidden fruit. "Apologies?" she breathed.

"Aye." His gaze slipped lower, down the velvet skin of her throat, over the soft, sweet swellings of her breasts. She was mesmerizing, enchanting, bewitching. All soft and firm and warm and cool. A thousand diametrical elements swirled together to make this magic. He reached out to touch her, to feel her against him. But thirty years of discipline stopped him. He swore in silence and snapped to his feet. She cried out and tumbled sideways.

There was nothing he could do but save her, catch her, bring her safely to her feet. Then she was naked and silent in his arms as she stared into his eyes. Her hips were pressed intimately to his and her thighs, long and cool as river water, cradled one of his own.

He closed his eyes for a moment as he grappled for control. But Catriona and control were not good bedmates. Desire roared through him like a pitch fire.

"Catriona," he whispered, meaning to tell her he must go, but finding that her name came out with the reverence of a prayer.

"Aye?" Her voice was as soft as the whisper of butterflies.

"I am . . ." Weak! God, so damnably weak! He could not resist her. After a hundred battles and a thousand hard-learned lessons, still, he could not resist this one burning temptation. But there were exemplary reasons that he must.

He was the king's captain of the guard. He could not afford to be distracted by her magic.

He had promised James he would guard her, not seduce her.

He could not bear to hurt her. And yet . . . She was

not Marcele. She was neither small nor frail, but strong and vibrant. And though it could not be possible, she seemed attracted to him. So perhaps—

From the floor, de la Faire moaned, breaking Haydan's introspection.

"You are what?" Catriona whispered.

Haydan snapped his gaze frantically back to her. "I am sorry. I must go," he rasped, and tearing himself from her, strode across the room to yank the Frenchman from the floor.

He had one fleeting impression of Cat's stunned expression before he slammed the door shut behind him.

"*I am sorry. I must go,*" he had said.

The words grated in Haydan's mind. Good saints, he had made it sound as if he were apologizing for leaving, instead of apologizing for having put her in such a position.

What the hell had he been thinking? She was an enchantress. Young, gifted, alluring beyond imagination. What would make him think she would be interested in a jaded old warrior with a broken nose and a limp?

The rain pummeled him harder. Good, he thought, leaning lower over his mount's withers as he urged the steed into the slanting rain. Maybe it would wash the insanity from his brain.

He had begun riding before dawn, visiting every garrison of soldiers that guarded Blackburn. He could not be too careful. Every road must be watched, every defense seen to.

He had to keep her safe.

Him! Haydan corrected angrily. He must keep *the king* safe.

But James's face was barely imaginable in his mind,

for every bit of his concentration was swallowed up by Catriona. She was there, like a dream dreamed so many times it was now part of his very soul.

He must keep her safe. But she did not need him. Nay, though she sometimes seemed soft and vulnerable, she was clever and strong.

Still, he wanted nothing more than to hold her again. Maybe it was her very strength that made him wish to protect her. Certainly it was her softness that made him hard.

Damnit all—he still ached for her! Even now, after ten hours in the saddle. It wasn't a healthy condition. Certainly not at his age; he was supposed to know better. But when he had seen her threatened . . .

For one fateful moment, he had had every intention of killing de la Faire. Indeed, if she had been hurt, if he had found the merest scratch on her, he might have.

But there had been nothing marring the perfection of her skin. It was flawless, feather soft, and—

He was doing it again! Daydreaming over her like a lovesick lad who had yet to know his first woman, when it had been more than twenty years since he'd given up his virginity. And there had been countless women since.

Well, perhaps not countless. A score maybe. A dozen for certain. Well, at least five.

He winced. How long had it been since he'd been with a woman?

It wasn't as if there weren't women who were interested or who interested him.

There was Lorna. She was bonny and bright and had made it more than clear that she did not find him repulsive. But she was young and healthy and deserved marriage to a man who would see to her needs today and three decades from now. His loyalty was to the king, and 'twas a dangerous position he was in. He might not live to see the morrow. 'Twould not be fair to such a lass.

Lady Aileen, on the other hand, was widowed and knew the ways of men. Indeed, she was wealthy enough to support herself and had never seemed to find either his occupation or his size a problem. He could visit Aileen now, but her manor house was nearly an hour's ride from Blackburn. Dusk was fast approaching and 'twas his job to make certain all was safe for the night. Indeed, Catriona might very well need . . .

He sighed at his own loss of will. Apparently, neither the ride nor the weather had washed her from his mind. And apparently there was no hope that either would.

Turning his steed away from the hard angle of the rain, Haydan gave himself over to fate and the rapid rush of desire that smothered him at the thought of her.

It had been raining all day. Catriona turned her gaze away from the window and back to the audience that surrounded her. With so many folk confined to the great hall, the day had been filled with tales and games and ballads. She had contributed her own stories, and they had been well received by all, especially the king, whose eyes lit with her tales of adventure. With the Hawk no longer hovering overhead, she had been certain to make her life of freedom seem wondrous and exciting. It was good that he was gone, and yet . . .

She lifted her gaze to the arched double doors. Where was he? She hadn't seen him since he had left her room on the previous night. Nor had she seen Lord de la Faire. But while she was thrilled with the cocky lord's absence, the hall seemed strangely empty without the Hawk's protective presence.

From a dark, gargantuan beam, Calum and Caleb hopped about to survey the crowd below them. Unwilling to venture out the window and into the rain, the birds had set to bickering, and so Catriona had allowed them to follow her down to the hall. James had been thrilled.

"Tell us another, Lady Cat," he said now.

She forced a smile. "Surely there are others here with more intriguing tales than my own."

"But none so charmingly told," said the black-robed priest. He seemed a good man, but there was something familiar about him. Something that she could not quite place. Something that niggled at the edges of her consciousness and made her slightly nervous.

"Indeed," said a man whose name she could not recall. "You cannot refuse the lad."

"Nay," agreed James. "I am the king."

The audience laughed. Catriona glanced at her grandmother. She sat beside Rory on a cushioned spot near the wall and nodded at her granddaughter's unspoken question. Catriona would spin her tales and Marta would "feel," hoping to find the source of the evil that had taken Lachlan.

"Very well then," Cat began. "I shall tell you a tale of Durril."

"Who is Durril?" someone asked.

"He is the greatest entertainer of all time," James said, and Cat smiled.

"Indeed, but he was more."

The hall went quiet.

" 'Tis said he could communicate with the beasts of the field and the birds of the air."

"And 'tis said that ale can cure insanity," Lord Hogshead said, raising a goblet so quickly that ale slopped over the brim. "I've seen no evidence as of yet. But I am still testing the theory."

All around him gentry glanced his way and chuckled.

Some yards away, Lady Fayette settled onto the seat next to Rory. Her gown was ivory in hue, flattering in design. She tilted her head toward his, and he laughed, his eyes already brightened by the thought of a possible conquest.

Something tightened in the pit of Cat's stomach. Surely not jealousy, she thought. But who could say for certain? Logic had no place in matters of the heart. For many years she had thought of Rory as her betrothed.

"I do not believe any man could communicate with the beasties," Lord Spectacles said.

Catriona drew her attention back to the business at hand. If Lady Fayette had abandoned the anonymous Matthew for Rory, she had nothing to say in the matter. "You are most probably right, Your Grace," Catriona agreed. "Even though Durril killed the leader of the wolves with no weapon, 'tis no reason to believe he was then granted the power to—"

"He killed a wolf without so much as a dirk to aid him?"

"Aye," said James, his tone sharp with the edge of impatient excitement. " 'Twas in the dead of winter when he saved the young prince, Endorai, from certain death. Continue, Lady Cat. What happened after he killed the wolf?"

" 'Tis said that because he fought so valiantly and so selflessly, the beasties gave him the power to speak with them." She raised one eyebrow and glanced skeptically at the nearby spectacled duke. "But truly, I do not believe a word of it. I think 'twas naught but good fortune that brought the next wild beast to him when he was in such dire need."

"Ho," said a nearby fellow. "Might you be kin to one called Roderic the Rogue?"

"Nay indeed," she said and grinned as she remembered meeting the man Haydan thought of as a father. "I have heard that the Rogue's tales are wild beyond belief."

The company laughed.

"Go on," urged more than a few.

"If you are certain. I've no wish to—"

"Continue," commanded James.

"Very well, then. As you know, Durril had a wee daughter. She was a bonny lass, hearty and happy, with her mother's entrancing eyes and her father's sense of wit. Even as a babe she performed, for she had the gifts granted her by her heritage. 'Twas when she was no more than five years of age that Prince Endorai first saw her perform. Graceful, she was, like a willow in the wind, with hands of magic and laughter like silver bells. But 'twas more than that which enchanted young Endorai. 'Twas her wisdom. Aye, even as a wee lass, she was clever far beyond her tender age. And somehow, in those early years, a bond was forged between the two.

"Though some thought the prince haughty and unfeeling, wee Martuska saw beyond his shortcomings to the depth beneath, and she loved him for it. As for the prince, he adored young Martuska and treated her not as a villein, but as an equal.

"Together, they would spend many of their days. Martuska showed him the freedom of her people, for she could ride as well as any man. Indeed, on her sixth birthday Prince Endorai gifted her with a small but spirited white palfrey that was faithful only to her.

" 'Twas a bonny autumn day that they rode down to a babbling burn. There they stopped by the water for the nooning, and there they played. With Martuska, Endorai could be anything—a pirate or a saint or a bold invincible warrior. There were no boundaries. But they had played hard all that day and wee Martuska was tired. And so, weary and at peace, she lay upon the grass to sleep while the young prince explored the rushes.

"His guards, of course, were watching him. After all, 'twas their duty to do so. But they were not commissioned to protect the wee lass whom he adored. Thus they did not see the evil that approached her through the grasses."

Catriona paused, her expression somber as she eyed her silent audience.

"A wolf?" someone murmured.

"Nay," said another. "A wolf would not be so bold."

"Unless 'twas fevered or—"

"His soldiers would surely see a wolf," said one of James's own guards. Glancing up, Catriona saw that it was the redheaded youth, the one called Galloway. He blushed now, but continued. "It must have been something small such as a—"

"For God's sake, let the lass tell the tale," Lord Spectacles insisted.

Cat delayed not a moment longer. " 'Twas a snake," she said. "Longer than His Majesty is tall, with a head that dove and weaved as he wended his way through the grasses. His evil yellow eyes were unblinking, his forked tongue hissing of death."

"Surely the guards see it," said Galloway, his tone agitated. "Who would not?"

"Maybe they were distracted because they had just lost their commission in a game of tables," suggested

Cockerel. He grinned as he eyed Galloway and jiggled the pouch of coins that hung from his belt.

"They did not see it," Cat said. "None saw it. None but Durril."

"The lassie's father." 'Twas MacKinnon who spoke the words, his tone solemn in the stillness.

"Aye, Durril had come to take his wee daughter home, for he cherished her so and could not bear to be parted from her a moment longer.

"As he drew near, he saw a movement in the grass. At first he thought 'twas naught but the wind ruffling the autumn blades. But then he saw it. The adder! Only inches away it was and prepared to strike."

"Surely the guards come now." 'Twas a woman's voice.

Catriona glanced toward Lady Fayette, but it was not she who had spoken, though her eyes looked uncommonly bright and her expression as solemn as MacKinnon's.

" 'Tis the prince that saves her," someone argued.

"Have you not been listening? She has a bond with the palfrey young Endorai gave her. 'Tis the beast that comes to her rescue."

"Nay, none of them saw, so none of them could save her," Cat corrected softly. "Durril knew that. Indeed, in his mind he saw the death of his beloved parents, and he knew in his heart that his wee lassie was about to die."

Lord MacKinnon scowled as if thinking of his own daughters, and Drummond turned his sleepy gaze from the pale Roberta to Cat.

"Broken and terrified, he screamed to the heavens. Ahhh!" Catriona's anguished wail echoed in the rafters.

Disturbed from his preening, Calum launched from his perch to circle near the ceiling.

"And then it came," Catriona said, her voice low with drama.

Not a sound broke the quiet.

"The great harrier."

There was a collective hiss of surprise and hope.

"It swooped out of nowhere." She opened her arms wide as if feeling the wind roar through her own feathers, as if tasting the rush of freedom on her face. "Like a loosed arrow it fell from the sky, its talons curved, its eyes glaring."

From far above, Calum saw her movement and dropped through the air to land as light as morning on her arm.

"But the adder was so near," Catriona continued, her voice quick and staccato. "Its head was drawn back, its fangs bared, its evil eyes steady. 'Twas only a moment to spare, only a heartbeat of time. And in that instant, the harrier attacked. It grasped the coiled body. The serpent writhed wildly. But the harrier launched from the ground and bore the poisonous adder away."

Reaching out absently, Catriona stroked the little greenfinch.

"Durril gazed up in wonder, wanting, nay, *needing* to thank the hawk. But in that instant . . ."

Lifting the wee bird from her arm, she hid it carefully between her cupped palms.

"It was gone," she said and spread her hands wide.

Calum was nowhere to be seen. Disappeared. There were gasps of surprise, nervous murmurs.

"Where did it go?" James was the only one either bold enough or young enough to voice the question.

"I do not know," Catriona said as if she thought he

spoke of the bird in her tale. "Mayhap Durril had called it out of nothingness, and to nothingness it returned. Or mayhap 'twas a magical falcon come only to save wee Martuska. 'Tis for you to decide."

James shook his head, still searching for Calum with roving eyes, but finally he pinned Catriona with a perplexed scowl. "To come just when Durril screamed as he did—it could not have been pure coincidence."

Catriona shrugged. "Perhaps you are right."

"Ho," said Cockerel, turning abruptly away. "Speak of the falcon, and see him land. 'Tis too bad you did not fly in sooner, Sir Hawk. You missed the lady's tale."

Against her will, Catriona turned toward Haydan. His hair was wet and dark, swept back from his sharp features, and around his immense shoulders, his cloak hung in damp folds.

'Twas the same cloak that had sheltered her the night before. The very sight of him swamped her with memories that began at her belly and spread outward in hot waves.

"Lady Cat," James said, calling her back to the present.

"What?" she asked, turning abruptly back to the king.

"I said, Sir Hawk can call in his birds just so."

"Can he?" She felt breathless.

"Aye," James murmured. "Tomorrow we shall go hawking together."

She could feel Haydan's gaze on her. Something pitched in her stomach. "Nay, I cannot," she said.

"Do you forget that I am the king?"

"Nay. 'Tis just that I have no wish to disappoint you at your birthday celebration. I must practice."

"I will not be disappointed. Not by Durril's kin," he said, and all around her there was agreement.

Chapter 10

"I felt it," Marta said, her tone hushed in the darkness of their shared chamber.

"What?" Cat set Calum on the top of the cage and turned toward her grandmother. "What did you feel?"

"Evil."

For a moment, Catriona could not speak, so intense were her feelings, but finally she found her voice. "Evil? *The* evil? Are you certain?"

" 'Twas directed toward the lad."

"James?" Catriona gripped the old woman's sleeve in fingers numb with emotion.

"Aye."

"Who was it?" Cat asked, barely able to force out the words for the tightness of her throat.

She felt more than saw Marta shake her head. "I do not know, lass. I could not tell."

"But—" Frustration screamed through her. "Nay! You must know. Was it someone near to the king? Was it—"

"In truth, lass, there could be many who hate the lad. 'Tis the way of lower folk to be jealous of their betters." The old woman's voice sounded tired even beyond her venerable years. "I do not know for certain if it was the one for whom we search."

"But it must be." Cat tightened her fingers in her grandmother's sleeve, her desperation so intense she could barely speak. "It must be. He has to be here. He said he would know if I told anyone his secret. He said he would immediately know . . . and that Lachlan would suffer." She forced herself past the fear. "Thus he must be close at hand."

"Perhaps he lied. Perhaps he would not know, but only told you that to make certain you did not give him away."

Catriona had thought of that, of course. Indeed, she had lain awake countless nights trying to determine how to outmaneuver the one she called Blackheart. The one who had stood in the darkness like an apparition and set forth his horrid demands. She had wrestled it every which way and still had no answer. Maybe Grandmother was right. Maybe there was no need to bear this pain alone.

Sir Hawk's sharp features flashed through her mind. "Shall I seek help?" she whispered.

"I do not know." Grandmother's voice, which had seemed old before, sounded ancient now. "Indeed, lass, I cannot feel that far."

Despair burned Cat like a hot poker. "Then there is no hope."

" 'Tis not so," Grandmother said, turning her gnarled hand to grip Cat's arm. "There is every hope."

"He is alive?"

"He is alive and he awaits your arrival," Grandmother rasped. "That much I know."

"Then we shall get him back?"

"Aye. We shall."

Drawing a deep breath, Cat turned and helped her grandmother toward the bed. Once seated there, they spoke again in hushed tones.

"Tell me now," Cat began. "Tell me all you know of the evil."

Marta closed her eyes, though in the dimness, there seemed little need. "All day I have sat in the great hall and searched for feelings. But the feelings were overwhelming, everywhere at once. It took me some time to separate one from the other."

"And?"

"And mostly it is passion."

Catriona shook her head. "I do not—"

"Passion of every sort," she said. "Lust, anger, hatred, adoration. 'Twas disorienting and bewildering, but then you began your tale, and I felt the emotions recede a bit. Even then it took me some time to tell one man's feelings from the rest, but finally I was able. None of the three men to your left was the one we call Blackheart. Of that I am certain."

"The first three," Cat mused, finding their faces in her mind. "The fellow with the spectacles. The guard called Cockerel. And the balding gentleman. 'Twas none of them? You are certain?"

"Aye."

"And the next two?"

"The fat fellow and the snaggle-toothed lad?"

Catriona nodded. Royal blood did not always produce a royal visage.

"The feelings were muddled there. But I do not think they held enmity for either you or the king. And after that . . ." She shrugged wearily. "I am old, Catty. When I was only ninety or so I would have known the culprit long days ago, but now . . ."

"Do not worry," Cat said, though her own nerves were stretched taut. "Rest now in the quiet. On the morrow you can try again." She rose.

"And you?"

"I wasted last night," she said, guilt gnawing at her. "I meant to search once I was certain everyone was gone, but I fell asleep."

"What do you mean when everyone was gone?" Marta asked. Even in the darkness, her gaze felt sharp.

Catriona turned rapidly away, remembering the feel of Haydan's hands on her skin. "There was . . . there were noises. I knew there were people in the halls." Turning quickly, she headed toward the door.

"Aye," Marta said, her gaze steady on the back of Cat's head. "There were people, and one raptor."

For a moment Cat thought of arguing, or at least of pretending ignorance, but there would be little point. Grandmother might have little use for honesty, but she was always astute. Slipping to the door, Catriona listened for noises on the far side, but none caught her attention. She opened the door quietly.

"My lady."

Cat all but shrieked as she jerked back into her room. "What are you doing here?"

"My apologies." Galloway's face reddened. "I had no intention of frightening you."

"Then why are you lurking here?"

The lad's color deepened. "Sir Hawk sent me. He told me to guard your door until dawn."

"Why?"

"You are most . . ." His words stuttered off into silence. "That is to say, perhaps Sir Hawk feels that men might . . ."

She glared at him as frustration burned through her.

"He worries for your safety," he finished.

Dear God, this couldn't be. She had things to do. Dozens of rooms to search. There was no time to waste. But she drew a deep breath and did her best to calm her wild worries. "We have met before, have we not?" she asked. In truth, she remembered him well from the time outside Blackburn's walls.

"Aye, lady." She had not thought his complexion could redden any more, but he countered his blush by deepening his scowl. "I am called Galloway. I was the one who delayed you before you reached the castle."

"Ah, yes."

He straightened his back and tucked in his chin to stare straight ahead. "I did not know you were a friend of Sir Hawk's. I should have made certain you had safe passage to Blackburn."

"Regardless of what you think of me?"

His lips moved as if he tried to find a response, but she spoke before he did.

"You are not the first to dislike my kind," she said. "Nor will you be the last."

"I will guard you well and faithfully," he vowed, earnestness clefting his brows and bunching his fists.

" 'Tis not that I do not believe you," she said. "Indeed, I appreciate your efforts. But the truth is this, I have no need for a guard. Hence, you are relieved of this tedious—"

"Sir Hawk said I am to stay beside your door, lady: last night, tonight, and every night so long as you are—"

"You were here last night?"

"Aye. I was here, though I was not called to this post until sometime after midnight." Shifting his gaze uncomfortably to hers, he drew a careful breath. "Sir Hawk seemed . . . distraught." He said the words as though it were a phenomenon never before imagined. "Was there some trouble?"

"Nay," she said, remembering de la Faire's sloppy advances, contrasted dramatically with Sir Hawk's disturbing warmth. "Nay. All was well," she said, and stepping quickly back, shut the door in his face.

She shifted her attention rapidly to the window. 'Twould be a much more difficult task now, but she had little choice.

Morning dawned earlier every damned day.

Haydan sat up in his pallet and rolled his right shoulder in an effort to soothe the ache there. It did little good, so he rose to his feet and let the pain in his knee battle for supremacy. If one had enough wounds, it was too difficult to tell which to pity oneself for.

There was his medical philosophy in a nutshell. Perhaps it was good he hadn't endeavored to become a physician.

It was his own fault that he ached, of course. He'd spent the entire previous day sitting a saddle in the rain, when there was no reason he couldn't have sent a younger man to check the outlying garrisons.

No reason except for her.

He winced at the thought. Damnit all. His knee didn't hurt nearly enough. Not enough to make him forget the sight of her—naked, in another man's arms. But through no will of her own. He had wanted to kill the cocky Frenchman. Indeed, 'twas only the tightest control that had kept him at bay.

And why? There was no reason for his overprotective instincts. Indeed, his second glance had assured him that she had no need of a hero, for she had held a dirk to the poor bastard's balls. One quick movement and Lord de la Faire would have become . . . well . . . he would have become less troublesome.

Still, 'twas not enough for Haydan to escort the drunken fool out of the maid's bedchamber. No indeed. He had felt a need to knock him senseless, then proceed to prove that he was no wiser than the fellow he had just tromped into unconsciousness.

Surely he was too old to be thinking with his wick. Hadn't he realized by now that he had neither the strength nor the discipline to resist her?

He might be as old as black pepper and have battled a thousand wars, but that experience seemed to do him little good where she was concerned. She was like a nettle under his skin—forever niggling, forever worrying him. And why? She was only a woman. Little more than a girl, really.

True, her eyes were as mercurial as the weather and seemed to hold a thousand mysteries. And yes, her lips were the very definition of sensuality—full and lush and berry red. Her rich velvet skin had felt as smooth and cool as marble beneath his hand, and when she kissed him—

Enough!

Haydan swung irritably away from the window. What the hell was wrong with him? He was mooning over her like a lovestruck hound. He was too old to be a hound. He was the Hawk now—captain of the king's royal guard, bold, disciplined, unflappable. But for a moment she had seemed so vulnerable. Soft and strangely sad, like a lost fairy princess . . .

He was doing it again!

Lowering his head, Haydan wearily scrubbed his face with dry hands. Even with all his years behind him he was not strong enough to resist her. Thus he had little choice but to avoid her.

King James deserved not only Haydan's loyalty, but his absolute attention. He had no time to worry over a Gypsy lass who already had every young buck in the palace panting after her like a roe in rut. Even young James was not immune to her charms, so Haydan could assume the lad would wish to spend some time with her.

He exhaled softly. His duty was clear. If the boy wished to be with Catriona, Haydan would simply send another to guard them, just as he had ordered Galloway to watch her door at night.

'Twas his best plan, for while he would still be fulfilling James's order to keep her guarded, he was also keeping himself safely out of her range. And Galloway was the perfect candidate. Not only was he still young enough to be awed both by a post at Blackburn Castle and by Sir Hawk's daunting and much embellished reputation, he also felt guilty for failing to guard Catriona at their first meeting.

Haydan was more than willing to use that guilt if it meant keeping her safe.

Scrubbing his face again, Haydan sighed. He might be neither as disciplined nor as unflappable as either his reputation or his age deemed appropriate, but at least he was wise enough to know his limitations.

Thus, he would avoid her, he decided as he belted on his plaid. 'Twas surely not such a difficult task.

"Sir Hawk!" young James called, his plumed cap askew as he bounded across the hall.

Haydan turned toward the boy. Though dressed in a red velvet doublet and soft deerskin hose, somehow he always managed to look rather unkempt, like a waif who had stolen the garb of a wealthy man's son.

"Lord Tremayne would insist that you show more decorum," Haydan said, but the bright flush of excitement on the lad's face made him smile. Too often the young king of the Scots was treated either as a trophy or as a pawn, when in truth he was nothing more or less than a high-spirited boy with the bad luck of being birthed by the queen.

"Lord Tremayne is not here," James puffed happily, "and since 'tis so close to my birthday, Ferrand has agreed to forgo my French lessons for the day."

"Indeed? Then I imagine you'll want to practice your Latin."

James had a gift for showing annoyance without saying a word. "Today we hunt," he said as if surely the whole world knew.

"Hunting is it?"

"Aye. We go to the meadows to fly the birds."

"We?"

"Lady Cat has agreed to accompany us."

Haydan stiffened. Lady Cat! Just the sound of her name conjured up lush, erotic emotions. But he had made a resolution to avoid her, and he would keep it—as much for James as for himself.

"My apologies," Haydan said, bowing slightly. "But I fear duty calls me elsewhere." Where, he didn't know. But he'd better think of somewhere quick.

"Nay," James argued, his bright face scrunched in disappointment. "Send another to do the task."

So the boy wished to spend time with him. A sharp pang of emotion smote Haydan's heart, but he stifled it. There was no place for emotion between a guard and his royal ward.

Perhaps he should have remarried after Marcele's

death. Perhaps if he had sired children of his own . . .

"I am sorry," Haydan said. "But I will send Galloway and Cockerel with you. And Russell, of course."

"But none handle the birds like you."

"I am flattered, Your Majesty." Far too flattered. "But I am certain the royal falconer can manage without me."

His words did nothing to soften James's scowl. "You were gone all of yesterday and I . . ." He halted, and in that instant it seemed Haydan could see the boy James wrestle with the man he would someday become. "*Lady Cat* missed you."

A double attack on his emotions. How clever of the lad. Haydan's stomach twisted into a tight knot. But he soothed the foolishness with a reminder of his astounding age, and refused to ask if she had truly spoken of him or if the boy was covering his own sentiments, and if she had said anything else, and where they had been when she'd mentioned his name, and how her face had looked, and—

A movement caught his eye. He glanced up, and she was there.

She wore a gown of russet hue that seemed to have turned her eyes to bronze and her skin to apple butter. The garment was laced up the front, showing a bit of pecan-smooth cleavage and a waist little wider than his forearm. But perhaps it was her grace that mesmerized him, for it seemed that she did not walk at all, but floated, like a wood fairy or an angel or a—

Nay! Haydan tightened his hands to fists and swore in silence. She was no angel. She was no fairy. She was a mere mortal like every other woman, and he would not weaken. He had determined to avoid her and avoid her he would.

But his muscles were cranked as tight as an ancient

crossbow, and his mouth felt brownstone dry. Still, he would not weaken. He was disciplined, bold, unflappable.

"So will you accompany us when we go hawking?" she asked, her eyes entrancing, her voice like a siren's song. It turned his will to oatmeal, his muscle to mud.

He tried to resist, but there was no hope. After all, if he were so tempted, so would every other man be. She was not safe alone.

"Aye," he said, and desperately wished that a modicum of wisdom had accompanied his astounding years.

Chapter 11

The day was cool and lovely in the full throes of spring. Calum and Caleb accompanied Cat for a ways as she rode from the castle, but they soon returned to flit about the bedroom window. Pipits sang from the trees, and beside the road, the grass was a green so fresh it all but begged children to run barefoot across its springy turf. The sky was a rain-washed blue that dazzled the senses. Birds soared through the heavens like errant spring breezes.

Catriona turned to glance behind her. Dozens of raptors were tied about the wooden bases that perched on the backs of even-spirited palfreys.

"It seems a pity that they cannot fly free on such a bonny day," she said. "Must they always be tethered?"

"Russell of the Mews says they must be confined and hooded so that they do not become overwrought," James said, then leaned closer and lowered his voice. "But Sir Hawk disagrees."

"Why the secrecy?" Cat asked.

"Russell is as flighty as a sparrow, so we must be careful not to wound his feelings, but I know that sometimes Sir Hawk allows his peregrine to fly unencumbered. He believes birds need to be set loose now and again, though he seems to have no such feelings about monarchs," he said, and glanced good-naturedly at the huge guard on his other side.

Calendine tossed her flaxen mane and did a little dance to impress any stallions that might be watching. Haydan's dappled gray cocked his head and rumbled encouragement, but Hawk gave a slight tug on the reins that quieted any further displays of emotion. Apparently neither horse nor rider was wildly ostentatious about his feelings. Hawk had been particularly quiet during their trip. Behind them a small mob of nobles and servants followed, jostling and talking and laughing. But Haydan the Hawk had barely said a word to her.

Indeed, he acted as if he had not even noticed her. It shamed her now that she could not forget how his arms had felt around her, or how her skin had burned beneath his fingertips.

Strange, how after all the men who had pursued her, she would become enthralled with the one man who avoided her.

She turned her gaze away, but she could still see him clearly in her mind's eye. He rode very straight in the saddle, his cloak thrown back over his massive shoulders and his knees bare between his black doeskin boots and his plaid. Higher up, his powerful thighs gripped his stallion with easy command. With no trouble at all, she could remember how those thighs had felt beneath her, how the muscles had tightened and bunched when he'd kissed her. Or rather—when she had kissed him.

Still, for a moment, she had thought he had felt the same breathless emotion as she. But she had been wrong. Indeed, 'twas only his good manners that had made him suffer her caress at all. In fact, he had been nothing but eager to spring from her touch at the first possibility.

What had he found so repulsive? Was it her mixed blood? She knew she did not possess the characteristics that most called beautiful. Her skin was not the smooth alabaster of a proper lady. She was too tall and strong. Few men would call her delicate. But—

Behind her, a boy laughed. The sound cracked through her, charging her with shame. How could she worry about such foolish matters when her only brother's life hung in the balance? It made no difference whatsoever if Haydan the Hawk cherished her or detested her. She was here for one reason only—to learn who had taken Lachlan. And until that goal was met, nothing else mattered.

The day wore on, and the birds were flown—merlins, falcons, peregrines, and goshawks, a wide array of handsome birds whose handlers were determined by their social rank.

There were too many rules for Catriona to try to understand them all. She knew, however, that James was the only one allowed to keep the great golden eagle he had received as a gift from the king of Spain.

Lord Tremayne and Lord Spectacles both flew saker falcons, and Haydan had brought a peregrine—a sharp-beaked bird with a gray speckled breast and eyes that pierced you in one glance, not unlike its handler.

Aye, the birds were breathtaking when they flew, but Catriona had little time to watch them. Instead, she stood on the outer edges of the assemblage and studied every man present, whether he was yeoman or duke. Blackheart could be anyone, but he was there. She felt it in her soul, so she listened and watched, studying every mannerism, every expression, every nuance of gesture or tone.

Lord Hogshead was talking to Lady Fayette somewhere behind her. A noblewoman and her small daughter were searching for wildflowers, and a half dozen others carried on conversations around her. On a distant hill, young Roberta of Perth leaned her head toward her mother's in earnest conversation.

"Have you never been hawking before?" asked Lord MacKinnon. He had brought a northern goshawk that was waiting nervously on its portable cadge, its wings sweeping wildly in the sweet spring air.

"Nay," she answered, and carefully watched his reaction. "Do not be so surprised. After all, is it not a sport reserved for the gentry?"

"Aye, it is."

She canted her head. "And I am not gentry."

" 'Tis not what I have heard."

She laughed. "Then you have heard incorrectly, good sir."

Rory had accompanied the crowd out into the meadow. She could feel his disapproving gaze on her, but it made no difference. She would do what she must.

MacKinnon's smile expanded shyly. "Gentlewomen are allowed to fly merlins. But a princess . . ." He shrugged. "Since I have never met one before I am not certain, but I myself think even a gyrfalcon would not be too bold a creature for you."

"Shall I take that as a compliment or simply deny any link to nobility once again?"

"Would a compliment have any hope of winning my way into your good graces?" he asked.

"It may."

"Then might I ask you to accompany me to supper this eve?"

"I—" she began, but a noise turned her attention aside.

Lifting her gaze, she saw a lark streak through the sky. In the next instant a merlin grabbed it with its hungry talons. The hapless lark let out a piteous squawk and fell wounded and dying toward the earth.

In the next crackling seconds Catriona drew in perceptions like fragments of dreams. There was a gasp from the small girl, a soothing word from the mother, tears in Fayette's eyes, a twisted expression on Hogshead's face, a rumble of approval from a group of men behind her.

And then the bird was dead. Life seemed to return to normal speed. Several men came forward to retrieve the lark and move away, praising the merlin's flight and their own birds.

The little girl was weeping softly, wrapped in her mother's arms.

"Lord Harrowhead," Fayette said, turning from the sight. "Are you well?"

"Aye." The young earl's voice was gruff. "Aye, I am fine," he said, but his tone sounded strange as he turned and walked away.

"Tears are naught to be ashamed of," Fayette said, her voice drifting off as she followed him.

Silence settled onto the hillock. MacKinnon cleared his throat. "Scotland's noble families," he said, his voice very low. "God save us all."

Catriona turned toward him with a scowl.

MacKinnon glanced away, but finally caught her gaze again. "Madness runs rampant."

"Are you saying that Lord Hogshead is mad?"

"In truth . . ." He smiled but the expression did not reach his eyes. " 'Twas myself I was speaking of. Douglas is but—" He stopped abruptly.

"Is but what?"

Anger flashed for a moment in MacKinnon's eyes. " 'Tis said the parent determines the child's worth. And indeed, the eldest son was as evil as the father."

"I do not understand," Catriona said, glancing surreptitiously toward Douglas. His head was bowed, but Fayette was still speaking to him as they wandered toward the woods.

MacKinnon's lips narrowed almost imperceptibly as he watched the couple disappear into the trees. "It serves him right that his scrawny youngest son gained the earldom."

There was something in his tone—anger, bitterness. Might Blackheart hide his true identity beneath such an innocuous facade?

"Who?" Catriona asked, nearly breathless with anticipation.

"What?" He turned toward her as if surprised to find her still there.

"It serves who well?"

He drew a deep breath. "Harrowhead's father was a hard man and cruel, preaching self-discipline and sacrifice while all the while . . ." He paused a moment, then said, "He was found dead some months ago. Stabbed a half dozen times."

"How terrible!"

"Do you think so?" he asked, glancing at her.

"Regaling the lady with tales of your family, MacKinnon?"

Catriona and MacKinnon turned in unison.

"Lord Drummond," MacKinnon said, his tone taut.

The handsome, narrow-faced man bowed shallowly, his dark half-lidded eyes alight with an unspoken humor. "Lady Catriona." Reaching for her hand, he brushed a kiss across her knuckles. Then, tightening his fingers over hers, he grinned. "I have not yet had the pleasure of your acquaintance, and here my chamber companion is already sharing his terrible woes."

Without Roberta to prompt his charm and hold his attention, his eyes were spooky and unmoving. Was there evil in their depths? She must find a way to search his locked room.

"Chamber companion?" she asked, pretending she did not know their sleeping arrangements.

Drummond laughed. "I suppose it is a hopeful sign that he has not yet informed you that he shares a room with me here at Blackburn. But then, you would have little reason to take her there, aye, MacKinnon?"

"Quiet, Drummond," warned MacKinnon, "or you shall regret your words."

Lord Drummond raised his hand to his heart and widened his eyes as if terrified. "You are frightening me. Indeed, I think perhaps the horrid rumors may well be true."

Catriona held her breath.

"Mayhap they are," MacKinnon said. "And mayhap I shall tell young Roberta why your past two betrothals did not come to—"

Laughter snared Catriona's attention. It came from somewhere behind her and traveled up her spine like a ghostly scream, raising the hair at the nape of her neck. Blackheart had laughed just so, as if her brother's life were no more important than the weather. She jerked toward the source.

A large group of men had congregated on a sheltered

hillock some distance away, but who had laughed?

"You are disturbing the lady," MacKinnon said.

"I suspect she is not so easily disturbed as you think. Are you, Catriona?" Drummond asked, but she had no time to waste.

Without a word of apology or explanation, she rushed away.

Nearly two dozen folk were gathered on the distant hill, five women among the men. Catriona catalogued them in her mind, trying to place names with faces, to remember what she had heard of each, to analyze each man's movements and voice patterns and manner.

But all that endless afternoon, she never heard the laughter again, and for that she chastised herself. She should have stayed with MacKinnon and Drummond, for surely there was evil there. But among the wealthy and well-dressed gentry of Blackburn, there seemed to be evil everywhere.

Still, the more she dwelled on it, the more Drummond's movements reminded her of Blackheart's—how he had lifted his hand to his chest, as if fondling some precious medallion. But though she had studied him often, it had done her no good, for she had no answers.

Finally, frustrated and tense, she watched as the last bird was called in, hooded, and returned to her cadge.

Bending to secure his falcon to its perch, Haydan caught her eye suddenly and stiffened.

"Lady Catriona," he said, his tone low and formal. "Is something amiss?"

For some reason she could neither discern nor explain even to herself, she found it difficult to force out a lie, but she had little choice. "Nay, all is well."

He straightened with a scowl and took two quick strides toward her. Her stomach fluttered.

His eyes met hers in a gaze no less piercing than that of the falcon he had just left.

"When a bird sings like a thrush but flies like a kite, which is it?" he asked, his voice deep and low.

"What?" she breathed.

He stopped only inches from her. "Your expression says that all is not well."

"Oh." She nodded once in concession to his riddle. " 'Tis a thrush."

He continued to watch her, his brows pulled low.

She countered with a smile. "You must believe the song, for a bird has no reason to lie," she said, and turning rapidly away, retreated.

The assemblage was preparing to return to Blackburn. Finding her steed, she tightened Celandine's girth. She could still feel Haydan's gaze on her. The heat of it all but scalded her back, but when she finally allowed herself to turn, he was gone.

'Twas good, she told herself, for the Hawk was certainly dangerous to any thrush.

"May I assist you, lady?"

For one heart-jolting moment she thought Haydan had approached her, but she turned to find Blackburn's dark-robed priest at her elbow. His face was shadowed by the lowering sun. She would have liked to refuse his offer, but there was something familiar about him— and until she learned what it was, she would turn aside no clues.

" 'Tis good of you to offer, Father. Thank you," she said, and gathering the reins over Celandine's flaxen mane, allowed him to boost her into the saddle.

His hand rested on her leg for a moment, but his gaze lingered much longer on her face.

"Is there aught I can do to soothe your melancholy, my lady?"

"Melancholy?" She laughed. Since when had her emotions become so obvious? She could not afford such honesty. " 'Tis not the case," she assured him. "I am naught but fatigued."

He was silent for a moment, but finally nodded. "Then I would wish you rest," he said, and walked away.

James rode up beside her. "Did you see the gyrfalcon's stoop when the fox was flushed out?"

"Nay, I did not," Cat said, turning her mare behind a line of guards.

" 'Twas magnificent," James raved. "She would have gotten him had the cowardly beast not ducked into the brush."

Fatigue wore at her. "Perhaps you would be cowardly too, if a huge bird chose you for its prey."

James grinned. "Is it always your way, Cat, to see things from a different angle?"

"If I do, 'tis simply because I come from a different place," she said.

The sun was sinking toward the western horizon, etching the sky in vibrant hues of magenta and scarlet. Beneath their horses' hooves, Scotland rolled away in verdant hills and dales.

"Still," James said, settling back against the high cantle of his saddle. "You must admit the birds are beautiful."

"I will admit it readily if you will grant me one favor."

"What favor?" he asked.

"I am a simple Rom lass who has been tending myself for as long as I can recall. I am not comfortable with a guard at my door at all hours of the night."

He stared at her. "Again because you come from a different place?"

"Mayhap."

"A freer place," he said.

She glanced at him, feeling a sharp twist in her gut for the deception that she must deal. "Would that I were in your place now," she murmured.

"Nay." He shook his head. "You could never give up your freedom, Lady Cat."

Up ahead, the guards nudged their mounts into the hustling burn that cut across their path. Catriona watched the water wash over the horses' hocks, then rise to their bellies. They struggled a bit against the current.

"You might well be surprised what I would give up," she said.

James laughed as his steed stepped into the water. At eleven years of age, all of life was still an adventure. "Not your freedom," he insisted. "You are the wind."

"I am naught but a stagnant breeze."

Their mounts sloshed deeper. The waves rose higher in curling, frosted swells. Catriona lifted her feet from the stirrups, attempting to keep her slippers dry.

"The wind," James repeated, his grin mischievous. "Come to blow me free."

"What?" she asked, suddenly realizing his thrust.

He grinned charmingly. "Sneak me away from Blackburn," he said, "and I will call off the guard."

The earth disappeared from beneath her horse's hooves, and suddenly Cat was falling. Water, cold as Highland snow, slapped against her. Celandine scrambled for footing, but the current was strong.

She heard James's hiss of surprise and someone's gasp, but there was no time for another single thought, for suddenly she was snatched away from her mare's thrashing hooves and lifted into the air.

She turned in shock and gratitude to stare into Haydan's icy eyes.

"Sir Hawk!" she rasped.

"Are you hurt?" His voice was as deep as the sea, his arm about her waist as steady as stone.

"Nay. 'Twas . . ." For a moment she could find no words, for there was something indefinable in his eyes. " 'Twas foolish of me to take my feet from the stirrups."

"Did she strike you?" he asked.

Beneath her, Haydan's stallion shuffled, stirring the water restlessly. The world seemed nothing more than a jumble of colors and sounds. "She?"

"Your mare."

"Oh."

He loosened his reins, allowing the stallion to make his way toward the opposite shore. Halfway across his hoof struck a stone, and he stumbled.

Cat hissed a sharp breath through her teeth, and Haydan's arm tightened protectively, drawing her against the granite wall of his chest. A cauldron of emotions stirred at the impact, swirling in her belly, tingling to her breasts.

In an instant, the stallion found his balance and soon they were across.

"Were you struck?" Haydan asked again.

"Nay. I do not believe so."

A bevy of folk were gathered about, talking and staring and jostling for a better view.

"Sir Hawk," said Galloway, his youthful face bright with emotion as he rushed across the burn toward them. "My apologies. I should have been watching her."

"Nay." Haydan pulled his gaze from hers to stare at the soldier. "You should have been watching the king, as you were."

But still Galloway scowled. " 'Tis my fault. Therefore she must ride my mount."

"I will ride my own mare," Catriona said. She felt foolish and strangely breathless.

"I fear not, lady," Galloway argued, nodding toward Celandine, who stood on the grassy bank, one foreleg bent to rest naught but her toe on the new grass. "She seems to be lame."

"Nay." Cat tried to slip from Hawk's grip, but his arm only tightened, bunching his corded biceps against the side of her breast.

"Andrew," he said to a nearby soldier. "You shall stay behind and bring the lady's mare in at a cautious pace."

"Aye, sir."

"Nay, I—" she argued, but her words were cut off by a nearby soldier.

"I would be happy to take the lass with me, Sir Hawk."

" 'Tis good of you to offer, Duncan" said the one they called Cockerel. "But I've no wish for you to strain yourself. The lady can ride with me. My steed is better suited to bear an extra load." His mount flicked back a nervous ear and pranced.

Duncan scowled, first at Cockerel, then at the restive black. "I would not put an Englishman on that twit of yours. My mount is much better—"

"She rides with me!" Hawk interrupted darkly.

Duncan raised his brows. Cockerel grinned.

"Close ranks about the king," Haydan ordered. "And wipe that foolish expression off your face, Cockerel. I am her guardian. Nothing more."

"Aye, sir," Cockerel said, but the grin remained.

Catriona said nothing as they passed the onlookers, nor did she glance at them, for she felt clumsy and conspicuous in the huge knight's embrace.

The company turned and hurried along behind them.

A breeze skimmed past the edge of a copse of rowan. Though it was chill, it felt good against her warm face. She cleared her throat.

"I did not mean to be a burden," she said, not looking up at him, but watching the country roll away in shades of winter browns and spring greens.

Haydan said nothing. Beneath them, the big stallion strode along in a heavy-footed walk. Even that easy gait jostled her, pressing her firmly up against Haydan's chest. From a barren rowan, a thrush trilled, his cheerful song in sharp contrast to Haydan's silent disapproval.

"My apologies," she said.

"Why are you here?" She could feel the words rumble from his chest, and tensed at the question.

But she dared not show her nervousness, so she remained facing forward, trying to calm her nerves. "I am here because James asked me to stay," she said simply.

He was silent for a moment. Her nerves stretched tighter.

"You did not enjoy the hawking?"

She could lie, but it seemed that he would know, would feel it in the contact of their bodies, her back against his chest, her buttocks pressed into the tight valley between his thighs.

"In truth, Sir Hawk, I do not like to see the defenseless suffer."

"But if the falcon does not eat, he suffers too."

"Perhaps I have a wish to see the hapless prey win sometimes. And see the fierce predator fail."

"The predator often fails."

"Does he?" There was too much emotion in her tone. She knew that, and yet she could not seem to quell it. She could only remain facing forward and hope he would not guess her feelings.

"Aye," Haydan said. "More often than not the quarry escapes."

"But what if the quarry is young and weak?" She could barely force the question from the constricted confines of her throat.

" 'Tis true that the falcon sometimes steals the young of others," he said, his voice quiet. "But there have been times that those same birds take the victim to their nests and do not kill them, but raise them to adulthood."

"Truly?" She turned. Her breast skimmed the coiled strength of his arm, their hearts inches apart, their gazes melded.

"Are we talking about birds?" he questioned, "or about something of more import?"

She tried to force out a lie, but his eyes were so intense that for a moment she forgot how. Still, her brother's life depended on her subterfuge. "Birds, of course," she said, and turned to hide her face from him.

The muscles that surrounded her tightened almost imperceptibly, and for a moment she thought he would call her the liar she was, but instead he fell silent again and turned his mount onto a cobbled road behind a fat earl with his retinue of servants. Ahead, Blackburn glared down at her in looming disapproval, as if even it knew her hideous plans.

"The dove does not have to fly alone. It might be that the hawk could help."

Her heart wrenched. "Help me with what?" she asked, but her tone didn't achieve the flippancy she had hoped for.

"I do not deny that I am a man," he said softly.

A thousand emotions flitted through Catriona. Fear, hope, and an aching longing to trust. But she must play the hand given to her, so she ignored the emotional and concentrated on the physical. Against her legs she felt the tautness of his thighs, against her breast she felt the strength of his arm, and against her buttocks, she felt the hard edge of his desire. She turned to glance up through her lashes at him. "Did you imagine that I hadn't noticed, Sir Hawk?" she asked.

He tightened his jaw and raised his gaze from hers. "Nay, you have noticed," he said. "And thus you do not trust me."

She frowned at his confusing words. "You think I do not trust you because of your sex?"

"Is there another reason?" His gaze lowered sharply to hers.

She shifted hers away. "Nay, of course not."

His muscles relaxed just a smidgen, though his thighs felt no softer against hers.

"Since your arrival at Blackburn, how many times have you been forced to defend your virtue?" he asked.

"Several times," she said. "And you?"

" 'Tis not a laughing matter." His tone was tight with anger, his body the same.

"You worry for me," she whispered.

She would not have thought it possible for his muscles to tense even more. "The king has commanded me to guard you," he said simply.

"Did he command you to worry?"

For a moment he did not speak, but finally the words came, as if he could not hold them back. "Let me help, lass. I will not fail you."

How desperately she wanted a friend, *needed* a friend. And this man, this Hawk—what power she felt in his hands, what caring she saw in his eyes. He had helped her before. He had saved Rachel and her Liam. He was trusted by a dozen powerful clans—the Forbeses, the MacGowans, the king himself. Surely she could trust him too.

" 'Tis my brother," she rasped, but just then she sensed the sweep of great wings and heard a small bird's terrified cry. Jerking her gaze upward, she saw Haydan's peregrine slam into its hapless prey.

The small bird spilled toward the earth and the peregrine swooped after it. Haydan spurred his great horse forward, and in that instant, Cat recognized the victim as her own pet.

"Caleb!" she cried.

Haydan pulled his steed to a skittering halt. Catriona slid to the earth and ran toward the fallen finch.

Frightened by the commotion, the falcon dropped onto the ground some yards away and glared at her intended prey.

Caleb lay inert, his eyes closed as Cat scooped him into her hands.

"Does he live?" Haydan was less than a stride behind her, his voice gruff. The falcon hopped sideways cautiously as he pulled his stallion closer.

"I'm not certain." Catriona felt tears tighten her throat. 'Twas only a bird, a contentious bit of beak and feathers. And yet she could not bear to lose . . .

"Give it to me," Hawk ordered and ripping off a glove, reached for the tiny greenfinch. It looked small and limp against his square palm.

There was a moment of silence, then he said, "Mount my horse."

"What?"

"There is still a heartbeat." Drawing his stallion in on a tight rein, he nodded toward the steed. "Go straightaway to the physician. Tell him James sent you with the bird."

"But—"

"Go!" he ordered and all but tossed her into his saddle before handing over the tiny finch.

Chapter 12

Catriona looked bedraggled and damp as she watched the king's physician examine the wee greenfinch held by his slim assistant.

Her brow was furrowed and her face pale. Haydan pulled his gaze from her with an effort.

Calum or Caleb, or whoever it was that'd had the bad judgment of soaring from Cat's window to find her, wriggled weakly.

"How does he fare?" Haydan asked.

"My patient?" The king's physician said the word "patient" with a distinctive lack of respect and did not deign to turn toward Haydan.

"Aye."

"A broken wing, I think. And perhaps a concussion." The healer was as lean as a winter reed and just as bent, with a nose like a scythe and a personality to match. "You are aware, I expect, that this is a *bird*?"

Haydan raised his gaze to the old man's rheumy eyes. He was called Physic to his face. Behind his back, the names were not so kindly. 'Leech' was Haydan's particular favorite.

"Aye, Physic, I am well aware—"

"And not a valuable bird," the physician interrupted with a lift of his blue-veined hand. "I suggested, in fact, that we finish the job your falcon began and allow the pig boy to feed it to his swine."

Haydan glanced at Catriona. Her eyes were too bright, her brow pinched, but maybe he could have borne that. It was her hands that broke his heart, for they were clasped tight and white in her lap, as if there was nothing she could do—as if, for the first time in her life, she was helpless.

"But the *lady* took offense to my suggestion," Leech continued. "She said *James* insisted that I mend the beast. *James*, she called him. As if—"

"Physic." Haydan kept his tone level, though it was more difficult than he would have thought possible. "Do you, perchance, remember meeting my cousin, Rachel of the Forbes?"

The old man's anemic lips puckered. "The one they call the lady saint?"

"Aye. That one. Perhaps you have heard of her healing skills."

Physic sniffed. "There are rumors."

Haydan allowed a bitter grin. "Be assured of this, old man. They are more than rumors. With a prayer and her armory of potions she could bring your shoes back to life."

"Do you have a point, Sir Hawk?"

"Aye, I do. She is a friend of the crown and a friend of Lady Catriona's. In fact, 'twas Rachel herself who brought the lass's brother back from the brink of death."

"I am quite impressed."

Haydan ignored the sarcasm. "Then add this to your list of thoughts to ponder—if Catriona but asked, Rachel would be here within a day's notice. And once here . . ."

He shrugged. "Who can say if she would stay?"

The old man stared at Haydan for a moment longer, then turned abruptly away. "I will wrap the wing to his body. It may mend."

" 'Tis good of you."

Physic sniffed as he lifted a linen strip from a table and began wrapping the bird. The process did not take long, for the patient was small and none too active.

" 'Tis done then," Physic said finally and nodded for his assistant to hand the bird to its mistress. "Keep him still if you can and . . ." For a moment he seemed to struggle. "Return him to me if he removes the bandage."

"You have my thanks," Catriona said, cupping the finch gently to her bosom.

"I do not want your—" Physic began.

Haydan cleared his throat.

"You are most welcome," the old man said, his tone still acid.

Putting a hand to Catriona's back, Haydan ushered her from the room.

The hallway was quiet, as was the girl. Haydan searched for something to say, to break the silence, to reassure her.

"You needn't worry," he said finally. "Physic's skills are far better than his temperament."

He heard her sniffle, but her hair, still wet and wild in long tendrils of gilded sable, had fallen forward and he could not see her face.

" 'Tis not too late for you to take back your words," she said finally.

"What words might those be?"

"I believe you said I could charm any man."

Haydan chuckled, relieved simply to hear her speak. "I meant any normal man."

"Normal?" Her voice sounded hoarse.

"Physic's tastes run . . . in an unusual direction."

"What—" Her question stopped before it had barely begun. Then she turned to him, her eyes wide with surprise. "His assistant?" she asked, her tone shocked.

"He particularly likes fair-haired lads. But you need not worry," Haydan hurried to add. "He was rendered incapable of . . . making a nuisance of himself some years ago."

"Oh."

There was silence except for their footfalls before Haydan found his voice again.

"I thought if you delivered the bird yourself, even he might be moved to decency. I fear I overestimated him. You have my sincerest apologies."

She turned toward him again, her eyes so wide they swallowed his world. " 'Twas you who convinced him to mend Caleb."

"Aye. And 'twas me who failed to secure my falcon properly." He paused. "I am sorry. I am not usually a careless man."

They had reached the door to her chambers and she turned, her face solemn.

"You are not careless, Sir Hawk. Indeed . . ." Reaching up slowly, she cupped his cheek with her palm. Feelings as bright as fireworks crackled through him, seeming to bring every dormant nerve ending to sparkling life. "It could be that I have never met a man so full of caring."

He tried to remain quiet, to back away, to run or think or . . . something! But he was rooted to the spot, frozen by the sadness in her eyes.

"Then let me help you."

"You have helped me," she said, holding the wounded bird closer to her breast.

Haydan ground his teeth. "Mayhap you think men cannot be trusted. And 'tis true that my behavior of the other night was . . ." He steadied his nerves as he remembered how she had felt in his arms, against his chest, against his heart. "It will not happen again," he vowed.

But somehow during his soliloquy she had moved closer still, and suddenly her lips touched his. Longing seared him like the touch of a hot lance, but he ground his hands into fists and remained as he was, unmoving, unresponding.

She drew slowly away.

"Let me help you," he pleaded.

Her eyes were as bright as dawn. "I need no help," she whispered, and disappeared into her room.

"Lass!" Marta sat up in bed as Catriona closed the door behind her. "What happened?"

Calum chattered from the top of the cage.

"Everything."

Struggling off the bed, the old woman hurried toward her granddaughter. "What happened to Calum?"

"It's Caleb," Catriona corrected, but her body felt heavy, her mind numb.

"I don't care if he's the devil himself. What happened to him?"

"The hawk. The hawk caught him. Just as he will catch me if I falter."

Marta shook her head in confusion. "I think too much time with these pale nobles has made you daft."

Details and fears and worries swirled together like dark water in Cat's mind. "He asked me to sneak him from the castle."

"The Hawk?"

"Nay. The king."

"God's balls!" Marta's voice was harsh in the dimness of their shared chambers. "However did you manage that?"

"I managed nothing." Going to the cage, Cat carefully set Caleb inside. Calum fluttered after to hover over his fallen comrade and Catriona. "I did not even suggest such an adventure," she added. " 'Twas James' idea."

"Then how did you answer?"

"I fell into the burn."

There was a moment of perplexed silence, then, "Why?"

"I did not mean to," Cat said and began to pace. Her skirts, still heavy with water, wrapped about her legs, seeming to drag her further into fatigue.

Marta watched her closely. "*My* great granddaughter fell?"

"I am out of my depth, Grandmother, floundering. I do not know what to do." She turned and dropped desperately to her knees, clasping Marta's cool, gnarled hand as she did so "I nearly ruined everything this day. I nearly told him the truth."

"The king?"

"Nay, the Hawk. He pulled me from the water, and I . . . I . . ." She searched for words to explain her weakness, but there seemed to be none. "What am I to do?"

Marta remained silent, her hand squeezed tight over Catriona's. "I see goodness in him, Catty," she said finally.

"Goodness!" Cat moaned. "Goodness is not on our side in this. Only necessity. I dare not trust him lest I end up like Caleb."

"The finch snared by the hawk," Grandmother mused,

glancing at the cage. "But the finch is not dead."

"Nay, not dead, but perhaps mortally wounded." Catriona rose abruptly to pace again. "Certainly unable to fly. I cannot afford to be winged. Not now. Not yet."

Grandmother sighed, the sound rusty and low in the sinking light of the room. "Then what will you do?"

"Tell me again that Lachlan is well," Cat pleaded, her heart twisted into a small painful lump.

"He is well, love. That I promise."

Catriona drew a deep breath, steadying her will, steeling her nerve. "Then I will plan to follow the orders given." She whispered the words. "But until I am certain there is no other choice, I will search for the culprit. And toward that end, I will need your help."

"Lord MacKinnon," Catriona said, stepping up to the young baron's side. At Marta's orders, she had bathed, then slept for several hours. The arrival of dinner, brought late and delivered by a servant bearing a well-laden board and two goblets, had awakened her.

Sleep and a hot bath had revived her somewhat. She'd dressed carefully, donning a deep blue gown with slashed sleeves that showed the white of her chemise beneath. She had dried her hair as best she could, then drawn it up to the top of her head with brass pins. It fell now in stray ringlets beside her ears and neck.

She'd felt nothing but relief when she'd found no guard at her door.

"Lady Cat." The young lord looked surprised as he turned toward her, drinking horn in hand. " 'Tis late. I thought you must have found your bed by now."

"I could not sleep," she lied.

He glanced uncomfortably about the vast hall. "Mayhap you should not be here at such a late hour."

Indeed, she did not want to be. The great hall bustled with life, but most of that life was male. She could feel dozens of eyes turn toward her, even while two men, bared to the waist, wrestled near a side door while well-clad noblemen placed bets and yelled encouragement. Several board games were being played at once, and beneath a pair of crossed spears, a score of men were participating in a loose variation of a time-honored sport known as wench-lifting. Judging by Lady Fayette's fey mood, she did not particularly care who carted her about and may very well have had an unusual prize in mind for the winner. Rory was nowhere to be seen, but Lord Hogshead seemed to have recovered from his earlier depression and was drinking and laughing with the others.

"Are you not the wench-lifting type?" Catriona asked, glancing toward the mob.

"Nay, I suppose I am not," MacKinnon said, and scowled toward the crowd of revelers. For a while he was silent, then, "She is not as . . . She is not what she seems."

Was anyone? Catriona wondered.

"Indeed," he said, "Lady Fayette has a good heart. There was a time after my wife's death that she cared for my daughters. They quite adored her."

For a moment he looked so melancholy that Catriona was certain that he could not possibly be the man for whom she searched. But in that instant a memory burned her mind.

"You will not know us."

She tightened her resolve. He was probably not Blackheart, but his room companion . . . She skimmed her gaze over the hall's occupants and found Lord Drummond. He was intent on the wrestling match and had not yet seen her. She felt a panicky need to keep it that way.

"I wished to give you my apologies," she said.

"Apologies? Surely not," MacKinnon argued.

"Aye. You were kind enough to offer to accompany me at supper and I did not even give you a response."

He glanced away. "After Drummond's words I was unsurprised that you ran away."

Reaching out, she touched his sleeve. "I have wounded you. 'Twas not my intent, I assure you."

"Was it not?" His eyes were wide and earnest. Cat's heart twisted. Surely this couldn't be the one she called Blackheart. She should leave him in peace, but she had so few leads, and how could she know how a madman would act in the light of day?

"Nay," she assured him. "I merely thought of something I had to tell Lord Tremayne." 'Twas an uninspired lie, but a safe one, since James's old councilor had taken a moment to remind her that he was keeping an eye on her.

"I saw you speaking to Tremayne," he said. "There was no trouble, I hope."

"Nay, all is well."

For a moment he was silent, then, "I did not do it."

"What?" she said, her mind racing.

"I did not kill my wife."

Shock spurred through her. What the devil was he talking about?

"Oh." Something akin to relief spurred through her. "I never . . . I never thought you did."

"Did you not?" He stepped closer, his expression solemn. Judging by his breath and his unsteady pose, Lord MacKinnon had been drinking for some time. So luck had not abandoned her completely. "You are . . ." He paused, momentarily at a loss for words. "You are kind."

She lowered her eyes, though her heart was beating

overtime, and her mind screamed that she must hurry. Already she sensed that others were approaching, and she could not afford to be interrupted. "You flatter me," she said.

"Nay. 'Tis not so, Lady Cat."

"Please, Lord MacKinnon—"

"I would be honored if you would call me Samuel."

"Samuel." She kept her eyes averted. If he was Blackheart, he was an excellent actor. Thus, she must be the same. " 'Tis a good name."

He watched her in silence, then, " 'Tis warm and too close in here," he said.

She had heard that line before and well knew the next request, so she nodded while in her mind she reviewed her plans, making certain she had everything she needed—Marta's tiny vial and the rolled piece of vellum hidden away in the pouch on her girdle as it always was.

"Might I ask . . ." He paused. "Might I make so bold as to ask you to accompany me to the gardens?"

"The gardens would be lovely. But if you would not mind . . ." She forced herself to meet his gaze. "I would rather go straightaway to your chamber."

Chapter 13

Samuel MacKinnon stared at her. "To my chamber?" he murmured.

"Aye," she said and slid her arm through his, steadying him as she herded him toward the door. "I simply . . . I must have some time alone. Away from—"

"The crush of admirers?" he guessed, then frowned down at her. A bit of ale sloshed over the rim of his horn.

"Do you mind?"

"Nay." His answer was solemn and hesitant, his gait a bit unsteady as he turned to the left. "You are welcome to use me any way you wish."

"My thanks," she murmured, and seeing Lord Tremayne approaching from the right, turned her face to the left and prayed to be ignored. She forced herself to go several strides before glancing back, but when she did Tremayne was still watching, his expression pinched with disapproval.

"Lady Cat?" MacKinnon said.

"Aye." She turned back with a frown, her heart beating overtime.

"May I voice a question?"

"Certainly." One more glance assured her that Tremayne was gone. Raucous noise issued from the great hall and she hustled him away.

"Why me?"

"What?" she asked, distracted and jumpy.

"Why me? That is to say . . ." He tried to pull her to a halt, but she would have none of it. She had a mission and precious little time to accomplish it. "I am hardly the highest-born among the assemblage here."

"Mayhap I care little for titles."

He frowned as they hurried along. "It cannot be my features. Though I do not frighten small children, still, you . . ." He lost the words and fell into silence.

"Perhaps tis simply because you are a good person," she said and stopped by his door.

He scowled. "How did you know this room was mine?"

Panic galloped through her. "I . . . Someone said Drummond was the kind to keep his chamber locked." She held her breath and prayed. "Do you have the key?"

"Aye. This room housed Blackburn's spices, I am told. But with the crush of visitors it was fashioned into bedchambers," he said and fumbled around his drink for his leather purse.

"Here then," she said, forcing the panic into submission. "I will take your goblet."

He handed it over before turning back to the door.

It was almost too simple to slip Marta's potion into his ale. By the time he'd wrestled the door open, it had been well mixed. She was inside in a moment.

He followed her, pulling the door closed behind. The room was as dark as mud.

"Well," he said. "Here we are, then."

"Aye." She frowned into nothingness. "In the dark."

There was a moment of silence, then, "Your pardon?"

" 'Tis dark. Mayhap you could fetch a light."

"Oh." He bumped to life, patted about on a nearby surface, and soon produced a candle.

The door creaked open. Light streamed through the crack, then followed his entrance.

She quickly closed the door behind him, turned, and handed him his drinking goblet.

"Lady Catriona," he said, not seeming to notice his drink as he stared into her eyes. "There is something you should know. But now, 'tis . . . difficult to say the words."

A confession? A clue? Was he Blackheart? Or did he, perhaps, know something about Lachlan's disappearance? "What do you have to say?"

He drew a deep breath. "Your—"

Footsteps sounded in the hall. Catriona froze. Momentarily distracted, MacKinnon glanced at the door. But the noise passed.

"My what?" she said, trying to relax.

"Your beauty astounds me. In truth, I have never seen a woman as enchanting as you. But—"

Disappointment swamped her. "Drink," she urged. Lifting the horn toward him, she touched her finger to the bottom of the goblet, tilting it toward his lips.

He finished the brew without more prompting. The room was utterly silent. Catriona stared at him, realizing suddenly that she had neglected to ask Marta how long it took for the herbs to take effect. Perhaps she should get him nearer the bed. If he landed on the mattress 'twould surely be quieter than if he hit the floor. She stepped in that direction.

He followed her slowly. "Are you real?"

"What?" She brought her attention back to him with a start.

He shook his head as if to clear it. "I mean no disrespect. But . . . there are those who say your beauty is not natural."

"Are you suggesting that I am a witch?"

"Not a witch. A fairy, perhaps."

"Nay."

"Then . . . how can you be so enchanting?"

" 'Tis a curse," she said and glanced quickly about the room. There were two simple iron-bound chests, a three-legged stool, and a small table. No small boxes that might house a favored medallion met her gaze.

"Your beauty is a curse?"

Honesty was hardly needed here, but he seemed so earnest. "I mean that my features seem to draw . . . the wrong kind of man."

He was silent for a moment. "Am I the right kind?"

She glanced impatiently toward the trunk again. "I hope so."

He stepped closer still, so that they stood side by side near the bed.

"There is a terrible truth, lady. But I must tell you."

"What truth?"

"I have not . . ." He paused. "What Drummond meant to tell you was . . .'Twas my wife Harrowhead was with, the night he was murdered."

She could not speak, could barely breathe.

"My wife . . . she was unfaithful. But I did not kill her. And I did not kill the old earl."

Dear God, she had never imagined that he had. Mayhap this man was no safer than Lord Drummond.

"She was returning from a night with her lover when she fell from her horse."

"I . . ." Emotions and questions and fears swirled around her. "I am sorry."

He smiled, but it did not touch his eyes. "I did not tell you for your pity," he said and cleared his throat. "The truth is this: I have not . . . I have been unable to . . . perform since I learned the truth."

If she had been forced to guess what he had been about to say, that would not have been her first supposition. She should say something, she thought. But nothing came to mind.

"With Fayette . . . Well, I owed her so much for her kindness with my daughters that I dare not disappoint . . ." He shrugged and took a scant step closer. "But I think perhaps with you it will be different." He caressed her cheek, then leaned close. "Thank you," he whispered, and then he collapsed, draped over the edge of the mattress like a wilted carrot.

Catriona winced. "Lord MacKinnon?" she whispered, bending slightly.

He didn't answer.

"Lord MacKinnon?"

There was no doubt about it: He was unconscious. But MacKinnon was facedown on the mattress. What if he suffocated?

Crawling onto the bed, she grabbed handfuls of his doublet, dragged him onto the pallet, and turned him over. Then she scurried over to the nearer trunk. Which was MacKinnon's and which was Drummond's, she didn't know. But that was not her immediate concern.

The nearer chest opened with a creak of protest, but her hands were immediately inside, fumbling through the clothes.

Nothing.

The other trunk was smaller but still goodly sized,

nearly three feet tall and bound by iron bands with strange gargoyle faces placed at intervals on the metal.

Cat rummaged through that just as quickly, but again she was disappointed. Where might he hide a precious trinket?

The bed.

Rising quickly, she hurried to the pallet and managed to drag the scattered blankets from beneath MacKinnon's inert form. Still nothing. She pulled up the edge of the mattress, but there were no treasures hidden between the tightly stretched ropes and the straw-filled tick.

Her heart was racing. There would be no reason to lock the door unless there were some treasure hidden inside, so where . . .

Her gaze fell on MacKinnon's limp form. On the girdle beside his hip, a pouch was tied.

Scrambling across the mattress, she reached for the leather thong that held his pouch in place. He moaned.

She snatched her hands away for a heart-stopping instant, but one glance at his face assured her he was still sound asleep, so she eased her fingers forward again. Once the pouch was free, she dumped the contents onto the mattress. Only coins, a chip of flint, and a stub of candle.

She must keep looking. But where? She skimmed her gaze past his limp form, then snapped it back.

His codpiece. 'Twas a good-sized thing and a likely place for a man to hide his jewels.

She winced at her poor pun and reached under his doublet. Her fingers skimmed his abdomen.

"Fayette," he sighed.

She nearly screamed as she jerked her hands away, but when she snapped her gaze to his face, found that his eyes were still closed, though a contented smile lifted his lips.

Still, her breathing came in hard gasps and her hands were shaking when she reached out again.

It was no simple task to undress him. She was forced to untie a half dozen laces that bound his hose to his doublet before she could even begin to drag the required garment from his flaccid body.

But when it came free, she found that his codpiece was entirely empty. 'Twas all she needed to know, she told herself—but curiosity coaxed her gaze upward. Rigid and reddened, his swollen penis lay stretched against his pale belly. She could not help but stare.

A rustle of noise passed in the hall, and she jumped. Realizing she had no time to spare, she hurried to the far side of the room, peering into the corners, behind the curtains.

Her gaze hurried back to the smaller trunk. It was quite a high box, taller than it was deep, and . . . A false bottom!

Certain she was right, she lunged back toward it. Throwing it open, she grabbed handfuls of clothing and tossed them out. Her knuckles thumped against the bottom. She frowned, searching blindly for a way to lift it up. But nothing untoward met her fingers.

Jerking to her feet, she snatched the candle from the table and shone it on the inside of the trunk. Still, she could find nothing.

She dropped back onto her heels in abject frustration.

Already she had been there too long. Drummond might return at any moment. She must hurry.

Her gaze skimmed the box in front of her. 'Twas then that she noticed one of the gargoyles was slightly askew. Reaching out, she touched the gnarled face. It turned beneath her hand. Her breath caught in her throat. Her fingers trembled as she rapidly turned up the other gargoyle and tugged at the sides of the trunk.

Wood slid against wood as, to Catriona's surprise, a narrow receptacle slid out of the bottom of the chest. And in that receptacle . . . She shakily lifted a piece of linen.

Jewels!

Her heart thrummed noisily against her ribs. This was it. She was certain of it.

She skimmed the drawer. A ring. A large, squarish brooch. There! The medallion! Lying on a large coil of silver chain was a round medallion set with rough stones. Her hands trembled as she lifted it out.

It must be the one. It must. But . . . Somehow it did not seem quite the same as the imprint she'd found. Holding the piece in her shaky hand, she fumbled for her pouch and pulled out the scrap of vellum. The medallion was approximately the same size as the item Blackheart had dropped, and the stones were in the same approximate position, but the vellum showed three stones at the top and bottom of the circle and an intricate Celtic knot in the middle.

The medallion had no knotwork and fewer stones.

Disappointment nearly drowned her.

A low, humming voice sounded in the hallway.

Catriona froze, her gaze locked frantically on the door. For a moment she was certain that it would open, that all was lost—but the voices moved on.

She breathed again, drawing air rapidly into her lungs as she covered the jewels with the linens and rapidly slid the secret compartment back into the trunk. The gargoyles leered as they fell into place. The clothing settled rapidly into sloppy piles, and the trunk closed almost silently.

Catriona rose quickly to her feet and glanced about, and then, unable to leave MacKinnon so exposed, she flipped the blankets over him.

Footfalls approached from the hall, stopping her breath, but again the sound traveled leisurely away. She heard a door open and close, further down.

The nobles were returning to their rooms.

Snatching up her vellum drawing from the floor, she rushed to the door and listened.

Nothing.

She pushed the latch and stepped quickly into the hall. All was quiet, and she hurried toward her own chambers. She was in no condition to search more this night.

"Catriona."

She almost screamed as she jerked about.

Haydan the Hawk stared at her with hooded eyes, then bent slowly. Breathlessly, she watched him retrieve her fallen vellum and glance at the sketch.

"A favored trinket?" he asked, his voice deep.

"What?" Her heart was in her throat, pumping wildly. Where had he come from? Had he seen her exit MacKinnon's chambers?

"The drawing," he said, lifting the leather. "Is it a sketch of a brooch you covet, perhaps?"

"Nay. Nay. I—" Her hands were trembling, so she clasped them together and prayed for calm. She had done nothing wrong. Stolen nothing. Hurt no one. Of course, if MacKinnon was found unconscious in his room, people would begin to ask questions. And if it was discovered that she had been rummaging through the young baron's possessions . . . Gypsies had been burned for less.

"Nay," she repeated and reached for the sketch. He let it go after a moment. " 'Tis naught of import. Just something I drew to pass the time."

"Pass the time?" He watched her very closely. Too closely. "Why are you not abed?" he asked.

"I . . ." She could not help glancing just once at MacKinnon's door, like a murderer needing to check the scene of his crime. But the door was firmly closed and all was silent. "I . . . Why are *you* not abed?"

He said nothing.

"Were you following me, Sir Hawk?" she asked. She made certain her tone was haughty, but her stomach twisted at the thought. 'Twas fear, of course. Fear and nothing else. The thought of him longing for her did not upset her equilibrium.

"Is there some reason I should?"

She forced a laugh. "Not unless you are enamored of me and refuse to admit it."

A muscle jerked in his jaw. " 'Twill be a dark day indeed when the lark leads an old bird like me a merry chase. But I would be your friend if you would have one."

Her stomach twisted harder. She did not need him, not as a lover and certainly not as a friend. There was no more certain path to death.

"Why do you wander these halls?" he asked again.

There was concern in his eyes, power in his hand, but she had nearly been weak enough to reveal her troubles to him before. She would not be so foolish again.

"I could not sleep," she said and turned away from him, heading toward her chambers.

"Something troubles you?"

His voice was deep and alluring. She could not help but remember the feel of his arms around her, the dance of his muscles against hers. But in the end he had drawn away.

Still, she could feel his gaze on her as he waited for an answer.

"Mayhap 'tis naught but your need to mother me that troubles me," she said.

He was silent for a moment. "You could ask any of my men," he said finally. "I am not the mothering type."

"Then why do you haunt my every move?" she asked. Reaching her door, she turned to face him.

They stared at each other, his brows cliffed above his raptor eyes.

"Why are you not abed?" he asked again.

His power, his maleness, the very timbre of his voice called to her. But she could not come. Frustration screamed through her.

"Maybe I search for companionship," she snapped.

He leaned closer. His nostrils flared for a moment. "If such is the case, methinks you would not have far to search."

Breathless tension snapped between them. Against her will, she took a step toward him. For a fraction of an instant he remained as he was, and then he turned and stalked away.

Chapter 14

The stables were dark and quiet when Catriona stepped inside. Midnight had long ago come and gone, but still she could not sleep. Her footfalls were quiet against the hard-packed earth, the light of her lamp feeble against the surrounding darkness. In the rafters overhead, a pigeon took flight, startling her with the noise.

But one glance assured her that all was well. In a moment, she was inside a roomy, high-walled stall.

Celandine turned her bonny head, nickered low in her throat, and stumbled a few painful steps toward her mistress. Never did she fully straighten the foreleg that was bandaged just above the fetlock.

"Celandine!" The name caught in Cat's throat. She hurried forward to stop the mare's progress with a hand on the animal's sleek neck. The steed turned soft, worried eyes to her mistress. "Nay," Cat whispered, tears choking her as her fingers tangled in the flaxen mane. "Not you, too." She was losing everything, everything she loved. Stepping closer, she wrapped her arm around the mare's neck and closed her eyes. The weight of the world seemed as heavy as a millstone upon her shoulders, and she wanted nothing more than to curl up in the shadows and forget it all.

"I am sorry."

Cat caught her breath and straightened abruptly. Lifting the back of her hand to her cheek, she dashed away her tears, then turned with hard-won composure to find Haydan filling the open doorway.

"Sir Hawk. Again. And I thought James had called off the guard."

She tried to lighten her tone, but his expression didn't change. His face remained in chiseled sobriety, limned and shadowed by the flickering light.

"It seems that everything you cherish has been compromised," he said.

"Compromised?" She forced nonchalance. "Whatever do you mean?"

"First your steed. Then the bird," he said finally, his tone deep.

"Oh." Relief flooded her with such strength that she had to turn aside. He knew nothing of her deepest troubles. Nothing of Lachlan's abduction or the horrible ultimatum. "A bird and a horse," she said, her tone flippant though her fingers were still tangled in the mare's mane. " 'Tis hardly everything I cherish."

"There is your brother."

She turned numbly toward him, unable to breathe as their gazes caught and fused.

"He is well?" Haydan asked.

"Aye." She tightened her fingers in the mane. "He is with his cousins, as I have told you."

Hawk took a single step forward, then clenched his fists and stopped. Silence echoed around them. "Why will you not tell me?"

"Tell you what?" She forced a smile.

"Tell me what worries you."

"Celandine is lame, and Caleb broken. Is that not enough for a little sadness?"

He stared at her, his gaze as steady as winter ice. But in a moment, he drew a deep breath and relaxed a mite.

"Aye. 'Tis enough, I suspect. But if you are concerned for the mare's well-being you had best help me see to her leg."

"Was it you who bandaged her?"

"I only made certain it was done," he said distractedly. " 'Tis a small wound for such a swelling." Reaching past the door, he retrieved a leather halter and a wooden bucket.

Water sloshed nearly to the brim as he stepped forward and placed it in the straw. In a moment, he had the halter fastened in place. Smoothing a hand over the mare's forelock, he straightened it between her seal-soft eyes.

Catriona watched him from close proximity. His brows were drawn low. His hand, which looked as if it had been crafted for naught but battle, seemed just as right here, soothing, stroking, as it slid down Celandine's throat and along her neck. How would that hand feel against her own flesh? How would it feel to be soothed and caressed by this man among men? Her breath stopped in her throat as she watched him.

Bending slightly, Haydan smoothed his fingers over the chestnut's forearm. The mare flinched and jerked it away in anticipation of pain.

Even from the side, Cat could see the tendons tighten in Haydan's neck, could see the fleeting expression of frustration that crossed his face. But not a harsh word did he speak. Instead, he drew the mare back toward him with a gentle hand.

"You are wise to be cautious, lass," he crooned, his words so soft they were nearly lost in the darkness.

It took Catriona a moment to realize the truth.

"Surely you know Celandine's injury is not your fault," she said.

He did not turn toward her, but she saw the telltale muscle flex in his jaw.

"Sir Hawk?"

"Aye?"

" 'Tis not your fault," she said.

"Then what is my purpose?" he asked, the words clipped and terse as he turned toward her.

"Your purpose?"

"If not to guard and protect?"

She laughed a little, startled not only by his response, but by the intensity of his emotion. "Is it, then, your place to guard everyone, *everything*?"

"Nay. Only those within my reach."

She was within his reach. But she shoved the traitorous thought aside. "You take too much on yourself."

"Nay, I do not." His expression was solemn, intense. "I could do more."

Their gazes fused, and though he did not say the words, she knew he was asking again for her trust.

But 'twas a trust she dare not give. She turned abruptly away. "What is it we do with this water?"

For a moment she thought he wouldn't answer, but finally he spoke. "We soak the leg to reduce the swelling." He sounded disgusted, then added, as if to the mare, "Lady Fiona would never be content with such a mean attempt. A few herbs and a prayer, and you would again bloom like the flower for which you were named."

Catriona tried to disavow the feelings his words evoked, tried to ignore the shiver of emotion that shook her. "The king's fierce captain of the guard—a poet?" she asked.

"Nay. Naught but a frustrated old warrior who dreams of tossing Physic into the moat."

"The water was his advice?" she guessed.

"Aye, and even that hard won. It seems he is not commissioned to treat the *familiars* of a—" He stopped, his brows lowering still more as he realized what he had been about to say.

Catriona only shrugged. "He was indeed enamored with me."

Hawk's expression softened with a hint of humor "You cannot expect every man to swoon at the sight of you, lass."

Not him, at least. He was not for her, and yet she was tempted almost beyond control to reach for him. "You said I could," she argued, careful to keep her tone light.

"It may surprise you to know that I can be wrong. It seems, in fact, that there are two among the crush who are not enthralled."

"Two counting you? Or two others?"

"Surely you do not begrudge me some dignity, lass. 'Twould not be right for me to act the fool when my very own nieces are no older than you. Quite unseemly for me to bobble about like a pin-feathered gosling in your wake."

Her throat hurt. "I think it would not kill you to bobble a bit."

The words came out without thought.

For a moment, Hawk stared at her in mild humor. "I will say this, wee Cat, I've not met another quite like you."

So little comfort there. In the past, she had found

men's adoration little more than annoying, but now all seemed different. Changed.

She lifted her chin slightly and set her mouth. "So if you were not so . . . ancient, you might find me appealing?"

His lips remained unbowed, but his eyes smiled. "Fear not, lass, there be scores of swains, both lads and men alike, who are breathless at the thought of a mere glance from you."

"I am indeed relieved."

" 'Tis good," he said. Their gazes met. Feelings as potent as wine swamped Catriona, but she swept them away, fumbling to find the bucket.

He did the same thing at the same time. Their fingers brushed on the leather handle and they froze, naught but their eyes moving as their gazes met and their breathing stopped. Catriona's heart banged like a restive steed against her ribs.

"Here now," he said, his voice a deep rumble in the stillness as he drew away. "We had best be started. Can you hold the mare steady while I remove the bandage?"

"Aye," Cat said, eager to set her attention elsewhere.

Not another word was spoken as he untied the bandage and began unraveling it from Celandine's leg. After a bit, it was adhered to itself. Drawing out a short, broad-bladed knife from his boot, Hawk carefully cut away the cloth, then dipped a rag from the bucket and began to wash the fetlock.

The wound was obvious, a patch of torn flesh about two inches long. But Hawk was right; it did not seem severe enough to cause the mare such swelling.

"Might there be something else that is troubling her?" Catriona asked.

"I have looked," Hawk said, bending still lower as he

ran his fingers past the horny ergot hidden in the fetlock's center. "But I cannot find—" The mare flinched. His words stopped abruptly as his fingers probed. Celandine recoiled and tried to pull away.

"What is it?" Cat asked.

"A small wound, no more than the size of your wee finger. But it has scabbed over."

"Might that cause the swelling?"

"Aye, if it does not drain properly. Once I was stabbed by a Spaniard's thin blade. 'Twas naught but the tiniest hole, and it seemed to heal quickly. But my arm swelled up tight as a ripening gourd . . ." He glanced up. Perhaps it was her expression that stopped him. "Mayhap you do not need to hear the whole tale."

"Perhaps not," she agreed, frowning at him. What the hell right did he have not to be enamored with her? Not that she harbored any great feelings for him, but he was large and hard and so unreasonably masculine that . . . She turned her thoughts abruptly away. "How does the story end?"

"I still have my arm."

"So I noticed." Her flippancy was becoming strained. "What was the cure?"

"Lady Fiona lanced the thing, then packed it with hot cloths."

Cat winced and slipped a protective hand down the mare's neck.

"I do not think we shall have to do the same here. The wound is low down, so once the scab is removed it should drain well. But in truth, the lady's scolding was near as bad as the lancing. She took it quite personally that I would be neglectful after she had toiled so long to see me healed in the first place."

"Healed?"

"I was frail," he said, and after washing his hands in the bucket, dried them quickly on his plaid.

She stared down at the tremendous width of his back and felt that now-familiar ache of desire. "I forgot."

"Aye, well, she has not. To this day she asks if I am eating sufficiently."

Cat laughed at the image, and Hawk straightened to stare at her.

"What is it?" she asked, made breathless by the intensity of his attention.

He squatted by the mare's leg again. "It has been a long while since I last heard honest laughter from you."

"I . . ." Tension knotted her. He was so close, as solid as the earth, as kind as the sunshine, and she wanted nothing more than to be held in his arms, to lay her fears at his feet, to trust him with her body and her soul. "The mare is dear to me. I am glad to know she will mend."

"You have had her long?"

"For some years. She was flighty and half starved when I first saw her. I thought 'twas surely a fool's errand to take her in trade. But Lachlan—" She stopped, her voice catching.

Haydan was on his feet in a moment, his hands warm as they wrapped about her arms. "What of Lachlan?"

"He . . ." She struggled with every weakness that was in her. She could not bear the worry alone, and yet she could not tell him the truth. "He insisted I could save her. He was forever like that—so certain all would be well."

"*Was?*"

"*Is!*" Oh God, she was going to cry. "He *is* like that," she insisted.

"Lassie," he crooned. "What is it?"

"I just . . ." She was afraid. So afraid and alone and

without hope. "I just miss him, is all," she lied.

"Please. Tell me."

He must believe the lie. "I have never been parted from him before. Since our mother's death he has been everything to me—the closest kin I have. I did not realize . . ." Tears tore at her throat. "I did not realize how I would miss him."

"Catriona—"

"Hold me." The words came out without volition. "Please." She squeezed her eyes closed and fought back the worry, but it gnawed at her like an evil beast. "If you could just hold me."

He hesitated for a moment, but finally his arms folded about her back and she was drawn against his chest. She didn't try to be strong. Indeed, she no longer could. Instead, she let her arms slip around him as she pressed her face to the hard, molded wall of his chest. And there, against the wear-softened fabric of his tunic, she cried.

But tears can only flow for so long, and hers finally dried. She sniffled without much charm, and realized he was stroking her hair with one broad hand. His touch felt like sunlight and peace. She drew in a few quivering breaths and let herself relax against the strength of his chest again.

Minutes ticked slowly by, but he never stopped stroking her.

She drew another shuddering breath and cleared her throat. " 'Tis I who should apologize now."

"Aye. 'Tis quite a hardship to hold a wee lass like yourself against me."

She smiled against his chest. "Is it?"

"Aye. Hard on an old man's heart."

"How old?"

He chuckled, then tilted her chin up to stare into her

eyes. "Old enough to resent your asking." The world went quiet. "Is it the truth, Catriona?"

She nearly winced at his words. "What?"

"You only miss Lachlan? Is that all that—"

She rose up on her toes and kissed him. Not a hard kiss or a passionate kiss, but a kiss of tenderness and thanks.

"Lass." His voice broke when he said the word.

"Aye?" Her own was throaty. It seemed the kiss was not so innocent as she had intended. Indeed, even now, she felt desire unfurl in her belly.

"I cannot . . ." He paused for a moment. His fingers had slipped to her throat and remained there against the thrum of her pulse. "I cannot bear to see you hurt."

"Then kiss me back," she whispered.

For one frozen moment she thought he would refuse. But finally he bent his head. His lips touched hers. Pleasure and hope and longing seared her. She tightened her arms about his waist, but he did not hurry the kiss. Instead, he drew back to wipe away the tears with his thumb, to kiss the corner of her mouth, her cheek, her eyelids.

It was she who found his lips again, who pressed up tighter against him, who longed for more.

And with that increased pressure, she felt the muscles in his back flex, felt his kiss slant harder against her mouth.

His hand slid down to her waist, pulling her closer. She answered with all the desperate longing that was in her.

"Lass!" He pulled away, his breathing harsh, his tone deep as midnight. "I would not take advantage of you."

"Why the devil not?" she asked. Frustration tore at her. All her life men had attempted to take advantage of her. Now when she wanted one to, he refused.

He was holding her arms, just as she was holding his. But his were thick-muscled and powerful.

" 'Twould not be right. You are so young. So—"

"I am aging every minute," she said and kissed him again.

She felt him try to hold back, but she had no mercy, for she needed him, needed his strength, his kindness, his nearness. Finally he wrapped her in his arms again and gave himself to the kiss.

His lips burned hers, and then they were moving, touching her cheek, her ear, traveling down the length of her throat. But it was not enough. She needed to feel, to drown, to be lost in his heat, and so she tugged at his tunic, longing to feel the warmth of his skin beneath her hands.

"Haydan, I want . . ." For a moment she lost all words as his lips met hers again. "I need to feel you."

She could not decipher his expletive, though it sounded like a plea to God.

"Take off your tunic. Please."

In a moment his torso was bare. She pressed her palms to his chest. It was hard as marble beneath her fingertips. She slipped her hands lower. Muscles danced, rippling beneath her caress as she worked her way down his abdomen.

"Lass . . ." His voice quivered.

"Aye." Her own was throaty.

She heard him draw a deep breath but did not raise her gaze to look at him.

"I thought I told you I was not enamored."

"You did," she said and pressed her ear to his heart.

"I am old and scarred and—"

She kissed his chest. He sucked air through his teeth in a sharp hiss.

"And disciplined and—"

She brushed her lips across his nipple.

"Well controlled," he rasped, and she suckled gently.

He jerked beneath her lips and rasped a faint expletive.

"Life is short, Haydan," she whispered. "Tomorrow may not be. I wish to feel."

Pressed up against his chest, she could tell that he ceased to breathe.

All was silent but for the steady thrum of his heart.

"Are you asking me to make love to you, lass?" he rumbled.

"I would rather not have to."

For a moment neither moved, and then he kissed her with all the tenderness and passion of a thousand years. The earth seemed to sink away below her feet. The straw cradled her back. His lips burned her throat, her shoulder, the high, aching mounds of her breasts.

She never felt his fingers at her laces, but suddenly her bodice was open and she did not care.

Nay, 'twas not true. She cared. She yearned. She needed. She lusted.

His hands burned her flesh. Against her thigh, she felt the hard length of his arousal. She arched into him. His kisses ravaged her, sweeping down her throat, over her collarbone, and onto—

"Cat!" someone whispered from the aisle. "Lady Cat."

Chapter 15

"James!" Haydan hissed.

Catriona stared at him, her eyes glazed and her hair a dark halo about her face. But he had no time to appreciate the scene, for he was already scrambling to his feet.

"Catriona," James called, closer now.

Haydan jerked upright, swore silently at the pain in his knee, and yanked Catriona up beside him. Her hands were already moving, rearranging, hiding. He almost cried, but there was no time for that either, so he nudged her behind him and stepped toward the door just as it was swinging open.

"Cat—" James's voice stopped in midsentence. In the teetering light of the lantern, his eyes looked as round as ptarmigan eggs. "Hawk!"

"Aye!" Haydan cleared his throat as he stepped through the doorway, driving the boy king before him. "Aye. What is it, lad?"

"I thought . . ." James began, then paused, trying to see around Haydan's towering form. "I thought to find Lady Cat here."

"Aye, well, she . . ." But it dawned on Haydan suddenly that the sun had not yet risen. "Why are you not abed? And where are your guards?"

"Where is your tunic?" James asked.

"I—" Hawk glanced down at his bare chest in some surprise. Good saints, he must be out of his mind. " 'Twas hot." Hot? A half-witted dolt could think up a better excuse than that.

"Hot?" James said. " 'Tis barely above freezing—and not yet dawn."

"My thrust exactly," Haydan said, parrying to win the upper hand against the quick-witted lad too fast approaching manhood. "What are you doing in the stable?"

James maneuvered easily around the query. "You look flushed. Are you feeling well?"

He was feeling like a randy spring buck, and damn his gimpy leg. "What are you doing out of bed?"

"I saw a light and thought mayhap Catriona needed assistance with her mare," James answered, and with that brief explanation, sped past Haydan and into the stall.

"Your Majesty!" Catriona's voice sounded ungodly breathy.

Haydan gritted his teeth and followed the lad inside.

"Lady Cat, are you well?" James asked.

"Oh, aye. Aye."

"You look flushed too."

" 'Tis warm in here."

Even from the side, Haydan could see the boy frown. " 'Tis not yet dawn and somewhat chilly," he said, bemused. "Mayhap I should waken Leech."

"Nay!" Haydan said.

"Nay," Cat echoed. "We've been working, is all."

"Working?"

"Aye. Sir Hawk thought . . ." She drew a deep breath.

Their gazes met for a fraction of a burning second before she yanked hers away. "He thought Celandine's bandage should be changed and her wound cleansed."

"In the wee hours of the morning?" James's tone sounded more and more incredulous, and the strange thing was that she had told the exact truth.

So why did it sound so ludicrous? And why did he feel so guilty? Haydan wondered. Surely he was old enough for a midnight tryst if he so desired, and she . . .

He skimmed his gaze to her, and all logical thought ground to a shivering halt, for before him stood a goddess. Bronzed by the flickering light of the tallow lamp, her hair shone like sable. Her face and throat gleamed like molten gold, and her eyes, wide as royal jewels, glowed like sun-struck topaz.

"Hawk?"

"What?" He snapped his gaze to the boy king and remembered to breathe.

James scowled. "I'm waking Leech," he said and turned away.

"Nay!" Hawk insisted. "I feel well. Did you ask something?"

The lad's scowl had deepened. "I asked if the mare is mending."

"Oh! Aye. Aye. She is. She is mending." A pause. Too long. Too uncomfortable. "See?" he hurried to add and stepped toward the mare. "I found a wee puncture wound near her fetlock."

"It will heal then?"

"Aye. It will heal."

"By the morrow?"

Haydan lifted his brows and tried to find his bearing. "Tomorrow?"

"Lady Cat promised to teach me some of her skill with horses."

"Oh," Cat said, still somewhat breathless, but better. "Nay, Your Majesty, I fear my Celandine will not be mended so soon."

"But 'tis my birthday soon," James reminded them as if it were news.

"Not to worry, Your Majesty, I can use my Bay."

"Then we shall ride tomorrow?"

"We shall have to see whether the rain—"

"Or shall I wake Leech?" James interrupted, his tone sly.

Haydan scowled, but Cat spoke.

"Twill be a pleasure to ride with you, my lord."

Though Catriona was certain she would be unable to sleep, the opposite had been true. Her dreams had been kind but forgotten, and against all odds, she awoke refreshed to Caleb's raucous complaints of hunger.

Rising from bed, she fetched a pouch and opened the willow branch cage where he was confined. Looking strange in his rough linen suit, he struggled onto her hand to peck at the offering while Calum, overjoyed by his companion's newfound appetite, promptly glided over from the window to steal the other's breakfast.

A fight broke out, and Marta sat up abruptly.

"He is better," Catriona said, breaking up the battle and glancing toward Grandmother. "I think 'tis a good omen."

"I dreamed a dream," Marta said, her voice low with sleep and reverence.

Cat caught her breath. "About Lachlan?"

"Aye. He was laughing."

Catriona felt the blood drain from her face, for suddenly she remembered her own kindly dreams. They, too, had been filled with her brother's laughter. "Where is he?" she murmured.

" 'Tis a room. A small room, and there are guards."

Cat's heart twisted. "But they have not hurt him?"

"Nay. He has charmed them." The old woman smiled and did not turn her gaze from her own dream world. "They tell tales and play games."

Depositing the grain and the birds inside the cage, Cat hurried to sit on the edge of the bed. "Where is he kept, Grandmother? Where? Is he near?"

"I . . ." Marta squeezed her eyes closed in concerted thought. "I do not know, Catty," she said finally and opening her eyes, reached for her great-granddaughter's hand. "I do not know the where. I only know that he schemes and awaits your arrival. I am sorry."

"Nay," Cat said, squeezing the gnarled old fingers. "He is alive and every day we get closer. I feel it. All will be well."

"Aye. 'Tis true."

Drawing a deep breath, Catriona rose to her feet. It did not take her long to don her garments for the day—a pair of gauzy, bronze pantaloons beneath a brown, serviceable gown.

She and Marta entered the great hall together not much later.

"So you ride with the king again today?" asked the old woman, sedately stirring honey into her sowens.

"Aye."

Marta nodded. " 'Tis good. 'Twill give me a chance to be alone with the men."

Catriona turned a horrified glance on her grandmother, and the old woman laughed, her mood lightened by her kindly dreams.

"I shall try not to excite the gossipmongers," she said.

"Grandmother!"

"You needn't worry," Marta soothed, "for I fear the one who interests me will be leaving with you."

"Who—" Cat began, but when she glanced in the direction of Marta's gaze, her eyes met Haydan's.

Warmth flooded her face as every moment of the previous night washed back into her memory. She pulled her gaze away with a start.

"Ah," said the old woman. "So that be the way the wind blows."

"Whatever do you mean?" Cat asked, fiddling with her own oat cereal.

"I mean . . ." Marta leaned closer. "Is all of the Hawk as well proportioned as what I see?"

Catriona's face burned. She refused to look up. "I have no idea."

"You soon will," the old woman said, and turning her attention to her breakfast, gave a heavy sigh for her old age.

Just past the drawbridge Catriona slowed her gelding to match pace with James's smaller mount.

"Did you order such a morn?" she asked, for the air felt soft and kind against her face and the sky was as blue as a robin's egg.

"Aye, I did," said the king, grinning impishly. "Do you like it?"

" 'Tis as bonny a morn as I've ever seen."

"Your Majesty," Hawk said, riding up on James's opposite side. "I ordered the nooning to be brought to High Lochan. Have you any objections?"

"Nay. Have you seen High Lochan, Lady Cat?"

"I have not."

" 'Tis a bonny spot," he said, and when they arrived there nearly an hour later, Cat had to agree.

'Twas not the lake that was actually high. 'Twas the land above it—an outcropping of sorts. Dotted with smooth, weathered rocks and scraggly gorse bushes, the earth fell steeply downward, giving way to the rolling countryside below. A small lake, sapphire blue and glassy smooth, lay beneath them. Rowans and chestnuts, just beginning to show the first signs of life, stood guard on the distant hills, making a russet barrier between the brilliance of the sapphire sky and the emerald turf.

"I have been practicing my horsemanship since your last visit to Blackburn," James said, sitting very straight on his placid cob.

"Have you indeed?" Cat asked.

She and the king were in the middle of a rolling dale. The guards stood at the top of a nearby hillock, and for reasons Cat had no wish to contemplate, Haydan had stayed with them.

"Aye, I have," James said. "Would you like to see what I have accomplished?"

"If you do not make me look the fool with my own poor attempts."

He smiled crookedly, a raggedy urchin who happened to be born king. "I would not worry on that, lady," he said, "the Hawk watches me like . . . well, like a hawk. If I do anything more dangerous than tie my own laces, he frets like an old hen."

She laughed as she shifted her gaze to the hillock where the Hawk sat his horse. His cape had blown over his stallion's croup, making him look regal and powerful, and reminding her how it had felt to be held in his arms. Although she knew she should be ashamed, she had hoped he would come to her after James was safely abed again, but he had not.

"Let us ruffle some feathers," she said softly.

James laughed out loud. "A fine idea."

She turned her smile on him. "You first."

"As you wish," he said, and tossing his cloak onto a nearby rock, slipped past the cantle, over his palfrey's rump, and onto the ground.

"Very good," Cat said, smiling at the simple trick.

"There is more," he said, and walking around to his mount's near side, grabbed the pommel and launched himself into the saddle. "Did you see?" he asked, beaming at her. "I did not use the stirrups."

"But your horse was not moving."

"What?"

"Your horse was standing still."

He gave her a peeved expression. "Do you know nothing about royalty? You're supposed to be quite impressed and tell me I am magnificent."

She laughed. "Come. Get off," she ordered, slipping from her own mount. " 'Tis almost simpler when the horse is galloping than when he is standing still."

"Galloping!"

"We'll try it at a walk first," she said, and leaving her gelding to graze, grasped the king's reins and led his palfrey forward. "Here now, you go on ahead and move toward us on the left side. Then when you're even with his neck, do not stop. Let your movement work for you. Grab the pommel and throw yourself upward."

He scowled. "As you wish," he said, but his tone was rife with skepticism.

Despite his doubts, however, the trick worked on the first try. The king beamed with pleasure. "Aha!" he crowed. "He wasn't standing still that time."

"But he was not trotting."

His scowl reminded her sharply of Haydan's frequent expressions of disapproval. "Are you always this difficult?" he asked.

"Frequently," she assured him, then, taking the reins again, she ordered him to dismount.

He did so in a moment. She tugged the gelding forward, trying to convince him to trot. But he was a mount chosen for his sense, not for his sense of adventure, and apparently saw absolutely no good reason to trot along beside her.

Catriona stopped to frown at the horse.

"You might use my mount," she suggested.

" 'Tis a grand idea," James agreed eagerly, and in a moment she was leading the taller gelding along at a trot.

On his third try, James managed to launch himself into the saddle and from then on there was no stopping him.

Catriona taught him terms and actions—how to make the gelding strike forward with his front feet on command, how to launch him into immediate motion, and how to make him rear. And through all this Hawk perched on the top of the hill, ready to fly down upon them at the first sign of trouble.

The morning breezed along with teasing and tricks and guileless praise.

"What a marvelous steed," James trilled, breathless with exhilaration and exertion. Bay danced in place, lifting his feathered forelegs high.

"Oh, I know another trick," announced the king.

"Do you?"

"Aye. But . . ." He leaned forward to pat the gelding's

neck before sliding from the saddle. "I had best use my own mount. He is somewhat shorter."

Catriona watched as James walked behind his own placidly grazing animal, his strides long and determined. But once there he stopped, pulled his bottom lip in between his teeth, and gnawed in earnest concentration. "You will not laugh if I fail?" he asked.

"That depends how amusing you look."

He scowled, but he was eleven and he was game, so he rubbed his hands together, hunched his shoulders, and launched himself toward his horse's haunches. His palms landed on the animal's rump, and the quiet cob, certain he was being attacked by a fanged adversary, sprang into action.

There was a moment of breathless terror as James flew through the air, and then it was over, with the king crumpled on the turf like a broken marionette.

Chapter 16

"James!" Cat gasped. She rushed forward, but Haydan rushed past her.

"Lad, are you well?"

The boy opened his eyes slowly. "I think I forgot to warn Courtier of my intent," he said, his voice raspy.

"Come," Haydan commanded. Worry gnawed at him with ravenous teeth. "I shall take you on my own steed."

"Nay. I am well," said the lad and managed a single deep breath. "I am well."

"We go to Blackburn," Haydan ordered.

James caught him with a hard, slanted gaze, though it lost some of its effect due to his position on the ground. "I did not interfere when I found you afevered in the stable."

"That was entirely different," Haydan said. "I was not trying to kill myself on my horse."

"What exactly were you doing?" asked James.

"I . . .'Tis not the concern here," Haydan countered. "Where do you hurt?"

James shifted his gaze to Catriona. " 'Twould not be gentlemanly to say in a lady's presence."

"Oh." Haydan settled back a quarter of an inch. Broken bones and head injuries were serious. Bumps to the privates rarely were. He knew, he had taken his share. But then, he was not the crowned king of Scotland. There were few folk concerned with the condition of his privates. "We had best have Physic see to you."

"Leech!" James said and blanched. "Do you think I do not know what's said about him?"

Haydan raised one brow. "What is said about him?"

James motioned him forward. Hawk moved as commanded, leaning down to hear.

"He . . . prefers young lads."

"Prefers them to what?" Haydan asked, aghast that the sovereign king would have been privy to such gossip.

"Don't *you* know?" James asked, disappointed.

Haydan stifled a grateful chuckle. Perhaps the lad wasn't growing up quite as quickly as he had feared. "You needn't worry about Physic's preferences," he said. "I'll stay in the room with you."

James deepened his scowl and sat up slowly. "This is not so serious. 'Tis not as if I am about to die from the affliction."

"I had hoped for more than your continued survival," Haydan countered.

"Such as?"

"An heir to the throne eventually."

James grinned wolfishly. "Then you'd best explain how I might achieve that end."

The sight of that mischievous grin did more for Haydan's peace of mind than Physic's assurance ever would. "Now hardly seems the appropriate time for that lesson, lad."

"Tonight?"

"Can you stand?"

"Tomorrow?"

"You'll stand now. I'll tell you in two years."

"Two years! I might well be a grandfather by then."

"You'll not even be wed by then."

"I've heard one does not need to be wed."

"You've heard too much of late. Have you been talking to Kitchen Elsie's lad again? Here. I'll help you up."

"I can stand." James did so without assistance, though he winced a bit before straightening. "I'll not be returning to Blackburn yet, Sir Hawk," he said arrogantly. Haydan cranked one brow up a notch, and in a moment James added, "Please."

"As you wish, then. We shall stay for a spell. At any rate, it looks as if our meal has arrived."

A troupe of servants were descending the hill toward them—cup bearers, servers, tasters, and pourers—and James was already hiking toward them. Hawk turned to speak to Catriona and stopped at the sight of her pale face.

"What is amiss?" he asked.

"I am sorry," she whispered brokenly.

" 'Twas my own fault. I should have been watching more closely."

"Nay, I—"

"Did you tell him to strike the saddle with his nether parts?"

She scowled at him, but her face had gained a bit of color.

"The Stuarts are a hardier line than one might think."

She stared at him in silence for a moment, then, " 'Tis a strange thing to hear from you, Sir Hawk. I thought for a moment that you might well faint dead away at the sight of him on the ground."

Haydan scowled and resisted the desire to shuffle his feet under her scrutiny. "He is my king."

"I think he is far more."

He deepened his scowl, though intimidation had failed to impress her thus far. " 'Twould be my head if some ill befell him."

" 'Twould be your heart," she countered.

He considered arguing, but there seemed little point, so he shrugged. "I have no wee ones of mine own to fawn over."

" 'Tis not too late."

His heart rate kicked up again, and beneath his plaid, he could feel a familiar tightening. Good Christmas, 'twas a sad state of affairs, when a wee scrap of a lass could set him on edge with no more than a bit of innocent talk of children. "I am an old man," he said, reminding himself as much as her.

"How old?"

" 'Tis time to sup," he said. Though he intended to hurry away, James had managed to walk with more ease than Haydan's desire allowed him.

The meal was sumptuous: mutton stew, white bread still warm from the oven, brie tarts, and cool, sweat mead. Although clouds began to gather in some earnestness, the air was warm and still.

"So this is how Durril supped?" James asked, lifting his silver-gilded horn to have it promptly filled by a solemn-faced pourer.

Catriona glanced at the liveried servants. "I think that generally there were fewer than a score of men to attend him on his journeys."

James scowled. "I would dine alone but I fear my council would not allow it. They are certain brigands would swoop from the sky and devour me like a kestrel does a field mouse."

"They are wise to worry," Cat said.

"But Durril did not."

"He was not the crowned king of the Scots," she reminded him.

"Aye, but even so, I wager he would not have allowed himself to be so . . ." He flipped a hand. His lace sleeve bobbled. "Coddled."

She laughed, both at his bitter expression and his words, for 'twas not difficult for a vagabond like herself to understand why he chafed.

"It so happens, Your Majesty, that Durril liked nothing better than to be coddled."

" 'Tis surely not true," James argued. "Durril reveled in his freedom."

"Mayhap, but he also gloried in Endorai's royal comfort."

James gave her a quizzical glance.

"They became friends you know," she said.

" 'Twould make sense," James admitted. "After all, he did save the prince's life."

"Aye, but 'twas more than that. They enjoyed each other's company. Indeed, quite often they dined together much as we are."

"Out of doors?"

"Aye, with servants and silver tableware and costly spices."

"And Durril enjoyed it?"

"Oh, aye." Catriona settled onto her haunches, curling her legs under her russet skirt. "Perhaps too much."

Off to her right, she could hear Hawk giving quiet orders.

"Too much?" James prompted.

"Aye, for he found that the abundance of food and wine made him sleepy and slow-witted."

"But surely the king's guardians were there to keep them safe," James said, and glanced surreptitiously at his own looming captain.

"Aye, his guards were there, but they had no intentions of keeping them safe."

"Why's that?" James asked, pausing just as he was about to sample a tart.

" 'Tis like this," Cat began, tucking her skirt beneath her legs. "The king's master guard was called Adder."

"Because he was as quick as a snake?"

"Aye, as quick—and as deadly."

"Tell me of him."

"His scalp was as bald as a serpent's hide, and he wore a band of gold in the lobe of one ear. 'Twas a gift from the prince himself for service well given. But in truth . . ." She lowered her voice slightly. "Adder did not love the prince. Indeed, he planned his murder."

"Nay!" The single word was breathy.

"Aye, for unknown to the prince, Adder was a descendant of their arch rivals, the house of Ruble. Years ago there had been a great battle between the powerful clans. All the country thought the Ruble line was well rid of. But alas, long ago Adder had been born in the deep folds of the mountains and there he was hidden away."

"No one knew he had survived?"

"Nay. None but those who cared for him. And through his growing-up years he was taught to fight and taught to hate, until finally he was old enough to work his way into the young prince's employ.

"Adder served the royal house well and grew trusted and admired, but all the while he planned the prince's death until finally it seemed the perfect time.

" 'Twas in a place much like this that he planned his

revenge. Where the sun shone softly on their shoulders and all the world seemed blessed."

She glanced momentarily about, and James did the same before flitting his attention to Hawk, then quickly back to Catriona.

" 'Twas a spring day. Winter was behind them and all manner of possibilities lay ahead. The world was being reborn, so they found a bonny spot high on a rocky slope that overlooked the emerald country beyond. Durril supped well, then leaned back to let the kindly sun warm his face. But in that instant . . ." She jerked, causing James to start also. "Durril saw a flash of steel near the prince's retinue of guards. He leapt to his feet just as the first man fell, but it was too late. Already a band of desperate brigands was swarming into their camp. He yelled for Adder to stop them. 'Twas then and only then that the hatred was revealed in the other man's eyes. 'Twas then that Durril knew the truth. Adder planned to kill the lad."

James tightened his grip in the blanket beneath him. "Durril will stop him," he murmured.

"But what could he do? Already Adder was between the lad and his mount, and Durril was unarmed. The traitor drew his sword. It was broad and curved and gleamed wickedly in the clear light of day.

"It was then that Endorai too realized the truth. The man he had trusted like a brother had turned against him. Terrified, he backed toward Durril. But the Rom had no weapon of his own and no hope of matching Adder's strength bare-handed."

Cat settled back as if the tale was finished, but James leaned forward in anticipation. "What did he do?" he rasped impatiently.

"Who?"

"Durril!"

"Oh." She shrugged leisurely. "He did the only thing he could do."

"Which was?"

"He grabbed the lad." She did so now, grasping James's wrist in a tight grip. "And with one mighty heave, he tossed the boy onto his mount's back."

James opened his mouth in a soundless mew of awe, then, "But Adder was standing between him and his steed."

"Aye." She abandoned her grip on his arm.

"Then how—"

"Durril threw him *over* the traitor's head. Adder screamed and tried to seize the lad. But Endorai set his heels to his steed. In an instant he was galloping for safety.

"Screaming his frustration and fury, Adder turned back to Durril. All around them men fought, but 'twas the battle between the Rom and the traitor that burned the hottest. 'Twas Adder's strength and hatred pitted against Durril's speed and goodness."

"But Durril has no weapon," James whispered.

"No weapon but his wits and his swiftness. Adder slashed at Durril with his terrible sword, but Durril leapt over the blade. The brigand slashed again, higher this time. Durril ducked below. But he was near the edge of the cliff with nowhere to run. Beneath his feet, tiny rocks rolled free and fell toward the lochan far below. Adder watched, and knew he had won. Durril had no way out, so the traitor grinned his evil grin and leapt at his hated enemy.

"Durril was certainly doomed," Catriona said, her words speeding along. "And in the moments when Adder was careening toward him, he saw his life slip away. But at the last instant before Adder struck, he threw himself to the earth. Adder skidded toward the edge of the cliff. He tried to stop himself, but his hatred was too powerful, his rush too forceful, and he fell, plummeting over the edge to his death far below."

James settled back with an audible breath of relief. "And Prince Endorai?"

"He returned posthaste, leading a troop of his guards to save what was left of his men."

For a moment James was silent, then, "Does goodness and wit always triumph over hatred?"

"You cannot win this tourney, Princess Cat. We are clever beyond your ken."

"I hope so," she murmured.

He grinned. " 'Tis a good tale," James said and released his tense grip on the blanket beneath him. "If a bit unbelievable."

"Unbelievable? Whyever would you think so?"

He gave her a look that suggested he was far too old to believe such nonsense. "No one could toss a lad over a man's head and onto a horse's back."

"Are you certain?"

"Aye, I am."

She shrugged as if unconcerned by his doubt and took a sip of mead from her leather mug. "I suspect it would be rude to prove you wrong then."

He stared at her in perplexity for a moment, but finally his curiosity won the battle. "Can *you* do it?"

"You said no."

"Could you throw me?" he asked, excited now.

From somewhere behind her, Sir Hawk cleared his throat. "Not with the Hawk circling overhead," she said.

The boy scowled, then brightened. "Could the Hawk throw you?"

"Me?" Memories of Haydan's hands on her skin warmed her face. "Nay!"

"But you said anyone could learn."

"I did not mean—"

"So 'twas all a lie for no good reason."

"Not a lie."

"Then show me."

She scowled, first at him, then at Haydan, who had stepped up beside them. But the latter spread his hands in front of him and said, "Nay," in a voice unmistakable in its determination.

"He refuses," Cat said, relieved.

"Then perhaps you could toss *him*."

She raised her brows and gave him a look of wry disbelief. "I believe in good," she said. "Not in fantasy."

"Galloway then?" James suggested. "Mayhap you could teach *him* the trick."

"Galloway?" She had not begun this tale so that she might be tossed about by some strange man who did not even like her kind.

"Aye," James said, and rising to his feet, looked about for the mentioned guard.

"And what might you doing, lad?" Hawk asked, his tone deep and suspicious.

"Finding a partner for Lady Cat."

A muscle jumped in the big warrior's jaw. "I thought you had injured your nether parts, not your head. You cannot go tossing the lass about like an overripe plum."

James grinned—the imp king personified. "But 'tis what she does. And Galloway is strong enough."

"Galloway cannot even *speak* to the lass without turning red as my blood. I've no wish to know what would happen if he attempted to lay a hand on her."

"One of the others then?"

That same muscle jumped in Haydan's jaw, and he mumbled something under his breath.

"What's that you say?" James asked.

Haydan gave him a peeved expression. "You know well and good what I said, lad."

"Nay, I do not," countered James.

"I said I will do it," Haydan gritted.

Chapter 17

This, Haydan decided, was the pinnacle of insanity. Hadn't he learned anything yet? He had no strength where she was concerned. Last time he'd been daft enough to touch her, James had caught him half naked in the stable. In the stable! As if he were some randy stud horse chafing to mount his first mare. It was embarrassing, mortifying, insufferable . . . exhilarating!

No. Not exhilarating. It was foolish. Idiotic. He was too old for such behavior. He knew that. She knew that. So why hadn't she been outraged by his actions? Could it be that she was not simply flirting with him, but that she actually found him appealing? Might she be as attracted to him as he was to her? Mayhap she felt the same hard, unearthly allure that he did.

But one glance in her direction told him no. He was a battered old warrior with little to show for his scares. While she . . .

She was magic.

"Sir Hawk." Her voice was soft with that lyrical mixture of deep sensuality and youthful innocence. "I did not mean to draw you into this. Indeed, I did not plan to perform this trick at all. But if I must, I can practice it with another."

No, she damned well couldn't. Not while he watched, at any rate. "I have no wish to see one of my men faint," he said. His voice was admirably steady. Unfortunately, he feared the same could not be said about his hands.

"Faint?" she said. Her lips curved up in a devilish bow.

"You know exactly why," he said. " 'Tis little reason for you to act coy."

"Ah, 'tis because of my astounding allure."

"Just so."

"But you are immune?"

Memories of the night in the stable popped into his head. And with it came a sharp ache in his loins. "I'll try to remember my age," he said dryly.

"Which is?"

"I would tell you, but I've no more wish to see you faint, than my men."

"It might well get you out of this performance."

The truth was, he'd rather pit his discipline against her beauty than reveal his age. Pride was a damnably heavy burden. "I fear your unconscious state would only delay the trick," he said. "James might very well wait for you to awaken, then insist that the show go on. Stubbornness is a hallmark of the Stuart line."

"Is that why you cherish him so? Because he reminds you of yourself?"

"Are you implying that I am stubborn?"

She canted her head at him. "We shall see if you accomplish this task."

"Let us not confuse stubbornness with foolishness."

"I never do. Squat down."

His stomach twisted at the mere thought of her touch. "Your pardon?"

"Squat down so that I may step on your thigh."

There were many things he would like her to do to any number of his body parts. Stepping on his thigh was not among them. "My thigh?" he asked.

"Aye. I will step on your thigh, then up to your shoulder."

"Ah. And then?"

"Then you straighten."

He gave her a narrow glance. "Forgive me. But I am uncertain what that will accomplish."

"Eventually you will straighten quickly enough to launch me from your shoulders and into the air."

"Ah yes. Something I've been longing to do since the beginning of time."

She laughed. " 'Tis for the king. Remember?"

"Nay," he said dryly. "But my forgetfulness may very well be caused by my astounding old—"

"Thus far I am quite unimpressed," James interrupted, scowling at them from some yards away.

"Squat down," Cat ordered.

Haydan did so, feeling his knee crunch and knowing he was a fool for refusing to refuse.

But her bare foot touched his thigh, torching a hundred hungry nerve endings and bumping his pulse rate into a gallop. She reached for his hand and he took hers. Her face skimmed past his. He felt her breath, warm against his cheek, felt her fingers tighten in his, felt her skirt brush against a hundred sensitized regions. But in a moment she stepped down.

He released her hand with an effort. Their fingers parted. He managed to breathe.

"You have . . ." She paused, but went on in a moment.

"You have uncommonly good balance," she said, wiping her palms on the skirt of her gown.

"Did you imagine that I might crash over like a felled oak?" It was more difficult to speak than he would have imagined. Indeed, he had done nothing more stimulating than hold her hand, and yet it seemed that the very scent of her was enough to set him aquiver. It was that realization that made him only more determined to act nonchalant.

"I did not know," she admitted, "since you refuse to give me your age." She stared at him expectantly, but he only scowled back, breathing in and out, in and out.

"Are we going to do this trick, or did you only begin this in the hope of seeing me topple over?"

"I do not think you would topple over if I weighed a hundred stone."

But she didn't. She seemed to weigh little more than one of her foolish birds.

'Twas not true. Haydan reminded himself. She was no delicate lass. Indeed, she could not be and have accomplished what she had in her meager lifetime. And yet . . . it seemed, in his demented state, that she was as fragile as a feather, and when she stepped back onto his thigh, the need to take her into his arms was almost overpowering.

Still, he forced himself to remain as he was, to take her commands and be careful not to touch anything that wasn't offered.

"What now?" he asked when they had tried the first portion of the trick several times.

"We will do the same thing again," she said. "But this time, if all goes well, I will step onto your shoulders."

He gave her a wry expression, but did as ordered. Again he squatted, and again she stepped onto his thigh.

They balanced for a moment, their hands clasped, and then she tentatively placed a foot on his shoulder. The slim muscle of her calf brushed his ear, but he remained as he was by the strictest of efforts, holding her hand as she turned to face the opposite direction and place her left foot on his other shoulder.

"Can you straighten?" she asked.

He did so carefully, still holding her hand.

"So you see, Your Majesty," she said, facing young James. " 'Tis no great feat."

"But you have hardly launched over a man's head and onto a steed," he argued.

" 'Tis a simple step from here to there. Surely you can see that it can be done."

"Nay, I do not."

She was silent for a moment, then, "Release my hand, Sir Hawk."

But she was so high up. A hundred things might go wrong. What if she fell?

"Sir Hawk," she repeated. "You may release my hand so that I can jump off."

Jump! The very idea made him go cold.

" 'Twas the plan at the outset," she reminded him.

He knew that. But she was so light and young, with skin as soft as a cloud and . . . He released her hand abruptly.

She bobbled a little and fear spurred through him. He jerked his hand upward, catching her leg. It took him a moment to realize that his fingers had skimmed under her skirt to the gauzy pantaloon beneath. The fabric felt silky soft, the muscle beneath, delicate and slim.

His desire solidified to rock hard consistency. Beneath the heavy woolen of his plaid, he throbbed painfully.

"You can let go," she said. "I am fine."

Haydan ground his teeth in roiling frustration.

"Sir Hawk?

"What?" he asked, startled from his preoccupation with his own hard needs.

"You can let go."

"Oh," he said and snatched his hand away.

She bobbled again, but wildly this time.

He made a grab for her, trying to snatch her to him, to keep her safe, but she was already falling in a tangle of fabric and limbs. He grappled, twisting her about and cradling her fall as they tumbled to the earth together.

They landed facing each other with his hand gripping her arm in a panicked attempt to keep her unharmed.

"Are you well?" he rasped, finding his voice with difficulty.

"Aye. I am fine. Did I hurt you when I jumped?"

"You jumped?"

"Aye. 'Twas—" she began, but her words stopped abruptly. Her gaze snapped downward.

It was then that Haydan realized their positions. She was cradled between his spread thighs with one leg bent beneath her and the other . . . Holy Christmas, the other was under his plaid. He could feel the slim muscles of her calf contract against the solid heat of his erection. And her ankle, thanks to his traitorous Highland garb, was pressed up warm and snug against his scrotum.

Their gazes snapped up and fused.

"Are you wounded?" James asked, hurrying up.

The sound of his voice snapped Haydan to his feet, but since he was still holding Cat's arm, she was yanked along with him. Her leg skimmed the length of his desire for an instant, then the pressure was gone.

"I am well!" Haydan rasped.

"I am well!" Cat gasped, but refused to meet his gaze.

The lad remained silent a moment, then scowled. "I think you should visit Leech when we return to Blackburn. You are acting strangely again."

Strangely? Haydan thought in rare panic. He was acting like a raving lunatic!

"Mayhap you can teach him the trick some other time," James suggested, turning his attention to Catriona.

"Nay!" Haydan answered.

"I think not," she agreed.

James's scowl deepened as he looked first at one, then the other. "But 'tis my birthday."

"I will do the trick later," Cat said. "Perhaps with Rory."

Against his will, Haydan turned to her. But still she refused to look at him.

"Do I have your vow?" James asked her.

"Aye. Before I leave Blackburn you shall see this trick performed," she said, just as the first smattering of rain began.

In moments it was no longer a sweet spring shower, but a hard, cold deluge.

Haydan yelled orders to the nearest guards, and in a minute they had mounted and were returning posthaste to the palace.

The hour was late, but Haydan lay awake and restless. He should never have agreed to such foolishness that afternoon. He was the king's captain of the guard, for God's sake. He should have some pride. But thinking of Catriona in another's hands . . .

Swinging his feet over the edge of the mattress, he rose to pace irritably.

Images of her flitted through his mind, but he swiped

them out with a silent curse. But the memory of her hand against his chest, her leg against his . . .

He had to see her. Jerking about, he lurched toward the door. But either the pain in his knee or some belated spark of good sense stopped him.

He couldn't go to her. Not only was she little more than a child; she was under his protection, his ward of sorts.

And if neither of those reasons were sufficient, she was sharing a room with her cantankerous great grandmother.

Frustrated by his own appalling lack of propriety, not to mention the hardening ache at the mere thought of her, he yanked his plaid from the mattress, hastily wrapped it about his waist, and stepped into the hallway.

A few words with the guards beside James's door assured him all was well, and he headed downstairs for the kitchens. Perhaps a horn of ale would help him sleep. Voices drifted up to him long before he reached his destination, but when he stepped through the arched doorway, he saw only a handful of late-night revelers.

A trio of men sat drooped over their cups at a table not far from the banked kitchen fire, and some distance away, Marta remained slumped over her own horn.

Haydan stopped abruptly as reality crashed in upon him. If Marta was here, Catriona was alone. He almost spun about and galloped for her room, then he stopped himself with a memory of her face. There was sadness there. Even when she smiled, he could feel it. She hardly needed another randy hound sniffing at her skirts. What she needed was an ally, a protector. But a protector from what? That's what he needed to find out. And who better to tell him than the ancient crone that bobbed over her drink?

Near the gargantuan stone oven, a keg of ale was set on a thick timbered table. Haydan wandered over, dipped out an ample supply, then made his way back between the rows of tables to Marta's side.

" 'Tis rather late for old folk like ourselves to be afoot, is it not?" he asked.

The old woman lifted her gaze to his. Neither surprise nor disorientation showed in her razor-sharp expression when he settled across from her on the trestle bench.

"You are calling yourself old?" she asked, her pebble-dark eyes small in her wrinkled face.

"If I am half so old as I feel, I am ancient beyond count."

Marta snorted and drained her cup. "My toes have corns older than you, lad."

He chuckled and, lifting his horn, filled hers nearly to the top with his own ale. "Then why have you come on this hard journey to Blackburn?" he asked.

Marta took a long quaff, then lowered the mug slightly and assessed him shrewdly over the rim. " 'Twas my granddaughter's wish to come."

"But perhaps 'twas not the wisest thing."

She drank again. "Mayhap you have not noticed, Haydan the Hawk, but my Catty has a way of doing as she will."

He nodded, for he supposed there were few who could deny the maid anything. A journey through hell in search of bluebells would not seem such an arduous task. "She is a persuasive lass," he admitted, "but could her cousins not have accompanied her?"

"Hertha is awaiting the arrival of another babe," Marta explained. " 'Twas best for her to remain behind with her family." Tilting up the mug, she scowled into the bottom, then mournfully licked the last drop from the rim.

Haydan stood, strode across the kitchen, hoisted the ale keg under his arm, and returned moments later to place the barrel beside him on the table. Dipping the wooden ladle into the brew, he drew out a bowlful and tipped it into her horn.

Marta gave him a nod, took a long sip, and sighed contentedly.

"How are Hertha and her daughters?" he asked.

"Here lad, drink up," she said and sloshed a ladle of ale into his curved horn. "Hertha is well, as are her lassies. Though they miss the Cat, I am certain."

"She is easy to miss."

"So you have noticed?"

"I only assume," he said.

Marta laughed, the sound low and rusty, like an old wheel. "Aye. Of course."

Haydan frowned. "The maid is young enough to be my daughter." He tried to sound offended, but the thought of Catriona only made him itchy and too warm, as if there weren't enough air in the huge, drafty room. "No older than my nieces, in fact."

"And I am old enough to be your grandmother," she said and shrugged.

He scowled, uncertain of her meaning. "I only wish to protect her." And feel her lie beneath him, and hear her sated sigh fall on his ears and . . .

"Untruths are most tiresome unless they are mine own. Lies do you little good," said the old woman and sighed before she drank again.

He thought about protesting, but she had not called him a liar . . . exactly, and he had learned long ago that those who protest the loudest oft harbor the most guilt. "Oh?" he said, his tone calm.

She nodded. "Aye. What I cannot see with the gift I can guess through uncounted years."

"And you think I do not wish to protect her?"

"Oh aye. You do. But you have other wishes as well."

He leaned back slightly to cross his arms against his chest and hoped to appear casual. "You think I am drawn to her?"

Her gaze smote him like dark fire, though her wrinkled lips quirked slightly with humor. "You would not be the first."

"Then why am I here now, Grandmother? After all, the lass is alone in her room. I could go there and plead my cause."

The old woman grinned. What few teeth she had left were hardly worth mentioning, but that did not impede her drinking, which she proved yet again with an impressive swig. "You are here to get me addled enough to tell you all I know of her," she said, and draining her cup, held it out to be refilled.

He complied readily.

"And why are you here?" he asked.

She scowled. "It might be that I am considering getting you addled enough to take advantage of your person."

He was not a man who was easily surprised, but he was quite certain his brows were firmly ensconced somewhere in his hairline. "Truly?"

"You're a fine specimen, Haydan the Hawk," she said. "But while the spirit is willing . . ." She sighed and shook her head. "The flesh is damnably tired."

He chuckled. "Hear, hear," he said and raised his mug in an informal toast.

She drank, then watched him do the same. "Be warned though, lad, if I get pickled enough, I may yet have the will to drag you under the table and have my way with you."

"If I get pickled enough I may not resist."

She gave him a rusty chuckle. "I fear there are not enough spirits in all Christendom to gain that end."

"You may well be surprised."

"I rarely am, lad." She drank again. "Fill me up."

He did so, then leaned his elbows on the table to watch the old woman in the ensuing silence. "She is sad," he said finally, for indeed, there seemed little purpose in skirting the issue. And too, she had already drunk half a keg of ale. Surely it had loosened her tongue by now.

"I assume we speak of my granddaughter again," Marta said, sipping the ale appreciatively, as if it were her first taste.

"Aye," Haydan agreed. "She is sad sometimes. I but wonder why."

"Think on it, Haydan the Hawk. Catriona has seen much hardship. She lost both her mother and her father long before she should have made that parting. 'Tis doubtful she shall ever see the land of her forebears, and the man she once called beloved is . . ." She sighed and drank again. "He has disappointed her," she ended simply.

"Rory?" Haydan guessed, ignoring the tightening of his gut.

"Aye. Rory."

"Then why is he here?"

"For the same reason you are. He could not stay away. Here." She shoved his horn toward him. "I do not care to drink alone."

He joined her. "If she is disappointed with him why does she not find another? I do not think she would have any great difficulty."

"Difficulties are drawn to the Rom like maggots to a dead ox," she said, scowling into her cup.

A charming analogy. "What kind of difficulties?"

"Have you not been listening, lad?" she asked and nudged his hand with her empty mug.

He filled it dutifully. "Listening to what?"

"To her tales," she said, sounding exasperated.

"Of Durril?"

"Of her kinsmen."

Haydan watched her closely. Surely she wasn't addled enough to believe the old wild tales. Just how intoxicated was she?

"Quite. But not yet intoxicated enough," she said, answering his unspoken question, then chuckling at his expression of surprise. "Do not give up hope, lad. I cannot remain lucid forever. As for yourself, Haydan the Hawk, do you think the maid looks as if she were born to Scotland?"

"Nay." She looked as if she were born in heaven, but that seemed unlikely, even in his incrcasingly foggy state.

"Nay indeed," Marta said and drank deep and long. "Nay indeed." Her thoughts seemed far away, but she spoke finally in a tone so deep he could barely hear her. "Black as midnight were his eyes and when he looked at me 'twas as if I were the only maid in all the world. 'Martuska' he would whisper and I would all but swoon with pleasure."

Haydan had no idea what she spoke of, but there was a soft dreaminess to her tone that entranced him. He drank again, watching her all the while and wondering if she had, in her youth, had the same unearthly allure as her granddaughter.

"She has my eyes and my hands," she answered. Had he asked the question aloud? "Her hair is like her mother's, wild mane that it be. But her smile . . ." She sighed and drank. "Her smile is his."

His being her great grandsire, Haydan assumed.

"When were you married?" he asked.

"For three years I was his first." She tipped the horn to her lips, found it empty, and pushed it out for him to fill.

Good saints, she had a hollow leg.

"His first what?"

"His first wife."

His brows, which had recently lowered, shot up again like a missile from a cannon. "He had others?"

"Seven."

Haydan remained silent. "I cannot decide if you are extremely intoxicated or simply jesting."

"You might ask," she suggested and drank again.

"Your husband had seven wives?"

She gave him an expression of disgust. "I would have thought a man such as yourself capable of ciphering. Last I counted, seven plus myself made eight."

Damn. He *was* drunk.

She laughed, supposedly at his expression of surprise, then continued with her story. " 'Twas a common practice for a man to take more than one wife. Certainly a prince had that right."

Prince Endorai? She *must* be jesting. And damned if she couldn't drink like a swine herder. "So he took other wives and you had no hard feelings?"

" 'Twas a different place and time." She shrugged and

winked. "And since then I have far surpassed his number of . . . partners."

Haydan sat in silence, trying to quell the question, but it came nevertheless, probably washed up on a wave of ale. "And your great-granddaughter?"

"I have had her share too. Drink up, lad. You're falling behind."

He did as told, then lazily considered how to rephrase the question.

"Ah, my Catriona," sighed the old lady. "For many years I thought she might be a changeling, but now . . ." She eyed him with a narrow gaze. "I now think there may yet be hope."

"What the devil does that mean?"

She stared at him a moment longer, then shrugged. "She has the Rom allure. You could hardly condemn her for accepting a few lovers, could you?"

His gut cramped. Too much ale?

"Could you?" she asked again, her eyes intense as she leaned toward him.

" 'Tis hardly my place to condemn or condone."

"Nay, 'tis not. But most men do. When they themselves are as loyal as hounds on a hot scent."

'Twas true, of course. And yet, thinking of her with another . . .

"And what of you, Haydan the Hawk?"

Haydan's elbow slipped on the edge of the table, causing his chin to bump down and his eyes to snap open. "Me what?"

"What woman lights your wick at night?"

"Lights my . . ." Some vague part of him wondered if he should be offended by her terminology. After all, he was a knight of the realm and the king's personal guard. But somehow he could not quite dredge up the appropriate emotion, for all he could think of in his blurry mind was Cat—her laughter, her sadness, her softness, her strength . . .

"Ah, so you still want her, no matter who she has taken." She nodded.

He raised his brows. Or possibly just one, since the other seemed unreasonably weary. "You are sadly mistaken, old one."

"And you were a poor liar when sober. Pathetic when intoxicated," she said and drank.

"Intoxicated?" he tried to sound shocked, but it may have only come out as groggy. "Nay. I am only . . ." He was only what? Only too old for her by a score of years and had been ordered by royal decree to guard her? "I only wish to protect her."

The ancient eyes were dead earnest as she leaned forward to gaze into his. "Protect her from what, lad?"

"I do not know." He shook his head. The room swayed. "I do not know. But I feel her sadness and I am certain there is something she is not telling me."

She stared at him long and hard as if judging his very soul. "And what if I told you that you are right, lad? That she needs your help? Would you forsake all to come to her aid?"

"I have already sworn to protect her," he said, baffled by her words.

"Aye, you have sworn. But when the hammer strikes the anvil, will you hold true?" she mused.

"What?" During the enforced inactivity of his childhood it had been *Haydan's* place to speak in riddles, but just now he could not seem to speak at all, and the table kept rising toward his chin.

Then he felt her gnarled fingers grasp his jaw in a

firm grip. "What are you made of, Haydan the Hawk?" she asked.

Even if he had known what she spoke of he could not have formed a coherent answer, for the room kept dipping strangely. Nevertheless, she spoke again.

"You may do, lad. You drink like a milk-fed babe, but when the fat hits the fire you may yet do," she said, and pulling away her hand, let his head drop to the table.

Chapter 18

Haydan awoke groggily. His pillow felt hard and strangely damp, his neck stiff, his head woolen.

"Sophie said there was something left over in the kitchens."

He sat up with a start to stare into Kitchen Elsie's amused eyes. For a moment all sense deserted him, and then reality struck. He had spent the night slumped over the table. And Marta? He glanced blearily over at the opposite bench and saw that spot had been vacated.

"Hard night, laddie?"

Good Christmas, he couldn't even outdrink an old crone. And what idiocies had he spewed before he fell into unconsciousness? Get her drunk indeed! Learn Catriona's secrets! More likely the old wench now knew he was having wet dreams over her great-granddaughter. He was lucky she hadn't smacked him over the head with the empty keg of ale. On the other hand, she very well might have, judging by the throbbing in his head. Lifting his hand to his aching cranium, he felt for any gaping wounds.

" 'Tis still there," Elsie assured him.

"What?"

"Your head," she said. Shifting the hollowed wooden bowl that rested on one plump hip, she grinned. " 'Tis still attached."

"I know it's still attached," he said, not daring to scowl at her, lest his skull burst open and spill his dubious brains onto the table. "It hurts like hell."

"Could be you're too old to drink the night through, Sir Hawk. What was wrong with your bed?"

"Besides the fact that it was empty?"

She chuckled low in her throat. "Empty of you or empty of another?"

"Empty," he said flatly.

"I think there might be some who could help you with the latter."

"That an offer, Elsie?"

Her grin was suggestive. "It may be. Didn't know you were interested. But I have a night available now and again."

"I may be too old to fight for the honor."

"Could be I'd do the fighting for you."

" 'Tis good to know since—"

"Elsie, I—"

"James!" Haydan choked and straightened quickly enough to make his head throb and his back creak.

"Sir Hawk!" James came to an abrupt halt, causing the guards behind him to do the same. "Hawk," he repeated, continuing into the kitchen. "You look worse off than you did before. What ails you?"

" 'Tis naught," Haydan assured him, but his voice cracked, so he rose abruptly to his feet and tried again, though his head clanged ominously at such an egregious offense. " 'Tis naught, Your Majesty. Why are you about so early?"

"To break the fast."

"Is there some reason the meal could not be brought to your room this morn?" What kind of luck would bring the lad here when he was in such mind-boggled disarray?

"I am bound for the stables," James said.

"And why so early?"

"Galloway said Lady Cat goes out in the morn to see her mare."

Haydan exchanged a glance with the young guard. "Did he now?'

"Aye," James said and took the hot scones Elsie had already fetched for him. "Galloway knows all about Lady Cat."

The red-haired guard cleared his throat. "I but noticed that the maid tends her steed just after dawn."

Haydan turned toward Galloway just as James turned away. It could very well be that the young guard might know something Haydan did not. "Anything else you have observed?" he asked, focusing all his attention on the guard's freckled face.

Galloway shuffled his feet. "There are a few things, Sir Hawk."

"Such as?"

The young man cleared his throat. "For a Gypsy she seems . . . quite honorable."

"And?"

The guard squirmed under Haydan's glare. "She has the most bonny eyes in all the world."

Good saints! Yet, if an old reprobate like himself was cast adrift by her slightest attention, how much more would this poor young swain be affected? "I meant have you noticed any of her other—"

But James turned back just then. "Would you like to accompany me to the stables, Sir Hawk?"

For a moment Haydan's heart sped along at a faster clip. All he need do was walk out to the stable and she would be there for him to see, to speak to, to make certain she was well. But his neck crinked, reminding him of his wrinkled appearance. He could hardly greet her this way. At the very least he would have to rid himself of his beard and . . .

He was acting like a hang-jaw lackey again. "Nay," he said. "I have . . . business to tend to. And a swordsmanship lesson to give a young king."

The lad scowled. "Surely it can wait," he said, his tone wheedling.

"I suppose it will not hurt to delay it a bit," Haydan admitted, but in his own traitorous mind he was already hurrying through the list of necessities before he too could rush out to the stables.

God help him, he thought as James exited the hall with his guards close behind him.

Back in his own chamber, Haydan hurried through his toiletry, taking a pumice stone to his whiskers, tying back his hair. A silent reprimand rasped through his mind for his hurry, but he stilled it. After all, 'twas his job to ascertain the young king's safety. 'Twas good for him to be at the lad's side, he thought and he hurried down the steps toward the stable. His boots rang against the flagstones in the courtyard. From a nearby alcove the sweet sound of a lute filled the air.

Haydan glanced in that direction and saw Rory strolling along with the bottle-shaped instrument against his chest. Nodding, Haydan continued on. The music stopped. "You are looking more the hawk this morn," said the Rom.

Haydan halted. "What say you?'

Rory gave a crooked grin. He was a handsome lad,

which did little to improve Haydan's mood.

"I could have told you you would get nothing from Grandmother last night."

"Get nothing?" Haydan asked, struggling to keep his tone casual.

Rory shrugged, his expression disarming. "She can be as tight-lipped as a monk."

"Hardly tight-lipped," Haydan said. "Indeed, Blackburn's ale supply is much depleted since last eve."

Rory laughed. "Oh, aye, she can drink her weight in ale. Yet still she told you nothing, aye?"

"Told me nothing of what?"

The Rom's gaze didn't flinch. "About Catriona. 'Tis what you wished to know, is it not?"

Haydan said nothing, but Rory only shrugged. "You are hardly the first mouse to be snared by the Cat."

"I think you are imagining things."

"Then you have no interest in her?"

"On the contrary, I owe her a great debt of gratitude."

"So you only wish to help her?"

"What help could I give her?" he asked, his tone tighter than he wished it to be.

"I think mayhap that is for my Catriona to decide."

Careful now. Careful.

"Mayhap your Catriona is too cautious," Haydan warned. "I would help her if I could."

The Rom was silent for a moment. "Nay, it seems she yet depends on me to mend her wounds. And 'tis right, of course. For despite her flights of fancy, I am the one she shall wed," he said. Giving Haydan a hard stare, he turned to walk away.

"Lady Cat."

Catriona turned abruptly from her gelding. "Your

Majesty," she said. "You are about early." 'Twas indeed early for the young king to be in the stables, but 'twas good that he was here away from the prying eyes of the nobles who surrounded him.

"I am come to practice my horsemanship," he said.

"Are you, now?"

"Aye." He grinned. "I thought I would see if I could damage the remainder of my person."

" 'Tis a lot to ask on an empty stomach."

"But mine is filled with scones and honey mead."

"Ah, then why delay?" she asked. "Unless Sir Hawk would object to more injuries."

"He gave his blessing."

"Truly?"

"Aye, so we may as well be started."

Catriona acquiesced, for her time was rapidly slipping away, and fate or God Himself had delivered the lad into her hands.

Though the hour was early and Bay was less than jovial about leaving his stablemates, James was an enthusiastic student and a determined horseman. With a little coaching he improved his ability to launch into the saddle and became increasingly adept at cuing the gelding for his spectacular leaps and strikes.

The sun was halfway up the morning sky when James slipped over the gelding's rump for the final time.

Galloway and Cockerel stood against the stone stable wall as they watched their young ward.

"So I am ready," James said, his freckled face still flushed from exertion.

"Ready?" Catriona patted the gelding's neck and loosened his girth. "For what, Your Majesty?'

"For our adventure."

Cat's heart bumped abruptly against her ribs as her

hands fumbled with the saddle straps. "Adventure?" she asked, skimming her gaze breathlessly toward the guards.

"Aye," James said, his own gaze cutting toward Galloway. "I've decided I want to do it on my birthday."

She tightened her grip on the stirrup leather. "Do what, exactly?"

His grin was effusive, his eyes alight with mischief. "We will sneak from the castle, of course. Just you and I."

For a moment she forgot to breathe.

" 'Twill be the perfect opportunity, with all the festivities. 'Twill be marvelous. No one will know that I am freed."

"But what if we are caught?" 'Twas not her place to dissuade him, she thought frantically.

"You shall bring him to us," Blackheart had said. *"Just you and the young king. Or your brother will know us very well indeed before he dies."*

"We will not be caught," James whispered. "You are of Durril's wild blood. Surely you can see this done in the dark of the night."

"I . . ." 'Twas what she needed to do, but terror and guilt gripped her in a tight fist. She spurred her gaze sideways as fear pumped through her, certain there would be a guard there to drag her to the gallows. "But what of the Hawk?"

James shrugged. "I am *here* alone. I think he has other things on his mind. Or perhaps he is ill."

"Ill?" she rasped.

Galloway removed himself from the wall to stride across the springy turf toward them. "Is something amiss?"

"Nay," they said in unison.

"Nay," Cat repeated, her gut burning with bile and fear. "I but wondered why Sir Hawk is not here. Is it true that he is ill?"

"I do not know," Galloway said.

"He did not insist on accompanying me here," James said. "And he looked the color of the moat in midsummer."

"The Hawk sick?" Catriona asked. 'Twould be best for her plans if he were well out of the way, and yet she was torn. "Mayhap I should notify Physic."

Galloway cleared his throat. "In truth, my lady, I do not think you need concern yourself."

"But if he is ill—"

"I believe 'tis naught more than a wee case of poisoning."

"Poisoning!"

"Ale poisoning."

"Oh?" The Hawk did not seem like one to drink to excess. She frowned at the guard. "Is this a common occurrence?"

"I have never known it to happen before."

Perhaps he was not drunk at all! Perhaps he had only pretended so that James would think it safe to discuss their plans.

"In truth, lady, I believe 'twas your grandmother he was drinking with," Cockerel said, joining their small group.

"Grandmother?" She had heard nothing of this. But then, Grandmother was well known for her tendency to divulge what she wished and keep the rest silent.

Cockerel's full lips quirked up suddenly. "I believe Sir Hawk was intent on matching your grandmother's considerable appetite and therefore—"

" 'Tis always a pleasure to hear my name on your lips, Cockerel," Hawk said.

Catriona jumped, and Galloway paled to the color of weak cream. Only Cockerel grinned.

"Sir Hawk," he said, nodding.

"Aye," said Haydan. "In the flesh."

"The lady was just worrying over your absence."

"And you felt it your duty to reassure her?"

Cockerel bowed. "I only do what I can, sir."

Haydan glowered at the dark guard for a moment, but finally turned his attention to James. "And what trouble have you found for yourself, lad?"

"Trouble?" Innocence, it seemed, was the boy's forte. Cat wished she could say the same for herself, but her heart was still thundering overtime and her head felt light. "No trouble, Sir Hawk. Lady Cat was assisting me with my horsemanship."

"Was she, now?"

"Aye," James said. " 'Tis my duty to improve my skills."

Hawk gave him a skeptical glance. "And you care?"

"Of course. 'Tis as you say—even the king of the sky must make his arduous journey west each day. No matter how weary or worn," he said, his tone dramatic.

Haydan scowled, then nodded toward Cat's gelding grazing placidly nearby. "And what has that to do with this horse?"

"Like the sun . . ." James lifted his hand skyward. "I too must fulfill my destiny and learn to conduct myself as befits my station."

The Hawk's brows lowered even further over ice-blue eyes. " 'Tis not the fact that you discerned the message that concerns me most, but that you listened to the moral at all."

James grinned. "Who can tell, Sir Hawk?" he quipped. "Pigs might yet fly. Who knows what the morrow might bring?"

Chapter 19

"On his birthday," Catriona said, abruptly pacing again. Caleb wobbled on her shoulder, but found his balance without the aid of his bandaged wings after a bit of scrambling.

"You will take him then?" Marta asked, her old voice rusty in the narrow room.

"Unless we can learn who the culprit is, I have no choice," Cat said. She turned hopefully toward her grandmother, but the old woman shook her head.

"For a time in the hall last night I thought I felt the evil. But the place was full and I could not determine the source, though I sat long trying to sort out the emotions. As the crowd diminished I hoped to identify the feelings. But even with only a few men left, the place felt filled with passions. The kitchens were less confusing." She turned shrewd eyes to her granddaughter. "Was it not the MacKinnon lad who you drugged and ransacked?"

"Aye. It was."

"It seems he enjoyed it."

"Noblemen are strange," Cat said, distractedly pacing again. "What did he say?"

"Something about your purity, and that only a lout would besmirch your name."

"Who did the besmirching?"

" 'Twas a dark fellow with half-lidded eyes."

"Drummond. He was speaking to MacKinnon?"

"Even as I left Haydan the Hawk asleep on the table."

"But why?"

Marta sighed from her place on the bed. "Ahh, lass. If every man who spoke of you was guilty of treason, there would not be an innocent left."

"There are no innocents left."

Marta was silent for a moment, then, "What of Haydan the Hawk?"

"What of him?"

"Is he innocent, I wonder?"

Catriona shook her head. "Innocent? Nay. Well-meaning?" She shrugged. "I do not know. But it matters not—I dare not trust him."

"Mayhap you have no choice but to go where your heart leads you."

" 'Tis not my heart that is important here," Cat said, fear spurring up inside her. " 'Tis Lachlan."

"And the king?"

"Aye." Catriona clenched her hands and paced again. Calum flitted through the open window to land on the cage and taunt Caleb with his ability to fly. "Aye, the king, too."

"When do you meet Blackheart again?"

"Two days."

"Where at?"

Cat shook her head. "I do not know. I go first to the livery stable in Burnsvale. There I shall be told what to do next."

"And tonight?"

"When all is quiet I will continue my search."

"You will be careful?"

"Aye," Cat said and forced a smile for her grandmother's worry. "That is exactly what I shall do."

Lightning slashed against the iron-bound window. Fractured light burst in the darkness, then subsided, throwing Catriona's life back into blackness. From the direction of the great hall came a burst of raucous laughter. The sound itself seemed to blow Catriona toward the nearest door. The inhabitant of this room was yet in the hall. That much she knew, thus her reason for being here.

His door opened noisily under her shaky hand, but she was inside in a moment. The chamber was bathed in darkness, but she risked no lamp. There was no sound but the noise of her own breathing, rapid and harsh as she hurried to the far side of the room. But the floor was cluttered and she tripped.

Startled, her heart beating like a wild drum, she turned to determine what had tripped her up, and in that moment she realized the truth.

'Twas a person on the floor! She recoiled. A servant had been left behind to wait in the darkness. But perhaps she hadn't awakened him. Cat turned to rush for the door, but lightning cracked across the ebony sky. Forks of silver slammed brightness into the narrow room, illuminating that space like the light of day and showing a narrow rivulet of blood on the face of—

"Lachlan!"

Catriona hissed his name in horror, and in that moment she awoke, but the nightmare pursued her.

Lightning crackled like the lash of a whip outside her window. She jerked wildly to her feet. Thunder snarled.

She whimpered at the sound as the image of her brother's bloodied face ripped through her mind. She must find him!

Flying across the room, she yanked open the door and launched into the hallway.

"Catriona!"

She heard the voice but did not stop. There was no time. Every moment counted. The floor flew beneath her bare feet.

"Catriona!" Something snagged her arm. She fought it off, but her captor was strong.

"Nay! Let go! I must—"

"You must what?" Haydan asked, his voice deep.

Reality slashed across her consciousness. "I must . . ." Words deserted her. Only fear remained, the rancid taste of terror on her tongue.

"What? You must what, lass?"

She winced, remembering. "I had a dream," she whispered.

"You shall be his only hope and you shall not fail him. Nay, you are the Princess Cat, willing to sacrifice all if needs be."

She shivered as dreams and reality melded in a confusing swirl of uncertainties.

"Dreams cannot harm you, lass. All is well." Haydan's hand felt warm and unearthly strong against her skin. "I will see you safely back to your room."

"Nay!" Lightning crackled outside. Fear exploded within her again. "Nay." She calmed her tone, but her heart still raced and in her mind she saw the door again. But now she realized that the hinges were twined with unruly vines. 'Twas not a room inside the castle at all, but the door of a crofter's cottage that she had seen. "I cannot go back just yet. Please."

Up ahead and around the corner a man murmured something indistinguishable and another chuckled.

Haydan scowled and paused a moment, then, draping his arm around her, he herded her away from the on-comers. It took only a few minutes before they stepped inside a small room. He closed the door behind her. Candlelight flickered in the draft.

Catriona trembled again.

"You can remain here for a wee bit of time," Haydan said.

"Is this your chamber?"

"Aye. 'Tis." His tone was low, the candlelight soothing.

The dream receded a mite, but she shivered again nonetheless.

"Are you chilled?"

"Nay. I—" she began, but he had already fetched a blanket to wrap about her. His fingers brushed her shoulders, sending a bit of warmth through her. Surprised by the shiver of feelings, she lowered her gaze and caught her breath. "Why were you at my door?"

He drew away to pace restlessly across the room, a huge man with a gigantic shadow cast in flickering detail upon the far wall. "I could not sleep, so I decided to make certain no one bothered you this night."

"I . . ." Lightning flared again. She drew an unsteady breath, glad that on her nights of searching, she exited the window. "I do not need a guard, Sir Hawk."

He clenched his hands into fists. "Mayhap 'tis my own need that I answer."

"Your need?" She raised her gaze, but he shifted his away.

In the corner of his room stood a narrow table. He went to it and brought her a horn mug.

"Drink," he insisted. " 'Twill calm your nerves."

She did so and felt heat course through her in tingling waves.

"What was your dream?" His voice was deep, quiet.

"There was a door. Entwined in leafy vines it was. And inside . . .'twas Lachlan," she whispered. Mayhap she should not tell him. But she was scared and lonely, and deep inside she needed to share the terror. "I dreamed he was wounded behind that door."

"Thus you rushed into the hallway to save him?"

She nodded. Hearing the foolishness of her actions made the terror less real, still, fear gripped her.

"Do you think the dream was an evil omen?"

Catriona raised her gaze sharply to his. Why did he not dismiss her nightmare as idiocy? 'Twould have seemed the likely thing for a warrior of his stature.

"Have you had premonitions in the past?" he asked instead.

She shook her head and exhaled softly, blowing a ripple into the surface of her ale. "Nay. Grandmother is the seer."

"Was *her* sleep disturbed?"

Catriona scowled, thinking of her own dark room, her grandmother's soft breathing. "Nay. She slept well."

"The dreams were naught but the monsters of sleep, then."

"What?"

"When I was small I would oft call nightmares the monsters of sleep. 'Twas the Rogue who said they were not really monsters at all, but sniveling cowards, afraid of many things. Light. Laughter. The warm touch of a loved one."

A loved one. Her heart wisted. Whom did Hayden the Hawk love? " 'Tis hard to imagine you as small."

"Good."

She laughed shakily at his emphatic tone, then sobered and glanced back into her drink. "Thank you," she said softly.

"I have done nothing."

"You have reminded me that all is well."

"Is it?" His voice was as deep as the night beyond his window.

"Grandmother assures me it is. 'Twas just a dream," she said. "Nothing more."

"Then why do you tremble?"

"Does nothing make you tremble, Sir Hawk?"

He was silent for a moment, watching her, his face solemn in the flickering light. "Many things make me tremble, lass."

"Truly?" she asked. Intrigued and soothed, she wrapped her hand about the smooth surface of the drinking horn. "Name one thing."

"You."

The room was as silent as death, his gaze steady on hers, and she laughed, though her eyes were filled with foolish tears.

"The day I make you tremble is the day I die."

"Do not say that." His tone was gruff, startling.

The candle sputtered.

"Why?" Her voice was barely audible to her own ears.

For a moment she thought he would answer, but instead he turned away.

"Perhaps you should return to your room. Your grandmother will worry," he said.

"Why do I make you tremble?" she whispered.

A muscle jerked in his jaw. "I think you know."

"In which case there would be no harm in telling me."

" 'Twould do no good to hear it said aloud."

She watched him in the uncertain light. "I think you are wrong."

"Nay. I am not."

She stepped toward him, and though she thought he might retreat, he held his ground.

" 'Tis not as easy for you to dismiss my presence as you say," she whispered.

His scowl deepened.

"Is it?"

"Would you have me say that I am no different than the others?"

"I would not believe it, for you are nothing like the others."

"I am a soldier," he said. "The captain of the king's royal guard. Do not confuse my position with concern for you."

"So you watch me only in an effort to keep the king safe?"

He scowled. "The king commanded me to keep you from harm. Don't you remember?"

"I remember two men who accosted me outside Blackburn. I remember their intent," she said and shivered.

He reached out but drew his hand back immediately.

"I remember you saved me," she added.

" 'Tis not how I remember it. It seems to me you had already saved yourself."

"Then why do you continue to look after me, if I have proven my ability to do so on my own?"

"Mayhap I hope to ingratiate you, lady, to win my way into your . . ." He paused.

"Heart?" she guessed.

"I was going to say 'bed.' 'Heart' implies that I have

feelings for you, instead of using you for my own carnal pleasure."

She laughed.

His brows lowered even more over his ice-blue eyes, and she noticed that his hands were clenched tightly at his sides. "Something amuses you?"

"You do."

The candle hissed.

"Oh?" he said, his tone dark.

"Think on it, Haydan the Hawk." She said his name distinctly, reminding them both who he was. "I have all but forced myself on you and still you avoid me—except to save my life now and again, of course. It seems a strange way to coerce me into your bed."

"Why?" The single word was tortured. "Why are you here? In this room? Why me?"

"Mayhap to lose myself for a short span of time," she whispered. "Mayhap to forget. Would that be so terrible?"

"Forget what?"

"Everything." She exhaled sharply.

He ground his teeth. "That your beloved has been unfaithful? That—"

"My beloved?"

"Rory."

She grasped the excuse with tardy desperation. "He has betrayed me a hundred times. So why should I not—"

"Why me?"

Because he was everything a man should be. Tough and tender, wise and witty. "Do I have to have a reason? Can I not simply . . ." Words abandoned her. "I need you this night," she finished weakly.

He reached out slowly. His fingers touched her cheek.

She shivered at that simple caress and closed her eyes.

He stepped closer. She could feel his nearness like the brush of a warm breeze, and then he kissed her lids, softly, tenderly before gently wrapping her in his arms. His strength surrounded her like a coat of armor. His warmth touched her like the light of the sun.

"Do not tremble," he whispered and lifted her into his arms. His strides were sure and steady. His chest felt firm and broad beneath her hand. The mattress sighed as he laid her on the bed. He watched her for a moment, his face shadowed and illumined by the fickle light.

But Catriona could not bear the separation, for her dreams were still monsters without him near. Slipping her hand behind the broad strength of his neck, she kissed him, then drew back to watch his eyes.

Against her hand, his muscles felt as tight as rope. She sensed his battle with himself, but she could not condone his cause, and so she kissed him again.

It was he who trembled this time. She felt him quiver, and then he was beside her, his fingers splayed through her hair, cradling her scalp.

His kisses strayed from her lips, traveling down her throat. She arched her back, granting him better access, letting the feelings take her.

His hands skimmed down her throat, over the swell of her breast and down to her waist, pulling her closer, drawing her nearer. His palm swept over her buttocks, curving her into him, and she slipped her leg between his. Flesh against flesh. Warmth against warmth as their garments were pushed upward. He eased her leg closer, snuggling her against him, sliding his hand down her thigh. She pressed into him, wanting more, her hands restless against his back.

"Too many clothes," she murmured against his neck.

"Aye," he agreed and slid her nightgown slowly over her hips. But she was already tugging at his tunic.

"I meant yours."

Her lower body was bare, but she did not feel chilled, for his hands smoothed over her, warming, stimulating, caressing, arousing a thousand feelings left dormant too long.

His fingers slipped down her buttocks and brushed her hidden core. Catriona sucked air between her teeth and pressed hard against him. He played her gently, and she thrummed beneath his caress.

"Haydan," she rasped, her own fingers tangled in the folds at the back of his tunic. "Take me."

" 'Tis not time yet," he argued. Cupping her buttocks again, he pulled her closer still.

" 'Tis," she said. Even through the bunched wool of his plaid she could feel the hard proof of his desire. Tightening her grip, she pulled his tunic free from his belt and slid her hands underneath.

He sighed, but, "Nay love. 'Tis not," he said and kissed her lips until the world spun wildly. "I have not even removed my boots."

" 'Tis not a problem," she whispered.

He chuckled and the sound curled smokily into her belly. "I will not be making love to you with my boots on," he murmured.

"Then for God's sake, take them off!"

He kissed her again and she felt his smile in his caress. "You will have to loosen your grip on my tunic then, lass." He nudged her arms gently, but her fingers were firmly tangled in his shirt.

"Oh." She loosened her hold and he drew her hands between their bodies and up.

Gently, ever so gently, he kissed each knuckle, then

opened her hands to kiss the hollow of one, then the other. "I shall be back shortly," he promised and turned away.

Cold panic splashed through her. She rose to her knees with a jolt, already clutching his arm. "Where are you going?"

"Just here." He turned to say the words over his shoulder as he reached for his first boot.

"Oh." She relaxed slightly, but her hand had fallen against his shoulder and she felt the intriguing bunch of muscle there. "Oh," she repeated and slid her fingers over that muscle and beneath his arm. Her breasts crushed gently against his back as she stroked the mounded muscles of his chest, and against her sensitized fingers she felt his nipple harden. His head dropped back slightly.

"Please lass, I—"

But she had already slid her hand lower onto the corrugated strength of his abdomen.

He sucked air through his teeth.

She kissed the side of his neck.

"Lass," he growled. "I've no wish to rush you. But I fear—"

"Rush me!" She breathed the words against his throat. "I have waited two and twenty years. I think that's sufficient time to—"

"What?" He twisted slightly toward her so that the tendons in his throat stood out hard and tight, and his gaze captured hers.

"I said I've been waiting—"

"You are a virgin?"

She scowled at his dark tone. "Why do you ask?"

He gritted his teeth. "You said . . ." he began, then

scowled and paused. "Your grandmother implied . . . Damnation!"

Catriona drew a deep breath. "You are not going to be difficult about this, are you?"

"Nay!" he said. "I am going to return you to your grandmother's tender care."

Chapter 20

"I will not return to my chamber," Cat said.

Haydan tried to rise to his feet, but Catriona had a firm grip on his tunic. He slumped forward and swore with reverent feeling.

She scowled at the back of his neck. "I thought virginity was a problem easily remedied."

"I have vowed to protect you. Not . . ." He groaned. "Not deflower you."

"Deflower." She sighed. "A silly word, when in truth . . ." Wrapping her arm about him, she slid her hand beneath the hem of his tunic and up. The muscles of his chest danced against her fingertips. "I do not feel like a flower at all."

"Lass!" He said the word like a warning.

"What?"

"Don't do that!"

"What? This?" she asked and skimmed her fingers light as air over his nipple.

He gritted his teeth.

She circled his body with her other arm and pressed up tighter against him.

"Please, lass!" he rasped, but as he turned toward her, she found his mouth with hers.

Heat seared her, burning a path from her lips downward. He moaned against the kiss. She heard the muffled clump of his boots as he kicked them to the floor. Then he broke away to face her.

"Not even Rory?" he asked. "Not even your betrothed?"

"Must I lie to convince you to make love to me?"

"It might assuage my guilt."

" 'Tis not such a terrible thing," she whispered and kissed the scar at the corner of his mouth. "You were a virgin once too. Were you not?" she asked and slipped her hand back under his tunic.

He closed his eyes as her fingers touched his ribs. "I do not recall just now."

"Think hard," she said and slipped her tongue, slow as midnight, across his lower lip.

"Where does a virgin learn such things?" he rasped.

" 'Tis not so great a secret, Haydan. It takes no training. Not like . . ." She paused as she kissed the corner of his mouth. "Not like Latin or ciphers," she whispered and slid her hands in tandem up his torso. The tunic followed. He lifted his arms grudgingly, breathlessly. She slid her fingers over his heavy biceps, releasing him from that bondage as she slipped the garment over his head and away.

He sat before her half naked, every sinew taut with tension, a massive man with arms and chest hewn hard by years of battle.

She stared at him, forcing her lungs to fill with air, and then, ever so slowly, she smoothed the flats of her hands over his pectorals. His eyes dropped closed. A scar ran from his sternum to his shoulder. Touching it with her ring finger, she gently followed its course, then slid sideways along the hard edge of his collarbone. Another scar began at the mounded muscle of his upper arm, slicing diagonally toward his back.

"So many injuries," she whispered.

His eyes remained closed. "You should have some bonny young swain, lass. Not a scarred and jaded—"

She kissed the scar that marred his shoulder, and his words rasped to a halt. "Who were you protecting when you received this one?"

"I do not know."

"Come now," she chided, the reprimand breathy against his arm.

"My sister's daughter has a gift for finding trouble."

"Ah." Catriona moved on, kissing the old wound at the center of his chest. Muscles danced on either side. "And this one?" she asked.

He set his teeth against the feelings. "The Rogue sometimes forgets to watch his back."

She slid her fingers slowly down his midsection. Muscles quivered to life in their wake. But a circular scar just below his ribs drew her notice. "This?"

" 'Twas a blade meant for the old king."

Bending down, she kissed it tenderly, then straightened. "I think *you* are bonny, Haydan the Hawk," she whispered.

He opened his eyes and his quicksilver gaze struck her with the intensity of flint against steel. The room was silent, then, "I would love you, Catriona, if you will let me."

She considered telling him that had been her plan for some time, but no clever words escaped her, for at that moment he kissed her. Her stomach coiled with hot desire. His hand cupped her chin; his kisses touched her cheek, her throat, the fragile hollow between her collarbones.

The laces of her nightrail sighed open and he kissed her shoulder. His hand slipped with satin tenderness down her body, over every quaking curve until it reached the hem of her gown. His fingers touched her skin and pushed the linen up before them, caressing her thigh, curving over her hip. She let it come, let his other hand join the quest, let the garment slip over her head until she was naked and vulnerable before him.

Catriona Baird was not a shy lass, and yet it was not easy to raise her eyes to his. Still, she did so, but his were lowered, skimming with slow consideration over her candlelit body. She shivered beneath his perusal.

"You are beauty itself," he said, his voice low and quiet. "Beyond words. Beyond imagination."

And she wanted him with burning desperation. She reached for his belt, but he caught her hands.

"Nay, lass, not yet," he said, urging her back onto the mattress.

"Are you certain?" she asked.

"Aye," he said and kissed her. His caresses were unimpeded by clothing now. His kisses slipped lower, down her neck, over the rise of her breast to touch her nipple.

She bucked beneath him as feelings hot as coal burned through her. "Now?" she gasped.

"Nay." He whispered the word against her breast but in a moment his kisses moved on. She held her breath as he skimmed her belly, only stopping for a moment to touch his tongue to her navel.

She writhed beneath the caress. But he was already moving on, his splayed hand shadowing his kisses, soothing and exciting, warming and chilling. It scooped around her hip as his lips touched the upper regions of her private hair. She froze in place, waiting. His movements slowed as he worked his way lower, and she arched appreciatively, wanting more, needing more. His lips skimmed her hair and touched the nub of her desire.

She sucked air into her lungs. "Now!" she demanded, but he did not even respond. Instead, he slipped lower still, his mouth warm against her thigh, her knee.

His fingers splayed around her calf, stroking, soothing as the other hand massaged her buttocks.

She groaned in an inexplicable combination of agony and ecstasy. "I am sure it should be now," she moaned and thought she heard him chuckle.

His breath tickled her toes.

She curled them toward her soles and tried to draw up her leg, but he held it firmly by the ankle, and now, with excruciating care, he kissed each digit. She tried to yank her foot away from the intensity of the feelings, but he would not relent. Then his right hand slid slowly down her backside to join his left.

Catriona wriggled against his concerted onslaught, but he had captured both her ankles and began to nibble his way up. Not an inch missed his ministrations—not her arches, or her shins, or her calves. The backs of her knees were massaged and her thighs encircled as he crept higher. Finally he reached the apex of his climb. His lips touched her inner thigh.

"Now!" The word escaped on its own.

His hands slid under her knees to ease them up and out. His lips touched her swollen desire. She rasped a jagged breath, but his tongue had joined the assault, and she could no longer speak.

Instead, she pressed against him, beyond caring for

anything but the feelings, beyond thought and concern and worry.

Her fingers found his hair. She pulled him closer, but he came too far. His kisses left her aching need and slipped slowly up her belly.

"Nay. Nay," she moaned, trying to urge him back down. But the hard expanse of his belly was already pressed between her legs. She pushed against the undulated muscle. "Well . . . yes," she sighed, but in a moment his lips took hers with bruising force. Fire burst from her loins to her belly to her lips.

"Now?" he whispered.

She panted against his mouth, squirming wildly. "I said 'now' a lifetime ago."

"I feared you were only trying to flatter me." He kissed the corner of her mouth. She turned hungrily toward his lips, but he had already drawn back a few horrendous inches. "Just trying to make me feel good."

"I am trying to make *me* feel good," she rasped.

He chuckled. The deep laughter came from down low, the sound curled through her like sweet wine.

"Now," she whispered.

He drew slowly away, rising to his knees, his huge body shadowing her. She watched his hands open his belt, watched him unwrap his plaid, watched his erection rear into view.

The air left her body in a hard rush.

"Are you well?" he asked, concern in his voice as he dropped back over her.

His nipples brushed hers.

"Aye. Aye. 'Tis just that I . . . didn't imagine you would be so . . . well proportioned."

He leaned closer. "Are you *certain* you're not simply trying to flatter me?" he asked.

"Quite certain," she rasped.

He pressed the thick blade of his desire against her and she stopped her breath and squeezed her eyes closed.

"Truly I . . ." She swallowed hard and wriggled just so, searching for the perfect fit. "I cannot bear much more or . . ."

"Or what?"

"Or . . . I do not know," she said, wriggling again.

He gritted his teeth against her artless movement, then rolling over, pulled her atop him.

Her legs spread, positioning her knees beside his hips and her groin over his.

"Oh, aye," she breathed.

"Now," he murmured and lifting her hips off his, slid inside.

She opened like a blooming rose, pulling him into her garden, throbbing with pleasure, bursting with anticipation until he was planted deep inside her.

She shivered wildly against the earthy feelings, then, placing her hands on his chest, she began to move, squeezing her legs against his hips as she arched into him.

It was his turn to gasp. He gritted his teeth against the bursting sensations and pressed slowly against her motion.

Pleasure bloomed, opening, budding as he gripped her tighter and increased the rhythm. She dipped her head back and rode the wind of desire, galloping madly along the cliffs of raw pleasure.

His hands tightened on her thighs, pulling her closer, making them one. She leaned down. Her hair cascaded onto his chest, melding with his. Her breasts draped over him and he raised his head and closed his mouth over her nipple. Razor-sharp desire sliced through her. Gasping for breath, she pressed into him with new intensity.

Haydan arched into her with taut need. Harder and harder they rode, gripping, gliding, sliding upward toward the crest of desire until, with one final gasp, Catriona found the pinnacle and fell, trembling against his chest.

'Twas only then that he drew out and pulsed his own need between their bodies.

Against her ear, Catriona felt his heart, like the beat of great wings. Panting, she curled her hand over the taut mound of his biceps and closed her eyes.

Peace sifted over her.

"Did it work?" His voice was a low rumble. She could feel it reverberate against her ear.

"What?" she asked, sleepy and sated against the heat of his body.

"Did you forget?"

"Forget what?" she murmured. Then, "Haydan?"

"Aye?"

She felt him stroke her tangled hair, and closed her eyes against the beauty of the feelings. "Is it always like that?"

"Sometimes it—" he began, then stopped. "Nay. Never." He sighed and skimmed his hand down her back and over her buttocks. "Not until you. Though I would like to think I have learned *something* in my doddering old age."

"How old?" she wondered, but whether she said it or merely thought it she was never sure, for in a moment she was asleep.

Catriona awoke in deep shadows. The candle had sputtered out, pitching the room into darkness. But she needed no light, for she could feel the Hawk beside her.

He was breathing deeply, the sound soft and lulling, his warmth soothing. Here in the darkness, sheltered by his strength, soothed by her memories, she could almost believe that all was well. But it was not, of course.

She had been weak and for a time she had borrowed his strength, his caring. He was like a mighty ship on a tempestuous sea. But she must learn to swim.

Moving slowly away, she tried not to disturb him, but he mumbled something and reached for her. She remained for a while, lying in the darkness, content to be with him, comforted by his presence as long as she could be. But finally she could wait no longer.

Easing carefully backward, she edged off the bed, then dropped to the floor to search blindly for her nightrail. She found it tangled in the blankets and extracted it carefully. Slipping it over her head, she tied the laces and glanced once more toward Haydan's pillow. But the kindly candlelight that had illuminated the room earlier had long since sputtered out, and the lightning had been doused, giving way to a soft, steady rain. Thus, she had no choice but to slip out with nothing more than the shallowest glimpse of his face.

The hallway was even darker than his room. But she knew her way well by feel, for 'twas not the first time she had traipsed these halls without the aid of a light. She felt more rested than she had for a long while. Rested and hopeful, and up ahead, from around the corner, the sconce beside her chamber glowed faintly in the night. All would be well. She felt it in her soul. She but needed to find the abductor and then—

"So there you are," said a voice from the shadows.

Catriona jerked, startled and breathless, toward the voice. But the flickering shadows cast by the distant candle would not part to reveal the man who spoke. "Who is there?" Her voice cracked shamefully.

"Don't you even recognize me, Catriona?"

"You will not know us."

"Who's there?" she asked again, panic ripping through her.

Chapter 21

"'Tis me."

"Rory?" Cat asked breathlessly as she peered into the shadows.

"Aye." He stepped out of an alcove. Muted light shone off the brass wires of the lute he'd balanced against the wall. " 'Tis me. Did I frighten you?"

"Aye. What are you doing about at this time of night?"

"I could not sleep, knowing you were not abed. Is something amiss?"

"Nay." She glanced toward her room and tried to relax. "All is well."

" 'Tis good." He sighed. "In truth, Catriona, I do not think I could bear it if some ill befell you."

"Rory—"

"Nay." He stopped her with a wave of his hand. "Do not bother to tell me again that you are not for me. I know. And indeed, 'tis my own fault."

She said nothing, for there was sorrow in his voice, and deep remorse.

"But it does not stop me from caring about you," he added.

"You needn't worry. I am careful."

"Are you?"

"Aye. But I have little choice," she murmured. "I must learn who has taken Lachlan before it is too late."

"Is that where you were then? Searching for the culprit?"

She hesitated for a moment as she remembered Haydan's hands against her skin. "Aye." 'Twas a poor lie, but the best she had.

"Does it take so long in every room?"

She scowled. "What—" But the truth dawned before she finished the question. "You were watching my room. 'Tis how you knew I was not abed."

"Aye." His voice sounded strained. "I watch you, and why should I not?"

"Because you are not my betrothed, Rory." Anger and frustration were building inside her. "Because if you cared, you would be aiding my cause, not worrying where I spend my time."

"So you admit it." He took a step toward her. "You were with him. I was your betrothed, your beloved, but not once, not *once* did you deign to lie with me."

"You did not need me, for you had others. Still have others," she said, remembering how he had looked at Fayette.

"Others?" He sounded stunned. "Do you speak of the widow? She means nothing to me."

Tense and suddenly weary, she only stared. It seemed now that they had had this conversation a thousand times.

"I only went to her because I cannot have you—the woman I love, the woman I will love for all time." His voice had gone soft. He reached for her hand. His felt cool in the darkness. " 'Twas always you, Catriona. But seeing you, being near you—I cannot bear having no one beside me at night, not when you are so alluring, so . . . magical."

She exhaled sharply, relaxing a little. " 'Twas a time when I believed that was true," she said softly. "A time when I hoped that if I gave myself to you, you would stray no more."

" 'Tis true. Even now I can prove it, Cat, if you will let me. Say you will be mine and I shall make everything right for you. Everything. Give me a chance."

"I gave you many chances."

"Chances!" he said, his tone harsh before he soothed it. " 'Tis no chance at all when you tease with your beauty then deny me all but the most meager of kisses."

"I am sorry." And strangely, she truly was, for he was wounded. She could hear it in his voice, feel it in the air. "But I cannot live like that, Rory. Mayhap I am too selfish. But I need someone who will be true."

"And so you go to him?" he asked, his voice rising.

She tensed.

"You go to him? That great, towering oaf? It may be *he* was the one who has taken your beloved brother."

She tried to pull her hand free, but he did not release it. "Let me go, Rory. I am tired."

"But not too tired for him, are you?"

"I told you I was searching."

"And you found it, did you not?" he snarled. "Was it as big as you had hoped?"

She jerked away and dashed for her room, but he lunged after her. His fingers tangled in her hair and she was yanked to the floor.

"You are mine!" he growled, pulling her to her feet.

She stumbled upright and fear mingled with her rage. "I was never yours!" she hissed. "And I never shall be."

Lightning exploded inside her head. She reeled backward, crashing against the wall.

"Get up!" he growled. He came for her, leaning close, his handsome mouth twisted in a sneer. She tried to scoot away. Suddenly there was a wild bellow and Rory flew sideways. The wall shook beneath his weight.

And then she saw Haydan. His chest and feet were bare, his plaid haphazard about his muscular waist.

Rory rose with a scream of rage and threw himself forward. The lute struck Haydan's ear and he reeled against the wall. Rory dodged in, swinging again.

Cat scrambled to her feet and lunged at Rory's back.

He swung at her, slamming her sideways, and then, even in the uncertain light of the hallway, she saw his knife.

She tried to scream, but Rory was already charging.

"She is mine!" he growled and struck.

Haydan gasped and jerked.

"Nay!" Cat cried, but in that moment Haydan's arm swung wide. The knife clattered against a door, and suddenly Rory was pinned to the wall by Hawk's hand on his throat.

Rory scrambled wildly, arms milling and legs pistoning, his feet inches from the floor. His strangling rasps became louder, like those of a rabid dog.

Footsteps pattered toward them, bearing lights and gasps of horror. But Cat's attention was skewered to the two men by the wall. Hawk's eyes were deadly cold, Rory's popping wide as his face turned pasty blue.

"Good God, he's going to kill him!" someone gasped. "Stop him! Hey there!"

Rory bucked again, but weaker now, and it was that weakness that snapped Catriona into reality.

"Haydan!" She ran to him. "You must not kill him! You cannot!"

"On the contrary." His voice was as cold and deadly steady as his eyes. "I can and I shall."

"Haydan!" She grabbed his arm, but the muscles there were as hard as hewn granite, unrelenting, unforgiving. "Please, have mercy."

"Why? Why mercy?" he asked flatly.

"He is my kinsman."

For a moment, she thought he had not heard her, but finally his arm quivered and withdrew.

Rory fell to the floor like a broken puppet, grasping his throat and wheezing for breath.

"Are you well?" Haydan turned slowly toward her.

"I—" She was shaking and nauseated. "I am fine. But you . . ." She reached for him.

He pulled away. Grasping the front of Rory's tunic, Haydan pulled him to his feet.

"You will leave this place." His voice was deep, unwavering, beyond rage. "And you shall not see the lass again."

"She is mine!" Rory snarled.

Hawk's opposite hand streaked out, grasping the other's throat. But in a moment he had gained control and when he spoke his voice was level once again. "You shall not see her," he ordered. "Not for the entirety of your miserable life. Do you understand?"

Rory managed a croak of agreement.

Hawk drew back his hands and Rory wilted against the wall.

"You will leave now," Haydan said.

"You shall regret this," Rory vowed, clutching his throat.

"I regret her mercy already. Go while you can," he

ordered, and Rory fled, stumbling away toward safety.

The hallway went quiet.

"My God!" someone gasped. "He's wounded."

"Nay." Haydan turned abruptly. " 'Tis the Rom's blood on me."

"Come, Lady Catriona, I will see you to your chamber," he said, and taking a lamp from the nearest man, touched a hand to her back.

Her door opened silently. They stepped inside together.

"Rory didn't bleed," she said, shifting her gaze to the blood smeared across his abdomen.

"What?" he asked, skimming the room before returning his gaze to her face.

"You are wounded."

"Do not worry. 'Tis naught."

"Another scar. Because of me." A quavering sob rasped between her clenched teeth, and because he could not bear her pain, he cradled her chin in his palm and tilted her head up.

"I shall never think of scars the same," he murmured. "Not after your ministrations."

"You're delirious. I am no healer."

"On the contrary," he said. "You have healed my very heart with—"

Marta suddenly awoke with a snort and a start.

"Catty. So you are finally returned," she said, then narrowed her pebble-bright eyes and sat up. "What happened here?"

Haydan dropped his hand and straightened. "I fear your granddaughter has been molested."

"Molested!" The old woman swung her legs off the bed with amazing speed. Her nightrail shimmied up, baring legs as scrawny as a peahen's. But she seemed to neither notice nor care. “Molested by whom?”

“Rory,” Cat answered. “Rory was waiting in the hallway for me.”

“God help us,” said Marta, hurrying toward them while she pinned Haydan with a dark glare. “And you let this happen?”

“I am sorry,” he said, guilt gnawing at him.

“ ’Tis not his fault!” Cat insisted.

“Where are you hurt?” Marta asked, ignoring her defense.

“I am well. ’Tis Haydan who is wounded.”

“Nay, I am fine.”

“Good God! What a pair of brave souls. Give me a coward any day,” she muttered, then waved vaguely toward the bed. “Sit down the both of you.”

“I cannot stay,” Haydan insisted. “The gossipmongers will—”

“Gossipmongers! What are they to say? That you seduced the lass while I was yet in the room?”

No one spoke.

“You would not do that, would you, lad?” she asked, her eyes ungodly bright in her wrinkled face as she stared at him.

“Nay.”

“Just as I thought,” she said in disgust. “Sit down.” He did so. “You too, Catty,” she ordered, but stopped Catriona with a hand on her arm. “He struck you?”

“Aye.”

The old woman shook her head. “I should have known. I should have felt it in him. ’Tis me own fault. Me own cursed old age,” she said and sighed. “Sit.”

Cat did so, settling meekly beside Hawk on the bed.

Marta stared at Haydan. “Blood,” she said, shaking her head. “I do not like blood. Did he stab you?”

"Aye, but—"

"Quiet. Stay there. I go to fetch a few necessities."

"Truly, I am—" Haydan began, but she stopped him with a glare.

"Would you rather I fetch Leech?"

"Nay."

"Then there is a little hope for you at least," she muttered and tottered from the room, closing the door behind her.

Catriona expelled her breath and closed her eyes. Sitting there, she looked like a wee weary angel. "I am sorry," she murmured.

"Nay. 'Tis I who should apologize."

"You?"

"Damn him," he said, his soul tearing at the sight of her panicked eyes. "I should have killed him."

"How badly are you hurt?" she whispered.

"A cut. Nothing more," he said, but he kept his left arm pressed to his side so that she could not see the wound. "I should have escorted you to your room. Why did you not awaken me?"

She met his gaze, then reached up. Her fingers felt like healing balm against his cheek. "If I woke you it would not have been to walk the halls," she whispered.

"Lass," he began, but at that moment she kissed him, gently at first. Then desire struck fear like flint to steel and passion flared.

He could not help but kiss her back. Her hand slipped behind his neck. He quivered beneath her touch and slid his arm about her waist, drawing her closer.

"Damnably slow!" They jerked apart as Marta stormed into the room. "Is that all you got accomplished?" She carried bandages and a bottle. "What a foolish waste of a good bed. Had I moved that slow, Catty's grandmother would be yet unborn." She shuffled closer. "Here, then. Lift your arm."

"Truly—" Haydan began.

"Lift!" she ordered.

He did so.

"Ah. Well . . ." Uncorking the jug, she took a swig before dumping a bit onto a cloth. "The lassies like the scars, aye?" she said and slapped the cloth to his wound.

He gritted his teeth against the sharp slash of pain and straightened abruptly.

"There now. We'll have no fainting," she reprimanded.

"I was not about to faint."

"We'll have no weeping, either. 'Twould be embarrassing."

He scowled at her. "I'll not cry."

"Nay?" she asked and dabbed harder at his injury.

"Nay," he said, remembering her implication of Catriona's vast sexual experience. "But I am thinking of tossing you out yonder window."

She stared at him for an instant, then threw her head back and laughed. "You've got spunk for a wee lad."

"And you lie like a Persian rug," he said with feeling.

She leaned closer, staring into his eyes, and then she grinned and nodded. "I needed to know if you would cherish the prize even if you thought it less than perfect." The grin increased. "Apparently you did," she said, then nodded toward Catriona and took another swig of whiskey. "Bandage him up. He will live."

But when Catriona reached for the strips of cloth, the old woman touched her cheek and frowned.

"Put a cold rag on it, lass," she said quietly. "And remember this. Life is short." With that, she tottered over to the far side of the bed, set the whiskey on the floor, and stretched out on the mattress with her face to the distant wall. In a matter of seconds she was snoring.

"I had best leave," Haydan said, beginning to rise.

But Cat placed a palm against his chest. Warmth radiated from his skin to hers, taking her breath for a moment, but finally she found her voice. "Nay. Let me see to your wound."

"What of the gossips?"

"We have a chaperone."

He gave Marta a slanted glance. "She is asleep."

"They will not know that."

"They will know she is odd."

Catriona laughed and Haydan leaned forward to cup her chin and kiss her lightly.

"Sleep well," he said, and rising quickly, left the room.

Rain slanted into Haydan's face, driven by a cold wind that whistled from the north.

"Did you see which way the Rom went?" he asked the guard at the bridge.

"Nay, Sir Hawk. What with this damnable weather blowing out the torches, I only know he has left Blackburn." The guard fidgeted. "Is something amiss?"

"Nay. Nothing," Haydan said, then paused. Damnable weather indeed. "Open the portcullis."

"What?"

"Open the portcullis. I have business in the village."

"Business? At this hour of the night? Oh . . ." said the guard and grinned. He'd lost a tooth since Haydan had last seen him. "Business. Aye." He winked. "The nights, they do get lonely, do they not? Especially with that Gypsy lass forever about, aye?"

Haydan lowered his brows. Temper and fatigue and burning pain were contriving against his usual effervescent humor.

"Not to worry," added the guard as he rapidly raised the iron gate. "I'll tell no one of your . . . business."

"See that you don't," Haydan said, and wrapping his dark cloak about him, rode into the storm.

'Twas a simple enough task to find the Rom's wagon even in the dark. They had unhooked the narrow cart in plain view of Blackburn, in a bonny spot by the burn. But when Haydan opened the wee door at the rear, 'twas clear Rory was not there. There were, however, fast-fading tracks leading from the contraption.

In the gray light of dawn, Haydan followed the tracks toward the village. But once there, the footprints veered off, tramping across the vale and into the woods beyond.

Beneath the shelter of the trees, Haydan's task became more difficult. He damned himself for his delay. He should have questioned the Rom before banning him from the castle. But it had been all he could do to keep from killing the man, and mayhap this was best, after all—for perhaps the Rom's destination would tell a greater truth than his words ever would.

Sometime in midmorning, the rain began again. The clouds lowered until they seemed to envelop the entire world in grayness. The trail faded into oblivion. Haydan rounded back, searched again, and finally found a place where the Rom had slipped and fallen.

The woods thickened. Rain dripped off the edge of Haydan's hood, finding its way with chilly fingers down his neck.

The footprints disappeared again. Haydan swore with growling verve and searched hopelessly. The forest was dense and dark here. Vines grew in wild profusion, choking a weathered hawthorn, then twining horizontally across a grayish branch. But when he reached that spot, he found that 'twas not a branch that supported the vine. It was a wooden door set in a cottage so ancient it was nearly lost in the foliage.

Silently drawing his sword, Haydan waited beside the door for a moment, then lifted the latch and stepped inside.

The place was empty. Haydan's disappointment swelled. But upon further examination, he realized that someone had been there. A leafless vine crossing the inside of the door had been torn asunder, and the years of dust on the floor had recently been disturbed.

So the Rom had been there, Haydan deduced. Judging by the scattering of dust near the door, he had rested there for a time. But why? Why here?

Sheathing his sword, Haydan returned outside to search for more tracks. But the raw, wilding weather, seeming determined to foil him, came harder until finally there was nothing he could do but return to Blackburn to nurse his knee and his foul mood.

Chapter 22

Nearly two full days had passed since Haydan had held Catriona in his arms. He stood in the lea of the stables now, watching as she turned Celandine loose inside a stone yard. The mare was healing well and frolicked now, kicking up her heels before running to the far side of the enclosure to call to the horses who were even now bringing their riders back from a hunt.

"What do you mean, your partner has left?" James asked. "You promised he would assist you with the trick."

More riders trickled back to the bailey. Laughter wafted on the afternoon breeze that had blown away the wilding weather, leaving sunlight in its wake.

"I am sorry, Your Majesty," Cat said, but kept her face averted even as a greenfinch flitted from the stable wall to a branch to her shoulder. "His departure could not be avoided."

"Of course it could be avoided. I am king." James pouted. "You must call him back and—"

Haydan stepped away from the building. " 'Twas a matter of life and death, Your Majesty," he said. And indeed, it had been, for his hand had felt so right against the Rom's throat.

Catriona turned abruptly toward him, her eyes too wide, the satiny skin beneath them dark with fatigue.

"Whose life and whose death?" James asked.

Haydan pulled his gaze from Cat with a solemn effort. " 'Twas a family emergency," he explained. "I am certain you understand. After all, the king of the Scots must always concern himself with his people's needs first."

"I understand naught but that you are keeping something from me again."

"What is it you would like to know, lad?" Haydan asked.

James frowned as if stymied by this rare show of compliance. "Who is going to perform the trick with Lady Cat?"

"As she said, the . . ." Haydan paused, hopelessly searching for a word more appropriate than "bastard" and trying to force his muscles to relax. "The *Rom* has gone."

"Then you must perform."

"I cannot." For she was lying, keeping something from him, planning something! What, he did not know, but he dared not let himself be distracted. And Catriona Baird was the very breathing essence of distraction. One touch of her flesh against his and all hope of coherent thought was lost.

"Then I shall have to choose another partner for her," James said and glanced toward the assemblage of hunters.

Haydan's gut clenched anew as he too skimmed the distant crowd. Drummond, with his devilish, half-lidded eyes and rumors of cruelty. Lord Hogshead, soft and undisciplined, but the only surviving heir to a wealthy title. MacKinnon, watching her with his mournful expression, while scandals whispered around him like malevolent ghosts. Shortsighted Ramhurst. Bitter Tremayne. Twisted Physic. Damnation! There wasn't a man among them that he'd trust with Catriona.

But the truth was darker still. 'Twas simply that he could not bear the thought of having her touch another.

"Well? What say you?" James asked.

Haydan turned his gaze to the king's, and deep in those mischievous eyes he saw an understanding far beyond the boy's meager years. So the lad was not so naive as he sometimes acted. He knew Haydan had feelings for Catriona, knew he could not bear to see another touch her.

"I say, such blatant manipulation is beneath your lofty station, Majesty," Haydan said.

James grinned. " 'Tis sadly true, I know," he agreed. "But 'tis my birthday."

Their gazes held. Seconds ticked away, and then James skimmed the crowd again. Haydan tensed like a drawn bow.

"Cockerel," James called finally.

Haydan lifted a dubious brow.

"You have need of me, Your Majesty?" Cockerel asked, hurrying up.

James shifted his attention from his captain to his guard. "Aye. I thought you might wish to perform with the Lady Cat at my birthday celebration."

The guard's dark eyes gleamed. A spark of a smile tilted his generous lips. "Perform?" he asked, glancing at Catriona. "Might you clarify—" he began, but in that instant Haydan cleared his throat like a menacing growl.

Cockerel shifted his gaze to Hawk's eyes. A moment

of frozen silence passed between them, and then 'twas Cockerel's turn to clear his throat.

"My apologies, Your Majesty," he said with a practiced bow. "But I fear I must decline."

"You cannot decline."

"I will not be able to join the festivities. 'Tis my . . ." Cockerel scrambled for an appropriate excuse. "My grandmother. She is ill."

"Then we must rush her to Blackburn for healing."

Cockerel winced. Hawk glared.

"I have injured my . . . knee."

" 'Tis a great coincidence. Sir Hawk has the same malady, and he was nearly able to perform the trick, even in his dotage."

Haydan shifted his glare from the guard to the king, then back.

"My arm!" Cockerel crowed, nearly giddy with the idea as he yanked up his sleeve to reveal a superficial wound on his forearm. "Galloway was too zealous during practice. I can barely lift it."

Silence echoed around them.

"That is the most pathetic excuse I have ever heard," James said.

"My apologies," Cockerel said, almost grinning again. " 'Tis the best I can do under the circumstances."

James sighed as he turned toward Haydan, but beneath the boy's martyred expression was the shadow of an impish grin. "And who now is manipulative, Sir Hawk?"

Haydan inclined his head. "I have learned what I can from my king."

The lad's grin widened. "Then you'd best learn what you can from the Cat—for 'tis up to you to perform with her. And I'll expect it to be spectacular," he said and pivoted away.

The silence seemed heavy after the departure of the lad and his guards. From the top of a nearby rowan Cat's greenfinches piped up.

"I was worried about you." Catriona's voice was soft.

"Me?" Haydan turned toward her, but if she could feel his perusal, she didn't lift her face to his. "Why?" he asked.

"I did not see you all day. I feared your injuries may have been more grievous than you had let on."

Emotions burned through Haydan. She was a wee lass, barely more than half his weight and age, and yet she worried for him. There were dark shadows under her eyes, and he knew why she didn't turn toward him. She was hiding the reddened bruise that swelled above her ear and into her hair.

Anger sizzled through him like a wind-blown fire. Damn it to hell! He should have killed the Rom bastard while he had the chance.

But no, that would not have banished the sadness in her eyes. So what would? With aching tenderness, he remembered the night they had shared. For a short time she had been relaxed, content. He would give much to grant her that again.

Oh hell! Who was he fooling? He'd give his right eye just to feel that heaven himself. Temptation made him reach out. Good sense made him draw back. There was something afoot here, and he dare not miss it.

"Nay, I am well," he said, crunching his hands into fists by his sides. "And you?"

"I am fine."

She was not. She was scared. Of what? He'd kill to know. But he turned away. There was no hope of forcing her to tell him. And getting Marta drunk had not been one of his more stellar ideas.

"I need to speak to you," he managed.

She stared up at him, her eyes as mysterious as Highland mist.

"Regarding the other night," he added, yanking himself from the bottomless depths of her gaze.

"Aye." Her voice was breathy.

" 'Twas—" There were no words for what they had shared. There was no description. And yet he could not do it again. He could not! Not until he learned the truth, solved the riddle, saved her. But from what? " 'Twas wrong of me to take advantage of you."

"Advantage?" she repeated, and in her tone there was a breath of shock. Indeed, seeing her standing there as straight and tall as a reed, 'twas difficult to believe she was the sort to be taken advantage of. And when he remembered how she had touched him—seized him really . . . God help him!

"Aye. You were . . ." He cleared his throat and tried to ignore the tightening in his loins. "You were lovely—*lonely*," he correctly quickly, closing his eyes against her beauty for an instant. "You were lonely. I was but available."

"Is that what you think of me, Sir Hawk? That every time I am lonely I find an available lover?"

"Nay!" Nay, indeed—she had been a virgin! The very idea that he had been her first made him shudder. All her wit, all her unearthly allure, all her breathtaking bold innocence had been his and his alone. He remembered the feel of her skin, the sound of her moan in his ear, the taut contraction of muscles around him, the—

He should not have lain with her, for now he could think of nothing but doing so again. And there was much else to ponder. "I place no blame on you, lass," he said. "I but meant . . ." He drew a deep breath. " 'Twas wrong of me, and I will not press myself on you again."

"Oh." She stared as if lost and disoriented, then, "Oh," she said, her voice stronger. "You are right, of course. We must not. I am sorry."

"Sorry?" The word escaped on its own. In his mind, she kissed him. The touch of her lips was an intoxicating as wine. "Would that I could be sorry."

"What?"

He straightened his spine and hardened his discipline. "I said, would you like to start?"

"Start?"

"Practicing the trick."

"Oh. Aye." Pulling the mare's rope from the post, she toyed with it for a moment. " 'Tis not a difficult feat, but 'twill take a bit of time. Shall we return to the glen where we practiced before?"

"Nay!" Haydan rasped. Damnit all, he would be lucky to withstand her charms here on the castle grounds with others about. If he were alone with her, God only knew what might happen. "Nay," he said, lowering his voice and feeling ungodly foolish. "There is an open area in the gardens where we can practice undisturbed."

"Good," she agreed.

They returned Celandine to her stall, then walked together toward the garden. As luck would have it, they passed the guard who had lifted the portcullis when Haydan had gone to search for the Rom, but he said nothing, only stared in wide-eyed admiration.

They reached the relative privacy between the gardens and there the torture began with a few soft directives, a few quiet suggestions. 'Twas easy enough to lift her. 'Twas letting go that was hell. Each time his fingers brushed hers, it felt like unbidden fire. Each time he looked at her, the flame was fanned. Foolishness. Idiocy! He could not touch her, yet he could not stay away.

She slipped and he reached out, quickly cradling her waist in his palm in a wild attempt to catch her, to save her, to hold her safely against his heart.

Their gazes fused.

"Haydan!" She said his name in a breathy whisper.

He drew back with a snap. "Aye?" His voice sounded panicked, like a guilty lad fearing punishment.

"I have to go."

"What?"

"I must . . ." She wrung her hands, then lifted one to her forehead. "I have a terrible ache in my head. I'd best lie down."

"Oh. Aye. You rest. I will see you to your chamber."

The journey to her bedroom was as silent as their journey to the garden had been. In a moment, they stood before her door.

He turned to face her. "Sleep well."

"What?" She looked disoriented again and nervous.

"Sleep well."

"Oh. Aye. My thanks."

He almost asked her again what was wrong, but he would not. Nay, 'twas his task now to find out on his own, so he forced himself to turn and walk away. But once around the corner all nonchalance left him. He hurried along, his mind rushing in concert with his steps.

He had very little time. In a moment he was in the barracks, beside Galloway's bunk.

"Wake up!"

The young guard sat upright like a launched arrow. "My lord captain. What—"

"I need you to watch the lady's door."

Galloway turned groggily toward the window. "The lady's—"

"Catriona! Watch her door. But do not stand directly by it. Stay in the alcove down the hall."

Galloway nodded. "In the alcove," he said and swung his legs over the edge of the mattress.

"And if she leaves," Haydan added, narrowing his eyes, "follow her."

"Follow her?"

Haydan leaned closed to the young man's face. "Is there some reason you keep repeating my words?"

"Repeating—nay. Nay, Sir Hawk," he stammered.

"Good. Then go."

Galloway stumbled to his feet.

"And lad," Haydan said quietly. " 'Twould be best if you did not fail me in this."

Galloway swallowed and hurried away. Haydan turned to do the same, but noticed Cockerel's dark, broad-brimmed hat hanging on a peg on the wall. Grabbing it up, he left.

Back in his own room, Haydan threw open his trunk and dragged a pair of dark hose from the depths. In a moment he had kicked off his boots, dropped his plaid to the floor, and replaced it with the hose. Then he glanced down at his shirt. 'Twas not a distinctive tunic, but still, she was accustomed to seeing him in it.

He dug inside his trunk again to produce a red doublet. It was slashed and puffed and ostentatious, and he felt like a crazed jester when he wore it. But it had been suitable for the king's coronation and it would do now.

Slipping it over his tunic, he fastened it in place, then tugged on his boots.

In a matter of moments, he was stepping into the alcove beside Galloway.

"Is she still in there?" he murmured.

Galloway started. "Sir Hawk?" he asked, trying to gaze past the shadow of the hat's broad brim.

Haydan scowled. 'Twas good to know his disguise was suitable, but rather disconcerting to find out that the man he'd trusted to guard Catriona was an idiot. "Has she left yet?"

"Nay." Galloway shook his head and dragged his gaze from Haydan. "Nay. Where is she going?"

"I do not know."

"Then—"

"You may leave now."

"Aye, sir—" he began, but just at that instant Catriona's door opened. Haydan slapped his hand over the other man's mouth.

Galloway turned wide eyes toward his captain and froze, but Hawk only noticed the girl. One slim hand was set to the door handle as she glanced down the hallway. Hidden against the wall of the darkened alcove as they were, she failed to notice them. In a moment she slipped from her room, off in the opposite direction and around the corner.

Haydan dropped his hand from Galloway's mouth and strode after her, but in a moment he heard footsteps behind him. Turning rapidly, he glared into Galloway's wide eyes. Haydan lowered his brows and sunk his head between his shoulders. 'Twas a stance that had served him well through the years. Galloway backed up a quick step.

"I'll just . . ." he whispered, nodding vaguely behind him. "I'll just return to my bed."

Haydan nodded once, then pivoted on his heel and continued on. When he reached the corner, he paused a moment before glancing around the turn. But the hallway was already empty, making him hustle to catch up.

'Twas some heart-thumping minutes later when he spied her next and darted back behind a wall to prevent being seen. But eventually, with spurts and starts and a few well-placed windows, he saw her heading toward the stable. He hurried down the steps to find a circuitous route to the same destination.

Stepping quietly through a side door of the stable, he strode quickly down the hard-packed aisle and into a stall not far from Cat's gelding. Once there, he remained absolutely still, listening until he was certain Catriona was in a stall. She crooned a few words. Metal jangled. So she was planning to ride, he deduced. He would have to hurry to saddle his own steed in order to follow her, but when he stepped from the stall, her door was already swinging open. Turning his back quickly, he strode purposefully in the opposite direction.

Haydan did not know whether she saw him, but in a moment he was rushing off to saddle his own mount. It took him a few seconds to realize the folly of that idea. There was little point in changing his attire if he did not change his mount. In a matter of minutes, he was astride Cockerel's steed and trotting toward Blackburn's looming gate. Guards stood with their backs to the towering stone wall as Haydan stopped his mount inches from the pair.

"Did the Gypsy maid pass this way?"

"The—Sir Hawk?" the guard said, belatedly seeing through the disguise. "Sir Hawk, is that you?"

Haydan ground his teeth. "Did the Lady Catriona come this way?"

The guard grinned. "Business in the village again, Captain?"

Haydan straightened to his full height. Beneath him,

Cockerel's stallion chafed and pranced like an emperor's cocky destrier.

"When was the last time you were on duty to clean the garderobes, lad?"

The guard looked duly affronted. "The king's guards do not clean the latrines, Captain."

"Keep that in mind," Haydan said and lowered his brows, though he feared the full effect of his displeasure may have been lost beneath the wide brim of his borrowed hat. Still, apparently the man grasped his meaning for he straightened and nodded sharply.

"Aye, Sir Hawk. As for the maid, she passed here only minutes ago."

"Which way did she go?"

"Toward the village."

Haydan nodded grimly. 'Twas the same path Rory had taken, he thought bitterly, and setting his heels to the chafing steed, set off after her.

Chapter 23

Restive and temperamental, Cockerel's stallion half reared before dropping back into a high-stepping trot. The bridge rattled as they crossed. Haydan's teeth did the same.

"Calm yourself, you flea-bitten nag," he ordered, but the steed shook his head, tossing his heavy mane and breaking into a snapping canter.

Haydan settled back into the saddle and resigned himself to the ride.

'Twas not many minutes before he caught sight of Catriona. She was riding bareback, hence the speed with which she had managed to leave Blackburn. Her skirts were spread over the mare's croup as she cantered down the beaten trail. He pulled in his mount, but the stallion only cranked his neck down and kept up his pounding speed.

Haydan tightened the reins until finally the recalcitrant beast slowed to a decent pace, allowing the girl to stay well ahead of him. A copse of wild chestnuts and hawthorn crowded the road, which wound and curled like a dark ribbon through the verdant countryside. 'Twas some minutes before he came to the top of a sweeping hillock. Slowing his mount to an unwilling walk, Haydan searched the road ahead. It branched off below him, the right fork mostly hidden behind a copse of trees as it led to the village, the left more visible on its course to the woods beyond. He should be able to see her in a minute, and 'twas to be hoped that he did, for he wanted to know exactly where she entered the forest.

But the minutes ticked by, and he saw nothing but empty road.

The truth dawned on him abruptly. She was not following the Rom's path at all, but had turned off for the village.

With a soaring heart, Haydan loosed the reins and swept down the hill after her.

The noise and bustle of Burnsvale struck Haydan immediately when he passed the wooden palisade. He hurried his gaze about the crowded streets. A tow-headed lad was pulling a two-wheeled cart, a stooped gentleman was squabbling with a cobbler over the price of shoes. All around him, vendors were closing up shops and packing away their goods.

Haydan skimmed his gaze over the cobbled street. Just past the mill he thought he caught a flash of chestnut hide. Concentrating on that spot, he set his heels to his mount and followed. But by the time he reached it, Catriona and her mare were out of sight. He wended his way along, Cockerel's hat pulled low and his gaze ever moving, until he saw a hostler leading a flaxen-maned mare into the stable.

"Celandine," Haydan breathed. The stallion nickered and pranced like a one-horse parade.

Haydan swore in silence, then glancing rapidly about, hurried into the stable. It was dark inside, for the sun had begun its dip past the western horizon and cast long shadows into the musty dimness. He had no time to delay.

In a moment he was free of the horse and scanning the crowd again. It did not take him long to find her, for she was like a princess among peasants. Poetry in her motion, magic in her wake.

He just had to keep her in sight while pretending not to. 'Twould surely not be such a difficult task, he thought, but suddenly he saw a familiar face.

Tipping his head down, Haydan pretended to examine the nearest wares until Blackburn's priest had passed.

"In need of a new chemise?" asked the wench behind the counter. Haydan glanced up. Above her own chemise, her bountiful breasts threatened to escape from the tight laces that pressed them high. Her hands were on her plump hips and there was wry humor in her eyes as she motioned toward the feminine garments. " 'Twould complement your hat, my lord."

"Nay," he said, and glancing sheepishly at the priest's disappearing back, he hurried on with the sound of the maid's chuckle following him.

For a few panicked moments, he feared he had lost Catriona, but finally he spied her stepping into the blacksmith's shop. He paused, but it was dark, and he could see nothing but the glow of coals in the open hearth.

Catriona stepped farther into the smithy's shop. All was dark and still but for the coals that glowed orange amid black in the circular hearth. Outside, she heard the friendly hum of townsfolk bound for their own firesides. Her soul cramped with longing. What she would give for the warmth of normalcy.

"So you have come."

Catriona jerked at the sound of the voice.

"Nay! Do not turn around. Not if you wish to live out the day."

She froze, her heart beating like a wild hare's in her throat.

"I have come," she said. "As you knew I would."

"Aye." She felt him step closer. "We knew. So . . ." She flinched as his fingers brushed her hair. "So eager is the Cat to please if one pulls the proper strings." His hand brushed her shoulder. She jerked, but his fingers clasped there. "The Cat is curious? *Now* you want to become acquainted. But 'tis too late for that, for the reward will come later." His breath hissed hot against her neck. She shivered, her stomach twisting. "Greater even than the promise of burying ourselves . . . burrowing deep . . . deep inside you. Soon, if we are resolute, we shall have the power we so richly deserve. Still . . ." He leaned closer, panting. She felt his face brush her hair, heard him inhale, and trembled at the sound. "Still, we are tempted." His hand slipped lower, over the curve of her waist and onto her hip. "What is your magic? Are you a witch?"

"Nay!" Her own voice was scratchy with fear, her legs wooden.

"Then why can we not forget you?" he asked, and curved his palm slowly over her hip and onto her belly.

She jerked out of his grasp but dared not turn around. "Mayhap 'tis because you have abducted my brother."

His chuckle was breathy. "Aye, we have your brother."

"Is . . . is he well?"

There was a pause, then, "Aye, he is well."

"How do I know that? How do I know you are not lying?"

"You do not."

"Then why should I deliver the king at all?" she whispered.

"Because you are the lad's only hope, and you cherish him above all others."

"I am no martyr." A sob burned her throat but she refused to loose it. She must concentrate, must think. "And I shall not deliver the king unless you swear he is safe."

Silence. She shivered.

"Swear it on your father's name."

"On our *father's* name," he said and laughed. "Aye. We swear it. He is safe."

"I do not believe you."

"He said you would not."

A tiny spark of hope glimmered in Cat's breast. She dared not breathe, lest she blow it out. "He did?"

"Aye. Bold little thing, he is. He said you would never believe he was unmolested, and that I should bring back a herring pie from the village, so we could feast together before I turn him free."

He was alive. He was well. Her hands shook with her certainty.

"We suspect we should beat him for his insolence, but he is such a pretty boy." He crooned the words. "And the guards think him quite clever. Indeed," he said, stepping close again, "They may regret hurting him. But if you fail . . ." His hands were on her hair again, stroking, caressing. "If you tell *anyone* . . . . If you do not come alone . . . he will suffer in ways that you can only imagine and that I can only enjoy."

His lips brushed her ear.

She squeezed her eyes closed. "I cannot do it. I cannot bring him to you."

"Then why are you here?" Brushing her hair aside, he touched his lips to her neck.

She shivered and jerked. "I cannot. 'Tis treason," she whimpered, but he only laughed.

" 'Tis treason," he whispered. "But nevertheless, you have convinced him, have you not?"

She said nothing. In the smothering darkness, she could hear her own heart against her ribs.

"Aye, you have convinced him. For you are a witch. No man is safe from the temptation of you."

"But he is not a man. Just a boy."

"Aye. And even he is ensorceled," he said. Curling her hair about his hand, he tugged it aside and kissed the nape of her neck.

Her stomach roiled. Nausea swamped her, but she fought down the bile.

"When will you bring him?"

"On his birthday," she whispered.

"His birthday!" His hands paused against her hair. "How delightful."

"Where? Where must I take him?"

"All in due time, pretty Cat. You will know soon enough."

"I cannot deliver him if I do not know where to go."

"Ride south to the river, then west," he said, pulling her hair back. "Someone will be there to take you to us."

"I will not turn him over to you until my brother is safe," she rasped, fighting to keep her head upright.

For a moment she felt his anger roll over her like an evil cloud and then he laughed. "So proud," he said and slid his tongue along the lobe of her ear. "But what would you do if I refuse to let him go, Cat? Who would save you? Your Rom friend? The towering captain of the guard?" He laughed. "So forceful they are. But you have them in your power, and I have you in mine. So who is the master here?" he purred.

Her stomach roiled. "I . . . I will not give James up till Lachlan is free."

"James?" He chuckled low in his throat. "You call him James? But of course you do," he answered himself. " 'Tis why our wee plan will succeed, because you are who you are, angel or witch. We are not sure. But you are enticing." His fingers tightened in her hair, tugging her head back.

She gritted her teeth against the pain. "What will happen to him?"

"How tempted we are to taste your treasure," he whispered. "To bury ourselves in you. We wonder, would it be heaven or would it be hell?" he asked and pressed his crotch against her buttocks.

"Let me go!" Panic rose with the bile in her throat.

"We could take you from behind. We know what that is like," he crooned.

"Let me go!" She twisted away, but he had his fingers tangled in her hair, stopping her escape. She felt a draft against her buttocks. He pressed his erection up against her.

"Nay!" she rasped, and swinging her arm frantically backward, slammed her elbow into his face.

He stumbled sideways. Catriona scrambled away, spinning wildly out of the shop and gasping for air. A large man leapt toward her.

Haydan! Relief swamped her, but he ran past.

Not him. Not him, and 'twas a good thing it wasn't.

"If you tell anyone he will suffer."

Lifting her chin, she strode on, her heart like thunder in her chest, her stomach heaving.

A pair of fishwives turned to watched her. She kept walking straight ahead, refusing to look back.

The stable appeared finally. She found Celandine on her own and hurried from Burnsvale.

Darkness cushioned her. Quiet surrounded her. 'Twas only then that she gave in to the nausea.

Hawk strode into his bedchamber. 'Twas only when he'd shut the door behind him that he allowed himself to limp.

Damn his knee! He'd almost learned the truth.

Maybe.

Struggling to his bed, he eased himself onto the mattress.

He had no idea what Catriona had been doing in the smithy. Mayhap she had done nothing more than inquire about replacing her mare's shoe. But if such was the case, why had she cried out?

Though he had vowed to stay out of sight, pure instinct had propelled him toward her. Good sense had made him run past when he knew she was safe, though it had required all his self-control.

But when he burst into the shop, he had found it empty.

'Twas obvious that whoever Cat had seen had no desire to talk to him. On the other hand, maybe any sane person would run for cover if an oversized stranger burst into his place of business growling a threat.

Haydan rubbed his eyes as fatigue washed over him. Sleep was what he needed to solve this puzzle. He closed his eyes to achieve that end, but Catriona appeared immediately in his mind. Her face was ashen, her smoky eyes wide with shock.

Why? What was she scared of? What were her plans?

She had seemed tense during their practice that afternoon, but in his own deluded mind he had hoped that mayhap she had felt a bit of the same passion that haunted him, had been plagued by the raw force of her needs. But then she had excused herself, saying she wished to rest—only to journey secretly to Burnsvale. What had she accomplished there? And why would she risk her own safety for such a sojourn?

True, she seemed to think herself invincible at times. But surely Marta worried. Yet even on the night Cat had spent with him, the old woman had seemed unsurprised by her absence. What had she said? 'So you finally return?'

Haydan sat up abruptly.

Return from what? Catriona had said that Marta was asleep when she left. Therefore she would surely be surprised to find her granddaughter gone. Unless her disappearance was a nightly occurrence!

But no. That could not be. Where would she go?

His stomach coiled. Was she with another? But nay, she had been a virgin in his bed. Surely she would not save her innocence for a score of years only to toss it carelessly aside now.

Surely not—but he was already out of bed and striding down the hall toward Catriona's chamber.

"Sir Hawk!" Catriona stopped abruptly, slamming her heart against her ribs.

"Good morningtide." He looked tired and sharp-edged and strangely dangerous.

"What are you doing at my door?"

He smiled, but the expression curved his lips and did not touch his eyes. "I trust you slept well."

"Aye. Of course."

"You must be famished."

"What?"

"You went to bed straightaway after our practice."

"Oh." Her heart cramped in her chest. Did he know? She stared at him, trying to determine the truth. He stared back, his gaze icy cold. "I am quite hungry."

"Then I shall escort you to the hall to break the fast."

" 'Tis not necessary, Sir Hawk. I have no wish to distract you from your duties."

"Don't you?" he asked, his gaze level.

She caught her breath. "Nay," she managed. Her throat felt tight with fear, but he only smiled.

"In truth, lass, young James needs more freedom. And 'tis good for him to be with younger companions. Mayhap I tend to hold the reins too tight."

" 'Tis only to keep him safe."

"Of course," he said and offering his arm, ushered her away from her door.

The great hall was lively and loud, but they found a spot not far from James's raised dais.

The lad sat with one slim thigh thrown over the arm of his chair as he and a fair-haired boy threw quail bones to the hounds.

Haydan and Catriona shared a trencher of quail and venison, and though her nerves were stretched as tight as a psaltery's strings, it had indeed been a long time since she had eaten, and her stomach cramped with hunger.

In a moment, her mug was filled with honey mead. Raising it to her lips, she drank.

"Lady Cat."

She glanced breathlessly to the side. Blackburn's pale-faced priest inclined his head.

"Sir Hawk," he said.

"Father Matthew," Haydan greeted.

Matthew? Matthew! Catriona's breath stopped in her throat as her gaze went to the priest's copper-bright curls. Her memory screamed of a throbbing member pointing at her like an accusatory finger.

Fayette's lover! Father Matthew. She coughed, choking on her mead as she tried to make sense of the swirling dichotomies. The warrior was kind. The physician was cruel. The priest was immoral. Was no one what he seemed?

"Are you well?" Father Matthew asked, concern in his eyes as he patted her back.

"Aye. Aye. 'Tis just . . . I seem to have swallowed wrong."

He nodded. "You gave me a fright lass. What with last night and now this morn."

"Last night?" Haydan asked, his voice a deep rumble beside her.

"Aye. Our Catriona is quite bold to travel to Burnsvale without an escort, is she not?"

Chapter 24

"Burnsvale?" Haydan said.

Catriona couldn't speak, couldn't move, couldn't think.

"Aye, I saw her in the village last eventide," said the priest, then turned to address her. "Indeed, I thought to make certain you had an escort for the return trip, but I lost you in the crowd. I am glad that the good Lord has brought you safely back to the fold."

"Aye." She choked the word. "Aye. I am fine."

" 'Tis a relief to hear it," he said and turned to stride away.

Catriona turned back to her meal, grappling wildly for something to say.

"You went to the village?" Haydan asked.

" 'Twas a fleeting whim," she said, forcing a laugh.

"But to travel after dark without an escort?" He shook his head. " 'Tis not safe, lass."

" 'Tis not every day that I perform for the king's birthday," she said. "I thought to purchase cloth for a new costume."

He was silent for a moment, his eyes steady as an osprey's. "And did you accomplish your goal?"

Memories flashed through her mind—damp lips against her neck, fingers pawing at her hair, threats whispered like endearments in the dark. "Nay." She stifled a shudder. "Nay, I did not."

His gaze didn't shift a mite.

What did he know? Had others seen her there? For one panicked moment of relief, she had thought it was Haydan running toward her when she'd left the blacksmith's shop. She wondered now if it had been one of his men. Cockerel perhaps, for his dress had been quite cavalier. But no. He had been too large, and no matter how hard she tried to visualize a face beneath the hat's bold, black brim, she could not. Dear God, she should have told Hawk immediately that she had gone to Burnsvale.

She forced herself not to squirm beneath his unflinching gaze.

"I fear I am too particular. I found no cloth that seemed suitable. But I did manage to speak to the smithy about Celandine's injury."

"Oh?"

"Aye. He thought it did not matter if she were shod immediately or not."

"He said nothing else?"

"About what?" The words quivered slightly despite her best attempt to smooth them.

"About your mare."

"Oh! Well, 'twas late. I did not want to take more of his time."

"But so long as you had gone all that way—"

"Lady Cat!" James interrupted, bubbling with youthful exuberance as he bounced up. "I wish to show Fletcher what I have learned."

She jerked her gaze gratefully to the lad, though she

could not, for a time, drag her mind with it. "What you have learned?"

"My new horsemanship skills," he said, his tone exasperated.

"Oh." She breathed the word in wild relief. "Of course," she said and snapped to her feet.

"You needn't go immediately," Haydan said, looking up from beneath lowered brows. "The lad can wait a moment or two."

"But I am the king," James reminded.

"Aye, he is the king," Cat agreed, and bunching her skirts in her hands, fled the hall.

Once outside, she drew the damp air deep into her lungs and prayed for strength. Haydan suspected something. But what?

"Lady Cat," James said, looking up at her with gleaming eyes.

"What?" she asked, glancing at him frantically.

"I asked how your Celandine is faring."

"Oh. Very well."

They reached the stables in a moment. The lad named Fletcher rushed ahead to open the gate and inclined his head when she stepped through with the king and his guards.

James chattered away as Bay was saddled, and soon they stood upon a mossy sward. James was astride in a moment and riding around her in wide circles.

"He is a grand steed," he called, grinning as he flashed by at a centered canter.

"Aye." Her stomach twisted at the sight of his smile. What evil did Blackheart plan for the lad? Surely not death. Surely not.

"We shall have the power we so richly deserve."

He only hoped to abduct the king, hold him for ransom. Nothing more, she told herself, but her gut cramped even harder with the pain of her treason. "James!"

"Aye?"

She had said his name more forcefully than she had planned and calmed her voice now. "What would you do if brigands fell upon you?"

He stopped the steed and drew an imaginary sword. "I would slay the bastards and—"

"Nay!" Panic again, like the flash of too bright lights. "Nay, Your Majesty," she said, lowering her voice and slanting her gaze to his guards, then back to the boy king. If she must deliver James into Blackheart's evil hands at least she would give him some hope of escape. She would take him on Bay and pray for his safe return. "You must flee."

"Flee?"

"Aye. Your steed's speed is your best defense."

"Am I mounted on Bay?" he asked and grinned.

"Aye." She pushed the terror from her mind, concentrating on what she could. "Aye. Bay is beneath you." Walking over, she grasped the gelding's reins. "He is powerful and you are light, but he will do as you command if you are forceful. You must flee."

" 'Tis what I am repeatedly told," he said, his tone registering his disappointment. "But if I am to flee at the first sight of trouble, why do I bother with the swordsmanship Sir Hawk insists on teaching me?"

"He is wise," she said. " 'Tis good to be prepared for any eventuality. But you must flee if you can. Promise me."

He shrugged, looking perplexed. "As you wish."

"But what if someone is holding your reins, just as I am?"

James scowled, then brightened as her earlier lessons came back to him. "The courbette?"

"Aye," she said, relief sluicing through her. "Though he is no horse of war, he is still stronger than any man. If he leaps, the brigand will forfeit his hold. Try it."

"With you holding him?"

"Aye. Try it."

He grinned, then catching his lower lip between his teeth, he concentrated and cued.

Bay settled back lazily on his haunches.

"Nay!" Catriona chided. "You must seize him by the reins even as you command him with your legs. Do it again."

James settled deeper into the saddle, his wiry body tense, his brow furrowed in concentration.

Bay flexed his neck, snapped his forelegs into the air, and leapt, yanking the reins from Cat's hands.

Her fingers stung.

"Excellent. Excellent!" she cheered, pacing back up to him. "But what if there are brigands behind you?"

"The capriole?"

"Aye. Aye. He will leap and kick out behind. But you must not delay lest—"

"Did you see me, Sir Hawk?" James asked, lifting his gaze past her head to where his guards stood.

Dread coiled in Cat's stomach as she turned her attention to the towering captain of the guard.

"I did." He stepped away from the other soldiers as he looked from her to James. " 'Twas quite impressive. But I have just heard news that you have more visitors arriving."

"Visitors?"

"Aye. They are some miles off yet. But Andrew thought he saw your mother's royal banner."

"Mother!" James was sliding out of the saddle and over the gelding's rump in a heartbeat. Then he was off, running toward the turrets with his guards jogging behind him.

Catriona caught Bay's reins and failed, though she tried, to turn toward Hawk.

Silence stretched to the breaking point between them.

She cleared her throat. " 'Tis sad that there must be a festival in order for him to see his mother."

"Politics dictate much," Haydan said. "The queen's marriage to the Earl of Angus has made many nervous. There are those who would not have her visit at all what with her husband's loyalty to the English."

" 'Tis sad," she said again. Her voice quavered like a loosened bowstring. "A boy should be with his kin."

Haydan stepped up close. His arms quivered with the need to turn her toward him, to demand that she tell him all. But he had made that demand innumerable items—it had availed him little. And if he touched her again all sense would be lost, burned away by the fire-hot desire she caused in him.

"Aye. A boy needs his kin," he said, struggling to keep his tone light. Her lips might have learned to lie, but her eyes had not. " 'Tis not too late to send for your brother, Catriona."

A tiny noise escaped from her.

"What say you?" he asked and caught her arm to turn her toward him.

But she had already pressed the back of her hand to her mouth. In a moment she gave him a painful smile. "If only I could."

He held his breath. The truth! He could feel it like an arrow in his gut. "Why can't you?"

Her eyes! So huge and sad it seemed that all the world was lost in them.

But in an instant she shook her head and laughed. He felt her drawing away from him as surely as if she had pulled her arm from his grasp. "I am but being silly. I will see him soon enough. He is happy with his aunt."

The truth had been so close—he wanted to shake it from her. "I thought you said he was with distant cousins."

Her gaze snapped back to his. For a moment, he could feel her fear as easily as he could feel her arm beneath his fingers.

"Nay!" she said, then calmed her voice and began leading her gelding toward the stables. "Nay. I said he is with Hertha and John."

"I must have been mistaken." He had lied, and for a moment she had feared that she had been tripped up. She was not telling the truth about Lachlan. But why? "Is that why you spend time with James?" he asked. "Because you miss your brother?"

"I think, at times, there is little difference between royalty and peasantry," she said. "He reminds me much of Lachlan."

"Have you taught your brother to escape from brigands?"

She stumbled. With his hand on her arm, he kept her from falling and, without thinking, pulled her up close to him.

Her rasped breath brushed his throat. Her eyes, impossibly entrancing, seemed to pierce his very soul.

He all but quivered with their silent appeal.

"Why do you teach the king to flee from brigands?" His stomach felt like a sailor's knot. What the hell did she know that he didn't? And why, oh God, why would she not let him help her?

For a fractured heartbeat of time, he thought she would tell him the truth. But finally she pulled out of his grip. His heart ripped with the separation.

"He is our king," she said, her voice flippant, her eyes haunted. "I thought there would be no harm in teaching him what I could."

He wanted to rail at her. But even if he had the strength to threaten her, he feared she had the strength to withstand him if her need was real enough. "No harm," he said. "I only wondered why."

"No reason." He could see the tension in the way she moved her hands. For a woman whose every movement was poetry, she looked as stiff as a wooden doll. "I am merely fond of him."

"And he of you. Since his brother, the Duke of Ross, died, I think he is lonely. Indeed, I believe he cherishes you much as he would a sister."

Did she blanch? And if so, why? Might she be planning the king some harm? But nay! 'Twas absurd. She had been fond of the lad since their first meeting. He knew that.

But something was afoot, and it was his task to find out what it was. All he need do was stay with her, remain by her side, and prevent whatever evil she was dreading. But when he glanced into her eyes, he remembered the problem with that plan. He had vowed to stay away from her, to keep his distance, for he could not remain within arm's reach and not touch her. Yet he had vowed to his king that he would protect her, as he had vowed to protect James. And whatever she had planned certainly involved the king in some way.

Therefore he had no choice, really.

Turning Bay into his stall, Catriona began to loosen his girth. But her movements seemed no more fluid than they had earlier.

"Here." Haydan nudged her hands aside. "Let me do that."

His shoulder brushed hers and he gritted his teeth against the impact. 'Twas just a wayward touch, nothing more. Nothing significant. He pulled the saddle from the gelding's back and set it aside before turning to remove the bridle. But in that moment their hands brushed, fingers against fingers, flesh against flesh.

Haydan drew sharply back, holding his breath and praying for strength, but when he looked into her eyes there was no strength in all the world.

"Haydan." She said his name like a prayer.

"Aye." He could barely force out the word.

"Was it so bad? Our . . . joining. Was it so wrong?"

Nay. It had been right. The most right of his life and she was so near, so close. He could have that perfection again. He had but to reach out and—

"Nay!" Haydan jerked back his hand. How had he strayed so close to her?

She started at his sudden movement, but he did not apologize. Instead, he paced the narrow, high-walled stall like a fractious steed.

"Nay?" Her voice was small, her eyes slanted like a wide-eyed kitten's. "Then can we not—"

"Nay! Good saints, Catriona!" He raked splayed fingers through his hair. "What do you think that I am? A stud to rent?" He paced the stall again. "A beast who can have you and care naught about either the morrow or the consequences?" He paused. "Not care about the sadness in your eyes?" He had not meant to say that.

"I am sorry," she murmured.

"Sorry!" he rasped, wanting to shake her, to hold her, to take her in his arms and kiss her until she told him everything there was to know about herself. Until he could heal her wounds, soothe her worries.

"I think it best if I return to my room," she said.

"Nay!" he growled and nearly winced at his boorish tone. What was it about her that forever made him act the fool? Perhaps he was entirely wrong. Perhaps she had no troubles beyond loneliness for her brother. "What of our performance?" he asked, carefully softening his tone.

She scowled at him. "You have been wounded," she said, her tone cool now. "Surely James will understand why you cannot perform."

She was drawing away, emotionally and physically. And Haydan's soul ached with the distance.

"But he is the king."

"Your pardon?"

"He is the king and it is his birthday," Haydan said.

She continued to stare at him, her expression haughty, but finally she closed her eyes and shook her head.

"I cannot make sense of you, Haydan the Hawk. I cannot—"

" 'Tis because I make no sense."

She did not disagree. She only stood in silence, watching him.

He blew out a hard breath. "I have fought battles and schemed schemes for king and country, and never have I been defeated. But when you are near . . ." He scowled and wished he had not started down this road, wished instead that he could pull her into his arms and lose the last of his shaky sense in her warmth. "When you are near I am besotted and lame and bumbling. Like a foolish lad yet to be tested in his first battle."

She still stared at him, her brows slightly raised.

He lowered his still more. " 'Tis not all my fault, you know. Not a man at Blackburn has had a grain of sense since your arrival. There are those who think you enchanted."

"And what do you think?"

He tightened his fists and wished to hell that he could take back the entire conversation. "I think 'tis time we practice," he said and forced himself to move closer.

"I think 'tis a poor idea."

"Why?"

"You are a wise man. I believe you know."

"I myself am often surprised at what I do not know," he countered.

"Do you want the truth then, Haydan the Hawk?"

He wanted to say no. But he was trapped in her eyes, in the husky tone of her voice, and for a moment he could not speak at all.

"Tell me truth," he said.

"I want to feel your magic again. I care little for your honor or mine. I want you as I have never wanted another."

The air made a painful escape from his lungs.

" 'Tis strange," she murmured. "All these years that I have fought for my virtue. And now, when I no longer wish to fight . . ." her eyes looked unusually bright.

"Don't cry." The words sounded panicked to his own ears. "Please. Truly, lass, I do not think I could bear it if you cry."

She raised her chin. "And what would His Majesty's fierce captain do if I shed tears?"

He tried to muster a wee bit of pride, but there was none to be found. "Anything you wish," he admitted.

She laughed, though the sound was wobbly. " 'Tis

unfortunate for me, then, that I am not the crying sort." She drew a deep breath, making him wonder how close she was to the end of her resources. "And just as unfortunately, I made a vow to the king."

Haydan nodded. "As did I."

They began their practice in a sheltered grassy spot immediately, yet every time Hayden touched her his will weakened a bit more until finally he found to his wordless surprise that he could not let her go at all.

They stood face to face, his hands on her waist as the world faded to nothing. There was only her, her sadness, her strength, her eyes, drawing him closer still.

"I think he is busy," said a voice from behind Cat.

Haydan dropped his hands and looked over Catriona's shoulder.

"Lassies!" he said, and his heart leapt at the sight of the three young women who stood before him.

Chapter 25

They came in a blur of colors and scents, three maidens rushing toward the Hawk with smiles and laughter as they piled into his arms.

Catriona watched in aching surprise, but in a moment the nearest maid turned toward her.

"Catriona," she said, her voice low and husky.

It took Cat a moment to realize that this lady dressed in silks and an elegant coif was the same woman who had danced barefoot and wild at her campfire a lifetime before. "Rachel?" she asked.

The dark-haired lady laughed even as the other two turned toward Catriona, and now she recognized them also—the auburn-haired Shona, and the sunlight that was Sara. A trio of stunning women who had loved a man called Haydan the Hawk long before Catriona had met him.

" 'Tis me," Rachel said. "But what might you be doing here?"

It seemed like many long years ago that this same woman had called herself Flora and traveled with Cat's gypsy band; long ago that she had saved Lachlan from sure death. Yet for a moment it seemed that those years were but minutes, and Catriona wanted nothing more than to fall into her arms and beg for advice, for help.

But she couldn't afford that weakness.

"I have come to perform for the king," she said.

"So we are to be privy to the Lady Cat's renowned performances?" Shona said, then gave Sara a slanted glance. "Mayhap you had best send your Boden off hunting on that day, cousin. You know how his eyes wander when there be a bonny maid around."

Sir Boden Blackblade, Catriona remembered, was about as faithless as a deer hound, dark, adoring, and looming.

"Mayhap 'tis your Dugald we'd best send to hunt," Sara countered. "What with your sharp tongue, he—"

"All is well, I hope."

Catriona returned her gaze to Rachel, who seemed to have no qualms about interrupting her cousins' banter.

"Aye," Cat's tone was surprisingly light, though Rachel's bright, otherworldly eyes continued to pierce her. "Aye. All is well."

"I do not have a sharp tongue," Shona said, then turned to look at Catriona and scowled. "Still, it would not hurt to keep Dugald otherwise entertained, I suspect. What of you, Rachel? Shall we invent something to occupy your Liam's time?"

But the woman did not turn from Catriona. "Your grandmother? She is doing well?"

Catriona forced a laugh. "Of course. She is as strong as a Highland gale." And just as eerie as this woman when there was a secret that needed keeping. "She will outlive the lot of us."

Rachel smiled, her eyes softening. " 'Tis glad I am to hear it."

"We might have an archery contest at the same time

as her performance," Shona suggested. "Dugald is far too vain to miss such an opportunity."

"Unfortunately, so are you," Sara said.

"So I am sharp-tongued *and* vain?" Shona asked, raising a brow at her fair-haired cousin. "I fear you have—"

"Haydan," Rachel interrupted smoothly. "I have spent many a weary hour with my vociferous cousins in the past few days. Mayhap you could take them to the great hall and . . ." She shrugged. "Get them inebriated?"

Haydan scowled, flicked his gaze to Catriona, then back to Rachel. "I fear I have duties to—"

"But surely nothing more important than entertaining your nieces," Rachel interrupted. Her gaze was sharp as a hunting raptor's in her angelic face. "Truly," she said. "If I have to spend another minute in their bickering company I shall not be accountable for my actions."

"Bickering!" Shona said, offended.

"You do bicker," Sara admitted.

"One cannot bicker alone," Shona said. "Indeed, you—"

"Ladies," Rachel interrupted. "And I use that term with the utmost levity. Can you not see what is afoot here?"

Sara grinned. "Our Hawk is falling in love?"

Haydan started in surprise. "What the devil are you talking about?"

Shona laughed. " 'Tis fairly clear, Haydan. She is talking about you and the Gypsy lass."

"I—" he began, but Rachel was already shooing them away.

"Go now," she ordered her cousins. "You see what you can wring out of him; I'll talk to the Cat."

For a moment Catriona thought he would argue; then he raised his arms to the women he called nieces.

"Come, lassies," he said. "I go to reprimand your husbands for turning you loose on Blackburn."

"What about getting us inebriated?" Shona asked, taking his arm. "Dugald would be quite jealous."

"Just what I want," Haydan murmured as he turned with them on his arms. "A drunken assassin angry at me."

"He's not an assassin anymore," Shona reminded him.

"I am so relieved."

"Aye," Sara added. "And he hardly ever kills anyone when his wife makes him jealous. I am certain you are quite . . ." Her voice faded as they walked away.

Catriona turned her gaze nervously to Rachel. 'Twas not on some silly whim that the Lady Saint had sent her cousins away. That much she knew.

" 'Tis good to see you, Catriona," Rachel said.

"And good to see you."

"Is it?"

"Certainly. Why would it not be?"

"I thought mayhap we were interrupting at a bad time."

"Nay."

"Then you've had plenty of other time for loving our Haydan?"

"You have more imagination than I gave you credit for, Rachel. Indeed, there was a time when you first danced that I thought you had none at all."

Rachel laughed. "You love him," she said without a hint of doubt.

Uncertainty coiled through Catriona, but she struggled to maintain the lie. "I fear you've gotten the wrong impression."

Rachel raised her dark brows. "I rarely do."

Her eyes were wide, amethyst in color, and all-knowing. Catriona turned her own downward. She had lived with her grandmother far too long to think she could look into that sort of eyes and not give up her secrets. Best then, to let herself be distracted by her feelings for Haydan.

"In truth, he does not love *me*," Cat said softly.

"Nay?"

Catriona shook her head. "He is a knight in the personal service of the king, and I am . . ." She shrugged. "A Gypsy."

"And for that reason he does not love you?" Rachel asked and hooked Cat's arm with her own. "Truly, it might be that you do not know our Hawk as well as you might think. Come, let us discuss him at length."

As Haydan strode down the hallway, candlelight flickered in his wake. The hour was late, but Catriona was finally safely abed, and he could wait no longer. Stopping before an arched door, he raised his hand to rap on the timber, but it opened before his knuckles struck wood.

Rachel stepped silently into the hall. "The babes are fast asleep," she murmured and motioned him to follow her. "Have you, perchance, seen my husband?"

"Aye. He is playing tables with my guards in the hall."

"How big are they?'

"Bigger than he."

She sighed. "Any sign of violence?"

"Not yet. I wished to ask you something."

"Aye. She is."

"What?" he asked, glancing down at her.

"Catriona." She hurried down the stairs. "She is in danger."

Haydan drew a deep breath. "I do not know if I should be spooked by your gift or horrified that you have come to my own conclusion."

"You've little time to be either spooked or horrified."

His gut clenched. "How much time?"

"In truth, I do not know." Hurrying through the doorway of the great hall, she came to an abrupt halt as her gaze skimmed the faces there—a few noblemen, old Marta, and a trio of guards who were scowling at a dark-haired man with a scoundrel's grin.

A sliver of a smile played over her lips as she watched her husband. Liam the Irishman, he was called. A bigger rogue was not to be found, and yet she had tamed him. "You love her, don't you?" she asked, not drawing her gaze from the gamblers.

"I fear you have your cousins' sense of the ridiculous. I am but determined to protect her, for I think of her like a daughter and—"

"Like a daughter?" She raised her brows at him. "If I thought that were true, I would be praying night and day for your immortal soul," she said and turned her uncanny eyes on him.

Still, he could not admit the truth—not to her, and certainly not to himself.

"What kind of danger is she in?" he rasped.

"Grave danger."

Frustration cracked through him like the lash of a whip. "What sort of grave danger?"

"I do not know."

"Do not know? You are your mother's daughter, as eerie as she. Surely you know."

"Why is Lachlan not with her?" she asked.

Haydan drew a deep breath, forcing himself to relax. "She said he stayed behind with Hertha."

"She adores the lad," Rachel said. "And yet she barely speaks of him."

"Could it be—" He paused, pain twisting his soul. "Could it be that he is dead, and she cannot accept it?"

Rachel remained silent for a moment, then shook her head slowly. "Nay. I do not think so. I did not feel that sort of empty sadness."

"Might he be ill?" Haydan guessed.

"She would never leave him."

"Mayhap he is wounded and recuperating."

"Then she would speak of his recovery, his insatiable appetite for herring pie, his smile." Her brow furrowed at her private thoughts. "He is a bonny child," she whispered.

Haydan stiffened. "You see him now?"

She didn't answer, but kept her gaze on the far wall.

"Rachel," Haydan rasped, gripping her arm. "Where is he?"

"Not among friends. And yet he laughs, though they keep him confined."

"Abducted!" Haydan hissed, fear snaking through him like hot venom.

Rachel turned her gaze on him, her expression flat.

"Why?" Haydan asked. "Who are they? What do they want?"

But in that moment she closed her eyes and shook her head. "I know not. It might be that I am entirely wrong."

"What would they want?" he repeated, his fingers stiff about her slim arm.

"She is special," Rachel said.

"Do you think I do not know—" Haydan began, but he stopped abruptly. "Are they holding the lad until she gives herself up to them?" His heart was slamming against his ribs. "Might she be the princess of her wild tales? Perhaps they want her for that reason."

Rachel scowled. "She did not turn her back on Liam and me when we brought her nothing but trouble. How much more easily would she risk her life for her brother?" She was silent for a moment. "Could it be that she is to deliver another in exchange for her brother's safe return?"

Haydan remained unmoving, unable to speak as his own horrid fears were voiced.

"Has she been spending time with anyone in particular?"

Darkness settled steadily into Haydan's soul. "Nay. It cannot be," he murmured. "James is watched every minute. As is she."

"Is she? Every minute? Who is watching her now?"

"Galloway."

Her eyes were unearthly steady. "I saw the way you looked at her, Hawk. I doubt you would trust any man to watch her sleep."

His body felt leaden and heavy, his mind as slow as a dirge. "What do you suspect?"

"The same as you."

"Nay!" he rasped. "She would not—"

"Sir Hawk." Liam's voice was casual, though his expression was no longer cheerful as he stood beside his wife. "I would challenge you to a duel, but me daughter is too young to lose the father she adores."

Hawk turned his scowl on the roguish Irishman.

"You are squeezing me wife's arm," Liam explained.

Haydan lowered his gaze to where his hand gripped Rachel's arm, then turned with a start and hurried away.

The floor rang beneath his heels. Darkness consumed his mind, and in a moment he stood before Catriona's door.

"She remains inside?" he asked.

Galloway straightened. "Aye." He did not ask where she might have gone, but Haydan could see the question in his eyes.

"No noise?"

"What?"

"You have heard no noise?"

Galloway frowned. "Nay."

"And the other nights?"

"Your pardon?"

Impatience rolled inside Haydan like a dark cloud, but he clenched his jaw and slowed his speech. "Have you heard noise any of the other nights?"

"Nay. All is quiet."

Haydan's mind spun as he stared at Cat's door. What secrets were hidden behind that solid portal?

"Is something amiss, sir?"

Haydan turned his gaze back to the younger man. "Guard her door," he said. "And do not, under any circumstances, fall asleep. Make certain no one goes in or comes out. Do you understand?"

"Aye, sir," Galloway said.

Haydan turned rapidly away, but the young man stopped him. "Sir?"

He turned back with a scowl.

"What am I guarding her from?"

Terror coiled in Haydan's belly. "Herself," he said and hurried away.

Outside, it was cool and damp. Mist lowered like a lace curtain over Blackburn's courtyard. Haydan wrapped his cloak about himself and waited. His eyes burned and his knee complained, but he stayed on his feet, for hunkering down against the stone behind his back invited sleep. And he could not afford to sleep. Not when he had no answers.

As the night dragged on, his muscles stiffened with cold and immobility. He shifted slightly in the shadows of the tower, flexing an arm and wondering for the hundredth time if he were insane. After all, he had no concrete proof that anything was amiss. The fact that Catriona religiously denied it should surely set his mind at ease. And even if it was not the truth, even if there were some trouble in her life, 'twas not *his* trouble.

But from the start her eyes had haunted him, and now he had collaboration. Rachel Forbes was not called the Lady Saint for nothing. She had seen something in Catriona's eyes, had sensed something just as surely as Haydan had.

There was a sadness there, a fear just below the surface. True, she smiled and she laughed, but it was not quite right, not quite true. He could hear it in the melody of her voice, could feel it in the touch of her hand.

Only on one occasion had she seemed untroubled. Only when he held her in his arms, when she had forgotten all and lost herself in pleasure, had she seemed whole and at peace.

Never, not if he lived forever, would he forget the feel of her against him. The satin-soft slide of her hair against his chest, the husky murmur of her sigh in his ear.

He could hear it now, he thought and reached for her.

Haydan awoke with a start. Good Christmas, he was losing his mind. Mayhap the rumors were true. Maybe she truly was an enchantress. Maybe she had ensorceled him and—

And what the hell was that?

A movement halfway up the wall?

He froze, his heart pumping hard and fast.

A shadow was slipping sideways not far from James's window. But it could not be, for 'twas several rods above the ground. He blinked, trying to clear his head, to focus his thoughts. But in that instant, the shadow was gone, faded into nothingness. 'Twas naught but his imagination.

But his gut told another tale. 'Twas Catriona, escaped from her room!

Chapter 26

Haydan launched himself from the wall. His knee locked, nearly spilling him to the hard-packed earth, but he caught his balance and hurtled toward the keep. Throwing open the door, he rushed inside.

The stairs flew beneath his feet. The floor echoed with his panic.

The king's guards jerked to attention when he charged into view. He delayed not an instant, but burst into the room. The door ricocheted off the wall.

In the midst of his gargantuan bed, James sat up with a start.

"Hawk?" His voice wavered in the near darkness, and by the light of a single flickering candle, Haydan could see the boy's wide eyes.

"James." His own voice sounded husky and breathless as he slowed to a walk. "You are well?"

The boy's brow puckered. "Aye. I am well."

Haydan paced to the windows. They were broad, stained in bright hues and veined in lead. They were also closed and locked.

Haydan checked each one before striding to the boy's bed.

"And you?" the lad asked.

"What?" Haydan calmed himself, forcing his movements to slow. One of the guards, he noticed, had followed him inside.

"Are you well?" James asked. "I could call upon Physic."

"Physic?" Haydan asked. The boy never called Blackburn's healer Physic. Leech was his favored name for the sickle-nosed physician. Suspicions bloomed like wild thistles in Hawk's head. It would not be the first time there had been an impostor in the young king's place. Could such be the case again?

"You do not remember who Physic is?" the boy asked.

Haydan stared at the boy suspiciously, but the lad had James's whip-quick mind and his sleepy eyes were full of growing mischief just as they should be. Still, he could not be too careful.

Haydan turned to the guard. "You may return to your post. All is well."

The guard nodded once and disappeared, though his expression showed some doubt as to Haydan's sanity.

James looked no more certain.

"Tell me, Sir Hawk," he said, bending his knees to circle his arms about the mound they made in the scarlet blanket. "Do you plan to tell me why you are here, or shall I guess?"

Yes, the lad had the Stuart attitude.

"Guessing might be more fun," Haydan said, trying to soothe his impatience. It refused to be soothed. "But I fear I have no time. So I ask you this, Your Majesty: Long ago, when your life was in danger, with whom did you travel to the Highlands?"

"You forget?"

"Nay." Haydan forced himself not to grit his teeth, but rarely had the lad's tongue been more annoying. "I but want to hear it from you."

James grinned as if this were some new game. " 'Twas Lady Shona of the clan MacGowan who took me under her wing."

Haydan nodded, but perhaps that secret had eked its way into common knowledge, so he frantically searched his mind for one more suitable question.

"And when you escaped from Warwick," he said, narrowing his eyes at the lad, "how—"

"I slid down the garderobe," interrupted James. " 'Twas filthy." He grinned. "But quite ingenious."

"I was going to ask how you were dressed," Haydan said and held his breath, for this was a part of the story that did not please the king so greatly. He would not readily have told another, even in an effort to use the impostor's identity for a night of sport.

The boy scowled. "This game is becoming less amusing."

"Forgive me, Your Majesty," Haydan said, every muscle taut with the wait. "But 'tis important."

James hesitated an instant, then, "I was dressed in naught," he said, his face coloring slightly. "Between the slide down the latrine and the river's wild current, my garments abandoned me completely, traitorous things. Now what is this about?"

"Your safety," Haydan said. Relief flooded him in a wild rush, but he held it at bay. Yes, the king was safely abed, but there was much else to learn. "Make me one promise."

"I shall not," James said, sitting straighter. "Unless you tell me truly why you are here."

He thought fast. "I heard Shona's foster son has arrived with his family. I but wished to be certain that you were still you and he was still he."

"Kelvin is here?" James spouted, swinging his legs out of bed.

"Aye," Haydan said and strode swiftly toward the lad to urge him back onto the mattress. "But he will not have forgotten any of his wayward thoughts before the morrow. There will be time aplenty for the two of you to cause trouble then."

"Does he still look like me?"

"Regardless how he looks, you will not be trading identities with him again," Haydan said, settling the blankets over the boy's narrow chest.

The lad smiled impishly. "You would not know if I did."

"I would know," Haydan assured him, and giving in to a weakness for one instant, he swept the boy's hair back from his brow. "Now for the promise. Say you will not allow anyone in through this window."

The lad's brows shot up. "Anyone such as whom?"

"Anyone."

He should have expected the grin. "But what if some daring lass climbs to my window and begs for my help? I can hardly turn her away."

"Are you expecting this lass tonight?"

James scowled as if disappointed by the truth. " 'Twould seem unlikely."

Haydan forced himself to relax. "Then promise you will let no one in, lad, I beg of you. At least until the festivities are finished."

The boy shrugged. "As you wish."

Haydan nodded. "Sleep then," he said and turned away.

"Sir Hawk," James called.

"Aye, lad?"

"You worry too much," he said and turned his back to the door.

Hawk stepped into the hall.

"All is well?" asked a guard.

"Aye," Hawk said and strode away, his mind spinning.

Was he insane? He had been so sure. So certain that Catriona's sadness somehow involved the king. But she had not been in James's chambers. Had he imagined the shadow on the wall? Maybe, but he had to act as if he had not. He did not know why Catriona was prowling the halls, but he would soon find out. First, he had to figure out where she was, though. He could go to her room and wait for her return, but there was no reason to believe she would ever admit to her activities. Nay, he must catch her in the act. But where was she?

He tried to remember where the shadow had been; where it had disappeared.

She was in this wing, but beyond that he knew little. He could only search. For one moment, he debated calling assistance. But he could not. Though his soul ached with his own weakness, he could not allow others to know of her activities, for if he was right—if she planned some evil against the king—

Haydan closed his mind grimly against the thought and continued his search.

The night dragged on forever as he listened for any sound, checked every shadow. But he found nothing, until finally, his mind burning with questions, he paced toward her room. There was naught to do now, but wait at her door and—

A noise! Just around the corner.

He stopped abruptly and pressed his back against the

wall. A creak filled the darkness. He waited, breath held. Was it she? Had she turned the other way?

But suddenly a shadow appeared. Without thought, without warning, he grabbed hold.

There was a gasp. She tried to jerk away, but the effort was small and he held on.

"What . . . what do you want?"

Coldness settled into Haydan's gut at the sound of her voice. He pulled her closer. "You!" he growled.

She stiffened, and then, like a wilted flower, she collapsed.

He felt her fall. She'd been wounded, he thought, and bent to lift her into his arms. But in that instant, she kicked out wildly. The first strike hit his thigh. The second was more effective. Fire burst in his knee. He staggered back against the wall with a rasp of pain.

It took him a moment to realize she was scrambling away.

"Nay!" he growled and threw himself after her.

His fingers tangled in something, and he pulled. She shrieked as she was yanked against his chest. "Let me—" she began, but he jerked his fingers from her hair and clasped his hand over her mouth.

From somewhere down the hall, he heard a door open. Squeezing her closer against his chest, he propelled her around the corner and pressed his back against the wall. Pain pounded his knee like the strike of a blacksmith's hammer. He gritted his teeth and tightened his grip.

She mewled against his palm.

"Quiet!" he growled.

Her elbow slammed against his ribs. He sucked in his breath, but kept his hand steady.

From around the corner, two voices piped up in question.

He had no choice but to propel her forward, his hand still pressed against her mouth as he steered her away from the voices and toward his room.

Hell would surely have been no farther, but he managed to force her inside finally and close the door behind them.

He turned her loose. She spun toward him and backed away.

"I'll know why," he said.

Even in the darkness, he could see her eyes widen, could hear her sharp intake of breath. "Haydan?"

"Aye." He filled his lungs with air and willed himself to disavow the pain. "I've waited a long while for the truth. I will know it now."

Silence answered him, then, "The truth?"

Anger made him take a step toward her. Fear made her back away.

"I don't know what you're talking about."

"Truly? So you always sneak from your window in the wee hours of the morn?"

He could hear her breathing. "I did no such thing."

"Aye, you did." He took another step. She retreated. "Repeatedly, I think. I will know why."

"You've no right to question me."

"I do, for I am the king's guard. Do you disremember?"

"I've done naught to disturb the king."

"Nay, only to disturb me, lass. Why were you in that room?"

"I am sorry." Her voice was breathy.

He scowled. "What?"

"I did not mean to hurt you. Indeed . . ." He could see her hands meet in the darkness. "I did not think you would find out."

"Find what out?"

"You cannot blame me, Haydan. I was not meant to be alone."

Silent moments ticked away as he debated her words. "Do you mean to say were . . . seeking companionship?"

"Aye."

He stared at her for a moment, and then he threw his head back and laughed.

"What is so amusing?"

"I have heard better lies, lass."

"You think I lie? Then here is the truth, Haydan the Hawk. I gave myself to you, thinking we shared something special betwixt us. But since that night you have repeatedly turned me aside. And now I find . . . I find I cannot bear to be alone after—"

"Don't!" he warned in a low hush.

Her breath hissed between her teeth. "Don't what?"

"Don't lie to me, Catriona. Not now. Not after you kicked me in the knee. 'Tis not nice."

She raised her chin. "I am not lying."

"Oh? Who were you with this night?"

A moment of silence, then, " 'Tis none of your affair. I gave you a chance, but you did not take it. Thus I will find another. 'Tis the way with women."

"What the devil are you talking about?"

"Lady Fayette offered herself to MacKinnon but he turned her aside—that's why she goes to others. 'Tis the same with me. I thought you cared for me, but it seems you only wanted my innocence. Others are not so choosy."

His stomach twisted at the thought of her with another. Rage boiled like black tar, but still he wanted her, whore or saint. Even now, when he was filled with anger and pain and roiling frustration, his senses were filled with her. "You forget," he said. "I did not think you were a virgin, and still I wanted you."

"You did not want *me*," she said. "You but wanted a few hours of my time." She paused, looking small and frightened. "I wanted more. I wanted your love." Her voice was little more than a whisper. "But I see I do not have that, for you cannot even bear to touch me." She took a step closer, but he tightened his grip on her wrist in warning.

"Who were you with?" he asked, his voice low in the darkness.

"Lord Drummond," she said.

"Drummond!"

"And why not? He is a handsome man."

" 'Tis said he raped his first betrothed. Is that what you want? A violent man who would lie with you even as he tries to win another's hand in—" He paused and drew a deep breath, then loosed her arm and stepped back a pace. "You lie," he said softly.

Quiet held the room, then, "Ask him," she said.

Pain ripped his insides, diminishing the ache in his knee, but he could not quit now. "As you wish," he said, and placing his hand on the latch, nodded toward the door. "You first."

She didn't move. "I want you."

"What?"

" 'Tis you I want."

He dropped his hand from the latch. Pain turned to agony.

" 'Tis the truth," she murmured. "I swear it, Haydan. Say you will forgive me and I will never again lie with another." She stepped up to him. Her nearness filled his head. She touched his cheek. He closed his eyes to the confusion, the temptation. She was promising to be his!

Why, he didn't know, but surely it didn't matter.

Her fingers trembled against his cheek. She was scared. Why?

Reaching up, he took her hand in his and kissed it gently.

"Let us talk to Drummond," he said and reached for the latch again.

"Nay!" She jerked out of his grip.

He watched her in the darkness. "Why not?"

" 'Twould be . . .'Twould be embarrassing."

"So you can lie with him but you cannot speak to him?"

She jerked a nod.

"Come," he said and grabbed her hand again.

She tried to pull from his grip, but he held on, drawing her closer.

"Tell me the truth, lass, and I'll not make you talk to Drummond."

" 'Tis the truth!"

Rage spurred through him. Taking her by the arms, he shook her. "Damn you, Catriona! You've no right to make me love you if you will not trust me."

"You love me?" she whispered.

"Tell me, God damn it, or I will lock you away until I know you are safe from whatever evil you fear."

Her face went white as death in the darkness. "You would not."

"I swear I will," he growled.

" 'Tis Lachlan," she whispered. "They have taken my brother."

Chapter 27

"Who?" Haydan rasped. "Who has taken Lachlan?"

"I do not know." She lifted her gaze to his. The truth shone there in all its dark misery. "I do not know who has him," she whispered. "But Lachlan will die if I do not follow his orders."

"What does he want from you?"

"Jewels!" She croaked the word and grasped his tunic in clawed hands. "He said he wanted jewels. I told him I have no jewels. I told him. He laughed. He said he did not expect me to own them, but to steal it. After all, Gypsies are all thieves."

"You have been stealing?" he asked.

She was silent for a moment, not breathing. " 'Tis not just any jewels he wants, but a special medallion."

"The vellum drawing I saw. 'Tis that for which you search."

" 'Tis for my brother's life," she whispered.

"Why did you not ask for me help?"

"I dared not," Cat whispered. Turning her face against his chest, she cried. "He said if I told anyone, Lachlan will die."

He squeezed her to him, pressing her against his heart, aching with her horror.

"I have killed him!" she rasped. "I have killed him."

"Nay. Nay!" He pushed her away far enough to see her face. "You have not killed him, lass. 'Tis not true." He shook her gently, forcing her to look up. "There's no way for the brigand to know you have told."

"He'll find out," she whimpered. "He'll find out and kill him."

"Not so long as there is breath in my body!" Haydan growled. " 'Twill be the villain that dies."

"Nay!" Her eyes widened in abject terror. "You must not try to learn his identity. I cannot risk Lachlan. He is all I have."

"Lass—"

"Nay!" She tightened her fingers like talons against his arms. "Please, promise you will not. I will find the medallion. I must."

"I will assist you," he said, tightening his grip on her. "We will find it together, and I will purchase it from him."

"What if he refuses to sell it?"

"I will find a way to convince him. But only if you vow to take no more risks."

"I must deliver it to him very soon."

"Nay. I will do that."

"He said I could bring no one."

"You will not. I will go alone."

"But—"

"Nay!" he said, gritting his teeth. "I will deliver the medallion to the bastard. Just as I will deliver the lad to you."

She opened her mouth as if to speak, but he shushed her.

"You have my pledge, Catriona. As God is my witness, I shall not fail you."

Her hands trembled against his chest as she rose to kiss him. Her lips tasted of salt. He cupped her face in his palms and allowed himself a brief glimpse of heaven, but in a moment he drew away.

" 'Tis time you return to your room."

"Nay." Her fingers clutched his tunic. "Please, Haydan." She drew a shuddering breath. "Life is short. There is no guarantee that we will see another tomorrow. And if I die this night, I would wish to die in your arms."

He tried to be strong. He tried to refuse. But she trembled again and there was nothing he could do but lift her into his arms and carry her to his bed. It sighed beneath her weight. He leaned over her, and she pulled him down beside her.

Their lips met, but her hands were already moving, tugging up his tunic, tossing it to the floor. She rolled to the top and pressed her face against his chest. Haydan felt his heart thrum against her ear. She remained there for a moment, and then, turning, she kissed his heartbeat before sliding down the midline of his body. He trembled beneath her, awed by her power.

Her hands freed his belt and plaid. He felt it give way and reached for her garments, but she captured his hands. Kissing each one, she nudged them aside, then with agonizing slowness, she undressed herself.

She seemed to shine in the darkness, like a beacon in the blackest night. He slid his hands about her waist, worshipping her, urging her closer As she leaned over him, her nipples caressed his chest. Her bottom lapped his erection, and then, like a goddess of yore, she welcomed him inside.

He sucked in his breath and pressed into her. Her eyes

fell closed and she moved against him. There was no delay this time. No thought of waiting, for they needed more than they could say with words, and so they strove to please and be pleased, to touch and caress and give until they were poised on the edge of relief.

She leaned over him, her breasts like fire against his chest as she increased her pace. 'Twas all he could do to await her pleasure, to see her fall over the edge of desire before he lifted her from him and found his own aching release.

"*That* is his lady?" asked Roderic.

Haydan turned a glare toward his half-sister's husband. The great hall was crowded with the noble families of Scotland. Haydan's own kinsmen, the MacGowans and the Forbeses, were gathered around him like bad apples, and there was none more likely to cause trouble than Roderic the Rogue.

"She is not my lady," Haydan said, but Shona had already leaned across the table to speak to her father.

"They are planning a performance together," she said.

Haydan gritted his teeth. The noise level had risen with the hour. 'Twas late now and loud, and most of the young folk had been ushered to bed.

Beyond the towering windows, the night was dark, but inside, a hundred candles blazed. Upon the center dais, not far from James and his multiple bodyguards, an elderly bard sang a melancholy ballad.

Tremayne listened with tears in his rheumy eyes. Lord Drummond pressed closer to Lady Fayette. MacKinnon watched. The Earl of Hogshead drank himself into a good-natured stupor.

And Catriona . . .

She was there, not far from the king's side.

Haydan's breath caught in his throat at the sight of her, but he forced his gaze away.

"A performance?" Roderic asked.

"Aye. On horseback, I am told," Shona added.

"Horseback?" Flanna asked. Though she was Haydan's half-sister, she had raised him as a son. Seated beside her husband, the lady flame of the MacGowans looked like an auburn-haired queen. 'Twas a well-known fact that her clan would have only half their power and wealth were it not for her own steeds. "I thought she was a tumbler."

"Oh, she is more than a tumbler, Mother," Shona said. "She is a juggler and an artist and a . . . a magician, is she not, Hawk?"

Was it the truth? Haydan wondered. Had Catriona told him everything? It seemed right. It felt right. And yet—

"Haydan."

"What?" he growled, and his family laughed at his snappish mood.

"It seems our Hawk has found his prey," Roderic said.

"From what I hear, she is more the huntress than the hunted," said his daughter.

"Secrets," a woman murmured.

Haydan spurred his gaze toward Rachel, but her own attention was captured by her mother, Fiona, the renowned Lady of the Forbeses. The two turned as one toward him.

Their combined attention hit him like a rock to the gut. He had spent some years with Lady Fiona. 'Twas she who had nursed him from a failing lad into manhood. And never in those years had he managed to keep a secret of any substance from her. 'Twas eerie, is what it was.

"What can I do, Haydan?" she asked softly.

The bard's song came to an end.

Haydan shook his head. "All is well, Lady Fiona."

"Are you certain?"

It was then that he noticed that Catriona was gone. Panic ripped through him. He snapped his gaze to the king, and there she was, seated beside him, their heads together as they talked.

Haydan was on his feet in an instant.

"Haydan?" Rachel said.

But he was already fighting his way through the crowd.

"Kelvin is here," James whispered.

Catriona sat very still, barely breathing. "Kelvin?"

James grinned. "My twin," he said, but then leaned closer still and laughed. "In truth, he is Lady Shona's fostered son. But he could be my own double."

She stared at him, her gut twisted in hard knots.

"When I sneak from the castle, 'twill be that much easier if Kelvin is in my chambers while—"

"Nay!" she snapped, then forced her voice to soften and her fists to open beneath the table. "Nay, Your Majesty. We must not involve others." Especially not Haydan's beloved family.

"Then how—"

"I will think of a way," Cat said, and her gut tightened another turn.

"When? 'Twill have to be soon. My birthday is only—"

"Your Highness," Haydan interrupted.

Catriona tried to look nonchalant as she turned her gaze to him. Dressed in a bright ceremonial plaid and deep blue doublet, he was bowing toward them.

"Your guests are requesting that you play the psaltery."

The boy made a face. "Now?"

Haydan moved closer. "The crowd is getting restive."

"Aye." Lord Tremayne appeared beside him. "It might be wise to remind them that we are a cultured lot and not a mob of wild barbarians."

James grinned. "I like wild barbarians."

Tremayne straightened, his cheekbones shining as sharp as blades in his parched face as he turned toward Haydan. "I have warned you to keep your savage kin away from His Majesty."

"There is naught like music to soothe the savage soul," Haydan said, and canted his head toward James. "A tune, sire? Mayhap sung in Latin?"

"French is more lively," James said, his eyes mischievous

Haydan bowed again. "French it is. Cockerel?"

The guard stepped up, psaltery in hand, as if snapped straight out of Haydan's imagination.

James took it as he rose to his feet.

Lord Tremayne cleared his throat and lifted his chicken-thin neck. "King James of the royal Stuart line will now gift us with a song," he called.

There were cheers and whistles before James settled onto the edge of a table and struck the first notes. They sailed clear and sweet across the wide hall, and soon his words joined in a language Catriona could not identify, but only appreciate, for he had a fine voice and a gift for emotion. Her own raw feelings welled like tears inside her—feelings of loyalty and love and honor.

"You are well?" Haydan asked.

She forced herself to turn toward him with a smile. "Aye."

Their gazes met. She caught her breath as a crush of new feelings and a hundred vivid memories assailed her. She could not betray him. There had to be another way.

"Haydan," she whispered.

But he lifted his gaze past her shoulder. "Is there something you need, Lord Tremayne?" he asked.

"We should have held the festivities at Stirling," said the old man. " 'Twould have been easier to guard him."

"You needn't worry," Haydan said. " 'Tis my responsibility."

"Aye. And your neck if anything should happen to him," Tremayne said. Turning, he wended his way through the crowd.

"Lady Cat," someone called. "Give us a performance."

"Aye," James said, his song finished. " 'Tis my birthday, you know."

"I've nothing prepared," she demurred.

"Then what has Sir Hawk been doing in your company?" someone called. " 'Twas said he was practicing to perform for the king."

There were several cries of assent.

"Nay," Haydan rumbled, but just then the great arched doors burst open. There was a clatter of hooves and suddenly Bay danced into the room. Atop his broad, bare back, Shona grinned. Firelight flashed off her auburn hair.

"Move the tables," someone yelled, and a dozen servants rushed forward to do just that.

"What the hell are you about?" Haydan asked, his voice grim as he strode up to his niece.

"What else but making trouble?" someone called. " 'Tis her right by heritage."

Laughter rolled through the hall.

"Your steed, Lady Cat," Shona said and slipped from the gelding's back.

James's eyes seemed lit from within as he trotted over. "Come, Hawk," he urged. "If you perform the trick now I'll call your vow fulfilled."

The gelding danced in place, lifting his heavy hooves in a spirited piaffe.

"Lady Cat," the king pleaded. " 'Tis no reason for you to wait for the actual day of my birth. Perform for us now."

She nodded, but Hawk shook his head as he stared at her. Still, she approached him. Their gazes locked. She could feel his emotion, and then he reached for her. His hands touched her waist, and he lifted her. The crowd fell silent, and he set her gently upon the gelding's back.

The onlookers laughed. Catriona pulled her gaze from Hawk's with an effort and took the reins from Shona. Riding sideways on Bay's broad back, she let the steed circle the narrow area at a mincing trot.

"I fear this has caught me most unprepared," she announced. "But as I've been repeatedly informed, 'tis His Majesty's birthday celebration," she said and glanced pointedly at James.

The boy grinned, others chuckled.

"So I will do what I can," she said. Setting Bay in a circular pattern, she tugged his head into a deep arch, then leaned toward his ear. "Steady now," she commanded. He rocked along, his mane swishing in a slow cadence as she slid toward the middle of his back. "Haydan the Hawk," she called. "I am a bit thirsty."

From the corner of her eye, she saw Hawk lower his brows.

"Might you throw me a mug?"

"Aye. And it might crack you on the pate."

"I had planned to catch it. There." She pointed vaguely as the gelding continued to circle. "That one will do fine. Toss it to me on my next trip round."

Her back was turned for several seconds, and when she faced him again, he had indeed retrieved the mug.

"Excellent," she said. "Now toss it to me."

"Is Physic in the hall?" someone asked.

Laughter rolled around them, but Hawk tossed the requested item. She managed to catch it as it soared over Bay's croup and raised it high for the crowd to see as they continued their circuit. "Another," she called. Another mug soared. The execution was better this time. The third, better still. In a moment she tossed them into the air one at a time, so that they flew in a circle as Bay continued his rocking course. The crowd gasped and stared. But she had not been sought by kings for such an elementary performance, and so she rose slowly to her feet. 'Twas no simple task, but finally she was standing, rocking along as the horse galloped and the mugs soared. The mob broke into a roar of approval, but she was not yet finished. Stepping cautiously backward, she balanced precariously on her steed's rolling rump. A hundred nobles held their breath. A hundred servants gaped.

The turn was not as difficult as it looked, yet when she pivoted about to catch her mugs in the opposite direction, she was grateful for the gasps of amazement.

The floor blurred beneath the gelding's clomping hooves, the mugs blurred before her hands, but she did not notice, for this next part would require all her concentration. She waited, letting Bay lope about the hall twice more as she gathered her courage and fortified her mind. Then, just before she was even with the king, she leapt.

Tucking into a ball, she spun into the air and landed on the dais only inches from the startled boy. The mugs fell into her hands like autumn apples. The crowd let out a single gasp of surprise and burst into applause.

Catriona bowed. "Your mead, Majesty," she said, and handed James the mug.

He gazed into it with wide eyes. " 'Tis full!" he gasped. The crowd echoed his shock.

Catriona smiled as she lifted her own mug to her lips, but at that moment a flash of movement caught her attention. She lifted her gaze to the back of the room only to see Lord Drummond escort Fayette from the hall.

'Twas nothing extraordinary about it. And yet, there was something about the way the two moved that sent a shiver of something down her spine. Where were they bound? Why leave now, when all the others were distracted?

"The mug was empty when you threw it, was it not, Sir Hawk?" James asked.

"Aye, it was."

"Impossible!" someone said.

Voices buzzed around her, but all her attention was focused on the distant door as she hurried through the crowd. A few questions and awed comments came her way, but they let her pass until finally she reached for the door. The hallway was empty.

Voices to her right. She spun toward them, rushed around the corner, and careened to a halt.

" 'Tis none of your affair, MacKinnon," said Lord Drummond, his dark eyes angry, his grip tight on Fayette's arm as she cowered against the wall. "The lady wishes to spend some time alone with me." He pressed closer to her, his gaze not leaving MacKinnon. "Don't you?"

She didn't speak, but her eyes were wide, her face ashen.

"Is it true, lady?" MacKinnon's voice was low.

Fayette opened her mouth, but Drummond tightened his grip on her arm.

"If you care not for your own well-being, then think of his," he snarled.

Silence echoed in the hallway.

"Release her," MacKinnon demanded.

"Who will make me? Her husband? But wait." Drummond's eyes narrowed. "She is not wed. Not to a single one of the bastards she has bedded. 'Tis a wanton she is. Free for the taking and therefore—" he began, but in that moment MacKinnon charged.

His roar of rage echoed against the stones, his fist struck Drummond's ear. The dark lord was slammed against the wall, and Fayette, finally set free, spun out of his grip with a shriek of terror.

Chapter 28

"Cat!" Haydan roared and pushing past the crowd that milled through the doorway, he leapt toward the source of the scream. Down the hallway, around the corner.

She was there, standing well out of harm's way. One glance told him that, freeing his attention to the two men who were locked in battle.

MacKinnon slammed his forehead against Drummond's nose. The dark lord screamed and stumbled back. MacKinnon leapt in, but Drummond sidestepped and swung. His knuckles grazed MacKinnon's jaw. He was knocked hard against the wall, but in a moment he was up. Rocking unsteadily on his feet, he stumbled toward Drummond. The dark lord swung, making a solid connection with MacKinnon's face and drawing back again.

"Samuel!" Fayette screamed, and at the sound of her voice, something seemed to spur through MacKinnon.

Gathering his balance, he lunged toward Drummond and swung in two rapid, solid hits.

Drummond tottered backward and MacKinnon leapt in with a snarl. But in that instant, Drummond pulled a knife and straightened, effectively stopping MacKinnon's rush.

The crowd gasped.

Fayette whimpered.

Haydan shifted his gaze to her. Her sleeve was torn, her tears for MacKinnon, that much was certain.

"Stop them," someone rasped, but in Haydan's mind, he saw Catriona in the same position. Terrified and hurting, awaiting a hero.

"Drop the blade, Drummond," Haydan said.

The dark baron only laughed as he circled his smaller prey.

MacKinnon moved with him, his gaze never leaving the knife.

"Drop the blade," Haydan repeated, and bending slightly, pulled his own dirk from his boot. "Or I'll kill you where you stand."

Drummond paused and shifted his gaze sideways, but in that instant, MacKinnon launched forward.

His blow pistoned Drummond against the wall. The knife sailed upward, struck the wall, and fell harmlessly to the floor.

MacKinnon struck again and again, and finally Drummond slipped helplessly to the floor.

"Samuel." Fayette stepped forward, her voice weak.

MacKinnon shifted his gaze to her for a moment, and then, like a drunken soldier, he stumbled through the crowd and away.

Haydan turned toward Cat, but she stood with her back against the wall, her eyes wide with horror as she stared past Drummond.

"What is it?" he rasped, reaching for her.

She said nothing. Faces blurred as he skimmed his gaze over the crowd. Lord Spectacles looked sick. Tremayne outraged. Father Matthew crossed himself, and Hogshead looked giddy with drink or incoherence as he fingered his own jeweled knife before slipping it back beneath his doublet.

"Catriona," Haydan said, rushing his gaze back to her as a trio of woman assisted Fayette through the crowd toward her chambers. "What's wrong?"

" 'Tis naught," she rasped, and jerked her gaze to his.

He gritted the word. "You looked as if you might faint."

" 'Tis just . . .'Tis just . . . memories," she whispered, and then her knees buckled, spilling her against him.

He wrapped an arm about her, steadying her as he guided her toward the door. But once outside, he could no longer resist lifting her against his chest. She slipped her arms about his neck and let her head fall against his shoulder. His heart ached at the impact, but he did not stop until he reached his room.

Depositing her gently on the bed, Haydan drew away, but she whimpered and reached for him, and he could not resist. Stretching out beside her, he pulled her back into his arms. She wriggled closer, pressing her face against his chest, as he stroked her hair.

"All is well, lass. You are safe with me. Sleep now."

But she did not sleep. Instead, she lifted her face and touched her lips to his.

Her kiss was tremulous, needy, her cheek warm as sunlight beneath his hand. She moaned against the caress and tugged at his shirt. There were no words spoken, no requests made. But somehow he was soon naked, as was she.

Their joining was peaceful, slow, building gradually. Satiation came in a rush of color and feelings, until finally she fell asleep, cradled in his arms.

Haydan lay silently in the darkness, listening to each soft breath. Her head was nestled on his arm, her hand soft against his chest, and at each point of contact, he burned with want.

But 'twas no longer a lust for her body, no longer a need to feel her beside him, near him, around him. It was a lust for truth that plagued him, for she had lied to him again. He knew it in his soul, in each aching breath he took when he was near her.

She had seen something in the hallway that had frightened her. The battle between MacKinnon and Drummond may well have terrified some women, especially if they had been in similar situations as Lady Fayette. But that was not the case here. He was certain of it.

Something had snared her attention, something horrifying. But what?

He did not know. But he would. That, he vowed.

It was nearing dawn when Haydan escorted Catriona down the dark hallway. Galloway started, then stared in open-mouthed shock when they rounded the corner toward her room.

Haydan scowled as he opened the door to let her inside. Their gazes met for a moment, and then she raised on her toes to kiss him. Heat spurred through him like forked lightning.

"Thank you," she murmured, and then she drew away, stepping into her room. Two greenfinches fluttered momentarily into view and then the door closed.

Galloway was still staring, his eyes as wide as brownstone boulders.

"She fell asleep in the stable," Haydan said, improvising poorly. "With her steed."

Galloway's stare never wavered.

"I found her there when . . ." His mind bumbled hopelessly. There was nothing in the world he wanted more than to follow her into her room. To take her in his arms again and make her believe that all would be right if she but trusted him. "I found her when I went to check the mare." A grown man should be able to lie better than that.

"She seemed most grateful, sir."

Haydan scowled. "Aye," he said, "Her mount was just about to trample her, and now that you understand her gratitude, there'll be no gossip about this, will there?"

"Nay, sir."

"Good. Now find your bed."

"But—"

"Your bed," Haydan interrupted. "I'll guard her door for the remainder of the night."

And so he did, though he knew there was little purpose to it. If she wished to leave, she would find another route. He could only hope she did not wish it, and he suspected that she would not tonight, so he slept for a time, wrapped in his cape outside her door.

Catriona skimmed her gaze over the crowd in the great hall. Lord Drummond was nowhere to be seen. He was in the infirmary. She knew that. Indeed, she had seen it for herself, for 'twas there she had gone to filch his key while he slept.

MacKinnon sat alone, his face bruised and swollen, his meal already finished. Lady Fayette was accompanied by a serving woman, and young Roberta of Perth had already been hastily rushed out of Drummond's life forever.

"I would see to James's well-being," Haydan said,

bending down as she seated herself on a bench. "You will be well?"

Flippancy? Concern? Laughter? She could no longer remember how to act. What had her last lie been?

"Aye. Certainly. I will be fine."

Haydan watched her for a moment, then finally turned to make his way toward the king.

There was little time to waste.

Slipping from her chair, Catriona moved through the hall.

"Lady Fayette."

"Aye." The woman glanced up, a handsome woman with haunted eyes.

"Might I speak to you for a moment?"

Fayette frowned. "I—"

"Please."

At her mistress's nod, her serving maid scurried away.

Catriona sat down beside her. "I wished to extend my sympathies for . . ." She drew a deep breath and glanced toward Haydan. He was leaning low, speaking with James. "For Lord Drummond's actions."

Fayette fiddled with her mug. " 'Twas my own fault."

"Nay!"

Fayette glanced up at the sharp tone. "In truth, Lady Cat, you know little of me." She pursed her lips, fiddled with her mug again and let her gaze flicker away. "Since my husband's death . . ." She paused and drew a deep breath. "He was very religious. Some thought him a good man. But in truth, 'tis amazing what atrocities can be done in the name of God." Pain haunted her eyes. "Mayhap he hated me because I could not bear children. 'Twas the Lord's punishment on me, he said. Still, he felt it important to help out the Almighty in that regard." She tried a smile but it was weak and tremulous. "And

I thought . . . Perhaps I thought to pay him back for some of the evil. And so, since his death, I have sought unlikely men—to shock him perhaps. Or maybe 'tis another I seek to shock." She glanced briefly toward MacKinnon. "I can hardly blame Drummond if he thought me—"

"I do not care," Catriona said.

Fayette's lips parted.

"I am Rom and I am beautiful," Cat said. "All my life, men have found that reason enough to blame their actions on me. But 'tis all muck and I've no wish to hear it from your lips. Drummond's sins are Drummond's sins, and not yours to atone for. In truth, I would not care if he stayed under Physic's kind ministrations until Yuletide."

A hint of a smile lifted Fayette's lips. "I myself hope he had a most miserable night."

Catriona glanced toward Haydan again, her heart thumping. "And what of MacKinnon?"

Fayette cleared her throat and glanced away. "He has two wee, bonny daughters. Did you know that?"

"He told me."

"Aye. He would." She drew a deep breath. "After his wife's death I stayed with them for a time. He has a good soul. For a while I thought he might care, but . . ." She stopped. "Whatever he thought, I fear my recent actions have pushed him away."

"It may be that he too has done things that give him no pride. It could well be that he has feelings for you."

"In truth, Lady Cat . . ." She fiddled with her mug. "I all but threw myself at him once upon a time. You might very well be shocked."

She almost smiled, but there was no time. "I rather doubt it. Am I to understand that he did not respond to your overtures?" she asked and glanced at Hawk. He was already rising from his seat.

"He has barely glanced at me since—"

" 'Tis because he cannot."

"What?"

"Since his wife's infidelity, he believes he cannot . . . respond. He had no wish to embarrass himself or you."

Fayette's eyes were wide. "How do you know this?"

"I am Rom. You would be surprised what people tell me."

"Then do you think he might care . . . ? But no. I—"

"He does seem like the hot-headed sort."

Fayette stared in bewilderment.

"Prone to starting fights with men larger than himself," Catriona continued, then paused. "Or perhaps he could not help himself because of his feelings for you."

Fayette turned her gaze toward MacKinnon, her eyes filled with tears.

"Go to him," Catriona said. "Take him to your room to talk in private, away from memories of Drummond. Tell him what you have told me."

For a moment, Catriona feared that her entire plan would crumble like a house of sticks before her eyes. But finally Fayette stood and then she was gone, weaving through the crowd toward MacKinnon.

One more glance toward Haydan, then Cat was gone too, striding toward Drummond's abandoned room.

In a few minutes she was inside. The gargoyle turned beneath her hand. The secret drawer slid out, and in a moment Drummond's medallion was in her hand.

Breathless and determined, she dropped it into her pouch and yanked the door open.

"What the devil do you think you're doing?"

She had known he'd find her. Still, she almost screamed from sheer nerves.

He glanced sideways and pulled her into the hall.

"I found it." It took no acting ability to make her voice breathless.

"What?" He scowled down at her.

"I found it. The medallion. 'Twas Drummond's," she whispered. Her hands were shaky, her heart too forceful in her cramped chest. " 'Twas he who took it from Blackheart in the first place."

"How did you know?"

"Blackheart said 'twas a brigand who seized it, and when I saw Drummond's evil revealed . . ." She shook her head, breathless. "Now I can fetch Lachlan."

"Nay!" he snapped.

She jumped like a startled lark.

He softened his voice and loosened his hands on her arms. "We have discussed this before, Catriona. 'Tis I who shall go."

"But Blackheart—"

"Is concerned only with the jewels," Haydan interrupted. "I will deliver the medallion to him."

"But what if—"

"I will return the lad safely to you. This I promise."

It was all a sham, a ploy to get him safely out of the way, yet hearing the words said aloud made her knees feel weak, her head light.

"Are you certain?"

"Aye," he said. "The task is mine to do. I leave before dark."

"Tomorrow is James's birthday."

"Aye. And soon Lachlan will help him celebrate."

Chapter 29

"A*nd when you see our face all will be worth the sacrifice.*"

Catriona hunkered closer to the trunk of the tree in which she hid. The festivities had begun in earnest early this morn. Marta had ridden Bay from the castle the night before, then returned afoot at dawn after the guards had changed. Amid the chaos of the celebration no one questioned her coming or going. No one suspected that the gelding was hidden deep in the woods, and with Hawk gone it had been simple enough for Catriona to slip unnoticed from the castle. Beneath her gown, she had donned a tunic and brown hose. 'Twas that which she wore now as she perched high above the forest floor.

Beneath her, on the rusty ribbon of road that spooled through the glen, the sound of horse hooves echoed up. She tensed, but 'twas naught but a pair of servants driving an empty wagon toward Burnsvale.

Catriona closed her eyes and prayed. Blackheart would come. He must come. 'Twas power he lusted for. He had been there to deliver her horrid sentence; surely he would be there to see it carried out. Surely he would be there to see the king delivered. Thus, he had to leave the castle today.

But what if someone had seen her turn into the woods and came to investigate? What if—

Something crackled near her ear. Catriona jumped, nearly losing her grip on the branch that supported her. But the noise was nothing more fearsome than a pair of squabbling birds.

Birds!

Calum flittered to her shoulder, perfectly at home high above the forest floor. Somehow her finches had followed her. What if Blackheart recognized them?

But nay, even if he saw them he would think nothing of a pair of harmless birds. He was too sure of himself, too certain.

Catriona huddled closer to her tree and redoubled her prayers.

The hours droned away. Folks came and went. Worry gnawed at her. Terror ripped at her. Perhaps she had guessed wrong. Perhaps Blackheart would not come this way. Perhaps . . .

And then, far away near Blackburn's bridge, she saw a lone rider. A shiver of apprehension shook her, and she held her breath, waiting. Closer and closer he rode until finally, after a hopeless eternity, she could see his face.

Lord Hogshead!

Gone was the foolish smile and vague expression, replaced by a narrow-eyed wariness and a twisted grin.

Something glinted in the setting sun, and she realized it was the very dirk she had seen during MacKinnon's battle with Drummond. The very dirk that she had, weeks before, mistaken for a medallion. The very dirk that had told her that the innocuous Earl of Harrowhead was really a blackhearted villain. He fingered the blade as he rode along, stroking it as another might caress a lover, then slipping it beneath his doublet and hugging it adoringly to his side.

Drawing nearer, he glanced about. Catriona held her breath. Fear sliced through her, quaking the leaves of the branch on which she sat. But he did not see her and finally he crested the hill and moved on.

Below her, the road twisted away mile after mile, hidden here and there by a turn or a hill. She held her breath when he disappeared. What if he turned off the trail while out of sight? But no. There he was again, until finally, just at dusk, she saw him stop his horse, glance down the road in both directions and turn beside a trio of boulders into the woods.

No time for fear. No time for second thoughts.

Slipping down the tree, she ran toward where Bay was hidden.

The gelding's footfalls seemed inordinately loud when he stepped out of the cover of the woods and onto the road. Terror splashed through Catriona like a cold tide, threatening to drown her. Her hands shook on the reins.

She now knew Blackheart's identity, but Lachlan wouldn't be lightly guarded. 'Twas a plot against the king planned by a man of wealth and power. For how many years had Blackheart convinced all that he was a harmless gentleman? Only a twisted but clever mind could do such a thing. What chance did she have against him and his minions? None. 'Twas not too late to return to Blackburn, to alert the guards. . .

But Haydan had long ago set out in the opposite direction with Drummond's medallion, and the guards' loyalty was to the king. If she informed them of this plot it would be their duty to capture the villains. Lachlan's safety would be secondary at best. And if there was a raid on the camp, the brigands would surely kill Lachlan first to eliminate any who might spill their story.

Nay. 'Twas safest to go alone, for she could be silent, stealthy, quick. Years of training assured that, if only she could control her panic.

Turning Bay back around, she pressed him into a walk, but she felt as if a thousand eyes watched her from the woods. Still, no one jumped from cover to accost her. Bay worried at the bit, eager to catch the horse ahead of him. With shaky uncertainty, Cat urged him into a trot and then a canter.

Miles slipped by beneath Bay's steady hoofbeats until finally she reached the three boulders where Blackheart had turned off. And there, with soul atremble, she reined her mount into the woods.

It was dark as sin beneath the leafing boughs. The gelding stepped into the forest. A branch snapped. Catriona jerked at the noise, yanking her mount to a halt. But in a second she realized it was only the sound of her own passing, and so she pressed on.

Fear smothered her. There was no trail, but Bay moved easily along, following his own gregarious senses.

Minutes ticked by. A half hour passed. They came to a vague trail that wended through the underbrush, but perhaps her mount only followed that course for the sake of ease and not because another had passed there.

Fresh doubts assailed her, but finally they came to a small clearing. The wind scattered the clouds from the moon, and there, upon the ground was a steaming scattering of horse dung. Overhead, she heard the faint flutter of wings.

Catriona pressed on with a modicum of new hope.

But finally all certainty fled. The trail dwindled away, and her mount stopped to pull at a frond of bracken.

Panic seized Catriona in an icy-cold fist. She was lost—she had failed. But Lachlan's laughter echoed in her mind. She pushed her mount on. He turned of his own accord, seeming to know the way. Though hopelessness still gnawed at her, fear would not allow her to stop until she came to the crest of hill. Again the gelding halted.

'Twas then that she saw the spark of light far off. She started as if the tiny speck of flame had burned her, but in a heartbeat it was gone. She stared until her eyes watered and ached, but only darkness surrounded her. She'd imagined it, she thought, her stomach churning.

But no. There! A spark of firelight, not more than a mile or so to the northwest.

She pressed Bay on with shaky limbs. Eternity stretched before her, and the night went on forever until finally a campfire winked at her through the trees.

Her legs threatened to spill her to the ground when she slipped from her mount's back, but she braced her knees, clung to the mane for support, and prayed for strength. Strength did not come, but weakness faded a bit until she was able to stumble to a tree. There, she tied her mount and crept forward.

She could smell the smoke of the fire now, could hear the crackle of the blaze. Crouching down behind a molding log, she prayed for courage. But that too had abandoned her, for it took all her strength to peek over the rotting timber.

Three men stood before her, but she could not recognize the two who faced her. The other was Arthur Douglas, the Earl of Harrowhead, Lord Hogshead—Blackheart! She knew him even from behind, could feel his presence in her soul, for he had thrown aside his false mantle of decency.

"We told you there was to be no fire." His voice was soft, low, a purr of purest evil. It shivered down Catriona's spine.

"The boy was cold. We thought we'd best dry him off, and 'tis no place for a fire in the cottage." The roughly dressed man nodded toward the ramshackle building to his left.

Absolute silence.

"Ah. And did you fetch him herring pie too, Pitt?"

Pitt shuffled his feet. "He fell in the burn, Your Lordship. A dead lad would do you little good."

"Neither would a dead guard," Blackheart said. "And yet . . ." His hand struck out. Firelight flashed momentarily along a crest of stone set in steel. There was a rasping hiss of pain and then the guard doubled over, stumbling toward the fire. Sparks flared, illuminating the dying man's shocked expression. "We have many more at Harrowhead."

The guard tottered sideways. Then, holding his gut, he fell to his knees before collapsing slowly onto his face.

The body twitched. Blackheart watched him, his eyes dreamy in the flickering light. From beneath his doublet, he pulled out a cloth to gently stroke the length of his blade.

"Very nice, my love," he murmured. "Not as wondrous as the old man's death, but satisfying just the same. We were undisciplined, were we? We were weak?" He chuckled. "Well now *we* are earl and soon we will be—" He paused, turning his head abruptly to find the second guard staring at him in wide eyed horror.

"Discipline is very important," Blackheart said, tipping his dirk toward the body. "Get rid of him."

"Shall I . . ." Sweat stood out like the cold dew of morn on the man's brow. "Shall I douse the fire?"

Blackheart smiled, his expression sleepy and sated. "Clever lad."

The guard stepped forward to do as bid, but Blackheart raised his knife. A trio of colors danced in the stones.

"But not yet, Bramble," Blackheart added, admiring the blade before turning his gaze to the body. "I wish to watch."

Bile rose in Catriona's throat. She pressed her mouth to her arm and squeezed her eyes closed, but the sound of the body being dragged from the clearing echoed in her ears until she found the strength to fight down the nausea and lift her head again.

"And how is our bonny lad?" Blackheart asked.

The one called Bramble had returned. "He sleeps."

"Has he attempted to escape?"

"Nay."

Silence, but for the crackle of the fire.

"Nay?" Blackheart's tone was dark, filled with mild surprise.

Another man stepped from the shadow of the tumbled cottage. "Where is Pitt?" he asked, his tone suspicious, his eyes bright as he searched the clearing.

A corner of Blackheart's mouth lifted. "Ah, Clive, so you have decided to join us."

"Where is Pitt?"

"He is resting. Bramble here was telling us of our lovely boy."

Bramble flitted his gaze toward the woods, where he had left his dying companion. "The lad says we feed him well, thus he will wait until we tire of the game and set him free."

"The old earl would have seen him hanged from his heels for such disrespect. But we have a softer touch, don't we?" Blackheart stroked the dirk. "And we like the pretty boy." He smiled. "What of the traitor?"

"He is causing no trouble—" Bramble began, but just then a noise exploded overhead.

Catriona's stomach twisted violently as she dropped her head onto her arm and waited for death.

But nothing happened.

Above the battering of her heart, she could hear no talking.

'Twas then that she recognized the sound. Greenfinches!

Had Blackheart noticed the birds? Was he coming? She dared not move, dared not breathe, and then she heard it. Footsteps crackling the leaves on the forest floor.

Dear God, no! She could not be caught. Not yet.

Bickering twitters issued from the treetops and then the finches took flight.

" 'Tis only birds." 'Twas Clive's voice that issued toward her from some yards to her right, then faded as he returned to the fire. "Buntings, I think."

"At night?"

"I do not control the birds." The guard's tone was terse as he sheathed his sword.

She could not hear Blackheart's response.

From a tree some dozen rods away, the birds began to squabble once more.

Footsteps again. Two pair. Were they coming closer?

"Why is he here?" Blackheart purred.

"He had to take a piss . . . Your Lordship," Bramble said.

"Tell me, if he wanted swan for supper would you ride to Blackburn and request the king's own?"

Youthful laughter rang through the darkness, sparking through Cat's senses. Lachlan! She would know his voice anywhere, and yet she could not resist rising to her elbows to fill her soul with the sight of him. The fire shone in his glittering eyes and along his slanted grin. He was alive and he was well. For a moment fear was forgotten, replaced by a hope so powerful it nearly overwhelmed her.

"I *do* like swan," Lachlan said, his voice clear and bright in the night. "I've only tasted it once, and it *was* at the king's court."

"Why are his hands not tied?" Blackheart asked, his voice low.

"They were," Bramble said, then paused to lift Lachlan's arm to show the dangling ropes. "But he needs—"

"I believe you told me of his needs," Blackheart interrupted.

"There is none here who wished to hold his willy while he dribbles," Clive said. "Leastways, none till now."

Blackheart's eyes sparkled in the firelight as he turned them on the one called Clive.

"I'll not escape," Lachlan said, his tone bright as if he did not feel the strangling tension. "I've no idea where I am and nothing to eat should I get away. Nay, I'll wait—"

But his sentence was interrupted again by the birds' squawking.

"In fact," Lachlan said. "If someone would shoot those bunting I could make a fine stew."

The guards and Blackheart turned toward the birds, and Lachlan flitted his gaze sideways to skim the darkness of the woods.

He knew! Though their gazes never met, though she was certain he couldn't see her, he knew she was there. His attention turned for one fire-quick instant to Blackheart's horse. It stood off to the side between her and the men, its reins trailing. 'Twas now or never. Now, while Lachlan was free of the cottage.

For a moment her knees were too stiff to allow her to rise. But she forced them into submission, creeping along, her heart so loud she was certain they would hear.

"Why are bunting out at night?" the first guard asked.

"Clive does not control the birds," Blackheart said, his tone silky.

"Pitt does." Lachlan's tone was effervescent, his expression cheery again. "I'll wager he could skewer them both with one arrow. Where is he?"

She was nearly within reach of the horse. Crouched in the bracken, she reached for the reins. Her fingers closed over the leather. She tugged the animal closer.

He came, snatching bits of fodder as he shuffled along. Closer. Another step. Another. He was shielding her view of the clearing now, but that meant they couldn't see her—at least she prayed that was true.

The reins trembled as she slipped them over the steed's neck. She turned the closest stirrup. It wobbled in her hand, but her foot found the opening as she crouched behind the steed. She reached for the pommel.

"What was that noise?"

Rory! 'Twas Rory's voice. Catriona froze.

"'Tis naught but buntings."

"Not buntings. Finches!" Rory said, but in that instant, terror broke free in Cat's chest.

There was no time for cowardice. She leapt into the saddle and slammed the horse into a gallop.

"Lachlan!" she screamed, but he was already running, sprinting across the clearing.

Men yelled; someone called her name. But there was no time. No thought.

Lachlan threw himself at her horse. His fingers tangled in the mane. Cat grappled, catching him by the tunic and hauling him up, never stopping. He was almost aboard, his hand on her waist, his leg behind the cantle.

Suddenly a guard appeared before her. He reached up, grabbing Lachlan.

"Nay!" she screamed, trying to pull him back. A few more feet and they would be hidden in the woods. But he was falling—she could not hold him. "Lachlan!" she screamed, but suddenly she was wrenched from the saddle.

The earth rose like a dark boulder and she fell, striking her head.

Chapter 30

Darkness swirled for an instant, then a guard's sneering face swooped through the fog toward her. Catriona kicked wildly with both legs and the brigand careened backward. She scrambled to her feet, pulling Lachlan with her.

"Get them!" Blackheart screamed.

She was yanked to a halt; Lachlan was ripped from her fingers. Her back slammed against something hard, slapping the air from her lungs. An arm was pressed tight across her throat. She struggled to breathe, to think.

"Let her go."

She heard the words through a growing haze. The arm eased away from her throat. She gasped for air, painfully pulling it into her lungs.

"So you saw through our little disguise." Blackheart stood directly in front of her, his fingers light on the blade of his dirk. "How clever of you."

"Why?" It was the only word she could find. The only one she could force out.

"Why what, *Princess Cat*? Why would we seize the king? Power, of course. 'Tis what every man lusts after. 'Tis what our father wanted. 'Tis what our brother wanted. Indeed, they thought themselves quite powerful. And Arthur? We were naught but a frail bit of a thing with an eye for the lads." He laughed silkily. "Disgusting, they said. Worthless. Soft. They did not know us well." He stroked his knife. The stones on the hilt glittered in the light of the fire and he smiled. The expression looked eerily benevolent. "They are dead now, you know. But 'twas an important lesson they taught us: One must never underestimate an adversary. And yet it seems we may have done just that with you. Mayhap we owe you our thanks for the reminder."

She must have croaked a sound, though in truth, she could not tell. Beyond Blackheart, she saw Lachlan, his arms locked behind him by the guard called Bramble.

"What say you, lady?"

"Why me?" she rasped.

He raised his brows and stepped forward as though mildly amused. "Do you not remember?"

She stumbled back, but a brigand was still behind her and more had appeared from the cottage.

"Remember what?"

"You performed for us some years ago." He was close now, within inches. "Aye. You danced. But 'twas more than a dance. You were enchanting us. We offered you money. Indeed, we offered to take you as our mistress. Our lads were quite offended, were they not?" He chuckled, then reaching out with the point of his dirk, he lifted a curl of hair from her breast. He was so close she could feel his breath on her face, the press of his body against hers. "But you turned away. From us! As if we were nothing. Just as our father had. 'Twas then we knew."

She tried to formulate a question, but she had no strength.

"You are a witch."

"Nay."

"Aye. You are a witch," he said, and pressed his crotch against her hand, his knife against her breast. She staggered back, but the guard behind caught her arms. "But unlike the other fools who lusted for you, we knew what you were. Sacrifice is what was needed. I could have taken you then, but nay. 'Tis sacrifice that gains our ends." His eyes burned with an insane light. "If you could bewitch *us*, you could bewitch anyone—even the king. All we needed do was to delay the pleasure of having you and your pretty brother in our bed. And then you would entrance the king for me. And you have done it, have you not? All you need do is execute the plan."

"Nay, I—"

"Aye, you will. But you have gone back on your promise, and we have kept ours. So now we think 'tis your turn to make a sacrifice," he said, and leaning forward, licked her neck.

She recoiled, but her arms were caught behind her, so she spat. The saliva hit him directly in the face. For a moment he froze, and then he struck her. She reeled out of the guard's grasp, hitting the earth hard. Blackheart came slowly after her, moonlight flashing off the stones in his dirk.

She would die by the very dirk that had led her here. But suddenly Blackheart stumbled sideways and fell to his knees.

"You vowed she would not be hurt!" Rory growled. He stood over the earl, his legs spread, his fist curled around his own blade.

Blackheart chuckled. The sound was eerie in the darkness as he rose slowly to his feet. "So you too are bewitched, Rom. And for no purpose, for she does not care for you. 'Tis why you betrayed her at the start. 'Tis why you brought the pretty boy into the woods alone, away from his bear and the old woman with the spooky eyes. 'Twas because she turned you aside. You mean nothing to her. Remember?"

" 'Tis not true!" Rory said and Blackheart laughed. " 'Tis not true!" Rory snarled and lunged, but in that second a guard struck him from behind.

Rory crumpled to the ground. Blackheart lunged in. His knife rose and fell, and in that instant Catriona's fingers curled around a fallen branch. She raised it without thought, lurched to her feet, and swung.

Bramble stumbled under the blow, and Lachlan burst free. They were running in an instant.

She heard Bramble rise with a curse. Footsteps thundered after them, and fingers snared her hair. As she was yanked to a halt, a roar issued from the woods and a gray horse lunged out of the darkness. A sword flashed. The guard fell with a gasp and a gurgle. But there were more of them, swarming at her from all directions.

The rider's sword flashed again. Another guard fell, cleaving her a path. Lachlan lunged into the opening.

"Run, lass! Run!"

"Hawk!" Even in the hellish chaos, she knew it was he. She screamed his name even as he hissed in pain. His steed lunged sideways. Haydan teetered and slipped from the saddle.

Catriona leapt toward him and stumbled over a body. Her fingers brushed against a sword, and it came away in her hands.

A brigand sprang toward Haydan, but Cat was already swinging. As the sword sliced across his back, he fell screaming.

Haydan staggered to his feet just as another hurtled toward him. Steel met steel in an arc of shooting sparks.

Haydan stumbled beneath the onslaught. The villain lunged in, but in that instant, Haydan sliced up from beneath. There was a gurgled croak of agony as the other man fell.

Too late, Cat saw the man behind Hawk. She tried to scream, but already he was raising his sword. A horse charged from the darkness. Its shoulder struck the brigand, knocking him forward. Haydan swung and the night went quiet.

The sword fell from Catriona's numb fingers.

"Haydan," she whimpered and stumbled forward, but suddenly she was yanked back.

"Haydan," a voice purred against her ear. "How good of you to come."

"Douglas." Haydan straightened. The blood-darkened end of his sword drooped toward the earth. "Let her go."

"Why? So you can kill us?" Blackheart laughed, the sound maniacal in the darkness. "We think not."

"Let her go," Haydan repeated. "There is naught you can do. You have planned treason against the crown. Once that is known, there will be no place for you to hide."

"On the contrary. Our place will be with her." He pulled Cat closer still. "She is not our . . ." He breathed in deep as if inhaling her essence. "Not our usual fare. But she is bewitching, is she not? And so long as we have her, you will tell no one of our intent, will you?"

There was no sound but the low groan of a dying man.

Blackheart laughed. The noise shivered down her neck. "Nay, you will not tell," he said. "For you too are bewitched. She is an amazing wench, is she not? I think that for her, even the great Hawk might deliver his beloved king."

"You are wrong."

"Others have underestimated us. We would not advise it," Blackheart said and pressed the tip of his dirk against her breast.

"What do you want of me?" Haydan rasped.

Blackheart chuckled. "First we would like you to put down your sword. Carefully."

Haydan bent cautiously forward. His sword fell from his fingers.

But suddenly Haydan's death flashed through Catriona's mind. "Nay!" she screamed and twisting sideways, she slammed her elbow into Blackheart's face, and spun away. He grabbed her back, but in that instant Haydan yanked his dirk from his boot. It spun end over end, hissing past Cat's face.

Blackheart spasmed against her. She twisted toward him, but he was already staggering backward, his hands grappling with the blade in his throat as he gurgled for breath. Gone was the insane light in his eyes, replaced by a childish terror.

"Help me," he rasped, and then his legs crumpled, spilling him face forward onto the earth.

Silence echoed around them.

"Lass." Haydan's voice was just a whisper in the darkness as he drew her to him. "Are you well?"

She wrenched her gaze from Blackheart, her hands shaking, her stomach heaving.

A groan issued through the darkness. Among the fallen bodies, a man struggled to sit up. Catriona grasped Haydan's sleeve. He pulled her behind him with a snarl, but no one rose to threaten her. Instead, a tortured whisper shivered through the night.

"For you, Cat."

Catriona's knees buckled, but Haydan held her up. "Rory?" she breathed.

"I did it for you."

She took a trembling step forward, but Haydan held her back, keeping her behind him until he had retrieved his sword. Then they moved in tandem toward the fallen Rom.

"I would have returned him to you," he whispered when she was close.

"What?" She knelt slowly jerkily.

"Lachlan." His voice was no more than a raspy breath in the darkness. "Always I planned to return him to you."

" 'Twas you who betrayed us." Lachlan spoke from the back of a nearby steed.

"Nay." Rory caught Catriona's sleeve in a clawing grasp. "No betrayal, Cat. 'Twas my love for you that made me do it." He paused, gasping for breath and tightening his hold for a moment. "You are meant to be mine. But you had forgotten your true feelings for me. Still, I knew . . . I knew you would realize the truth when you lost one of your own. And when it was me who saved him, then you would love me again."

The night was quiet but for his rasping breath.

" 'Twas all going as planned . . . until him." Another tortured breath as he shifted his gaze to Haydan. "You should not have gone to him, Cat. I could not bear the thought." His lip curled in contempt. His grip tightened. "But I forgive you. I forgive if you will come back . . . to me."

"Rory . . ." Her throat was tight with horror. "How could you—"

"Out of love." His body spasmed. "He does not cherish you as I do. No one ever shall." Rasping breath. "You believe me, don't you?"

She struggled for words.

"You think I lie." Rory's voice was low, barely audible in the depths of the night. "Because of him, you think I lie."

"Nay, Rory, 'tis my own—" she began, but in that second he jerked up and struck.

She screamed as the knife slashed past her.

Haydan grunted and staggered back. Rory snarled something, then, listing drunkenly sideways, he fell to the earth.

"Haydan!" Catriona stumbled toward him. "Haydan, are you—" But even in the darkness she could see the dark blood pumping from his side. "Dear God!" Bile rose in her throat. She fell to her knees. "Nay, dear God, please!"

"Catriona." Haydan's voice was low. "Get up." He reached for her, then steadied himself for a moment on her shoulder.

"Haydan."

"Nay." He wobbled against her. "Do not speak. Just fetch the horses."

The return to Blackburn was hell. Catriona wanted to stop, to pull Haydan into her arms, to nurse him, but he pressed on, riding hard, his face pale in the darkness as he slumped over the pommel of his saddle. More than once he teetered to the side. She reached for him, but he pulled himself up and forced them on.

Tears burned her eyes when she saw the lights of the castle. The drawbridge echoed beneath their horses' hooves.

"Open up." Haydan's voice was no more than a growl.

A guard squinted through the portcullis at them. "Who goes there?"

"Open up," Haydan repeated.

There was a muffled gasp of surprise. "Sir Hawk?"

"Damn it, Andrew—" he snarled, but in that moment he swayed. His hands dropped from the reins, and then he slumped onto his mount's crest and toppled to the bridge.

"Nay!" Catriona was beside him in an instant. "Nay, Haydan! Haydan!" she cried, leaning over him. He didn't stir.

The portcullis creaked open.

"Sir Hawk!" the guard gasped.

Cat turned to him with a jerk. "Fetch a healer!"

"Wake Physic!" Andrew yelled.

"Not Physic." Haydan's voice was a low moan.

"Haydan." Cat breathed his name. Her fingers trembled against his cheek. "I am sorry."

His gaze caught hers, but his eyes were only half open, his breathing shallow.

"You were supposed to take the medallion to Glasgow," she whispered, the words painful in her throat.

"Is that why you laid with me?" His tone was raspy, labored. "To keep me occupied? To keep me distracted?"

Her throat burned. "He is my brother.' "

"And what am I, Catriona?" He hissed in pain for a moment. "Just another fool?"

"Nay." He was everything.

"Another fool to bend to your will?"

"Haydan—"

"Your brother is safe now," he said, his lips pale as the dawn. "My vow is complete."

"Don't die!" Her fingers shook against his bloody tunic. "Don't die, Haydan. Please."

He raised a hand. It nearly touched her cheek, but then it slipped away. "Sorry," he rasped, and his eyes fell closed.

Chapter 31

"Hawk." The voice was soft, calling him from the darkness. "Hawk. Awake."

The images of Haydan's scattered dreams shifted as if blown aside by a strong wind, but the folds of oblivion were deep and comfortable, calling him back.

"Sleep if you must, then. But know this. While you sleep, she suffers."

He awoke suddenly, his eyes wide open in a sunlit room that smelled of thyme and heather.

"Rachel," he rasped. "Where is she?"

"Who?" His dark-haired niece drew back as though confused.

Pain speared him from all sides. "Catriona."

Rachel scowled. "Mother was right: You are far too conscientious for your own well-being."

"Where is she?"

"Here." Catriona stepped forward.

She was alive. She was well. Relief swamped him, only to be washed away by a tide of worry. For her movements were stiff, her eyes red.

"What is amiss?" he asked and tried to sit up, but Rachel pressed him back down.

"If you tear out your stitches, I'll turn you over to Physic. I swear it."

"What's wrong?" he asked again, unable to move his gaze from Cat's haunted eyes.

Rachel leaned closer to tuck the blankets beneath him. "You are not the only one who can care. 'Twould be wise for you to remember that," she murmured.

"What?" He flashed his attention to Rachel, but she was already drawing back.

"Be patient with him. He is not usually so daft," she said, and turning away, left the room.

Haydan shifted his gaze to Catriona. All was quiet.

"So . . ." Her voice quavered. "You will recover?"

"Aye." But the sight of her made it difficult to breathe. For a while she had been his, for she had needed him, needed his strength, his prowess. And that made every aching scar worth the having. But how would he live without her? "Aye. I will recover."

"Rachel said you would. But I thought . . ." Her voice broke. Haydan clenched the blankets in fretful hands.

"Tell me what is wrong. Is it Lachlan?"

"Lachlan? Nay. He is well."

"Marta is not—"

"Do you truly not understand?" Her back was stiff now, her brow furrowed. "Do you think me so terrible?"

"Terrible? Nay." In fact, he ached for her, to hold her once again. But 'twas not to be. Long years ago, he had learned to let go.

"Well, you are wrong." She whispered the words. "I am terrible."

He shook his head, but she continued. "For 'twas not enough to know that you will heal. 'Twas not nearly enough." She took an uncertain step toward him. "I know I lied to you. I know I am naught but a wandering Rom. But—"

A single tear slipped down her cheek. She had reached his bed and crumpled the blankets in her fingers beside his.

"Catriona." He kept his tone carefully level. "Young James is safe. All is well. I will tell no one of the part you were to play in Blackheart's evil plan. You need not worry on—"

"Damn you!" she swore. "Will you make me beg?"

"Beg?" He wanted to touch her, to feel her against him, to press his hand against her flesh and know that she was his, but he did not dare.

"Very well." She drew herself up. "I want you, Sir Hawk. I know I do not deserve you. But I want you nevertheless, like I have never wanted before."

His heart did an odd twist in his chest. But he forced himself to remain lucid, to think. "Catriona," he said. " 'Tis my duty to protect. You owe me nothing."

But her hands had left the blankets and twisted in his tunic.

"I want you, damnit! Not because I owe you my life and my brother's life and my very own soul. I want *you*. Surely you would not be so cruel as to turn me away."

"I cannot—" he began, but she interrupted him.

"Perhaps there was a time when I was prideful. But I have little pride left, and so I tell you this. If you do not marry me, I will tell your family that I carry your child, and that you turned me out."

The air left his lungs in an odd mix of relief and pain. "You would not."

"I swear I would."

He tried to think of a way to dissuade her, for a *reason* to dissuade her. There were hundreds of them, he was certain of it. But just now he couldn't think of a single one, and Lady Fiona would never forgive him if he turned away the mother of his unborn child.

"You leave me little choice," he said, feeling foolish and giddy and strangely numb all at once. "I suppose I will have to marry you."

He watched her eyes widen and then her lips met his in a clash of warmth. He slipped trembling fingers beneath her hair, pulling her closer.

"Are you trying to kill him?" asked a calm voice from the doorway.

Catriona drew slowly away and turned. "Liam," she whispered. "He agreed to marry me."

"Of course he agreed to marry you. He is a martyr, not a fool. But you'd best cease kissing him. He already fainted once and if me wife finds you she will—"

"I did not faint," Haydan rumbled.

"He fainted again?" Rachel was through the door in a moment, her eyes intense as she scanned the room. "You didn't kiss him, did you, Catriona?"

"He said he would marry me," Cat breathed.

"There'll be no more of that," Rachel insisted. "Not until he is completely healed. He's not as strong as he looks, you know."

"He isn't?"

"How are you faring, old bird?" Roderic asked as he crossed the room.

"She was kissing him," Rachel chided.

"Quite well then," Roderic deduced and grinned.

"I told you so you would discourage him, Uncle," Rachel said. "Not so you would pat his back."

"I suppose this means you will not be performing this night?"

Haydan turned his gaze to the doorway, where James

stood with Lachlan and another troublesome lad who looked to be his twin. "My apologies, Your Majesty. Mayhap Catriona will perform the trick with her brother."

"I think mayhap you got yourself wounded just so you would not have to perform," Shona said, stepping into the room.

"I think he did it for pity," Liam said, then shrugged at their quizzical expressions. "She was kissing him."

"Truly?" James asked, his eyes round.

"Well, 'tis about damn time," said Marta, tottering into the room. "The lass is beyond two decades of life, and not a lover to be had. Not until this one here."

All eyes turned to Haydan, and then everyone began talking at once as more family squeezed through the door until Rachel finally called for everyone to leave.

Haydan lay in the silent darkness, waiting until it finally came—the slight rustle of noise at his window.

It took only a moment until a shadow darkened his window, a little longer until it stood beside his bed.

"I am no martyr," he said quietly.

He felt the shadow start.

"What?" Catriona breathed.

"Liam said I was a martyr. He is wrong."

"Oh?"

She stepped into his line of vision and he turned slightly to see her better. "I will not let you change your mind, no matter what excuses you may have thought up."

She settled onto the edge of his mattress as softly as a sparrow. "About what?"

"Marrying me."

"You think that is why I came? To tell you I have changed my mind?"

"That and the fact that you seem to be unable to remain in your own chambers for the entire night, yes. But . . ." He drew a deep breath. He could not live without her. That much he knew. "I have given the situation a good deal of thought. There is little else I can do as I lie here, and I have decided that this is the best thing for you."

"Marriage?"

He nodded. "I know that I am neither wealthy, charming, nor particularly bonny to look upon, and . . . well, you have met my family, such as it is." He sighed. They could at least have given her some time before they converged on her like a bad-tempered flood. "Neither am I a young man, and you are . . ." Her almond eyes gleamed at him in the darkness. "You are the Lady Cat." He tried to keep the reverence from his voice, but she was so near. He could imagine her skin, warm as sunlight, beneath his hand. "But I will offer what I can."

"Which is?"

"My protection."

"Ah. And you think that is why I wish to marry you?"

"Do you still?" He did not mean to voice the question, and certainly not in that odd, breathy tone, like a besotted lad awaiting a single word from his beloved. After all, she'd agreed to marry him once. He'd given her every opportunity to change her mind. He need not do so again and he would not. He was a selfish man at heart.

"Aye," she said. "I wish to marry you."

For a moment he forgot how to breathe. "Then you have my loyalty for eternity and beyond."

"I know," she said simply.

He swallowed the lump in his throat. "And my sword

arm to guard against all that may threaten you."

"What if I want more than your sword arm, Sir Hawk?" She leaned forward and kissed him. Flame touched his lips. "What if I want your kindness?"

It was difficult to breathe with her so near, but he managed. "I am not a kind man, Catriona. You should know that by now."

"Truly?"

"Aye."

"Then mayhap I shall marry you for your sense of humor," she said and kissed his bare shoulder.

He tilted his head back. "In truth, I have none."

She laughed. The sound was like the bells of Christmas or the song of birds at first light. Immeasurably soothing. "Then it must be your body that tempts me so," she said and slipped her hand down his chest.

"I have one of those," he rasped and pulled a sharp breath between his teeth.

"Aye, you do." She stretched out beside him, her breath warm against his bare skin, her fingers feather-soft as she traced a scar across his shoulder. "Am I hurting you?"

His chuckle sounded a wee bit insane, he thought. "Nay."

She was silent for a moment. "How did you know?" she murmured.

He stroked her hair for a moment, thinking. " 'Twas a fair enough lie you told about the medallion," he said. "And producing Drummond's piece—'twas all but a stroke of genius. But you gave in too easily. The Catriona I have come to love would have fought to the death before letting me deliver it to Blackheart alone."

"But I saw you leave the castle."

"I did not go far. Just out of sight, and then I waited.

'Twas following you through the woods that was difficult. But the finches are not known for their silence." He tensed for a moment. "I should have found you sooner. I should have known they planned to take Lachlan to the cottage where Rory had gone. But when you are near, I cannot seem to think of ought but . . ." He shook his head, his words a whisper in the darkness. "You should have told me, lass. It breaks my heart to think you endured that alone."

"I was so scared. So confused. Blackheart said I must tell no one, for the very person I trusted might be him. No one was what they should be at Blackburn. Not Physic, or Father Matthew, or Drummond—"

"Father Matthew?"

She lifted her gaze to his. "Might you remember when I went charging around the corner and you nearly beheaded me in the hallway?"

"Aye."

" 'Twas the priest I saw . . . coupling."

"Well, that's it then, lass," he rumbled. "*He'll* not be marrying us."

She chuckled, but the sound was jagged and uncertain as she turned her face back against his shoulder. "The Earl of Harrowhead, he seemed so—"

She shivered and he tightened his arm around her. "I should have known, lass. I should have seen through him. I had heard tales of his father's evil, but I thought he had weathered the storm. I can almost pity the poor bastard—a frail lad unloved by his father. It might turn any mind septic."

"It didn't you."

"What?"

"Your childhood was somewhat similar to his, it seems. But while he was all that is evil, you are all that is good." She shivered. "And I almost lost you."

He gazed down at her, letting the intoxicating emotions sink into his soul. "But you did not lose me," he said, and curling his fingers under, he stroked her cheek.

Silence settled in, soothing in the darkness.

"Samuel MacKinnon asked me to thank you," Haydan said. "For everything." A pause. "He blushed when he said it. Is this something I should worry on?"

"If you like." She sighed as she brushed her fingers, feather-light, across his chest. "Another wound."

He let himself be distracted, for he had a feeling that forever and always there would be worries where Catriona was concerned. "Aye. Another wound. I only hope it does not mar the perfection of my skin."

"Me too," she said and kissed a spot of flesh that was bared above a swath of bandage.

Peace flowed through him, but one worry niggled. "Tell me one thing, lass," he said, forcing himself to voice the question he was certain he should not. Leave well enough alone—she had agreed to be his. But honesty was a hard habit to break. "Do you marry me out of guilt?"

"Guilt!" Her gaze met his in the darkness. Against his shoulder, he could feel her heart beat in time with his own. "Nay, Haydan, not out of guilt."

"For gratitude?"

She hesitated a moment, then nodded. "Aye. Out of gratitude. Every day of my life, I will be grateful that you are the best, the kindest, the wisest man I have ever known. I will be grateful for the sound of your voice, the touch of your hand, the fact that you do not realize that you are too good for the likes of me." She pressed against him. "I love you, Haydan the Hawk. Not because of what you can do, but because of what you are," she whispered.

And as their lips joined, so did their lives.

Author's Note

James V was born in 1512 and crowned king of Scotland at seventeen months of age when his father died in the battle of the Field of Flodden. In 1525 he was seized by his mother's husband, the Earl of Angus, and kept in comfortable captivity while an English faction took over the government. Three years later, he escaped and seized the political reins. But for many years he would often disguise himself as a peasant and travel about Scotland visiting his people. I like to imagine it was my fictional characters who first introduced him to the wonders of being "average."

Dear Reader,

If you loved the Avon book you've just read, rest assured next month are four terrific love stories that I know you'll keep an eye out for.

Historical lovers won't want to miss Karen Ranney's *My True Love*. Her heroes are men you'll never forget. Here, meet masterful Stephen Harrington, the Earl of Langlinais—he's battle weary and longing for peace. Instead he rescues a beautiful woman who stirs in him feelings that are anything but peaceful . . .

Here's a name you'll need to remember: Christie Ridgway. She's destined to become a star, and her first full-length contemporary romance Wish *You Were Here*, will show you why. Yeager Gates is a hot-shot flyboy, grounded by injury but still very much a full-blooded man. Zoe Cash is a life-planner extraordinaire, a woman who leaves nothing to chance—until she meets Yeager. This is a memorable love story written by an author you'll be seeing more of.

He's a rascal and a rogue, the favorite of all the ladies of the court. She's prim and proper, determined to live a quiet life in the country. But when the king forces Richard Blythe and Elissa to wed, the passion that flares between them surprises them both. *A Rogue's Embrace* by Margaret Moore is a delicious confection of a book.

When the townspeople of Burr, Wyoming see a big, broad bed being pushed down Main Street, they know that Jack Donovan's looking for a woman to share it with. But no one expected that woman to be Sarah Calhoun. Debra Mullins' *Donovan's Bed* is a battle of the sexes where everyone wins!

Until next month, happy reading,

Lucia Macro

Lucia Macro
Senior Editor

AEL 0100